Pritty

Pritty

KEITH F. MILLER, JR.

HarperTeen is an imprint of HarperCollins Publishers.

 For information address HarperCollins Children's Books, a division of HarperCollins Publishers, 195 Broadway, New York, NY 10007.
www.epicreads.com

Library of Congress Control Number: 2023933848
ISBN 978-0-06-326492-2

23 24 25 26 27 LBC 5 4 3 2 1
First Edition
Art by Sogo Arts
Book design by Alison Klapthor

This book is dedicated to the youth leaders who dare to heal, grow, and thrive through trauma—and, in doing so, teach all of us how to do the same.

Spring

1

JAY

It's Leroy, and I think he's going to kill me. So I do the only thing I can: swing first.

Well, not exactly. I've never fought anyone, except my older brother, Jacob, and even those couldn't be called fights. They are more like physical arguments that turn into one-sided tantrums I lose before a single punch is thrown. But Jacob did teach me one thing after I failed miserably at learning to throw a football straight (never happened), to hit a baseball (not even off a tee), or to dribble a basketball (does carrying the ball with two hands count?): how to tackle and run.

Honestly, I don't know how I could have done anything to Leroy; I've always kept my distance, steered clear of him and the crowd vying for his attention, whenever he would drive by. When I heard a couple of guys say he'd been asking around about me, I thought it was a joke. I've only ever heard rumors about him, since we don't even go to the same school. I couldn't think of any reason why he—the younger brother of Taj, one of the leaders of the Black Diamonds who reign over K-Town—would want anything to do with me, so I said, "Whatever," and walked off.

How was I supposed to know he was *really* looking for me?

I think about making a run for it since we're next to a makeshift field in the back of a church, a shortcut I always take home on the way from school. If I run left, he could push me into the canal. If I run right, there's only woods, and I'm far from anybody's Mowgli. If I run in the opposite direction, he's close enough to grab me, which means the only way out of this is forward, through him, by any means necessary.

I remember Jacob's words: lower your stance, shoulders down but back, and then—as fast as you can—explode forward while pushing up. I charge toward him with everything I have, fearless and fear-full at the same time.

When I crash into Leroy, I smell peppermint gum and Cool Water cologne, but he doesn't fall. Instead, he crouches low and holds fast. Pushing and pulling, we grasp for legs and ankles to take each other down. He smirks, as if me fearing for my life is amusing. Then, I take my chance.

With all my weight, I pull him close in a tight embrace and then barrel forward, throwing us both off-balance. We topple over Spanish-moss-covered tree roots that punch our bodies like iron fists in satin du-rags until we land in a bed of pissed-off twigs.

On top of him, I flail could-be punches with great effort and little form. Beneath me, his arms are right angles that dodge and slap away every blow. He chuckles, but I am serious.

Every closed- and open-handed hit that makes contact whispers a fervent prayer to whatever god will lay away me a miracle, because I need it. I'm not stupid; I know damn well Leroy is bigger, tougher, and faster. If the rumors are true, he's also dangerous, like his older brother. I just need to escape so I can run home and never look back.

"Aye . . . yo . . . aye . . . ," he repeats between swats, grabbing at my hands and wrists.

Suddenly he smiles, and then lifts me up with his hips. I lose my balance and fall to the side. He climbs on top of me, but he's let his guard down.

Slap! The sweat on his face licks fire into my palm—I hit him hard.

Leroy glares, and in one quick motion, he slams me into the ground. "Chill," he says.

I thrash about as hard as I can and barely graze his face.

"I said chill," he yells. Leroy catches one of my wrists and dodges a punch from the other. I clutch at his throat but miss. I claw at his face and miss again.

Leroy finally grabs both of my wrists and pins me down. "Are you deaf? I said chill out!" He growls the words into my neck.

Sweat drips from his face and arms, which glisten even in the shadows of the trees. A silver chain dangles in the space between us, against the backdrop of a tattoo peeking from the top of his white beater. Something stirs in my chest, a different kind of fear. My body freezes. I hold my breath without knowing.

"You gon stop tryna hit me?" he asks.

Fuck you, I whisper over and over in my head.

No matter how this ends, I won't give him the satisfaction of hearing me utter another word.

His eyes soften. "Aight, I'm bout to let you go, but you hit me again, you aint gon like what I do."

I believe him.

He loosens his grip, but our bodies are too close for comfort; my shorts are hiked up in the scuffle, waist and thighs exposed. Somewhere between us, the friction lights a spark. And in the stillness, our bodies are a cocked gun, our labored breaths are fingers stroking the trigger. I try to pull away, but the more I move, the bigger it grows.

He looks down, jumps up, and turns away, tugging at the front of his basketball shorts.

Before he can say anything else, I scramble to my feet and run down the field toward the church. I hear him behind me yelling, "Jay . . . Jay . . . I didn't mean . . . I just . . . ," but I keep running past the parking lot until I'm out of sight.

I don't run home; I double back and hide between the pink azalea bushes at the front of the church and watch him. For a while, he stands there looking in my direction, his disappointed silhouette ablaze in the blushing sun.

Even after Leroy walks away, I stay, drowning in questions

while standing up. Every muscle throbs, wound tight like a fist, waiting for him to jump out the nearest bush of pink azaleas for round two. In my mind, we clash into each other again and again, unafraid, until our bodies are a breath on the cusp of a moan.

I dust off my school uniform as best I can. Get all the leaf bits and twigs until only the faint scent of fight and dirt and close calls and shame cling to the tattered seams of my khaki shorts. I walk until it all makes sense, which means until my calves ache, my mouth goes dry, and the bottoms of my feet burn. Until the only sense to be made is that I'm fucking tired and I have no fucking idea what the fuck happened or what it means. I want to know why I still feel the heat of his palms, the weight of his body pressing down just hard enough that I know it's there.

When I see the chain-link fences and hear basketballs licking palms and headbutting hot concrete, I know I've walked too far. I'm on the other side of Reeds Gate, somewhere near the lip of Peach Street. Any farther and I'll cross the train tracks into K-Town, where I'm not allowed to go unless Jacob walks with me. Across the street, the "City Kitty" bus hisses and then curses as it kneels near an orange bus pole with letters scraped off, so it reads, "Bop." When the bus huffs away, all that's left: an old man on the corner clutching a brown paper bag, sipping and singing to the cars.

I turn around and walk back until I stare at home. Jacob

and Momma haven't made it in yet—and won't since both work until late in the evening. Relieved, I file away the story I concocted in my head. I don't want Jacob or Momma to know what happened between me and Leroy because it will only lead to more questions. I want to keep it to myself because I don't know enough of the truth to trust it, to risk whatever meaning might be waiting for me on the other side.

I walk through the front door and plop onto the couch but eventually get up and reheat the lasagna Momma must have cooked before she left for work. I scarf it down, outrunning the thoughts replaying me and Leroy wrestling. Afterward, I fall asleep waiting for something, anything that can answer the questions I'm too afraid to ask.

The next morning, while I'm trying to focus on trigonometry, Leroy's face flashes in my mind, melanin crowned in sweat. In the middle of AP History, I remember his lips, their fullness. During chemistry, I'm struggling to balance chemical equations on both sides of the equal sign as I confuse coefficients with our bodies colliding, grabbing.

I want it to stop, but the questions keep going: If Leroy wasn't looking for me to hurt me, then what did he want from me? What did it mean—him getting hard? Does it mean he likes me? Like, *like me,* like me? Does me thinking about it mean I like him? Whether I do or don't, I already know I don't like this.

I want to forget it ever happened because since Dad left

nearly six years ago, nothing's been what it should be. Even though we didn't have anything to do with it, Dad's deeds still haunt us long after he was locked up. This—whatever it is—I don't have time for it. To think about something that I never thought would happen could happen.

Jacob turned down a full-ride track scholarship to his dream school, Northwestern University, and decided he had to work tirelessly to be the man of the house our father once was. And Momma has worked two and three jobs just to keep the house. I've had only one goal: make it up to Jacob (and Momma) by earning the highest grades, acing the SAT, and then getting a full-ride scholarship to the same university so Jacob no longer has to give up his dream.

The truth is, no one has ever liked me, not really. I do get compliments, but they always come with a "catch"—to "borrow" last night's homework, to lean over just a little during the exam so they can copy my answers. And when it isn't school-related, the ask always revolves around one thing: my lips. Not like how people are with Jacob's—big lips are a Dupresh family trademark—I don't get long, handwritten letters or Pretty Ricky–style songs about the things they would do to me, if only I'd let them. Jacob gets the poetry, I get the rude, romantic-less version of what's left: them begging to feel my lips on places only their hands are brave enough to touch.

When the bell finally rings, I try not to accidentally scuff the back of anyone's shoes and risk starting a fight in my rush to make it outside. The scent of ripe dates rides a cool breeze through the trees, making everyone drunk in the sweet. It is the only treat after a day that has been long and hard, a blessing you can only smell on the Southside in spring. For a second, I forget that all day I've been beating the memories of yesterday away with a stick.

Then I trip, almost face-planting on the concrete but crashing into the girl in front of me instead.

"Get off! What is wrong with you?" she yells.

I mouth an apology, but no sound comes out.

"Oops, my bad," someone says, and a whole crew of guys laugh behind me.

I freeze. I know that voice: it's Rouk. For the little bit of time I've known him, he's always been nice. But since his older brother, Faa, was killed last fall—some say by the Black Diamonds—he's changed. Now he's mean and always searching for a way to make himself feel powerful by making someone else feel powerless.

He laughs loud, looks like he's going to try to knock me down, but my words strike first.

"Don't touch me!" The words are hot on my tongue. I'm scared, but I want him to feel the burn.

A nearby instigator makes matters worse, sealing my fate. "Ooo, you gon let dat nigga diss you like dat?"

People turn around and more eyes settle on me, but I straighten up and keep walking, ignoring all of them. All

I know: I'm tired, tired, and guess what? Tired. I didn't do anything. I don't know anything. I don't even understand why any of this is happening to me. My junior year is almost over, and I haven't had any issues. Why now?

The farther I get from the school, the more steps I hear gather behind me, which means Rouk now has an audience.

"Jay, where you headed?" he sings behind me.

No matter how I look at it, Rouk is bad news—I can feel it in his voice, hear it in his smile. But just ahead, I see Leroy standing near a powder-blue Cadillac, dapping up a group of guys in front of two other cars, donning fitted caps and extra-long basketball jerseys.

Up until Faa was killed and they fell out, the only person I'd ever heard Rouk brag about or saw him around was Leroy, which means he might be the only one who could stop him, the only one brave enough to speak up and make Rouk actually listen.

"You ignorin me?" Rouk yells louder.

I don't answer. I just keep walking toward Leroy, hoping my gut is right—that he'll save me.

Leroy sees me, tilts his head up, a greeting. I try to lock eyes with him, to say something, but can't. It feels different to be seen by him. Instead, I walk past him, embarrassed.

"Fuckin faggot," Rouk spits.

I wince. His words hover like yellow jackets waiting for a second chance to sting and then bite. I want to swat his words away, tell him to fuck off, but I know better—it will only delay the inevitable, maybe even make it worse.

The crowd coaxes my demise into being, worshipping it like a god. They don't care what happens to me, as long as it doesn't happen to them first.

I feel my future humiliation drawing closer. I shut my eyes and brace myself, welcome it. It was stupid to think Leroy would stop him or care at all.

The sound cracks the air, stunning everyone into silence.

I flinch, stop, and then stand still, confused.

Around me, the crowd roars, and when I open my eyes, Rouk is holding the back of his head, his face turned over into itself in pain. He lashes back, exploding, "Who the fuck—"

A hush strangles him.

Leroy stands, chin angled up, enough body to end a war.

"Oh, it's like that?" Rouk says, a statement, not a question.

Leroy doesn't answer, just looks. If Rouk's body is a question, Leroy's is an answer, a bullet craving supple flesh. This isn't the Leroy I met yesterday. There is no smirk, no wrestling, no asking.

"You know what?" Rouk clenches his teeth, slowly walks toward Leroy and—

"Rouk! Wait!" a voice yells from behind us, running in our direction. It's Lyric Bryson, the Brazilian poster child of Providence Prep, also known as "Rich Kid Prep," on the other side of Avalon Park. The only time I've ever expected to see him on this side of town is for a track-and-field meet—he used to compete against Jacob—but here he is, stuck to Rouk's side and breaking up fights between friends turned enemies.

"Just calm down, it's not worth it," Lyric says, pulling Rouk back.

When I glance at the crowd encircling us, I see that I'm not the only one surprised at Rouk and Lyric's sudden closeness. If anybody else had touched Rouk or tried to stop him, Rouk would have stomped him into the ground by now. But he hasn't. In fact, when he sees the hellfire burning behind Leroy's eyes as he glares at Lyric, Rouk steps back, as if to protect him.

For a split second, it's as if Leroy is hurt, offended Rouk would do such a thing, make him out to be the monster.

"Jay," Leroy says, clenching his jaw, eyes still locked on Rouk.

"Huh?"

"Let's go." He looks at me, then at his car, then at me again. I don't want to, but he isn't asking.

Lyric eventually calms Rouk down, and they walk back toward the school, but it isn't over: Rouk's eyes burn a hole into me as Leroy's gaze tattoos questions into him. Both seem suspended in disbelief at the other, angry and heartbroken from a distance, as an argument I don't understand struggles silently between them.

Leroy gestures for me to get in. When he closes the door, he seems lost in thought before he starts the engine. The music blasts, and I jump.

"Too loud?" he asks.

I can't hear him, so I read his lips. I shake my head.

Leroy smiles, turns it down anyway. He pulls his seat back as far as it can go and props himself up on his right elbow over the armrest, so close he can whisper a secret in my ear. He never does, though.

He never says a word.

In my mind, I carry on my own conversation: Where are we going? (I don't really want to go home yet.) Why were you there? (You saved my ass, you know that?) If I needed you to do all of that again, would you? (Not that I would, I'm just sayin'.) Wanna talk about what happened yesterday? (Oh, okay, me neither.)

We're riding for what feels like five minutes, when he pulls up to the same church we fought at, cuts the car off, and sits silently. I want to ask him if he knows why the church never had a steeple and if a church without a steeple is less holy, but the silence swallows would-be words and converts them into gestures. In the space between us, a conversation ensues: he drums his fingers on the steering wheel and smiles; I stare at him in the reflection of the windshield; he catches me looking, stares back, until I look down; he rolls down all the windows, inviting the world outside in to witness, then stretches out his arms and legs, ending in a moan; I close my eyes, place my hands between my knees; he rests one arm behind the headrest, a hug by a different name.

Leroy cuts the car back on, nods. I gather my things and then get out.

He turns the music up to its original volume, waits, and when I am far enough away from the car, he nods before peeling out of the parking lot. Then it finally hits me, what I wanted to say the whole time we were in the car: *thank you*. I say it now, knowing he can't hear me.

With the glimmer of the sun at his back and the world rushing by, I hope he feels my words chasing him, like a prayer on the wind.

By the time I make it home, I can almost perfectly mimic Leroy's motions, the way he licks his bottom lip first, then the top; the way he rubs his waves, then massages the sheen into the leather of the steering wheel, as the faintest smirk appears then disappears, never making eye contact.

After I kick off my shoes at the door and swipe some fruit snacks out of the cupboard, I run up the stairs and plop down on my bed. I close my eyes, replaying everything one last time.

I wake up to the room trembling, terrified, until there's the waft of Old Spice. It's Jacob, and he's shaking me. When I turn over to face him, he grins, with his wrists crossed on his lap, as if he's just been sitting there patiently.

"Dinner ready." He grins. "Ma said come down."

For a second, I consider asking the obvious: why didn't he just yell that from downstairs, but he's already tied on his du-rag and changed into his white ribbed tank and gray basketball shorts, which means he's plotting something. I'm too sleepy to care.

"In a minute," I mumble, turning over.

He shakes me again, but when I look back, he's sitting there calmly, this time with his legs crossed, pretending he's admiring my Aaliyah poster.

I stare at him, waiting for him to get the hint and leave, but I know better. Beneath everything that made him the handsome (former) golden boy of the Daniel Lee High School Spartans—the mischievous charm, the muscles, the perfectly manicured waves that made everyone walk up to him and ask if they could stroke them, as they stared into his light brown eyes—I was the only one who knew the truth about him: he was the biggest teddy bear prankster and took pride in being the reigning tickle monster. And I don't stand a chance.

"No . . . no, Jacob," I repeat, trying to sound serious.

He nods, begins to tuck his chain beneath his shirt.

"Okay—I'm up—I'm up." I try to sit up, but it's too late.

Jacob's hands are already near my armpits. I'm fighting for

what little slivers of pride I can hold on to before I become a shrieking soprano.

"Quit—I just need a minute." I push his hands away, then try to hold them in place. No use.

"It's been a minute," he chuckles.

"No, it hasn't."

"Yes, it has."

"No, Jacob."

"Yes, Jay."

"Gimme five, then."

"Why?" He smirks again, tilts his head, as if he's really going to hear me out.

I say the one thing that *might* just work: "'Cuz you love me."

He smiles. But Jacob has something else in mind.

Before I know what's happening, he jumps on top of me and presses me down with all his weight, letting out a fake snore all up in my ear.

I squirm, but it is useless. Jacob's two hundred pounds to my one hundred and forty means, at best, I can only hope to survive. It takes forever just to get him off me, especially when he accidentally falls asleep for real.

"Jacob? Jay?" Momma's voice shoots up the stairs and finds us.

"Coming," we sing in unison as Jacob runs down the stairs by twos and threes, holding himself up on the banister so he barely makes a sound. He waits for me at the bottom of the stairs, then grabs my wrist and pulls me toward Momma in the kitchen.

When Momma sees my face, she giggles. I am beyond irritated—I'm fuming—and Jacob is enjoying every minute of it.

"Awww. Hey, sleepyhead," Momma says, rubbing my head.

"Hey, Momma," I say, kissing her on the cheek. I sneak a peek under one of the pots and grin at the smell—collard greens. My eyes grow wide as I see a plate of fried chicken just out of the grease next to a bowl of Momma's special sauce. She smirks, knowing.

"Noooo. You furreal?" I chuckle.

"Maybe . . ."

"Henny wings? Whaaaat? You only make these for special occasions. Am I missing something? What happened?"

"I just got off the phone with Lin—remember her son, Will? Y'all used to be tight."

"Tight?" Jacob says, smiling.

Momma giggles, retying the bow in her apron. "Whatever . . . it's a phrase I'm bringing back . . . well, she was telling me about some things that have been going on with Will, like him losing interest in things he used to like, being moody—all the stuff I went through with both of y'all at some point—"

Jacob and I look at each other, suspicious.

"And, since my two strong boys are here doing well and Lin could use the help, I proposed that Will come down from New York and stay with us for the summer. Plus, Lin said she can stay for a few days before heading back north, and we could all go do a few things together, like we used to. What do y'all think?" She smiles nervously.

It's been a little over ten years since I've seen Will—since the summer I'll never forget, especially the last night, when he kissed me on the cheek and said he'd miss me. I never saw him again, don't even know what he looks like now. But a part of me has always held out hope that we'd meet again, that I'd experience another ray of unexpected sunshine, from the boy who glows like the sun.

"You askin' for our permission?" Jacob says.

I'm just as confused as he is. Momma only decides; she asks for forgiveness, never permission.

"Yes, I am, actually." She turns the burner to low, stirs the collard greens, then motions for Jacob to check the Henny wings. "It's only right since y'all would need to, you know, spend time with him, make sure he's comfortable. And if he likes it here, if he wants, since he's got enough school credits, he could stay a little longer—they both could, if Lin wanted to come down again."

That's when I feel it: Momma's hope. She hasn't mentioned Miss Rosalind—"Lin"—her best friend since middle school, in forever. Not long after Dad got arrested, they stopped talking as much as they used to, and I never knew why. They still keep in touch, here and there, but Momma misses her best friend. If Will starts feeling better, it means Miss Rosalind might come back, too—and stay.

Momma finally takes the Henny wings out of the oven now smothered with sauce, after we've set the table and even moved the dessert over to the dining room table. After we say a quick prayer, I look at Jacob, wonder if he realizes these Henny wings, in their honey-glazed glory, are a bribe. After the first bite, neither one of us cares. When we ask for seconds and she says "Of course," we agree to show Will a good time, whenever he arrives.

2

Leroy

No matta what I do, errthang keep goin wrong. This morning, I went from bein five minutes late to bein thrown round by Coach White and damn near expelled; Rouk spoke to me after months of ignorin me, but only after I slapped fire into his neck for tryna jump on Jay; and I finally got Jay to notice me, like furreal, furreal notice me, but ioeno what to do next or if he feel the same way. It's like errthang is crowded, like the wall are closin in and errthang is too big, too heavy, and too hard for me to handle.

I floor the gas pedal, up the hill, and as I speed down the otha side and across the train tracks, it's like I'm fallin—no flyin—higher and higher till all of it falls offa my shoulders and I can finally breathe.

Outside of K-Town, errthang feels fake, wrong. Aint nothin right if you aint smellin freshly baked bread from Durst n Em bread company on Mills B. Lane, if you aint seein the Chucks ova power lines in Oak Boulie, where the railroad track flows next to Freedom Parkway. That's when I pass by the back roads where Figya and Eight's crew, the

Black Rydas, do chicken runs, after-parties up the street at the Where House.

Befo I turn the corner at Peach Street and East Lake, I see it: an old "Missing" poster. It's taped to the middle of a streetlight pole, Faa's face faded into the wood, a reminder: aint no pretendin in K-Town. Errthang is what it is: simple, till it aint—like me and Rouk.

We used to say we'd be boys fuh life, but when Faa was killed, errthang changed. At first, me and Rouk got even closer, but when the popos rolled up, talkin crazy and callin Taj a suspect, Rouk stop answerin my calls. Even when the charges was dropped cuz aint nobody had no evidence, he wouldn't open the door when I knocked. And even when the detective who tried to put errthang on Taj was brought up on charges, Rouk still aint speak when he saw me in the streets. Next thing I know, he hangin round Lyric nonstop—pretendin we aint neva know each otha.

Taj keep tellin me to give him space, give him time, let him figure out who he is and who he aint cuz Faa won't just his big bro, he was his whole world. But whatchu supposed to do when someone you known most of yo life tryna be someone who hurts othas for no reason?

I couldn't believe the person baggin on Jay was Rouk cuz we always had a code: don't hurt nobody who aint hurt you. That's why, when I saw Jay's eyes, I aint had no choice but to handle it. But what fucks wit me the most is what I saw in Rouk's eyes: he was drownin. But instead of sayin somethin, he hid behind Lyric. But Lyric aint one of us. He don't understand what we been through. Thinkin bout all this just gives me a headache—it's just too much. So Imma go to the one person who know how to make sense out errthang that don't: Trish.

I turn round the corner from me and Taj's house, past CJ's Junkyard till I'm in front of Trish's, a yellow brick house that has seen better days but that still shines in its own way.

"What's good, Lee?" CJ Jr. blows circles of smoke on the patio of the house next door.

"Whaddup, Jr.?"

"Chillin, you?" I look at Cee Cee, the blue-nose pit. Behind the chain-link fence, she listenin, waitin on my response wit her two puppies standin beside her.

"Same ol, same ol. Could complain, but I won't. You know how it is." He coughs smoke, then smiles. "Tell Taj me n my pops in on that thang he was talm bout and we bringin a few mo folks wit us, too."

I nod, promise to pass the message along.

I flick one of the plastic blades of one of the rainbow-colored windmills. I peek in, see the door open but the screen closed. Outkast's "Humble Mumble" wit Erykah Badu is boppin from the speakers in the livin room. I look ova to CJ Jr., who already grinnin.

"You know how many times she played it or she doin the whole album?" I ask.

"Just that one."

We chuckle cuz we know what it means: Trish Dibbs-Stanley of Providence Prep, the up-and-comin men's clothing designer, is in the zone workin on her senior collection. It's a big deal after she won a national competition that flew her to New York Fashion Week last year. She aint just a talented designer, she the princess of K-Town, which means she protected and respected cuz of who she come from. Her uncles run D&D's Grocery in the neutral zone; her pops is a foreman at the ports; and her grandma Mrs. Odette runs the most popular wedding dress shop in K-Town. Not to mention, she been my best friend, too, since fourth grade.

"Don't be out here hatin." Trish's voice comes from behind the screen door. She opens the door and steps out in a white camisole and light-blue jersey shorts, smile wide, eyes squintin, suckin on a sour apple Blow Pop.

"Aint nobody hatin. Errbody in Savannah know you on ya grind when you got Outkast on repeat."

"What can I say?" She walks to the edge of the steps, waves at CJ Jr., Cee Cee, and the pups. Even in the shade, she glows and glistens.

"Where mine at?" I reach for her sucker, but she dodges me.

Like magic, she pulls a grape one, my favorite flavor, from her white fanny pack.

As we walk inside, I twist the wrapper, then put it in my cheek all geeked for the sweet. Now in the livin room, Trish changes the song and turns up the stereo. "Ms. Jackson" jukes outta the speakers and we rock and sway, rappin as our own duo—her as André 3000, me as Big Boi. In between the mocha love seat and the powder-blue recliner, our hands "wax on" and "wax off" to our own slo-mo version of the chicken-head dance.

It feels good to not have to think, even just for a sec, to just be here, havin a good time. But aint no amount of dancin gon make all the thoughts cloudin my head go away. Errthang just keep pilin on top of me till it's so heavy iono where to start, what to say, or how to say it. So I just keep dancin wit Trish, hopin the words will come out the way I want them to.

"I needed that," she says, stretchin out her legs.

"Me, too." I keep tryna focus, but I keep gettin lost in my thoughts, not sure. Yeah, I'm worried bout Jay; yeah, I'm worried bout Rouk. But what I really need to figure out is how I'm gon fix how bad I fucked up this mornin at school. When Taj find out . . . he gon—man, I can't even think bout it.

"Ready to tell me what's botherin you?" Trish words bring me back. "You got that look when you thinkin real hard bout somethin, chewin the inside of yo cheek."

I frown, actin like iono what she talm bout.

"Unh-unh, don't try to stop now." She pulls her legs in under her and watches me even closer, wit her hands under her chin.

I turn toward the window. For a minute, we just sit in the quiet till all I can do is hear the truth screamin at me and the fact that she the only one who can help me figure out what to do.

"Trish, I fucked up." Ion even try to hide how I feel. "Like . . . furreal. . . . I got suspended for ten days, and they tryna expel me from high school."

I aint gon lie, I wanna tell her errthang bout Jay and Rouk so she can help me make sense of it, but I stick wit school shit. The words aint perfect, but at least they there.

"What? Why?" She sits up.

I can already see her thinkin, tryna figure it out befo I even say.

"Don't tell me . . . Coach White?"

My eyes say it.

"He get in yo face again?"

"Worse."

"Did you keep yo cool like we talked about?"

"I tried. But he just kept yellin, askin why I won't wearin my ID. I told him I accidentally left it in my car. Next thing I know, he draggin me to ISS. When he got me to the room, and I got up and tried to leave, he push me so hard I fell ova one of the desks. I got up, tried to hold it all in, but when he did that shit again, I pushed his ass back."

"Lee . . ."

"I just shoved him a lil bit, no harder than what he did to me. Then he started talm bout how Taj a murderer, said he belong in the electric chair for what he did to Faa. I just saw red; I tore up errthang I could get my hands on."

I know I fucked up. She know it, too. I can tell by the look in her eyes. But I woulda neva did that if he aint put his hands on me or say nothin bout Taj—neva. But he stay tryin me, cuz he can. They call it a school, but Buford High aint nothin but a jail wit a different coat of paint—don't matta they aint got no cells or bars on the windows. It's bout how they treat us.

"You said he did all that in front of errbody, right?"

I can see her thinkin, puttin together pieces.

"You remember if Miss JohnaMae was there? The counselor?"

I think as hard as I can. "Yeah, she was in the front office. Prolly saw the whole thing."

"Okay. I think I know how you can fix this but it aint gon be easy. Coach White is connected to people all the way up to the school board. He aint goin nowhere. And you and I both know, aint nobody tryna go work at Buford High on purpose. It's like they send people there who can't work in none of the otha schools."

"Whatchu want me to do?"

She gets up and stands next to me, wit her back against the sink. She quiet for a minute and I don't do nothin to distract her. She the only one who can help me figure out how I can fix this befo I gotta go home to Taj. She puts her hand on my shoulder, pulls me close to her. "I'm sorry he did that to you."

It's like she lookin through me, talkin to the part that don't nobody see: the real me. But it still hurts when errbody see me, the tats, the chain, the muscles—they automatically assume Imma problem they gotta fix or get rid of. I let out a breath, didn't even realize I was holdin it all in. Then, she pushes me toward her room, hummin Outkast's "Morris Brown." Together, we think through a plan of what I can do next.

It takes almost an hour, but she calls her godmomma, who works real high up at C-Pote Tech, and she talks to the person ova the GED program who also knows Miss JohnaMae. Turns out, when she saw errthang, Miss JohnaMae already called her, said I was a good fit for the GED program. All I gotta do: get my transcript, letters of support, and a creative essay. Iono how to do that last one, tho—Trish don't, eitha.

After she hang up, we both stop errthang and just sit quiet, thinkin bout who could help. Iono how much time pass but it's enough for Trish to get back to makin magic on her sewin machine as I lay across the bed, starin up at her favorite poster of Outkast, the one wit André 3000 standin next to Big Boi, his hands reachin out, pullin you in. Then Trish sewin machine stops and she turns round wit the biggest smile on her face, and for some reason ion like it.

"What about that boy you been crushin on foreva? Jay, right? You eva find out what school he go to? I know you been askin round."

I jump up but don't meant to. "Whatchu mean?" I try to keep my cool, play it off. But something kicks to life in my chest.

"You heard me. . . ."

"Why you askin bout that . . . bout him?" Should I tell her? And if I tell her, do I gotta say errthang, like even bout me wrestlin wit him and gettin hard? Nah, iono bout that.

"If you would tell me what's goin on, I might be able to fix yo love life . . . now that I done saved yo life."

I shake my head. We'll see if I live to see tomorrow once Taj find out.

I brush it off, try not to think bout it. "My love life don't need fixin," I say, knowin the truth: yeah, nigga, it do.

"It don't?" She props her elbows up on the back of her seat, does her starin again.

I hide from her eyes and stare into André 3000's, but my thoughts immediately go to Jay, thinkin bout when we was in the car together, how much I wanted to say but . . . iono, I was just—

"Scared?" Trish's words slap me outta my thoughts. There

she go, readin my thoughts.

"Go on somewhere wit that," I grumble. She gets up and jumps on the bed, shovin me into the corner.

"Aint you supposed to be sewin?"

"I'm just doin like you said . . . you told me to go somewhere wit that, now I'm here . . . wit that. Next to you and my boo." She blows a kiss to André 3000.

"You sure you don't need help witcho love life?" I say.

"Don't do me." She cuts her eyes. "You and I both know you neva make the first move. Am I right? Or am I right?" She play-nudges me wit her shoulder. When I don't say nothin, she sits up and watches me. At this angle, her chin pulled back like a bow and arrow ready to strike.

Ion say nothing—my eyes and body plead the Fifth.

"Wait." Her head shoots straight. "Naw . . . you didn't."

Shit! The truth always finds Trish.

She squeals, grabs a small square purple pillow, and throws it at me, her smile wider than a slice of watermelon. I can't help but laugh.

"That's what I'm talm bout. Hold on . . ."

I sit up, confused. "Yo, T, where you goin?" Then I hear it: Mark Morrison's "Return of the Mack" blastin through the livin room speakers.

She two-steps into the room, forward then backward. She tries to get me off the bed. "We gotta celebrate."

But when I won't, she just keeps dancin.

"Whatchu waitin on? Gimme all the details. Whatchu say? What he say? Don't leave nothin out."

I look at her, then wonder why I been trippin this whole time. If anybody can help me get my head on straight when it comes to Jay, it's her. So, I tell her errthang—well, almost.

"I see you . . . I see you," she sings. "Whatchu say when he got out of the car?"

"Nothin."

She squints. "Okay . . . Silence can be game, too. How you ask for his number?"

Shit, I aint think bout that. My heart was beatin so hard, it's like I was thinkin bout errthang and nothin at the same time. It's kinda always been like that eva since I saw him behind the church. I aint even expect to see him that day. I had parked on the otha side and was walkin to my favorite spot, a secret garden not too far from the canal. When I turned round, he was there.

"That's alright. It's kinda perfect that you didn't say much. Keeps the allure errbody likes bout you . . . we can use that."

"We?" I chuckle.

"Mhmmm . . . Don't be actin brand-new. I been helpin you wit yo love life since the fourth grade, since you stood up in front of the whole class and asked Mrs. Wanda to be yo girlfriend."

"Ahh . . . here we go. You aint neva gon let me live that one down, huh?"

"Nope. And you know why?"

"Why?" I say, ready to say her reason verbatim.

"Cuz that's when I knew . . ."

"We was gon be best friends or worst enemies," we say at the same time.

"Betta act like you know." She giggles. "Furreal, tho. I think it's cuz we got the same taste in women, but also when you put yo mind to something, don't matter how big or scary it is, you do it, no matter the cost—and we have that in common."

"Aww . . . you gettin mushy on me, Tee-Tee?"

She rolls her eyes, politely smiles as she flicks me off. I can't help but laugh cuz she aint the only one that the truth always find. I jump on her, wrap my arms round her real tight. "I love you, too, Tee-Tee. I love you, too."

I open the door, expectin Taj to be sittin in the front room, but he aint. I walk up the stairs, each step creakin louder than the next. There he is, on my bed, quiet, starin at my *Love & Basketball* poster behind my weight bench. He midnight black wearin all white: a white du-rag, white tank, and white basketball shorts.

When he look at me, I expect him to throw me through a wall or slam me through the floor till we land in the livin room. But that aint what his eyes say—he worse than mad, he feel betrayed.

He stands up, looks me dead in my eyes, and steps forward.

I step back, a reflex.

"Why, Lee?" His voice is soft—the calm befo the storm.

My left leg shakes. My body wants to run. "Lemme explain."

He crosses his hands in front like he listenin, but I know betta. When the words don't come, he steps forward.

I step back again.

"Wait, wait, wait," I say.

"Nah, aint nothin to say, *Lee*roy."

He only calls me by my full first name when he is pissed and ready to whoop my ass.

"It was Coach White. He got all up in my face—"

"So. What dat mean? Anybody get up in yo face, you gon act a fool?"

"No."

"And when you start fuckin up classrooms and walkin outta school, like you aint got no home trainin?"

For a second, I see it: the pain and disappointment again, that look when Ma used to say it's gon hurt her mo than it's gon hurt you.

"That's aight," he says, steelin himself—shuttin out any feelings that would make him hug me instead. "Get in here and put em up!"

I freeze. Try to think of a betta way to explain it. "I—"

Pop, pop! I barely block his first and second hit. They are open-handed, but his hands always been like bricks—even a slap can knock yo head clean off.

I step all the way into the room, notice he already moved my shoes, barbells, and clothes to the side on my desk. I get in the stance: hands up, palms forward, thumbs tucked.

Taj don't believe in one-sided ass whoopins. He always say, "Among men, you gotta have tha right to defend yaself, state yo case. It's the only way to learn how to be strong, even when you wrong." At least that what he says.

Dad aint round no mo, and Ma always been in and out, so Taj taught me to scrap so I know how to protect myself wheneva he aint there. But it always feels one-sided, even tho he say it aint. Taj trained under boxing legend Zeke Wilson. Some say Taj coulda went toe to toe wit the original Pritty Boy Floyd Mayweather Jr., if he kept at it, but Taj had to stop so he could take care of me and help Auntie Rissa when she took us in, even tho she told him not to.

"What did you promise?" he says.

Taj fires off three jabs. I block em, but the force knocks me back into the door. My belts and hats hangin from the door hook fall.

"What did you promise?" he says again.

"I said I wouldn't fuck it up."

"Then, why did you, Lee? Huh? Why you lie? Why you act like you don't care bout me, bout errbody who sacrificed?"

He slaps me upside the head. When I flinch from the

pain, he locks me in his grip and smacks me a few mo times, until my ears ring.

I break free, but barely. "I do care, Taj. I do," I yell back, tears in my eyes.

"Then show it—do betta! And the next time—"

Jab. Cross. Cross.

"I hear bout you—"

Jab. Block. Counter. I slip, almost get clipped again.

"Fuckin round—"

He slaps harder and harder, keeps comin. I take a few hits and counter, but I put too much weight in one, accidentally get in one good slap.

"Oh shit! I aint mean to!" I can still feel the sweat from his face in the palm of my hand.

I run down the stairs and outta the back. It aint the first but I'm afraid it will be the last. He darts outta the front to cut me off at the side gate.

"Lee," he says, winded, as we circle round the bush Ma used to make us pick our switches from right befo she used them. I can still picture her all giddy, singin as she snips off the leaves.

"Get ova here. Quit runnin!"

The switch bush is up to our chest and ova four feet wide. We can try, but neither of us can reach ova without the thorny leaves drawin blood, that's why I nicknamed the bush Savin Grace.

He lunges, but I'm too quick.

I can't match his skills in boxing, but my ass was born runnin. Suddenly, his phone rings. When he pulls it out of his back pocket, his whole body changes. He don't say much, just listens, clenchin his jaw the whole time.

"We gotta finish this later," he says, wavin me in as he walks to the front door.

I can see it on em, the weight of errthang he gotta hold as a Black Diamond.

Befo our pops went missin, he created the BDs—a network of OGs (olders and elders) and YGs (those younger) from all ova the city, mainly K-Town—to protect errbody from bein bullied by people in positions of power who try to use the law howeva they want to.

Since then, Auntie Rissa grew it into an underground activist organization errbody know exist, but don't nobody really know how they operate—on purpose. To errbody who need em, the BDs an open secret, always there to help you get yo rent paid, family fed, legal support. And to those outside of the community—lyin politicians, crooked popos, and anybody doin our people dirty—the BDs are a black box you know exist but can't see inside of.

Dependin on who you talk to, the BDs been accused of bein errthang from a violent gang to a secret drug enterprise to a newer version of the Black Panthers. But the truth is mo simple: the BDs one of the few groups that keep they promises and don't expect nothin from the people they protect but to keep each otha safe.

Technically, if you had to break it down, Auntie Rissa is the one the OGs elected to be president and Taj was elected by the YGs to be vice president. And together, they two sides of the same coin—in charge of the whole network. But lately, Taj role in the BDs been weighin on him, hard. Even tho he neva say what it is, I know it aint good.

Taj breathes in deep, then sighs, as he closes the front door behind us. A second don't go by befo he reachin for the phone vibratin again in his back pocket.

"Imma wash up and change real quick, but when I go, lock the door when I leave," Taj says.

"I know, I know."

When Taj comes back down, he in his new Chicago Bulls Jordan jersey wit all-black Girbaud jeans wit the red tabs, lookin like Treach, from Naughty By Nature. He grabs his keys then heads toward the door, while I follow close behind. "When I get back, I need to know how you gon make this right," he says, then pulls me into a loose hug.

Cool Water always smells different on him, mo grown-up, wit swag—that's why I wear it. Even though I'm eighteen and he just turned twenty, I keep tryna figure out his secret, how he can carry himself like he grown—and errbody believe him.

I stand in the doorway and watch as Taj walks out the front door to his Cadillac SUV. He nods when he wants me to go in the house but not befo sayin, "Aight, Lee. Love you."

"Yeah, yeah, yeah," I say, blushin.

He disappears behind the tinted windows, and I wonder if he feels some type of way bout me neva sayin it back. Does he know that "I love you" sounds too much like goodbye, that's why I can't say it?

I close the door and lock it like he always nags for me to. At first, I'm good, but the longer I stand there, the mo I feel it: the quiet, a silence so loud it's screamin.

I run upstairs and take a shower to drown out my thoughts. But all I keep thinkin bout is how, when Taj turned sixteen, he told Auntie Rissa he aint just wanna be a BD, he wanted to do somethin nobody eva did: unite the gangs and bring them under the BDs. She looked at him and hugged him tight. She knew why—it's cuz of what happened when Pops and Auntie Rissa got attacked and she woke up after bein knocked out and saw that Pop was gone, missin. We neva found him again.

Eva since then, Taj knew, activism won't enough to protect us. So he neva stopped fightin, tryna get errbody to see his vision, and got the scars and broken bones to prove it, until the heads of the different gangs joined the BDs and agreed to a truce and neutral zones. Now, the BDs don't just help, they protect—so in case that white mob shit go down, we ready and then some.

Anybody on the outside lookin in would assume Taj some dealer. But he don't deal drugs, he deal hope and tough love. That's why he my hero, my world—and I wanna make him proud.

I gotta plan. All I need to do now is get Jay to say yes.

For a minute, I think I'm dreamin or trippin. But I hear it again at the door, harder: *Bam! Bam! Bam!*

I sneak into Taj's room, reach behind the headboard, feel for the tape. I slide the bed ova, unwrap the Glock, and hold it at my side as I run down the stairs as quietly as I can. The closer I get to the back door, the faster my heart races. Taj always tells me to be prepared for anythin, but the steel don't feel right in my hands; it's too cold under my fingers.

"Lee, open the door."

It's Taj, but he don't sound right. Somethin wrong.

I put the Glock on top of the fridge out of sight and then unlock the door. When I open it, he barely standin up straight, wit one arm hooked round a guy's neck I neva seen befo.

I step back, confused.

The guy carries Taj in, and I point him to the livin room sofa. I slap away pillows and help him lay Taj down. Taj winces in pain. Then I see the bloodstains on the guy's white beater and the dried blood on Taj's face.

"What happened?" I ask, pullin at Taj. I need to see how bad it is, to know if this is the last time I'm gonna see him alive. I aint ready for him to go, and I need him to know so he can hurry the fuck up and tell me how to fix it.

"I'm fine," he mumbles. "Aint even that serious."

"Can you get me a rag or something I can clean him up wit?" the guy asks. He is calm; they both are. "I need to see if he'll have to get stitches. I've seen my fair share of wounds, so I can at least tell you that much. He wouldn't let me take him to the hospital."

He looks for a light. When he finds it, the dark is swallowed, and we stand there, dumbstruck versions of ourselves.

"You a doctor or somethin?"

"Lee, stop askin so many questions and get the kit."

I listen, but I aint convinced.

I bring one of the first-aid kits from the cabinet in the kitchen and hand it to the guy slowly. Aside from a cut on his lip, above his temple, and the back of his head, Taj is okay. At first, I think the guy could be somebody from Taj crew, but the longer I watch him, the mo different he seems—somethin bout him glows, even in the dark, like the silver chain he wears that has a class ring on it.

"He'll be good," the guy says, after glancin at my face. He throws the words ova his shoulder, as he moves to the otha side of Taj and slips his hands down his shirt to feel his ribs. Taj don't even jump, like his body is something he already knows.

I don't say much, just watch him patch Taj up, put him back together wit Band-Aids, gauze, and tape. The whole time, I'm wonderin: Why is he here instead of Taj's homeboys—Night, Brown Brown, and PYT? How he get this kinda power wit Taj? Aint a place on Taj body he afraid to touch.

"You gotta shirt?" the guy asks, still not lookin up.

"Yeah," I say, still lost in my questions.

"Let me borrow it. I'll give it back to you tomorrow."

"Why you need it?" The question come out befo I can stop it.

"To wear," he says, smirkin. "I can't go home lookin like this. Would cause way too much attention."

"Go get him one of mine and get me one too," Taj says. He calm and relaxed, like he gettin his hair braided, not like he just been wiped clean of all that blood.

While I'm comin down the stairs, I hear Taj whisperin and pullin at the guy, tryna see if he injured, too. But Taj don't have the same kinda power ova him. By the time I make it to the foot of the stairs, Taj is sittin still but starin in his eyes. I can feel where Taj comin from, so I try to help.

"What boutchu?" I say, handin the guy a shirt. "You good?"

He seems surprised I even ask. He don't respond right away, just smiles.

He slips Taj's white beater off and pulls the clean shirt I gave him ova Taj's head. I hide how impressed I am. Taj woulda neva even let me put his shirt on him without puttin up a fight.

"I coulda put on my own shirt," Taj says after the fact.

We both ignore his ass.

I hand the guy the shirt meant for Taj.

"Thanks for askin, man . . . I'm good," he says, peelin both of his shirts off. He's a lighter shade than Taj, but just as muscular, which means you can see the bruises on his side mo clearly but he aint got no cuts. The blood on his shirts musta been from Taj. He flips the clean shirt ova his shoulder but don't put it on right away. He stays focused on Taj.

"Yall gon tell me what happened?" I ask.

If somethin like this can happen to Taj bein in the BDs, somethin goin down in the streets—and if he can't fix it, things might get worse befo they get better, like they used to be, a time when aint nobody feel safe and even fewer could be trusted.

The guy glances up but keeps patchin and pushin. "Aight, you should be good now," he says. He holds Taj's face in his hands, movin his head in different directions to see if he missed anything else.

Taj grits his teeth a few times, but neva stops starin in his eyes.

"You got any painkillers?" the guy asks me.

I nod.

"Don't need em," Taj replies, still starin at him.

"You will," the guy says.

He takes the shirt off his shoulder and puts it on. When he winces, Taj jumps up. I kinda wanna reach for the guy, too—and iono why. Maybe he startin to grow on me. I try to play it off, just like Taj.

The guy balls up the otha shirts and places them in the trash once he makes it into the kitchen. He leans into the doorway so we both can see him.

"I'll be back tomorrow to check on yall." Befo closin the door, he says, "Leroy . . ."

"Huh?" How he know my name?

"Make him take somethin for the pain so he can sleep. They beat him up pretty bad, and you know yo brotha aint easily beat."

I nod, wonderin.

He closes the door and disappears. He gone, but it feels like he is still standin in the livin room, bossin both of us round. A part of me still waits for him to give me a command or some shit from the shadows. It aint errday somebody I don't know rolls up in the house and can order Taj round.

"Go get me some painkillers." Taj shakes his head and chuckles, as he unfolds his body across the couch, wincin but keepin quiet.

I grab the pills out of the cabinet and give him two.

"Unh-unh, one mo."

"The bottle say two."

He stares holes through me, and I give him anotha pill.

"Kill the light," he says.

He kicks off his shoes, nothin else. Tests the bandage on

his head to see if it will stay, if he lies down on it—it does.

"Can you get me a—"

I lay a sheet across him. Pull out a pillow, too. He looks up, surprised. I push the coffee table ova near the TV and make a cot on the floor next to him. I pull out anotha blanket and pillow.

"Aye, whatchu doin? Go lay in yo bed, Lee. Unh-unh . . . aint no need for you to be layin on the floor like that."

"I'm good."

"Lee . . . Lee, get up," he threatens. "What if I gotta take a piss and forget you down there?"

"Don't."

He sucks his teeth, stirs a bit in the dark, and tosses like it's enough to make my win feel any less great.

Later, when he thinks I'm sleep, I feel him bury his head between the pillow and the couch. He breathes in long and hard but stays quiet.

I don't say nothin, barely even breathe, cuz every man, at some point, needs to cry in peace, and fall apart, so he can put himself back together again without words.

Six years is too long and too hard for a boy to carry all our pain as a man and only be expected to smile.

3

JAY

It has been a little over a week since I last saw Leroy, and my world has turned upside down. It was Leroy's fault. Well, technically, it was Rouk's, but Leroy was to blame.

At first, I assumed Rouk would spread rumors to make me public enemy number one: unwanted, unlikable, unevery-thing. I even expected him, pride bruised and still stinging from humiliation, to get even, but he isn't.

Lyric must have convinced him to do the opposite, because there's a rumor that it was a misunderstanding, that the three of us squashed it and he was the one who made it happen. I don't confirm or deny it because this version of the truth has its benefits: Rouk keeps it cordial. But there is a downside.

As a result of what happened, I'm suddenly the topic of every side conversation or rumor at school. I've gone from being treated as "just Jacob's little brother" to people asking if I'm connected to the BDs, like Leroy's and Rouk's brothers.

Since I don't say anything, people come up with their own stories, literally. There's even a fictional action saga in the school newspaper that vaguely references me, Leroy, and Taj as vigilantes out there punishing crooked cops and getting revenge against all who cross us (if only my life were that exciting), while running a secret drug enterprise (my mom would kill me first).

Walking through the double doors, everyone is standing around as they erect a new memorial trophy case for Faa, one of the most popular graduates of Daniel Lee High and the same year as Jacob. In the golden-embossed "Rest in Power," they've listed all of his awards in the community as editor of the school newspaper and the youngest beat reporter for the local news station. Everyone thought, in ten years he'd be one of the youngest news anchors in Savannah history, he was such a talented investigative reporter. But tears and sniffling in the hallway reveal a painful reality: hopes and dreams can only do so much when you piss off the wrong people.

I turn up the volume in my headphones and weave in and out of others, trying to ignore the truth that gets harder to admit every day, especially after what happened with Rouk: I don't feel safe—and I only feel lonelier.

I know I'll be hurt by someone, but what I'm most afraid of is that I'll find myself in another situation like what happened with Rouk: I'll be hurting, and no one will care; I'll need help, and no one will lend a hand. The hell that is high school hurts less when you have someone to depend on, share everything we all know we must survive but can't talk about openly—the three "L"s: "love," "loss," and "loneliness."

Could Leroy be that person, someone who will be there no matter what? Or is he like everyone else, lost in the idea of who I might be but not interested in who I really am? Then, I think of Will's face—or, at least, the one I can remember. Outside of Jacob, he was the only one I felt safe around, the person who also just wanted to be around me because of who I was, not who everybody wanted me to be. When he visits in June, I wonder what he'll be like, if he might at least be the friend I've been hoping for.

As I sit down at my desk in Mrs. Jaxon's AP English and Composition class, Princeton, the resident charmer of Daniel Lee High, is practically performing the latest installment of the newspaper series when he sees me walk in. He never says my name, never says the story—his series—is about me, Leroy, and Taj, but the oohs and aahs of curiosity and perfectly timed looks in my direction give more than enough hints.

The only thing that matters: Christina Chisholm, our school's Aaliyah, is front row and center, listening—and every time she giggles, she looks over at me, her eyes lingering. She's smiling, a vision of what perfection could be, and she's doing it because of me. Well, the story is *about* me and the words Princeton's, but gimme a break (I'll take a win however I can get it).

Mrs. Jaxon watches me quietly over her slender red

frames, curious. Can she tell that a part of me likes that he'd care enough to make up stories about me? Princeton, the all-star track athlete, class president, and irresistible ladies' man is the most popular guy in our class. In fact, he's the ten inches (don't ask . . .) most boys seem to measure themselves against; he can do no wrong, which means even if he is wrong, he can redefine "right" and change people's minds, turning rejection into unconditional acceptance.

Princeton *is* popular opinion but, he, too, must walk the tightrope of people's expectations or risk losing his crown. The difference is everyone wants him to be king . . . well, prince, because it's easier to follow someone else, give him the power to be everything they secretly want than dancing to the beat of their own drums.

Mrs. Jaxon brings Princeton's passionate performance to a close, making her way to the front of the room. I hide from her eyes, knowing she can spot a lie as it's forming in your mind before it even makes it to your lips. For a second, though, I grow bold, fearless, daring her to read my thoughts.

I'm not complicated; I want to be wanted, liked. I want to be more than someone defined by who does or doesn't protect me. I want a friend—someone who can like me for me and choose to stay without me having to pretend I can get them Jacob's number or that I might have access to a secret crime-fighting organization that doesn't even exist. I'm just Jay, and, for once, I want that to be enough.

Like every other time, my courage disappears into thin air before anyone knows it's there, and I slide down into the metal trap that is my desk. But not for long. On the board, Mrs. Jaxon writes in cursive a title and a name:

"a song in the front yard"
by Gwendolyn Brooks

We don't know what it is or what it means, until she speaks. The words flutter from her lips as she slowly strides across the front of the room and down the aisle, and I imagine her walking, followed by a train of peacock feathers and chandelier earrings, her voice fanning our ambition. She's barely five feet tall, but her voice towers over us, and by the time she lands at my desk and says the last of the poem, everyone—including myself—is speechless, wondering.

With a flick of her wrist, she breaks the spell, triggering rounds of applause. As she walks past my desk, she taps me on the shoulder. It isn't much, but it's enough to make me feel better, until she drops the bomb. For the next few weeks, she's assigning us in pairs. Once she calls our names, one of us has to go to the front to pick our theme and we have to create a series of written works together. I'm not the biggest fan of group projects, but I don't mind it, until I hear her say, "Princeton and Jay." I look across the room feeling betrayed.

Princeton jumps ups, giddier than I expect him to be. As

everyone plays a game of musical desks, he grabs the slip of paper and does a charming bow, before sitting in the seat next to me. He pushes his desk close to mine, leans in too close for comfort, and proudly smooths out the folded piece of paper on my notebook, so I can read the verdict written in perfect cursive. I stare at him in disbelief. It reads: *Love*.

Immediately, I run through every conceivable excuse of why this can't work, but it's pointless. I try to give myself a pep talk, speak possible where it feels impossible. It's not like I don't know Princeton, he practically worshipped Jacob and followed him everywhere when he was on the track team. In fact, he's still trying to beat all the state records that Jacob set. We've always known of each other, it's just . . . complicated.

Mrs. Jaxon gets everyone's attention, then explains, "You have the remaining forty-five minutes of class to figure out what you will create today based on your theme and how today's piece will inform the other pieces you will create together." She pauses, looks over at me. "Before you ask, partners are permanent."

She winks, confirming my suspicion. The moment Princeton began his show, she'd already made up her mind, we would be partners, and there is absolutely nothing I can do to change it.

For the next few minutes, I don't say anything. I just ignore Princeton staring at me, waiting to get us started.

"Why dontchu like me?" He locks eyes with me, serious.

I don't like it. It makes me uncomfortable, like he can see parts of me he shouldn't, without my permission. "Where's that coming from?"

He takes his time answering. "I'm just sayin'. All these years I been runnin' track with Jacob, you barely eva look me in the eye or give me the time of day. Barely even speak."

I shrug. We're from two different worlds—the popular and the invisible. Plus, I'm just starting to figure out what it means to live outside Jacob's shadow now that he's graduated—and that's hard enough.

In the silence, we write, our eyes dodging one another until he puts his pencil down and slides me his notebook. Without asking, he pulls mine toward him. I don't stop him.

As I read his writing, a different Princeton unfolds in front of me, speaking of yearning, fear, and loneliness. I'm struck by his last question, one we both wrote: *What is love?*

"Damn, I knew you was deep, but I ain't know you had it like that," he says, mid-laugh.

He works a pen between his thick lips and straight teeth and nods. With bushy eyebrows, perfect waves, and long eyelashes, he is the picture of confidence—blemishless brown swirling in red tints that glow in any light—where every word out of his mouth seems like a pickup line. "Whatchu think about mine?"

I pause, not sure what to say. If I tell him the truth, he

might think of me as soft, or worse, accuse me of trying to flirt with him (wait, am I? I've never done it before, so how would I know?).

Overwhelmed, I just say what I think. "You're a beautiful writer."

"Really? You think so?" His eyes light up, glimmer.

"Yeah, I wish you talked more about this stuff." The truth feels awkward, like words jumping the fence between my mind and my heart.

He hides his smile, taps a beat into the desk with his pen. He takes the pen top out of his mouth, as if he's about to say something, but he stops himself. His feet finish the cadence he started with his hands, softly.

"I'm sorry . . ." He breaks eye contact.

"For what?"

"'Bout what happened . . . wit Rouk." He speaks barely above a whisper, his giddy smile now lost somewhere behind his lips.

"It's not your fault." I draw circles and stars outside the margins of my paper, trying to avoid the memory. "You weren't the only one there . . . who didn't stop it."

Something in the silence threatens to crush us. We squirm in our seats, trying to escape by getting closer.

"I wish I did." He puts the pen top back in his mouth, fits right in the center, where his lips are the pinkest. His eyes are a pair of hands reaching for mine.

"It's cool. Don't worry about it."

"I'm tryna make up for that. Nobody should have to feel that . . . helpless."

The word lingers between us, as if it knows us more than we care to admit. I want to ask him what he means, if he has ever experienced it, but I don't. I can't. Our worlds must remain different, our lives separate, or I'll be sucked into the black hole that is him and his seductive charm and be destroyed.

"You really good wit' words," he says, resurrecting the smile—and the dimple in his left cheek. "It's like . . . I can feel your emotions. I try to do the same thing, but I like how you do it." He pauses. "I'mma ask you somethin' kinda weird."

I nod, like it's a choice.

"Just hear me out," he says.

His hands are big like he is. I hide mine, so I don't feel so small.

"Okay," I say.

"Ever wrote a love letter? Like to a girl . . . or a boy . . . anyone?"

I frown.

"I ain't mean nothin' by it. I'm just sayin' . . . you never know. . . . You should try it. Might be fun."

"Being with a boy?" I say, half joking, half serious.

He almost chokes on the pen top, takes it out of his mouth as he catches his breath.

"Or writing a love letter?"

He smiles, puts the pen top back where it belongs. Doesn't answer my question. Even flustered, he finds a way to remain in control, to keep his crown. I stare at him, impressed.

Mrs. Jaxon saunters past us. She smells of flowers and something soft, but her presence is bold, like a hand clenched in a fist.

"Might get us extra points," he says. "Mrs. Jaxon said if we went above and beyond, she'll reward us. Write one and lemme read it in class tomorrow." He whispers "reward" like it's a secret, a gift only she can give.

I wonder if it's worth a try: writing a love letter. "Who should I write it to?" I ask, accidentally out loud.

Princeton smiles with both rows of teeth, the pen top fit snuggly between. Then, he takes it out. "It don't matta; who-eva help you get the job done."

The bell rings.

"If you need somebody, tho, you can always use me." Princeton smiles, then slowly struts away. He turns around to see if I'm watching him—I am, but not for the reason he thinks. I think about telling him that when he tries to strut too hard, he walks less like a Casanova and more like a bowlegged peacock. I chuckle the more I think about it. Princeton grins, not knowing, then darts into the hallway.

I zip all the papers into my binder and drift into the hall-way, lost in my thoughts. Do you have to be in love in order to write a love letter? What if you don't know what it feels like? I flow into the traffic jam of Jordans, pleated skirts, and khaki pants in the hallway toward the double doors, hoping they'll lead me to an answer smelling of peppermint and Cool Water, to Leroy. Again, he's nowhere to be found. I follow my silent longing all the way home and try to sleep it off, hoping that when I wake, the ache in my chest will have gone away.

The front door slams so hard Momma's pictures snap back on the walls in protest. I jump up, quickly rubbing the sleep out of my eyes as I run to the hallway to see who it is. But I already know—I feel it—there's only one person that brave or that stupid: Jacob.

He storms up the stairs, his steps hard and reckless. He stands at the top, winded and surprised by it.

"Hey," I say softly, walking toward him. "What's—" I stop as my words crash into the invisible wall he's erected between us.

Suddenly, fear flashes across his face. He won't look me in the eye. That's when I see the signs: his shaky breathing, the muscles in his forearms flexing as he grips the banister tight like it's a lifeline, the beads of sweat suddenly gathering on his forehead. He's having a panic attack.

"Let me—"

"No . . . don't do that," he snaps. "Just gimme a minute."

I do what he says, but I inch closer, looking for a way to lend him some of my strength.

The door opens and closes again: Momma.

"Jacob, you done lost your damn mind slamming my door like that."

Her voice shoots up the stairs and yanks at him from behind. As he falters, I close the gap between us and grab him. He trembles under my touch. I tell him I'll handle Momma. He nods, holds on to me when I loosen my grip, then lets me go.

Downstairs Momma mumbles under her breath, cleaning an already spotless kitchen. I stand there quietly, not sure of what to say or do. She's more upset than I thought.

Her eyes lock onto me, a vise grip that won't let go. "Can I help you with something?" Translation: If you say the wrong thing, you'll feel my wrath, too.

I shrink. "No, ma'am."

She wipes one last circle into the counter, then throws the rag into the sink. "Make some Oodles of Noodles for you and your brother when you hungry." Then, just like Jacob, she stomps up the stairs, down the hall, and slams her bedroom door—a physical last word to whatever conversation she and Jacob were having in the car.

When Momma and Jacob get along, the house is sunshine and rainbows and music and dancing, but when they don't, it's dark and cold and sad and unbearable. Jacob is Momma's kind of stubborn; he'd rather pass out in hunger than tell Momma she's hurt his feelings, and Momma would rather him speak his truth than do what our dad used to and hold it all in. So everything happens as nothing happens, and I'm left in the living room sitting on the couch, staring at the wall, waiting for a sign to let me know which one of them I can talk down first.

But there's no sign to be found, so I climb the stairs anyway, hoping Jacob is at least willing to talk to me when I knock on his door.

"Who is it?" Jacob's voice is gruff; he's still mad but not as mad as earlier.

"It's me."

"Who's me?"

"Jacob," I say, turning the handle anyway. I peek my head in. "It's me, *me*."

He's on his bed smiling with a notebook in his lap. "I know who it is. Ma don't ask."

As I enter, he moves over, pats the space beside him. I sit down and lay my head on his shoulder and watch him flip back and forth in his notebook. Since he seems to be in better spirits, I finally ask. "What did Momma say to make you so mad?"

He stops flipping but still doesn't look at me. "Trust me, you don't wanna know."

"I do, though. If you know, I wanna know. Maybe I can help."

"You can't. Just take my word for it."

I turn to face him. "Come on, just tell me—"

"Jay, what I say?"

"Nothin'. That's the problem. Guess I'll assume it's just another one of your secrets."

He stares at me as if he's hurt, but I won't be silenced. Every secret he keeps is like a void between us, a space I'm not allowed to be. It scares me. I get ready to ask him again, to be stubborn on his behalf, even if he won't like it.

"J.D.'s getting out of prison."

Whatever words I plan on saying evaporate. All I can do is look at him. "Dad?"

He nods. He hasn't called him "Dad" since that night, since he hurt both of us.

There's a knock at the door—it's Momma.

When Jacob doesn't answer, she opens the door slowly.

In her hands is a peace offering, a bag of thrills, my and Jacob's favorite flavors: red and blue raspberry. She sits in the middle of the room, calls us to her. The three of us sit cross-legged on the floor in Jacob's room, scraping and crunching the frozen Kool-Aid with chunks of fruit to the sound of crickets beatboxing in the moonlight.

"I told him so you didn't have to. . . ." Jacob's soft words trail off, get lost somewhere in the light blue fluff of the carpet.

"You didn't have to . . . but thank you." Momma's eyes are open arms, waiting. But Jacob won't look up, just stares at the bottom of his cup.

"Jacob . . . look at me," Momma says, but he won't.

She scoots closer. "Unh-unh, look at me." She gently lifts Jacob's chin so his eyes meet hers. "I know you don't like this. I'm not saying you have to. But as a family, we should at least talk about it, okay? It's been six years, we knew this day would come."

"You gon' let him move back in?" Jacob asks.

"Do you want him to?"

He shakes his head. Then looks over at me.

"Okay. . . . What about you, Jay? Do you want him to live with us?"

I shake my head as well.

"Then the answer is no."

"What if he comes anyway?" I say. "What if he—"

Jacob's eyes hold me, calm me down.

"It don't work like that, baby. If we as a family say no, it means no."

I can see the questions forming in Momma's mind, why we've never wanted to see Dad, why we never talk about him or miss him the same way she does. I wonder if this is the time we should tell her what happened before he got arrested, the truth. But Jacob's eyes remind me of why I can't: she still loves him, misses him, wants us to be a family again. We won't do that to her. We can't.

"I need both of you to promise me something," she says, pulling us closer to her. "If something is wrong, I need you to promise to tell me the truth. Okay?"

Jacob and I look at each other and do the only thing we can: lie.

Mrs. Jaxon is a promise that today will be better than yesterday, in a baby-blue blouse and a white skirt and white-rimmed glasses to match. This morning was the first time I wasn't hoping to see Leroy. I still think about him all the time, but after the news about my dad getting out of prison soon, I feel different.

Suddenly I wonder if everyone you care about has the capacity to hurt you, to let you down, no matter how much you like them. Growing up, Dad was the strongest man I knew, the fearless protector, kind of like Leroy, but if even he turned his strength on us and used it to hurt us, would Leroy do the same? I shake the thought off, wait for it to fade away as quickly as it appeared.

Mrs. Jaxon announces we will have to be in our groups for the whole period. As Princeton dances over to the desk beside me, I pretend to ignore him. Then he drops a stack of some of the most beautiful watercolor-painted envelopes I've ever seen. They look handmade.

"What's this?" I hold one of them like a fragile treasure, a white envelope covered in light-blue-painted azaleas.

"For the letter."

"Did you make these?"

"Whatchu think?" He shows me his paint-stained cuticles

as proof. I stare at him in disbelief. I knew he was many things: a smooth talker, track all-star, secret homework doer (even though he pretended to be too cool for it), but a painter? No idea.

I hand him the letter I scribbled together this morning. It was the only thing I could do to distract myself. "You should give it to Alicia, the cheerleader everybody says you have a crush on."

"Don't believe everything you hear," he spits. "Ion like her like that. Got my eye on somebody else."

"Just read it."

"Wait, it looks like my handwritin'. How you do that?"

I glow in triumph. He isn't the only one with secret talents. "I can just about copy anyone's handwriting if I stare at it long enough—don't get any ideas."

He smiles, thinking about something he should keep to himself.

It was two pages front and back. He reads it, face almost to the page, as he chews on his bottom lip, smirking between bites. He puts the letter down and stares at me. His lips curl into a sly grin. If he wasn't the color of chestnuts, I would know if he is blushing or not.

"Hmm . . . ," he says.

"You don't like it?" I ask, unsure.

He fumbles with the edges of the paper, folding and unfolding until he makes a square, and then slides it into the envelope I'm cradling in my palms. He scribbles something on the front before walking across the room and giving it to a girl. He pimps back over and slides into his desk.

"What the hell? Why'd you give it to her?"

"Shhh. Watch."

She reads, hanging on every word until her face turns crimson. She looks back at him. He nods, sends a message with his lips but no sound.

"Wait till the bell rings," he tells me.

I don't think much of it as he shows me all the different kinds of envelopes he's made: some inscribed with heartfelt quotes or lyrics from songs, some even poems. Together, we decide to create a series of handwritten letters with handmade paper as our final assignment, which means we have tons of work to do. And I need to learn calligraphy almost overnight so I can write perfectly the letters based on poems and lyrics. When the bell rings, a boy walks in. The girl Princeton gave the letter to runs up to him and tongues him down so hard in front of everyone that Mrs. Jaxon threatens detention.

"I said it was from her boyfriend," Princeton says, snickering. "We both on the track team and kinda got the same handwriting. At practice, he stay whinin' 'bout how he can't tell her how he feel. Said he thought she was 'bout to call it quits on him. Guess they good now."

I watch, bewildered.

"I wanted to test it." Princeton turns toward me, leans in.

"Test what?" I lean away, suspicious.

"Your words. See if they hit someone else like they hit me. I think you can do betta, though. You were holdin' back a little. I felt it."

"Huh?"

"Iono, I just know. Write me anotha one. Make it how you feel 'bout me," he says, and winks, a period to his sentence.

"If I did, it wouldn't be a love letter, and you don't need any more hate mail."

"Dayum, it's like that? Aight, aight. You got me. Well, write it like it's to someone you really like, and don't hold back. Say the thing that scares you—ain't that what love is?"

I fight back a smile, surprised but not surprised at his brilliance.

He bops his head. "I'mma make us some more of these. We 'bout to get all the hearts."

"We?"

"Yup. *We.* You ain't gon' be able to get rid of me that easily." Princeton is genuinely serious, and I don't know how I feel about it.

The bell rings, and everyone hops up and tosses their papers in the basket in front of Mrs. Jaxon's desk.

Princeton taps me on the arm. "Aye, gimme thirty minutes before you leave."

"What? Thirty minutes? That's too long. I'm going home—it's been a long day," I say, irritated.

"Jay, come on, man. Just thirty minutes. That's all I'm askin'. If I ain't back by then, you can leave and forget I even asked. Furreal, furreal." He sways side to side, hands at his side, pleading with the blue pen top still in his mouth.

I think about it hard. Then I nod.

Thirty minutes come and go, feeling more like an hour and a half—and Princeton never shows. As I walk down the halls, I swear, when I see him, I'm going to give him a look that turns his ass to stone.

Outside, the sun slaps me on the forehead, but the smell of green apple Jolly Ranchers and Shock Tarts kiss it better. There's still a stream of cadets from JROTC out on the lawn who just got their boxes of chocolate and candy to sell, and everyone who would have been gone already is flocking toward the newly sugar-rich. Word must've gotten out that they were getting their boxes.

I ride the swarm until I'm almost through the crowd. That's when I see my classmate-now-nemesis, Princeton, the boy soon to become stone. He's smooth-talking three of the most popular guys in school: the captains of the basketball, football, and soccer teams.

When he sees me, he gets them to stuff something in his hand and jogs to catch up to me as I speed-walk by. I would have preferred it if he was at least wearing something other than his track uniform, which shows *everything,* making everybody we pass blush and then some. I do the only thing I can do in the face of a guy with the body of a demigod: ignore him.

"Jay!" he says, jogging in front of me. I ignore gravity fondling him in plain sight.

Eye contact, I chant in my head. "What?" I try out my death stare on him, but he laughs, refusing to turn to stone.

"Jay . . . come on. Don't be mad, I was on my way over to you."

"Yup, just what it looked like."

He stands still, looks me over, and shakes his head. "You been holdin' that in the whole time you been waitin', huh?"

I walk around him, but he stops me. "Hol' up, hol' up. Just hear me out. I got somethin' that'll make it worth the wait."

"A Snickers and two rolls of Shock Tarts?" I stare at the merchandise in his other hand.

"Something better."

I stare at him, unamused. "Alright . . . fine." Surprisingly, he hands me the sweet merchandise and an envelope with three crumpled sheets of paper stuffed in it.

"What's this?"

"It's three people who want you to write love letters to they girls."

I push them back in his hands. "I can't do that. Nobody's gonna pay me to—"

"And here's the money: a twenty for each, so sixty. The sheets of paper they wrote so you can see their handwriting, and I wrote a li'l somethin' 'bout each couple so you know the backstories."

“Why did you . . . This is a lot of money for just three letters.”

“No, it ain’t. You gotta gift, and it’s gon’ save they relationship. Least that’s what I told ’em.”

I shake my head.

“Look, I know we ain’t been the closest, but we’ve always known each other, right? Even you can admit it, though, I ain’t neva been one to lie—not furreal, furreal. The newspaper series is fiction, so it don’t really count.” He winks.

When I don’t respond, he gets even more dramatic. “Trust me, even if right now you don’t trust yourself.” His words hit me, pull a nod out of me, even before I realize I’m doing it.

He’s right. Maybe it’s worth a try.

Some guys in tracksuits like his run toward us. They grab Princeton. “Nigga, quit mackin’ and come on. I ain’t runnin’ no extra laps ’cuz a yo’ ass.”

They drag him away. He struggles with a smile.

Stunned by the money and envelope in my hand, I slide them in my pocket and look down the street where I’d seen Leroy just days ago. I don’t say anything, just keep walking until I’m at the school sign. As I cross the street in front of the school, I look for Leroy again. He’s nowhere in sight. What if he got in trouble after standing up to Rouk? What if something happened to him, and Rouk is looking for me next? What if it’s all my fault? What if—

Suddenly it feels too hot, so hot I could sweat through my shirt in a matter of seconds. It’s hard to breathe.

I hear Rouk's voice again. "Jay," he sings. "Jayyy." His voice echoes louder.

I can feel the heat, hear the laughter and all their voices. I stop near the same tree where Leroy's car was parked, where I wish it was now. I look over. He's still nowhere to be found.

It's happening all over again. I want to run, but my feet won't move.

"Jay . . ." His steps approach faster than before.

I need to get out of here.

"Jay." He reaches out to "help."

"Don't—" I snatch my arm away, try to hide how bad I'm shaking, and back up until I feel the tree shielding me from Rouk's voice and the dangling noose of their laughter.

"Whoa, whoa." It's not Rouk.

"Princeton?" I ask, unsure if what I'm seeing is real. I thought he was being dragged away by his teammates, but now he's standing in front of me with his hands up, surrendering.

"Yeah, it's me. You good?" He steps closer. "You don't look so good."

I back farther into the tree trunk—a reflex.

It happens so quick; I don't realize he's doing it until the heat suffocating me melts away and all that is left is a cool breeze and the smell of Palmer's Cocoa Butter and Big Red gum.

"Take three deep breaths," he whispers. "I'll do it with you." He's wrapped his arms tight around me; his lips tickle my ear. As he breathes in, the trees and the wind around us do it, too.

We breathe in, his arms around me tighten.

We breathe out, he releases.

We breathe in, my arms around him tighten.

We breathe out, my body sighs in relief.

We breathe in, our arms around each other tighten.

We breathe out, both of us release.

"Better?" he asks, still holding on to my elbows with his fingertips.

I nod, unsure of what to say.

Something hangs in the silence between us, a truth on the verge of being spoken. Then, someone calls his name. The team captain—and he doesn't look happy.

"Shit!" he yell-whispers. "I gotta run."

"Thanks." I smile, meaning it.

"No problem. I gotchu. Didn't I say? You and me a we now." He winks and jogs away, disappearing as quickly as he came.

Out of nowhere, music blasts, almost shaking the trees. I look across the street. It's Leroy, and his face says it all before he drives off, leaving the smell of burnt rubber. Even though I've been looking for Leroy every day after school, hoping to see his car out front, the one day he does show up, he sees Princeton—and now, somehow, I'm the one in trouble.

4

Leroy

Ion fuckin like it. Not one bit.

Since I been gone for a while, I swing by to check on Jay and make sure Rouk aint givin him no problems. Instead, I pull up to see Jay lettin some otha nigga be all up on him. I shoulda said, "Fuck you," to him and that nigga, and then drove right to Keisha's or Jessica's or Shayla's.

But the mo I think bout him, the mo I wanna see him, so I do the opposite and turn the car round.

By the time I get back to the school, I see him walkin to the intersection of Bee Street. I'm bout to pull ova and hop out, but it's a one-way. I honk the horn, but he don't turn round. Iono if he don't hear me or if he aint tryna hear me. I flip a U-turn and park across the street in front of the gas station. I get out the car, lean on the hood, and wait, watchin the old-timers buy lottery tickets. In the window, the Powerball jackpot is trapped in bubble letters: $12,100,000.

As soon as the light turns green, I feel Jay's eyes. He stops right in front of me, pissed wit his arms crossed, sittin in his right hip; eyes mo narrow than I remember, while his hand blocks the sun.

I wish I knew what he was thinkin so I could let him know: sometimes I run, but I always come back. But it aint easy layin yo feelings down at somebody feet when you don't even know if he feel the same.

Jay walks right by me, don't even speak.

I watch him.

Then I see that he aint leavin, just walkin behind the car ova to the passenger seat. He opens the door, gets in, and closes it. Somethin inside me shifts, like it's makin room for him.

I start the car and am bout to pull off when I hear him say, "Seat belt."

I look down and then look ova at him. He unbuckles his, reaches ova for mine and buckles it for me, shakin his head. I thought he was bout to grab somethin else.

"Now we can go," he says.

I drive down the road like last time, headed to the church. I go hella slow cuz ion wanna let him out yet. I got so much I wanna say, but I keep ovathinkin shit: Am I goin too fast? Too slow? Am I bein too quiet? Should I play music?

I aint neva been much wit words but it's not like I don't have nothin to say, it's just people use my body to speak. That's how I got good at listenin wit my hands, feelin what people need befo they even know to ask for it.

Ma used to say, "Lee, one day you gon meet a real pritty

girl and she gon be the reason you speak." That aint happen yet. But wit Jay starin out the window, I wanna try. It's just the words keep gettin stuck in my throat, and when I hype myself up enough to speak, all I do is choke.

"Haven't seen you in a while," Jay says.

"I know. Had some family stuff come up—my bad."

"Oh, is everything okay?"

"Yeah," I say, but the truth is ion really know; I can't stop thinkin there's a lot mo Taj and Rissa aint sayin bout the BDs lately, somethin they keep hidin.

I look ova, and he still starin, waitin on me to say mo, but iono what else to say. All I know is I aint ready for this to end yet. I wanna take him somewhere but can't take him to my spot. Then it hits me: I know exactly where to go.

"You gotta go straight home?" I ask.

"Depends. Where are we going?"

"You'll see." I turn down a different street, head away from the church.

"Oh . . . this isn't going to turn into a fight like befo? I don't know if I'll be able to win this time," he says, smilin.

"You aint win the first time."

"Yeah, I think I did, actually."

"How? Runnin aint winnin."

"Says who?"

"Man, you buggin."

A laugh fills the car. It takes a second for me to realize it's mine. I shift in my seat, tryna hide the hope growin where it shouldn't.

Auntie Rissa's Chicken and Waffles is empty, but it aint gon be for long. Come 4:00 p.m., errbody and they momma gon come runnin to the shop wit the pink sign that has a waffle in the shape of a bootie. The shiny blue button seats and slick-smooth booths will be crowded wit people yellin and climbin ova each otha to order and make Rissa laugh while doin it.

When we walk in, Rissa's back is to us. Her hair is in a bun that has little gems in it to match her flowy black dress wit pink dots. She is already the tallest woman; except for long shifts in the diner, she wears heels. No matta the conversation, she talks wit her long, colorful acrylic nails to prove a point: can't no man, woman, or chile on this earth forget her—and once they meet her, they can neva get enough. That's why she's been talkin to investors and they lookin to make her diner a franchise—they already tryna negotiate a deal to get her to take her diner to otha cities like Chicago, Atlanta, and DC.

She turns round, yells, "Ooh, chile, look at this tall glass of a man walkin up n heah."

"Wuss good?"

I smile, bigger than Jay has eva seen me and he gettin a kick out of it—his eyes say it all.

"Boy, come ova here and gimme a hug." Rissa won't lemme go till it feels right, till she can feel what's wrong that needs to be made right and she knows how to fix it. It's why she has so many customers—she has two recipes: one for touch and one for food.

"Mmm." She looks at Jay. "And who is this?"

Jay smiles, and that sends her ova the top.

"This Jay," I say. "Jay, this Auntie Rissa."

"Oop! You hear Lee, Benji? Callin me Auntie like he mean it?" She shouts back at Benji eyein her from the kitchen. "Hey, Jay, I'm Auntie Rissa."

"Nice to meet you . . . Auntie."

"Oh Lawd, let the church say . . . Boy, you just as cute as you wanna be—aint bout big as nothin. Get on ova heah and gimme a hug. If you special nuff fuh Lee to bring here, you family and don't even know it yet."

Jay giggles when Rissa squeezes him.

"Aye, don't hurt him," I say, laughin. "And naw, you can't keep him."

"Whateva. . . ." She rolls her eyes. "Okay, I see you witcho lil muscles, Jay. You keep on and you might become my type."

"And what's that?" asks Benji, her longtime boyfriend who works in the kitchen. He is taller, bigger, and tatted mo than any nigga I know. I used to call him Schwarzenigga. He a former Marine and been wit Rissa as long as I can remember.

"Benji, you know there's enough of me to go round."

"You must not know my appetite. I'm neva full, baby, neva," Benji says.

Rissa blows him a kiss.

Jay and I look at each otha and grin.

"Whey ya brotha at? I aint seen my Bittersweet in bout a week," Rissa asks.

"He restin up."

"Hmm, sound like trouble."

"He—"

"Unh-unh, too many eyes and ears in heah. Is my baby okay? That's all I wanna know."

"Yeah, he good."

"Alright. Benji! Pack up three boxes of them oxtails and greens for my Bittersweet. Watchall tryna eat?" Rissa asks.

"You know I love whateva you fix me," I say.

Her eyes take me in and give me back. "Benji, let me get some of dem ribs, fried chicken, and some sweet potato mash. Put my special sauce on it—and a lot of it.

"Jay, whatchu thinkin?" Rissa asks. "I got some catfish and sweet tater fries, they what I'm known for. And I got three desserts today: apple crisp, banana puddin, and monkey bread."

"I'll have that and banana pudding. Thank you!" Jay smiles, showin off his dimples. Part of me gets jealous—he aint neva smile at me like that. Not yet.

"Where you live?" Rissa asks.

"Over near K-Heights." He smiles, like it's somethin errbody asks when they meet him. "But I grew up in K-Town."

"Po baby, I know they musta chased you all up and down them streets." She laughs.

Jay's face says it all: Rissa's words hurt.

"I'm just kiddin, baby. Keep ya head up, okay? I'm not laughin atchu—I'm laughin *witchu*. There's a difference, okay?" She strokes his chin, dots him on the nose. "Speakin of, is Leroy bein good to you?" Rissa pulls Jay in, a secret she wants to keep close.

"Of course I am," I say.

Rissa winks at Jay, tellin him somethin only they can understand.

"Aight, now. I gotta get ready, mo customers comin who need my love. Yall find a seat and Imma bring the food when it's done. Oh, yall want sweet tea, soda, or red Kool-Aid?"

"Sweet tea," we both say at the same time.

When Rissa finally bring the food, me and Jay eat and laugh natural like breathin. I aint neva seen him smile so big. I crack up when he hums wit his eyes closed while he eats.

"Like it that much, huh?"

He smiles wit his eyes, almost got me shiftin in my seat again. "It's really good. Rissa can burn," he says. "I've never been here before. You come here a lot?"

"Enough for her to know what I wanna eat."

"What made you bring me here? Could you tell I was

hungry?" Mo hummin wit his eyes closed.

"Kinda—but errbody get hungry when Rissa cooks. That won't the only reason, tho. I wanted to ask you somethin." I stuff the last bit of apple crisp in my mouth, take my time chewin it, so I can find all the right words. "Some stuff went down at my school and I'm gon apply for this GED program, but I need somebody to help me work on an essay. I was wonderin . . . you think you could help me wit it? You know . . . not write it fuh me but help make sure my words together like they need to be. I can pay if you want."

He don't respond right away, and he don't look at me, eitha. Did I fuck up? Say it wrong?

"Instead of money, could you bring me here when we work on it? Well, from time to time, in case it's too loud in here for you to concentrate."

"You sure? I got the money if you want it. Aint a problem."

"I know. I just like this better. It's more special. You seem more comfortable here. It's the only place I've ever seen you laugh and smile. You should do it more often."

"Aight . . . Dats wassup." I feel my face gettin warm, and it aint cuz I just finished eatin spicy fried chicken.

"Plus, I already got a lil money coming in," he says. "So, one of these days, I'm going to have to take you out for a bite to eat."

"Where you work?"

"I can't tell you. You're going to laugh."

"Nah, I won't."

"Okay. Some guys at school pay me to write love letters to their girlfriends."

I try to stop it—but it aint happenin. I laugh so loud he does, too.

"See? I told you. . . ."

"I aint mean it, my fault, my fault. You must be a beast wit da pen, then."

"I wouldn't say all that. I guess I'm just pretty good with words and feelings. Well, good with everybody else's but my own."

"Whatchu mean?"

"I guess, lately, I'm realizing some words just don't exist for the way I feel, or I haven't learned them yet. But I seem to be able to find the words for everybody else. Guess that makes me a little more complicated."

"Nah, it makes you mo special, that's all. Plenty a words in this world, but findin the right ones is the hard part. I'm workin on that, too." I look down at my empty plate and then back up at Jay. "You gon let me read one? One of ya letters?"

"No, I can't. That would be too embarrassing. I already can't believe I'm doing it."

"Why not? What's wrong wit whatchu do? Sound like a gift to me. Errbody can't use words like you do. If it's helpin people, why not?"

"Maybe. But I bet you're just as good, you just don't know it yet. I'll prove it to you. Then you can do whatever you want to do next."

"Werd?"

"Watch. I've got a feeling, and I'm rarely wrong . . . with feelings."

There's somethin bout the way he moves his spoon, works it in his mouth so he can pull it out clean. Has me chewin on ice just to keep my cool.

"How you get to writin letters? Was it a teacher or somethin?"

"Kind of. Our English teacher split us into groups, and we all had to pick topics written on these little pieces of paper. When my classmate picked for us, it said, 'Love.' After he read some of my writing, he asked me to write a love letter, and I guess he really liked what I wrote."

I nod. Can feel the irritation comin.

He sips from his iced tea, sucks a lil too loud by accident, then laughs. I like it.

"I just started, but Princeton, my classmate, seems to think it can go somewhere. We'll see how it goes."

I play wit my straw, tryna keep myself from explodin. Who is this nigga, Princeton? Is he the guy who was huggin all up on him? I try to focus, try to listen, but it's gettin hard.

"I never got love letters myself," Jay says, "so I never thought I'd ever be good at writing them, but I guess that's why it's kind of fun to do. It's like I'm writing what I always wanted someone to say to me. You know?"

I nod but won't look at him. The bell rings as a big group comes in—tourists. They loud like all they wanna do is be heard as they spend they money. Last to come in is a boy that kinda looks like Jay, maybe same age and errthang. He winks at me, won't stop starin.

"Cool," I say, still not lookin at him and tryin not to look at the Jay look-alike, eitha. I try to ignore all the bad shit I wanna say, try to find somethin good, but it's gettin harder every second. Iono why I can't just come out and say it: *I aint tryna hear bout no otha nigga you like. I don't even wanna know bout no fuckin letters if they connected to him.*

"You okay?" he asks. I can feel him readin my face. He looks round, sees the Jay look-alike starin at me.

"Yeah, just the itis," I lie, tryin not to look at eitha of em.

"Can I ask you something?"

"Sup?"

"You still mad at me?"

His question catches me off guard. I don't even know what to say. The truth aint pritty, and I aint in no mood to lie. "Mad bout what?"

"Princeton."

So that's who it was?

"I don't know. I just figured . . ." He keeps lookin ova at his look-alike, aint even eatin no mo, like somethin botherin him.

"Figured what?" I lean in, try to get his eyes back.

"Ever since I said Princeton's name, you're being cold toward me . . . again."

"Whatchu mean, again'?"

Jay shakes his head, won't answer, but I need him to. I want him to say it, tell me he don't like that nigga, that he only like me.

"Never mind."

Tha fuck? Never mind? I shake my head, sit back. "It's cool. You do you. He aint got nothin to do wit me. You like him?"

"Princeton? No. We're just friends."

"Friends hug all on each otha like that?"

"It wasn't like that. He was just helping me out. . . ."

Shit. I *am* mad, but I don't wanna be. "Let's get outta here. I gotta get home. I'll drop you at the church."

He aint gotta say it, I already know. He like Princeton . . . maybe the same way he like me.

"Leroy . . . It's not—"

"Come on, I aint tryna be late," I say, and I walk off.

Behind me, I hear him.

"Okay. Some other time then."

By the time I get home, errthang that had me feelin good is gone. When Jay got outta the whip, he barely said bye. I walk into the house mo confused than when I left.

"Aye, give me back the salt and pepper. Seriously, Taj, don't mess it up!"

"Look, I told yo ass, I can cook too. And even if you don't trust that, I gotta tongue, so I know how to taste. Just let me sprinkle some of dat in, I gotchu."

Taj and Jacobee—the guy who fixed Taj up a few nights ago after he got jumped at the club—damn near wrestlin in the kitchen. At first, Jacobee said he would only check on Taj the day after to make sure he was healin and eatin right. Then Taj begged Jacobee to cook for us—since he cared so much—and now, he been stoppin by, cookin dinner for us the past few nights. It took me fuheva, but Taj finally said what his name was but neva told me how they knew each otha.

Havin Jacobee round has been good for Taj—for both of us—but I still catch Taj every now and then starin off into space or up in the middle of the night, like somethin eatin away at him. Even though Taj's been keepin his secrets, the news been talkin bout the gangs. I know it means somebody been violatin the truce.

I wonder if that's why Taj try to keep Jacobee round, so he can know there's mo to livin and bein than just solvin errbody problems. Iono if Jacobee know it, but he aint just somebody Taj care bout, he Taj sanctuary, his peace.

After I close the front door, I'm watchin Jacobee playin goalie in front of a big-ass soup pot on the stove that has the whole house smellin like Rissa's. Taj has a saltshaker in one hand and a pepper shaker in the otha, threatenin to throw extra shakes in the pot when Jacobee aint lookin.

"Wuss good?" I say.

"Sup, Lee?"

"Hey, Leroy! Getcho brotha. He's bout to ruin a family dish I made just for yall. I keep tellin his ass it doesn't need no damn salt or pepper."

"Look like you handlin it pritty good yaself. You don't need my help."

"But I have to take a piss," Jacobee says. "Come on, Leroy. Help a brotha out. Well, not yo brotha, *a* brotha," he say, laughin.

Jacobee has a smile like Jay's, but it's different. He knows its effect on people, how it can change errbody round him for the betta. He even has Taj goin from protective to the prankster he always been when we was kids. I don't know how long it's gon be befo he gets called out to the streets again, so I get in on some of the action. Taj should laugh a little mo befo then.

I jump in front of the pot. Jacobee guards the sides, and I protect the top: we look like a weird-ass four-leaf clover.

"Where yo loyalty at, Lee? Ol traitor," Taj says, swipin at my hands, since Jacobee has already proved he's faster.

"What? You always tell me to stand up for what's right. Aint nothin right bout messin wit perfection."

"You aint even taste it. It need a lil mo salt n peppa." He keeps shakin and shakin. It's hard for eitha of us to know when he tryna get it in furreal or when he fakin.

"Aight, Leroy." Jacobee grabs my shoulders. "It's all in yo

hands. I'm trustin you wit my family's recipe. Guard it wit yo life."

He runs to the bathroom down the hall.

Taj swipes at my hands, and I block him. It's good to see him smile.

"Whey you been? Back in school yet?"

"Nope—"

He frowns.

"But I got a tutor who gon help me wit my essay for the GED program, so I can get back on track."

"Werd?"

"Yup! Told you I was gon make it right."

"Well, it's still talk till you back at school or you got that GED in yo hand."

"I know, I know. But watch me work."

He stops movin, leans in closer. "Aight. Time for the truth. Iono what it's called, but it's good as hell. Come on, taste it. Furreal. I aint playin. Hurry up befo he gets back."

"Nope."

"Whatchu mean? It's good."

"Who fool I look like to you? I aint stupid. You raise me betta than that. Aint bout to let you trick me."

Jacobee shows up in the nick of time and swipes one of the shakers from Taj hand. Distracted, I swipe the otha.

"Yall just gon gang up on me like that?"

We grin, victorious.

Jacobee hands us both spoons. He wearin an apron, and it looks good on him. He pulls out soy sauce, vinegar, and ketchup. Me and Taj look at each otha, confused.

"Trust me. It's gon be the best thing you eva tasted."

Me and Taj look at each otha and smile. "Prove it."

After he does his thing, we chuckle and bring the pot and bowls into the livin room so we can put errthang on the table and eat. And when we taste it, we realize he won't lyin—shit is fiyah!

It's been a long time since me and Taj had someone cook for us besides Rissa. But Jacobee don't just know how to cook, he know how to make the house feel like a home. What me and Taj always had was close, but since Ma left and we moved out of Auntie Rissa's, it feels like somethin is missin.

This whole week wit Jacobee swingin by errday just feels right. He can't neva stay long, but he always comes back. It feels like one of the only things Taj looks forward to, especially when he come in late at night exhausted.

At first I was a little suspicious. I aint understand why Taj neva told me bout Jacobee—and he still don't say much, even when I ask. But even when Taj aint home and it's just me, Jacobee still visits and cooks, so I aint home alone the whole time. It feels good to have somethin and somebody to look forward to.

"So, Leroy," Jacobee starts, "why did you have the long face when you came in? And what was that bag you brought in wit you? It smelled really good."

"Oh, it was oxtails and greens from Auntie Rissa's Chicken and Waffles."

"Nice. And the face you were wearin wit it?"

"Huh?"

It's like Jacobee can sense a tack in a tire a couple of states away. Can't get shit past him.

"Who is it?" Jacobee smirks.

"Whatchu mean?"

"Looks like you in the early stages of love, my man, right after 'like' but befo you even know what it is. That's when it still clings to you, keeps you daydreamin, barely able to sleep at night."

"Naw, if it's bout me sleepin at night, it's cuz Taj snores too loud."

Taj throws a chicken bone at me. "Nigga, ion snore, so you can keep that fuh ya troubles. If you took yo ass upstairs like I said, you wouldn't be worried bout my quiet sleepin habits."

"I'm used to it now. Hard to go back."

"You betta sleep in yo bed tonight. I'm fully healed. Aint no need for you to keep watch. I'm back, bayybee," he sings, until Jacobee throws a bone at him, and then swipes a half-eaten drumstick wit a chunk of meat off his plate and sucks it clean. Taj lets it happen, seems proud to, like Jacobee eatin somethin that had been in his mouth is all he needs to make his night.

"And don't change the subject. You aint slick. Who is it? Who got yo nose wide open?"

"Nobody."

"Aww, you blushin." Jacobee grins. He sips his soup extra loud to make his point. Reminds me of Jay a lil bit.

"I aint blushin. How would you know?"

"Well, I have a superpower: I know when people are in love or close to it," says Jacobee.

"Bullshit." I dodge anotha chicken bone. It barely misses my face.

"Quit. Fuckin. Cussin," Taj says.

Jacobee and I laugh. Taj smiles a different kind of smile, one I aint really seen since Ma. It's happier than happy, like a lil kid wit a crush.

"If you know when people in love, am I?" Taj asks, puttin his bowl down.

Jacobee ignores him.

"Want me to tell you?" Taj says.

Jacobee's face goes blank. Somethin happenin, and I aint got no clue what it is.

"Taj, stop playin, alright?"

"I'm not. You want me to tell you or nah?"

"Nah," Jacobee says. He gets up, squeezes by me, and heads for the door. "I'll see you tomorrow, Leroy."

"Aight, Bee."

Taj jumps up and barely catches Jacobee's arm. "Aye, aye.

I'm just fuckin witchu."

"No, you not, Taj."

"Whatchu mean? I *am*."

"Taj, my superpower, remember?"

They stare at each otha, and then I see it, too. Iono when it happened, but somethin like love snuck up on Taj, and it's standin butt-ass naked in front of all of us wit no plans of puttin no clothes on.

"I told you this wasn't a good idea." Jacobee leaves, closin the door behind him.

Taj stares at the door in shock, then runs out to catch him.

The longer I sit listenin, feelin the weight of Taj tryna say anything to make Jacobee stay, the mo I see what I'm afraid of: bein the only one in like, or in love.

Taj walks back in and closes the door. He don't have to say nothin cuz it's already on his face, the look of bein scared, left all alone. He climb the stairs, quiet. And, for the first time, I realize, if Jay did me like that, ion think I could take it. Naw, I *know* couldn't.

So I make up my mind: I gotta do somethin befo this shit gets outta hand.

5

JAY

The house feels as empty as I feel lonely. Momma is out, and Jacob is either working or in class, which means it's just me and my thoughts—the last thing I really want right now.

After Leroy, all I want to do is talk to somebody, to explain how much I don't understand how I feel about him. I don't know how to do this, how to say "I like you," because whenever I have gathered up the courage to say it before, no one has ever wanted to say it back. No matter who I like. They either never like me back or they never come back.

I throw myself into writing the love letters for Princeton, because it's the only way I can make sense of everything I feel and don't know how to say. Only as I stare at the twenties cuddling on my desk next to the empty envelope, I second-guess why I'm doing it altogether; the first letter to Princeton was a challenge, a point I needed to prove that I was more than just an invisible junior with high grades who only had his right hand to serve him up when he was lonely. But now, it's different.

I can't shake what I felt sitting across from Leroy, even as he looked at the other guy and as so many other people in Rissa's restaurant stared at him. I need to be needed. Outside of that, the words stop. The only way I can write these love letters is if I stop thinking and feel it for myself, to ask my own body what it already knows. But there's only one way I know how to do it. I look at the clock: I have a little over an hour before Momma and Jacob get home.

I lock the door, turn off the lights.

In the dark, I close my eyes, until my body is a hard invitation with a soft request. My right hand finds the rhythm, and that's when I see Leroy standing next to the powder-blue Cadillac. He has something I don't, even though the words of what that is escapes me. But here, in my room, in my mind, explanations are no longer needed.

Leroy steps forward. He doesn't speak, just leans in close and watches me. He moves with me, on the brink of touch. He slips his hands around my waist, until they find their home against my hips. He leans forward, until there isn't even enough space for a breath between us and all I can taste on my tongue is peppermint.

Leroy's lips and hands are keys, unlocking parts of me I always thought were off-limits, and together they rattle the broken chains against the fences, giving my body a new purpose. It feels like everything happens at once, and it's hard to breathe when I feel Leroy's lips and the weight beneath his hips. Suddenly, it clicks; I understand now.

It's hard writing a love letter when I've never been in love, but love letters aren't really about love; they are about want, luring a future fantasy into the present, so you can feel it—or at least the promise of it—between your fingers, against your lips. I have been looking at it all wrong. It isn't about what I have but what I'm missing. Like a prayer that has no god to hear it. Everyone calls it love, but I think it's something deeper, and the word "love" is just a placeholder.

Before I know it, I've written four letters: three to the boys' girlfriends and one to Leroy. In them, I churn everything I don't know how to say into touch, hoping for something like a miracle but a little less grand; no spectacle is needed, just hope, proof that things can be different, better.

I go to bed a prince and wake up a pauper—at least, it feels that way. If last night was a breakthrough, this morning feels more like a breakdown. On my dresser is the evidence: four letters that are probably the most prolific, heartfelt things I've ever written.

The first three letters are my job; the sixty dollars on my desk proves that. But the letter to Leroy is different. Shame slaps me around and makes me its bitch. I can't bring myself to pick them up and put them in my book bag. There is a little too much truth in the letter to Leroy, and my world feels like it depends on lies to feel safe. I don't just lay everything out on the table in words to Leroy—I set it with expensive china, make a full-course meal, and flip the table over.

Once Leroy reads his letter, there is no turning back, and I desperately need to be able to say "Just kidding," if he doesn't feel the same way. I want to risk it, to know where it leads if we don't try to stop it, name it, but I'm also afraid of the potential consequences.

I don't want to get the same look I got when I finally mustered up the courage to tell some girls I liked them. I hated how the pending rejection started in their face long before it came from their lips. First, the smile in their eyes, the look of feeling flattered, then that damn glimmer, the look you give cute, adorable things that don't know any better: pity.

I eventually take the letters and stuff them deep into each of my pockets: the right with the three letters for Princeton in one envelope, the left for Leroy. I trust the decision will make itself. I just pray I'm strong enough to handle it and leave the house.

As I jog to school, I remember Rouk's words from that day: *fuckin faggot*.

It wasn't the first time I heard the word, and he wasn't the first person to call me it. Most of the time, I thought I knew what it meant to other people. A faggot was a guy who liked other guys, and in a way that made them less than a man. At least, that's what I got from them. The proof was in the sneer and venom that dripped like molasses from the person's lips, as if saying it made them taller, bigger, more valuable than the person they were saying it to.

I've never said it out loud, but the first person to ever call me a faggot wasn't a stranger—it was my father.

I was around eight years old, and even though I didn't know what it meant, I knew it sounded wrong. Momma always tells me and Jacob that any name other than the one you choose is a poison others try to use to kill the best parts of you from the inside out. The parts of you that scare everyone else because they represent a power you have over them, a strength and freedom they can't handle. She says it is a hateful thing people, who are insecure in themselves, do to feel better, more whole. I don't know if this is really true or if it's something parents say to kids they know might be broken, unfixable.

I don't know if there is a name out there for me or how I feel—or if I will ever answer to it, even if there is. But I am afraid, and each step brings me closer to my fear so I can see it in all its glory. I'm afraid of Leroy saying those words with the same molasses venom dripping—and worst of all—believing him.

Princeton was so excited yesterday about me writing the letters, I expected him to be waiting the moment I got to school or at least sitting on my desk with some kind of charming joke to initiate the letter exchange. But by the time the bell rings at the end of Mrs. Jaxon's class, he's still nowhere to be found, which is odd. Then, a pair of hands cover my eyes.

I know the voice and the scent—Palmer's Cocoa Butter and Big Red gum. It's Princeton.

"Miss me?" he asks.

I smile, probably too big.

"You got them letters?" he asks, his smile a reflection of mine.

"What letters?"

"The letters for the three couples. It's Friday," he says, blowed. "You know people tryna get somethin' poppin' this weekend. You ain't write 'em?"

"Yeah, I did. I'm just playin'." I hand him the envelope.

He rolls his eyes, then opens it quickly, moves his lips as he silently reads. "Dayum, dayum." He stops in front of me, puts his hand over his chest, dramatically. "Oooweee . . . I shoulda charged way more than that. With this shit right heah, you might have niggas gettin' married an havin' babies by the end of the week."

"Hush, it's not that serious," I say, walking toward the door. Princeton tags along, refolding the letter he read before placing it into one of his special-made envelopes: all pastel colors with different designs, like flowers I've seen somewhere but can't remember.

"Whatchu doin' tomorrow night?" Princeton asks out of nowhere.

"Depends . . . why?"

"You should come to my party Saturday night to celebrate us goin' to state, and you knowin' one of the fastest niggas in Georgia." Princeton dances like everybody's watching.

"I don't know. Parties aren't really my thing. Different kinda crowd I'm not really used to."

"Bring Jacob, then. He'll know just about everybody there."

I mull it over. Jacob has been MIA lately, but if he is there, at least I would feel safe. "I'll think about it. Let me talk to Jacob first."

"Bet! Might have some more letters for you by Monday, too—word is gettin' 'round fast, so you gotta come to celebrate."

His words are a period posing as a question mark as he jogs toward the gym. Before I know it, I'm walking out the double doors, across the street, and down the promenade, as if I'm being pulled. Then, I realize why.

In front of the school, I see Leroy's Cadillac and, instantly, my heart starts racing, and I realize I have his letter in my hand, which shocks me. In my body, a decision about Leroy has already been made and there's no going back now.

When I cross the street, I see him more clearly now, he's in the cleanest outfit I've ever seen on him. A black fitted cap, black beater, black Air Force 1s, and the kicker: all-white Girbaud pants with black tabs—and on his arm, a girl I don't recognize. She has long burgundy microbraids in a bun, a tight white shirt tied at the stomach with "Heartbreaker" in pink glossy letters, and Apple Bottom jeans showing off every curve she has, and on her feet: powder-pink 1s that match the letters on her shirt. She's one of the prettiest girls I've ever seen and stands, leaning into Leroy, as if she owns him. Beside her, Leroy looks perfect, they look perfect, and the crowd gathering around them knows it.

At first, I think she is just flirting with him, but when Leroy sees me, he pulls her close by the hips. She stares in his eyes, giggles like all girls giggle in front of someone they like. She strokes his chin, and then she puts her finger on his lips, teasing him with words I can't hear. Then Leroy does something I never expect: he kisses her. Then, she mooshes his face from hers.

"What I look like to you? You takin' it too far," she says, rolling her eyes.

He laughs, tries to weave his fingers into hers, a couple fist, but she pulls away.

I want to turn around, but my legs are hell-bent on my own destruction. Before I know it, I'm standing in front of them, waiting for something that will never come.

Even though I've never been in love, I always wondered what heartbreak must feel like. I imagined it was like a vase suddenly crashing in the center of your chest, you speechless and in shock. Leroy proves me wrong—it's far worse, a slow smothering, hand over mouth and nose, right after he lets me take a deep breath of hope. His eyes say it all: there is no escape, no change of heart; this is all there is—all there ever will be.

"Sup, Jay." He wipes the commingled sheen from his lips. Any boy except me would envy him, but I just stand there, speechless and helpless, wishing somebody, anybody would save me.

"Hop in," he says, nodding.

I don't nod back—can't even pretend. I stand still, thinking about what it all means.

She introduces herself as Trish, but I hear "truth" and believe it to be true—the meaning of her name, and the hole in my chest it leaves behind. The more I think about it, it's like Trish can bend anything or anyone to her will, as if she knows a secret—and the power of keeping it. She is everything I can't be for him—a reminder that I'm just Jay.

"You comin or what?" Leroy says. Trish watches me from the other side of the car, but her eyes avoid mine, like she's hoping I'm smart enough to tell Leroy to go straight to hell lathered up in Crisco in gasoline drawers. I'm not.

Every muscle in my body begs me to walk—hell, run—but if I don't open the door and sit, I'll probably fall to the ground and only humiliate myself further. Plus, a part of me wants to know what I don't know. So I do the one thing I never expect, when someone stabs you in the heart: I don't cry, I don't scream, I wrap my hands around the handle and pull the blade deeper.

I get in the car, suffering silently and invisibly in the back seat.

As the bass bullies my heartbeat and the scent of Trish's cherry lip gloss hitches a ride to the back seat, my eyes keep meeting Trish's in the side-view mirror. It's possible I am the one staring, but it feels like she understands me, pities my dreams from the vantage point of someone who knows better. That's when I see the words etched on the mirror:

OBJECTS IN MIRROR ARE CLOSER
THAN THEY APPEAR.

Suddenly it all feels like a cruel joke and, yet again, I'm the punch line.

I overestimate myself, feeling every thought I've ever thought and every feeling I've dared to feel dying in my chest. I can't take it. It's too much. I open the door, hop out, and run across the street. I hear him call after me, yell as if I was the one in the wrong. But I never stop, and I promise I'll never look back.

6

Leroy

I wake up on the couch feelin like shit. I been stressin all weekend, barely sleepin waitin for Monday to finally get here, so I can find a way to apologize to Jay. I fucked up, and I know it. I aint mean to do Jay like that. It's just . . . I just . . . won't thinkin.

When I texted Trish that night, errthang was goin down between Jacobee and Taj, so I asked her to pretend we was datin so I could make Jay a lil jealous. She told me it was a bad idea, but I begged her, and she won't gon leave me out there on front street like that.

When I saw Jay comin my way in front of the school, I was gon back out, but errtime I see him, I feel myself fall harder and faster—like there aint nothin I can do bout it—and I aint gon lie, it scared me. And I do stupid shit when I'm scared.

I know it sound like an excuse, and it don't make what I did right, but I neva thought he would hop outta the whip in the middle of traffic and dip. And when I was callin him, tryna get him back and apologize, he ignored me. It wasn't till I hopped back in the whip that I found the letter on the floor in the back seat.

After I read it, I felt like my heart was gon fall out my chest. Errthang I wanted to avoid feelin, I felt it anyway *and* it's my fault. How was I supposed to know Jay felt that way bout me? Errthang in his letter, he aint neva said to me in person. If I woulda known he was afraid of the same shit I was, that all he wanted was for me to just be there for him like he wanted to be there for me, I woulda neva did nothin like that.

When Trish read it, she told me to find him and make it right. Only I aint know where he live, so I gotta wait till later today when I know he'll be at school, but I don't know what to say, eitha. I feel like aint nothin I can do to get him back, to make him forgive me. There's only one place I can go, only one person who can tell me what to do to make this right.

I pull up in the parking lot and see Benji on the side of the restaurant receivin some last-minute deliveries. When he sees me get outta the car, he waves and points to the otha side to let me know Rissa somewhere back in the kitchen. I stand in the parkin lot and, outta nowhere, imagine Jay walkin up to me like that day he crossed the street and got in my car. I breathe in real deep, smell the sweet hoverin in the heat, then I go inside.

As I walk through the door, the bell rings, and all I can smell is somethin sweet bakin. I'm so hungry I get light-headed; I aint ate much this weekend, just read Jay's letter ova and ova like it had a clue or somethin of how I could get to him.

I sit at my favorite stool, one of only two pink button seats, wit me and Taj initials.

I can hear Rissa nearby on the phone and she aint happy. "So you tellin me you gon take my property and offer me money, knowin it's barely pennies on the dolla? Don't be callin me actin like you doin me no favors." She slams the phone down on the receiver, then walks somewhere else.

I can hear her slammin things and Benji whisperin, tryna calm her down. Don't take long till she walkin in from the back. She still aint happy—and she aint tryna hide it—but her words still come out sweet like honey when she see me.

"Who done gon and broke yo lil heart?" Auntie Rissa says, stockin some glasses nearby befo she come closer. "Benji! Got anotha heartbreak on aisle seven. Lee need a plate of yo shrimp n grits. While we at it, gon head and bring a few clusters of dem Dungeness crabs. This gon be a big one, I can tell."

It's hard as hell to tell somebody what you can't tell yoself. I put my head in my hands.

"This got anything to do wit my boo?" Rissa says.

"Who?" I put my head down, peek up at her from between my arms.

"Boy, don't play wit me. You know who I'm talkin bout: Jay. I guess it does cuz he clearly aint yo boo no mo."

I don't have the words. So I give Rissa the letter. I can't

bring myself to say it, but if she reads it, I know she can connect the dots.

I can sell out a stadium's worth of tickets just to the show of Rissa readin Jay's letter. I aint neva gon hear the end of this, I already know. But it's the only way.

"Lee, whatchu not tellin me? Spill the tea." She gives me that look, which mean she aint gon ask again.

"I kissed Trish in front of him. . . ."

"What? Why? Aint Trish yo . . ." She sighs, shakes her head. "What were you thinkin, Lee?"

"I aint wanna—"

"Unh-unh. Don't even finish whateva you bout to say." Rissa hands me my plate of food. "Just eat that food and shut up till I figure out what Imma do witchu."

I smash the grits and smile at Rissa while I start on the crabs.

"Whatchu smilin fo? You in trouble. See? That's part of the problem right there. I spoil you and yo brotha too damn much. Imma stop feedin yall."

I laugh, keep eatin my crabs. It aint makin the pain in my chest errtime I think bout Jay go away, but Rissa know how to hit the spot.

"I eva tell you the story bout how I was born?"

"Nah. Why?"

"Cuz I was born twirlin."

"Whatchu mean?" I ask, confused.

She laughs. "I mean what I mean. I came out of the womb

twirlin. I was a breech baby."

"Feet first, right?"

"Yup. Ion really rememba tha details—it's prolly like all the best thangs, a little fact and fiction—but the way yo grandma told it, I was born in this gawdfuhsaken world feet first."

"Aint that dangerous?" I crack open two claws, slurp out the juice.

Rissa grabs one from my plate, does the same.

"Yeah, very. But my momma managed it somehow. She used to say that's how she knew I was gon be special . . . and stubborn." She laughs, workin her way through mo claws, pickin ova all the meat I seem to leave behind. Once she done, she squeezes lemon juice ova her hands and rinses them at the sink.

When she comes back, she folds some napkins into a shape, then put em in her apron. "I used to tell people I was born heels first to get a laugh, but the truth is that I was born runnin. From what people thought. From what I thought they'd say. Even from what I thought they'd do.

"I was Lawrence Booker the Third, right after yo grandfather, from the moment I was born until I was twenty-seven years old. And won't nothin gon change that. At least, that's how I saw it. It don't matta what I felt, that I knew it won't really who I was, who I wanted to be."

"Grandma aint accept you?"

"Did she? I think she and yo dad knew long befo I did.

I was the one that was scared. But when she died, I was so brokenhearted, I decided I was eitha gonna die a man or finally live as the woman I know my mom wanted me to be, in her honor. Then, somehow, I met Lady Chablis. She was in that movie *Midnight in the Garden of Good and Evil* and she really inspired me. It wasn't just her, tho, it was all the otha women in our community, too. When I was tryna figure it all out and wasn't good at it, they brought me in, put their arms round me, and showed me it was okay. It was hard at first, but eventually, I was proud to be myself, phenomenally.

"Aint that right, Benji?"

"Damn right!" he yells from the kitchen, hearin errthang.

"Now dontchu think it's time you get outta here and get to that boy school? You got some work to do, too, boo—and best believe, you gon have to work real hard to get him back after the stunts you done pulled."

"He aint gon wanna—"

"Befo you fix yo mouth to say what you is and you aint gon do, lemme put this anotha way: I'll be dead and twirlin in my grave befo I let you make the mistake of runnin from yoself like I was at yo age. Now, get outta that seat, hop in that car, and go tell that boy how you feel."

"Iono how I feel, tho."

Rissa comes round the counter, leans up next to me. Even wit all that grease and seafood, she still smells of flowers and pritty shit. "That aint nothin but the fear talkin. You aint gotta know. You just gotta say whateva you feel to Jay. He can't decide blind, baby. You know that."

"What if he don't care?"

"You and I both read that letter, Lee. Feelings that strong don't just disappear in a few days. But you won't know if you don't try. Now gon head. And don't you come back without our man."

I know aint no reason to be scared, but I am. Errtime I see Jay, it's like he got anotha piece of me I don't rememba givin him. I park in the same spot I always do and hear the bell begin to ring.

As soon as I spot him walkin down the long sidewalk in front of the school, I'm already chokin on my words cuz he walkin right toward me wit a look that could kill.

"Sup, Jay," I say.

No answer. He looks me dead in my eyes but keeps walkin. There it goes again, that feelin, anotha piece of me gone that I aint give him.

"Aye, Jay." I walk ova, step in front of him to stop him from walkin away, but he just walks round. I reach to grab his arm.

"Don't touch me!"

He yells it so loud my body freezes. Befo I can say anything else, he runs down the street faster than I eva seen him run.

It's one thing to live my whole life neva really bein heard, but it's like Jay helped me find words, the strength to stand up and grab em so I can feel them in my mouth, taste what I been missin. Jay gave me mo than speech, he showed me what the words represented: what it feels like to finally be understood. As his legs pull him farther and farther away from me, I neva wanted to be heard mo in my life, but the only one who matters is the only one not willin to listen.

I hop in my whip and go where I know he'll be—or at least where I'll be able to run into him: the church. When I pull up in the parking lot, I hop out and wait. I get close to where I think he walkin from, and when I see him, I step out so he can see me.

I don't say a word befo he almost takes flight again, but I'm ready. When you know what you can lose, you find any way to keep it. I mean to be mo gentle, but the fear of losin him fuh good gets trapped in my fingers, and I pull him to the ground.

He swings round and slaps me so fuckin hard I almost forget who he is.

"Jay . . . wait . . . stop," I say.

His eyes say it first, then his body. *Fuck you*.

Befo he scrambles to his feet, I climb on top of him, and then it's like muscle memory takes ova. The look in his eyes now is different: no fear. But ion wanna fight him, not like this.

If he don't wanna be here, I don't wanna make him. I stop

tryna hold him and wait, hopin he can see I just wanna talk. If he runs, I won't chase him. But I pray he'll stay even if it's only for a minute.

Jay stops tryna fight. And even though I'm between his legs and can feel myself gettin hard again, he don't look scared—he pulls me closer, adjusts his hips. I lean in closer to his face and he doesn't turn away, but he won't let me get any closer, neitha. He just holds me there, like his body is askin me a question I can't hear.

I want Jay. I want him to feel how good I can be, when I'm his. There is a lot I aint neva felt good at. But here, I know I can do him right, if he let me.

I kiss him, and it's a one-sided battle I'm happy to lose as his mouth pulls out all the words and sounds I've been tryna say. Under his touch, between his legs, I wanna become whateva he wants me to be. I reach into his shorts from his thighs. On the outside, he becomes stronger and takes control, but when my hands go further, he is all gasp and moan. For a second, he lets me find my way, see him better, but then he stops, pulls my hand away but stays there, underneath me, seein parts of me I aint neva showed nobody.

Wit him still, wit him listenin, I speak, "I know I fucked up, and you got a right to not wanna fuck wit me. But I aint know you felt that way bout me till I read yo letter."

He looks scared and surprised. That's when I understand: he don't know he left the letter. He tries to pull himself away, not look. But I don't let him. I hold him tight, like I imagined I would in Rissa's parking lot. That's when I realize I'm scared cuz if he asks for it, I'll disappear or turn into sand—anythin he wants. He just has to ask.

"What I'm tryna say is, I think I mighta known how you felt bout me, but I won't seein clearly cuz I was so afraid of my feelings. I aint gon lie, me sayin this don't mean I got nothin figured out. I'm just sayin, I know I can love you, if you show me how. Except fuh Taj and Rissa, I aint neva been really loved right." I lean up a lil, try not to hold him too tight. "You aint gotta say nothin right now, I just want you to know, if you let me, Imma run to you, not from you."

I pull back but gently hold on to his waist. We sit, wit each otha face-to-face, doin the only thing we can: not say nothin but still say errthang. When he is ready, he gets up, dusts off his clothes, and waits for me to do the same, takin me in wit his eyes.

As we walk, I see him listenin for where I am beside him, how close or how far away I am. I know cuz I test it. When I stop, after a few steps, he stops. If I keep goin, after a few steps, he keeps goin—we in sync, two parts learning how to move like a whole.

When we get to the front of the church, he says, "How'd you get here?"

"I drove. Parked ova there."

He sees, nods, sittin in his right hip.

When he walks in the direction of my whip, my chest knows what my body has always known. I'm not just close to somethin like love, I'm waist-deep in it, and the water is risin. For the first time in a long time, I'm swimmin, wadin in the water, without the fear of drownin.

When I pull up to the house, I tell Jay I been meanin to bring him here since we first met. Wit my hands on his hips, I tell him the story of Savin Grace, the thorny bush, and to watch out for the tree roots in the white dirt of the lawn cuz they like to trip unexpected guests; my hand on top of his on the screen door, so it don't slam but closes soft; and my chest up against his back, I explain the stack of comforters on the couch, even though we got three bedrooms upstairs.

The house is too quiet, but iono if it's cuz Jay here and I'm so focused on him or it's somethin else. Jay slowly walks by the wall unit, tracin the wood corners and hoverin ova one of the only pics of me, Ma, our pops, and Taj. He smiles, leans closer, mumbles somethin I can't hear, so I move closer. He smells a different kind of sweet from befo, like somethin that's just been cooked, like cookies—ginger snaps?

I slide behind him, ask, "Can I kiss you?"

He giggles, doesn't answer.

"Can I touch you?" I softly reach for his hand, then rub his arms.

He turns round, leans back onto me. "Only if you teach me how to see you wit my hands like you do."

I nod, then move closer, kissin his neck. I hold his hands,

then guide them down my stomach, past the waistband of my shorts, so he can feel all of me and how bad I want him.

He stops me, puts his hand on my heart. "Teach me from here," he says, then slides his hand under my shirt, so he can feel my heart knock at him from the otha side.

We stand, starin in each otha's eyes, like foreva on the edge of a smile. I kiss him on the lips, soft at first, then get lost, till it feels like the room is spinnin. His hands feel errwhere at once, my chest, my side, his nails press harder the deeper I kiss him, till we're breathin the same breath. When Jay lets out a moan, I can't hold it in and pull him on top of me on the couch.

We hear a sound and both of us freeze.

There's heavy breathin and moanin, but it aint us. Sounds like it's comin from upstairs.

Taj? But I aint see his car out front and he neva parks in the back unless . . .

Me and Jay grin at each otha, and for a second, we lil kids, sneakin up the stairs to hear the freaky sounds. When we get to the top of the stairs, the door is halfway open and it hits me: the sweet smell aint Jay. It's freshly baked cookies, which means the only person Taj could be wit is—

"Jacob?" Jay says.

Jacobee turns round, freezes between Taj's legs. When he sees Jay, he jumps up, reaches for his pants. Taj grabs for his shirt.

"Jay, wait," Jacobee yells, pullin on his shirt.

Jay runs down the stairs, I run after him to make sure he good.

When I get down the stairs, he frozen, starin at the front door. No, not the door, the window next to it, where two figures just walked by. We can see one of em in the triangle window in the door, but they look funny, like they wearin red African masks.

"Jay, what's—"

Bullets rip through the curtains, the windows, the front door. I drop down for cover. Jay's screams cut through it all, and befo I know it, I'm already on top of him, shieldin him wit my body. I look down to see if he okay.

There's blood.

When mo shots bounce off the walls, I grab hold of Jay's arm and pull him past the wall unit into the kitchen. Shots come from inside the house, and I turn my head to see Taj firin from the stairs.

Mo shots go back and forth.

"Jay, Jay . . . you okay? Talk to me," I say.

He nods, tryna hide the pain wit tears in his eyes. "Where's Jacob?"

None of this woulda happened if I woulda pulled Jay away, covered his mouth so the real name neva came out, and Jacobee and Taj coulda stayed Jacobee and Taj, not Jacob and Taj. They woulda neva jumped outta the bed, tried to hide who they were and what they meant to each otha. Jay woulda neva ran down the stairs by himself, and I woulda noticed faster that somethin won't right.

I look up just as Jacobee scurries into the kitchen. That's when I see it—the outline of a third figure in a black-and-white African mask peek through the back-door window.

"Back door," I scream, covering Jay as best I can.

"Who?" Jacobee says, lookin back again. The figure is gone.

His hands shake as he pulls at Jay's clothes tryna find where the blood is comin from.

"Jay, I'm here," Jacobee says. "Can you hear me?"

"I can hear you," Jay says, squintin in pain.

"Show me where it hurts," Jacobee says. Jay tries to move, but he can't. When he shrieks in pain, Jacobee freezes, scared, then snaps himself out of it.

"Lee, help me lift him a little, so I can see."

I try to, but Jay feels heavier than normal. I do what I can, while Jacobee keeps pullin at his clothes, shakin mo and mo by the second. He sees somethin, keeps lookin while Jay tries not to scream.

"Just a little longer, hold on," Jacobee whispers to himself—and to us. "You hit anywhere?"

"Nah, I'm good. I'm fine." I try to wipe the tears from my eyes, but I can't wit all the blood on my hands.

"Okay . . . it's okay," Jacobee says, lookin at me. "We'll get through this, we just need to . . . Hold on, lemme just—" Jacobee shuffles through his pockets for his phone, but he can't find it.

"I got mine," I say. "It's in my . . . in my . . ." I can't get my arm to—

"Is it in yo pocket?" Jacobee asks. "Front?"

I nod. He checks.

Somewhere, I hear car doors slam shut and tires peel off. I can hear Taj cussin, the front door open and close.

"Did Taj just—" I can't get the words out.

"Lee . . . you okay?" he asks, lookin at me, worried.

Jacobee is on the phone wit 911. He nods, leans down, lifts Jay's shirt while he talks. But this aint the Jacobee who made Taj as good as new; his hands are still shakin, and he keeps wipin tears from his eyes as he explains what he sees ova the phone.

"Yes," he says into the phone, "there are two, one is seventeen, the otha eighteen. One has two possible gunshots. The otha—"

"Jacobee? Lee?" Taj runs in from the livin room, aimin toward the back window, checkin to see if there's anybody else lurkin nearby. When he sees us and all the blood, he drops down next to me. "Lee, what's . . . I don't . . . are you—"

Jacobee looks at me, pulls at my clothes.

"I'm okay," I say. "Just focus on Jay, I'm fine I just—"

"Yes, he's shot, too."

"What?" Taj yells. "Lee, where? Show me."

Shot? No, I aint. I would know. "I'm fine . . . Jay, are you okay?" I ask.

"Taj, help me move Jay so I can check Lee."

"No," I say. They try to pull Jay from my arms, but I won't let em. And then, my arm lets go without my permission. I hear Taj yell the address into the phone so the operator can catch it.

"Lee, Lee," Taj shouts, movin to the otha side of Jacobee, so he can check my clothes and shirt. My leg feels like someone's stabbin it. I look down and see Jacobee's hands.

"Shit, shit, shit," Taj says ova and ova. "Okay, I see somethin . . . Jacobee . . . I think he might be shot in the arm but it's . . . it's too much blood." He cryin but tryna keep it together. "What? How? Lee . . . Jacobee, tell them to fuckin hurry up—they got his leg, too. What's takin so long? Hurry. The. Fuck—"

"Taj," Jacobee roars. "Eitha help or get the fuck out."

The blood is errwhere, I can't tell if all of it is comin from Jay or not. If it is . . . if it is . . . aint no way he can—

"Jay . . . Jay . . . ," I say.

"I'm okay," he says.

But I can't hear him straight, can't feel Taj like I normally do, even tho he right behind me. Errthang is goin in and out, and that's when I realize I mighta been bleedin the whole time.

"I can't . . . I can't . . ." My lips are movin, but no sound is comin out. I watch as Taj panics, screams for the ambulance as he holds me in his arms; Jacobee tries to keep all of us calm, wit Jay in his arms, but the mo Jay cries out the mo Jacobee falls apart, till he screamin into the phone, too.

I keep reachin for Jay, tryna apologize, but my arm closest to him can't reach, won't move, even tho the only thing I wanna do is touch.

I hear sirens, see Jacobee pointin and explainin as the EMTs crowd round us. I reach for Jay again but can't really see or feel him. I keep gettin confused by they questions. I answer what I can and try to keep my eyes open till I can't, till all I can hear is beeps and sirens, and strong boys cryin to the soundtrack of sorry.

Then it all goes quiet, and all I can hear is my own thoughts, my regrets.

If I woulda listened, believed Taj when he said be careful, stay alert, and always know who watchin, I woulda seen the signs, realized Taj won't in the streets tryna squash no beef but in the middle of a full-on gang war—not even knowin who the players are yet—neva tellin us really how bad things had gotten.

And maybe if I woulda known how little time we really had, I coulda told Jay the only thing I want in this whole world is to stay by his side like he wanted me to—always there to hug him, love him, and make love to him—so none of this otha shit woulda happened, endin us befo we even get the chance to start.

Summer

7

JAY

All dreams about that day of the shooting start the same way: in Leroy's house, in the dark with strings of light from the curtains, the stairs stretching far into eternity. With Leroy at my side, we hear it: the moaning, the groans, voices so low they twist into a growl grating every wall.

Instantly I'm running down the stairs, but they won't end, no matter how tired I get from running, no matter how many times Leroy screams my name. Then I'm there, in front of the door, the shadow of African masks stretching and warping light around them. Some are black-and-white asymmetrical with distorted lines, others are a flaming red with jagged, serrated teeth, but all of them stare at me, under full-bodied hoods. And then I hear it: the hard, cold, steel scraping, then tapping, against the wooden door, calling my name. I never answer, I never make a sound, even though I know they see my reflection in the shards frozen in midair of the triangle window in the door.

I stare at Leroy, his voice always on repeat, asking, "Jay,

what's wrong—" after each shot pierces the door over and over. Once you've heard it, you remember it in your bones, things that shouldn't make sounds at all: the strain of tears on the verge of falling; men's screams breaking the sound barrier until they're a hoarse squeal; flesh being jumped and ripped apart by lead alloys in soft copper jackets.

To wake up, I always have to beg my body as its being cradled by Leroy, pulled on by Jacob, and protected by Taj. I tell my body, my eyes and their dimming gaze, "I can change, I can be saved," even though I don't remember what I've done wrong or what I need to be saved from.

So I sit on the kitchen floor, in a pool of my own blood as Leroy fights, Jacob cries, and Taj screams for help from somebody, anybody. Sometimes, I wonder if this is what the pastors mean by hell, a never-ending wait for what's next, never knowing the right order: Are we fighting to live or living to fight?

I come to, half-asleep, half-awake but eyes still closed, on the floor.

Jacob whispers my name like a prayer. As he lays hands, my body jerks with each shot in my dreams, until I claw at my throat, unable to breathe, eyes wide with fear.

"It's okay. . . . It's me." He repeats it gently, until my eyes soften. I try to sit up but can't.

In the hall bathroom, Jacob grabs a washcloth and runs cold water over it. Then he puts my arm over his shoulder, helps me up to the edge of the bed. He wipes my hands, my arms, my chest, my abdomen free of lint and sweat. He crouches down in front of me and quickly wipes my thighs and legs. When he gets up, I grab his hand.

"I'm not leaving—I'm cutting on the fan," he says, folding the washcloth inside out, placing it on my shoulder. Then he puts the box fan in front of the window. He turns it up to the highest setting and twists it in my direction until we are trapped in a lukewarm wind tunnel.

Scattered moonlight weaves a net of night across his face, and as the fan purrs cool, I eventually turn and face him. I want to respond, to say something clever, but all I can wonder is what other secrets Jacob might be hiding. That day, I would have never thought he was there with Taj, but what shook me was how I remember him calling Leroy "Lee"—a name reserved for special people—and everyone calling him "Jacobee."

As the thoughts pull me deeper, I can't make light of a moment when both of us are so clearly searching—him with his hands, me with my eyes. Will he finally tell the truth—or at least more of it—now that we are haunted by the same ghosts?

I don't wake to the sound of beautiful chirping. Nope.

It is Yung Joc's "I Know You See It" blaring from a boom box that should have been banished from the Dupresh household years ago but, instead, is going up and down on Jacob's shoulder. In fact, I'm convinced it is not a boom box at all but a torture device from the Inquisition.

I stare at Jacob, my charming, loving, older brother and imagine all the cruel ways I will make him pay for waking me up out of a pleasant slumber for once. But he isn't alone. Princeton is dancing in a white beater and canary-yellow swimming trucks announcing dance moves as he does them—the sprinkler, the mailbox, the running man, the Bankhead bounce—all of them for some reason ending with a hip and a body roll.

I don't know if this is meant to be a scintillating strip-tease or a kids' dance-along. What I do know: this is only the beginning. If I don't get up soon, the oiled, muscular bodies of both the former and current golden boys of Daniel Lee High will eventually climb into my bed. So I do what any sane person not in the mood for being dry-humped would do: I shimmy from the sheets, up and back, until I have enough energy to slide a leg out and do a frozen twerk (hands on my knees, making the most vigorous facial expressions, as if I'm popping so fast you can't see it).

After the shooting, Jacob wasn't the only one who visited me every day I was in the hospital. Princeton did, too. I didn't expect it—can't even say that I wanted it, at first. But Princeton has a habit of growing on people. He even got me to open up to him about Leroy and what happened between us—well, just about everything. Now that I'm back home, he's pretty much been here every other day.

As he dances, all I can do is wonder what life was like without him and his almost-funny jokes, his snarky remarks, constant flirting, and sexual innuendos. But the real magic is his charm and willingness to make everyone around him as happy as he can. His and Jacob's Saturday dance party is meant to convince me to go to the pool with the both of them, and neither one is taking no for an answer.

I try to tell Jacob we can't because Momma said we gotta be ready for Will and Miss Rosalind when they get here. But as he eloquently explains, they won't arrive until 6:30 p.m., which means we could spend the whole day out, make it back home, take our showers, get dressed, and still be ready to welcome them both with big smiles and open arms.

By the time I'm gone and finished brushing my teeth, I've been guilted into saying yes.

"Mission accomplished!" Princeton says, doing a special handshake with Jacob I've never seen before. "I'll meet y'all there."

"Why?" I'm being nosy, and I know it.

Princeton grins. "Aww . . . you miss me already?"

"Of course. I don't know how I'd live without you," I say, batting my eyelashes Betty Boop style.

Princeton is stunned to silence. "Duty calls—Ma needs me, and she ain't exactly the kind of woman you wanna make wait. Don't have too much fun without me."

On our way to the pool, I'm already wading through the heat as my body is pulled by the childhood red wagon of Jacob's smile.

It's the first day of June in Savannah, which means it should feel like spring—(not!) it's hot as hell. The weather forecast warned us—ninety-nine degrees with 100 percent humidity. I wonder if the bright orange floaties I'm wearing on my arms might explode from the heat. I don't know what I'll do without them.

Everywhere feels like you are trapped in a hot car with the windows rolled up. But water gives and saves. Mrs. Gilroy's three kids are proof, galloping in an overflowing water hydrant. Up the street, more itty-bitties run as fast as their arms and newly mastered legs can take them as they join in the fluid sweepstakes.

"What are you thinking about?" Jacob says, breaking me out of my heat-induced trance.

We are a block away from the pool when I hear the voices and splashing, but my shoulder aches with every heartbeat, and the thought of Leroy slips through my defenses. I tell myself it is best to forget, but I can't help remembering him screaming my name as he held me, trembling. I shake the thought off, instead ask Jacob a different question.

"What do you think Will looks like now?"

Jacob shrugs. "Iono, it's been . . . what . . . over ten years. Who knows? Back then, I just remember his chubby cheeks and that laugh. I could recognize that anywhere."

I giggle, remembering it being a Woody Woodpecker meets gleeful squeal—and it'd been contagious and made your day better just by hearing it. I nod, wondering if he'd recognize me or if I'd recognize him. But then again, he's hard to forget. He's the first boy who kissed me, back when I was six.

"What are you thinking about?" I ask Jacob.

"Them damn floaties you wearin'. Take them off. You don't need them. I'll be with you."

He doesn't get it. Why I really need them. I don't want to be saved; I want to save myself.

"What's wrong with them?" I say.

"Everything. They're damn near fluorescent, and you're seventeen. Just don't come in the deep end. Keep it shallow and leave those traffic cones where they belong—on the ground."

He laughs; I don't. "Nope. I'm coming with you in the deep end, whether you like it or not. I don't care if you're embarrassed of me."

"Whoa, where'd that come from? Why would I be embarrassed of you? It's the fuckin' floaties, Jay, not you. Don't twist my words." He shakes his head, frustrated. Eventually, he takes a deep breath and says it differently in a softer tone. "All I'm saying is . . . at least let me work with you some more. You know how to tread water, right? Remember what

I taught you last time?"

"Yeah, I think so, just a little bit." Enough to drown slower than if I couldn't swim at all.

He shakes a budding smile off his face. I wonder if he's reading my thoughts.

At the pool, the need to look like I can swim overrides my desire to save myself. There are just as many people in the deep end as the shallow end. The bright-ass floaties have to go.

I can wade, jump, and—if need—flap and throw myself in the direction of safety. If none of this works, better to die quietly than to arrive with these bright-ass plastics on. Jacob reads my mind; he holds out his hand, unplugs them, and squeezes them flat—social disaster averted. We take off our shoes, so the chlorine water won't mess them up. There isn't a table in sight to put our stuff on, so we hang our shirts on the fence and cover our shoes and socks with our towels.

Once his white beater is off and his feet are free of shoes, Jacob is midair in a dive, slicing into the deep end with barely a splash. By the time he comes up for air, he's already swam the full length of the pool, despite how crowded it is.

I am different; I have a ritual of stalling. Defeated by the thought of the cold water, I distract myself with our shoes and socks, making sure they are perfectly covered by our towels. I retie the drawstring on my shorts three times and fold our T-shirts before laying them back on the fence. A sharp pain runs down my left shoulder again, and my body becomes stiff. The pain grows, a forest fire of neurons chewing at my left side.

I stand, waiting, staring at the pool. I need to be saved, and I hate myself for it. I remember the glass shattering, the cuts on my back and hands when I tried to crawl, trying to get as far away from the door, but the fire trapped in my bones wouldn't let me. I was going to die. I was dying. I almost died when—

A guy nearly knocks me over as he runs and leaps into the air in front of me; he is a bright sun caught in the blue lips of the sky.

Cold water slaps my face and body, drenching me from head to toe. I gasp, staring through the ripples for the body swimming underneath. Revenge will be mine.

As he comes to the surface, I jump in the air and land with the biggest splash I can muster. It seems like a good idea, but the water is so cold I think my soul has been snatched from my body, and every bubble of air spews out of me like a geyser. I shoot through the surface, trying to hide the fact that I am choking. I fail miserably. I flail and slap clumsily at the wall of sealed concrete. I hold on to the sides, trying to breathe, but the air won't get into my lungs fast enough.

In the distance, I hear Jacob laughing. "I see you're serious about playing with the big boys, huh?" he says. I splash water in his direction, still struggling to catch my breath. I wipe my face and try to breathe normally.

"If I didn't know any better, I'd think you were trying to outdo me in a diving contest," the guy's voice says behind me, raspy and sweet on the ears like iced tea with lemon.

I turn around to see his face—there's something familiar about it, especially its glint of sadness even when he smiles. But there's something about his voice, too. Well, not his voice per se, his lips and how they bend with his smile as his golden-dust peach fuzz glows in the sun. On his neck, perfectly nestled between his clavicle and his cheek is a heart-shaped tattoo with the words "Kiss me."

I shake my head, still failing at not panicking. "I wouldn't say all that," I say, taking in more water than I mean to. I try to smother a cough, play it cool; the cough punches back instead.

"You good?" His eyes glimmer, adding extra subtexts and syllables to his words.

"Yeah . . . I think . . ." I hang on to the side of the pool for dear life.

"Sure 'bout that? You should lemme teach you."

"Teach me what?"

He shows instead of tells, glides through the water, like a hot knife through butter.

"I can do that." I almost glide—well, until water gets in my nose and all I feel like I'm good at is flailing and sinking sideways.

"You gotta stop panicking." He moves closer to me. All I see is his wet sandy-brown curls turn into a halo and a promise to me that he can do no harm—and I believe him.

I know what he is asking me to do, and it feels impossible.

"You ready?" He gestures toward the wall of the pool.

My eyes say it first: I don't know if I can do this.

"Just try it, come on. I won't let anything happen to you. I promise."

"Yeah, right. I barely even know you."

"Ouch," he play-winces. "How 'bout I introduce myself?"

I nod.

"But after I go, you go. Aight?" He finishes all of his sentences with a smile, like somebody I used to know when I was younger. It can't be him . . . can it?

"We'll see," I say. "But if I drown, you better die trying to save me."

"Trust me, I gotchu." He searches for my hand but accidentally touches my dick. "Oh, my bad, I was tryna—"

He blushes, avoids eye contact. Suddenly, he seems almost human. I pull my hand above the water. "I'm Joseph, but people call me Jay."

He grabs it. "You can call me Will."

There's no way it could be a coincidence. "Wait, Will, is your mother—"

"I'll show you how to dive first," he says, then winks. Before I can repeat my question, he's already swam to the other side of the pool and is hoisting himself onto the ledge.

As he pulls himself out of the water, his light-blue trunks hang heavy with wetness, revealing the outline of everything underneath. I try not to notice everyone else noticing, but Will's body gives sight to the blind.

"You paying attention?" he says, grinning.

I nod, speechless.

"Okay. All you gotta do is pick a spot where you want to dive. Once you dive in, swim under and straight to the other side. That way, you don't feel like you're drowning. Got it?"

He is concentrating as he turns around. Then, he pretends he's going to dive but doesn't.

"You see what I just did?"

"Yeah, I did," I say, laughing.

"What did I do?" By the way he sways his hips, I can tell he's enjoying this—the show and being the center of attention.

"Nothing. You did absolutely nothing."

"Right. Just making sure. Alright. Watch closely furreal this time."

He gets in position, turns around, and I see the change in his body: his shoulder blades flex strong like wings before taking flight, and his legs turn thick and muscular. He jumps into the air, turning with his knees tucked close to his chest and falling into the water.

The younger kids in the shallow end cheer, "Do it again, do it again!"

He swims over, a beacon of gold in blue, gleaming. He's so

close, I have to back up to stop him from accidentally kissing me. "Alright, your turn."

Something pulls at my chest. Then a phantom scent on the wind: Cool Water cologne and peppermint. I ignore it, pretend I don't feel anything. It'll pass, even though parts of me don't want it to.

Every time I think of Leroy, it hurts. I remind myself of his words scribbled in the note he gave Jacob a week or two after I got home from the hospital:

Im sorry. We can't be togetha. Not now. It aint safe to be round me. And I gotta protect you.

He didn't ask how I felt, didn't even give me a choice. And I never got to tell him: outside of Momma and Jacob, he was the only person I felt safe with. The only person I *wanted* to be safe with—now he's gone. And what the hell does he mean by "now"? Does it mean he still likes me? Still wants me?

All I know is that I don't know because he never told me to my face. I don't know if the pain will ever go away, or if I'll ever stop missing Leroy, but around Will—and there's no way it isn't *my* Will—under the warmth of his smile, it hurts a little less.

That's something. And, right now, that's more than nothing.

I hoist myself out on the ledge, blushing. Even though Leroy has my heart aching, Will's smile is enough to hold me, and despite the pain, I can feel his eyes, like hands, guiding me. Every muscle in my body begs me to stall, to stop altogether.

I take a few steps back.

He grins.

I take a few more.

He narrows his eyes, curious, then grins wider.

I've always loved the water, but I never trusted it. I realize now it was never about the water but about me. Sometime over these seven weeks after being shot, I lost something, offered it in place of the bullet in exchange for my life. But with each step I take toward the ledge, water as sky, I want to make a different offer.

I, too, let it start in my body: three steps, then I jump, legs outstretched, torso tight with want, a deep breath filling the ache where the bullet last kissed; I am an apology taking flight, my body folds in the air, both barrel and chamber, arms wide like wings and then out in full embrace, falling and flying at the same time. The water catches me, holds me tight, ushers me to the bottom; and with what little air I have left, I push off the pool floor toward a shimmering gold. I split through the water and reach for the pool ledge.

"Almost a front flip? You kiddin' me?" Jacob yells.

I don't know how he makes it over here so fast, but he

pulls at me with pride. I slap away his arms, but eventually he gets what he wants and bear-hugs me. He pauses, grins at Will.

"I take it you're the person responsible for this?" Jacob asks.

"What can I say? I'mma good teacher."

I splash water at Jacob. He chuckles, knowing where and why I'm doing it. "What? Oh, my bad, man. I'm Jacob, the big brother to this little brother."

"Nice to meet you . . . big brother to his little brother. I'm Will."

Jacob looks at him a little longer than normal. "You from 'round here?"

Does he see what I see?

"Nah, just got here, actually. Visiting."

"Oh, okay . . . from where? I hear a li'l somethin' somethin' in your voice . . . like an accent."

"From New York but been all over." He smiles.

"Wait . . . New York?"

Will nods.

Jacob squints, looks at him closer. Then his eyes light up—he sees it, too. The moment he does, Will lets out that laugh, as if he's been holding it in this whole time, trying to keep up the act.

"I knew it!" I say half out loud, half to myself.

Our eyes lock, and I hear Will say, "Me, too."

Jacob unleashes his full Kool-Aid smile, then pulls him over to him, ruffles his curls. "We can save the full reunion for later. In the meantime, you ready for an encore?"

Our nods are a "hell yeah," and with it, bodies of all shades of hope and joy and laughter jump in after the other, over and over, climbing higher into the first sky with rough grace before falling into the second, knowing we can fly without wings. Together, in the blistering heat and the blessed cool, we are Black portals between two worlds, up and down, pushing and pulling, racing to be swallowed whole.

After hours of splashing, my eyes lock with Jacob's and, instantly, we know where to go next: Edda Nae's, the candy lady. Since Will tells us he's never been, his attendance is mandatory. But he needs a second to get his stuff, so we wait for him up the street under the shade of a date tree. Jacob plucks a few yellow-orange fruits from the tree, and we suck and chew, spitting pits till we smell sweet. We are about to pluck a few more when we hear the roaring scrape of a skateboard.

It is Will, all smiles, with a book bag, his sky-blue trunks, and a white tank in his hand—and half the folks who were at the pool trailing behind. But next to him is someone who was supposed to be there but never showed up: Princeton.

When Will and Princeton make it to us, we join them

at the front of his band of dripping fluorescent bikinis and butterfly chests to the soundtrack of dozens of conversations happening at once. Princeton puts his arm around my shoulder and immediately catches me up on why it took him so long to get to the pool when he left the house before we did. But his story is interrupted when we pass a candy-apple-red '75 Chevy on thirty-inch rims being washed by a group of guys all shades of swagger with tats, grills, and more game than any of us can handle.

D4L's "Laffy Taffy" blasts through their speakers. It is only a minute, but time seems to stop. Even as everyone does their own rendition of the dance, all eyes are on Jacob and Will and Princeton as they shake their shoulders, pause, and then body-roll to the beat, sealing each direction with a snap. Together, they are a Snickers bar—nougat, caramel, and milk chocolate—and on the side, watching the show is me, the wrapper.

When the dancing ends, we keep moving, swaying in the swelter, chasing shadows of lanky clouds. There are too many people vying for Will's attention for me to get a word in, and Jacob has his own fans fluttering their eyelashes, flexing their muscles, licking their lips, and popping gum to show off their tongue skills. But Princeton doesn't miss a beat. I don't know if he senses it, but he pulls me close, so I know I have his full attention.

"So . . . you want me to go over there for a minute so he

can ask for your number?"

I look at him, confused. He nods over toward Will.

"What? No, it's not like that."

Now it's his turn to look confused. "Don't tell me you that blind. You 'on't see how he look atchu? I mean, he was just talkin' 'bout you when we was walking from the pool."

Will glances over at me—at us—and I see his eyes focus on Princeton's arm, as if he'd rather him move it so he could replace it with his own. Then he looks away. I wonder if I'm seeing things, overthinking it.

"Really, what did he—" I catch myself. "He's a family friend. It's not . . . it's nothing like that."

"Right," Princeton sings. "Well, I'mma go over there and let's see which one of us is right. If he come over here tryna spit game, you owe me twenty bucks. Better yet, you gotta promise to come ova my place before school start, so we can talk about getting them love letters back up and runnin'. Deal?"

He removes his arm and moves away before I can say no, which means, in his mind, the bet is on. But is it really, if I never said yes? I'm convinced that he just made all of it up so he could finally talk to the girls who have been gawking at him this whole time. I mean, Princeton in canary-yellow swimming trunks is about as subtle as a Category 5 hurricane in the Atlantic—and let's just say, their eyes are refusing to evacuate, praying for the storm.

Abandoned, I hover just out of reach of Jacob and Will but still stuck in their gravitational pull. To fill the space and time, I count the yellow stripes on the burning asphalt.

I pretend every compliment and question for Will is meant for me: "Can you teach me how to skateboard?" (Sure, but it's harder than it looks.) "Those yo' real eyes?" (Yup, all me.) "Can I touch your curls?" (Only if you rub 'em right.) "Whatchu bench?" (Two hunned, squat three—I wish.) "You single?" (Maybe.)

"You thinkin' 'bout me?" a voice says.

"Maybe I am, maybe I'm not," I reply to myself.

"So is that a yes?" Will's lips are suddenly so close to my ear that I jump.

I look at him in shock.

"I ain't mean to scare you. I thought you were talkin' to me."

I try to find words from somewhere, anywhere. "Oh—yeah—I mean, no . . . I was talking to myself." I shake my head, praying for either the power to rewind time (I only need a few seconds) or invoke selective non-life-threatening amnesia.

We both keep walking down the street, stealing glances of each other. For a second, the heat turns cool, as if it's Will's breeze.

"You ever get tired of it?" I ask. Another thought, half serious, half joke, but something I really want to know.

"Tired of what?" His arm brushes mine again. He flexes, then releases his abs before I can finish counting.

"The same questions over and over."

"You prolly the first person to ask me that," Will says. He relaxes his smile, lets a squint sneak in.

"I'm sorry, don't mean to be weird."

"You not weird at all . . . you're just like I remembered."

I nod, speechless and blushing.

Princeton is in my peripheral, motioning with his lips, *You owe me.* I pretend I don't see him.

We stop at the corner. As we wait for everyone to catch up, I shield my face from the sun. Will adds his hand to block the rays I can't.

"Thanks," I say. "Not tryna get any darker."

"Why not? I like it."

"Hmmph. Yeah, okay . . ."

"Jay," Jacob says, frowning—turning our duo into a trio. "Cut that shit out."

"What?" I don't even know where he came from. I thought he was much farther behind us.

"You know what. Quit baggin' on yo'self. I done told you 'bout that." Jacob's heat drags us forward, our line of three turns into an arrow—he's the point.

"I'm not, I'm just sayin'—"

"Well, now I'm sayin'. You fine just the way you are."

I follow, staring at his heels, afraid to look over at Will.

It means something to hear Jacob say that, and for Will to nod in agreement, even if I don't like how Jacob says it. But it doesn't hide the truth I've always lived with: all attention went to those with lighter skin, "pretty" eyes, wavy hair, and pink lips. The only time people liked darker skin was when there was proof you were an exception to an unspoken rule that dark meant less than.

The truth even plays itself out with Princeton. As charming and brilliant as he is, everybody's eyes are focused on one thing, seeing if what's between his legs lives up to his nickname, "Prince Ten." They aren't hiding it because if you're darker, you're expected to be more, just to be enough: what hangs between your legs has to be the biggest; your curves need to be the thickest, your skin the softest, your body the strongest, your brain the smartest—you have to fight harder, have sex the longest, be tougher than anyone else. But even my "more" isn't enough: I am too skinny, my voice too soft, my lips too big. I'm too smart, my face too young, my look too different.

Jacob means well, and I love him for it, but he doesn't know what it feels like being an Icarus born so close to him, the blinding sun.

We barrel left and arrive at the mint-green house with purple trim. Hanging baskets of purple pansies match the purple-and-white Holy Ghost shouting "God Bless You" sign in the yard. They look new, freshly set, still dripping, hanging from a special, hand-braided rope of the same colors.

It's older, less bright than the flowers but still strong. I don't remember seeing it the other times we've been here.

I lean closer into Jacob, hiding from the memory of the man who likely gave it to her years ago: our father. Pansies mean loving feelings, he used to say. Jacob turns around, asks what's wrong. He follows my eyes to the pansies, sees the rope, then puts his arm around my shoulder. He doesn't say anything, he doesn't have to. He remembers, too. Quickly, we try to forget.

There is already a line on the wheelchair ramp that wraps around her house. As we join, girls wrap towels around their waists and boys of all ages magically climb into shirts. Will looks over at me, confused. Jacob and I look at each other and grin.

"Edda Nae don't serve 'hoochies' . . . ," I say.

"Or 'hounds,'" Jacob finishes, and Princeton pulls on a white beater, even though he's usually the exception to every rule.

When Edda Nae waves us over, the icicles growing in my chest thaw in the warmth of her smile. Edda Nae is under five feet but her love is a beacon that towers over us all; in the fall and winter, she has jogging suits with matching visors every shade of purple, and in the spring and summer sundresses that look the same. Even though her eyes aren't what they used to be, she never forgets a face, a name, or your folks.

With our faces in weathered hands, she asks about our

mom. When she sees Princeton, she immediately asks him to pass on a message to his mom, Lady Tee. But when she looks at Will, she covers her mouth with tears in her eyes and waves for him to come closer.

"Oh my word! Will, is that you?"

Will looks at both of us, confused. "Me?"

"Yeah, boy, who else would I be talkin' to? Get on over here and let me love on ya. You don't remember me, do you?"

"I don't think so." He grins and blushes as she cups his face. We can't tell if his cheeks are turning red because of the heat or the extra attention.

"You Rosalind's baby boy, right?"

"Yes, ma'am."

"I knowed it! I took care of you back when you were in Pampers until you were old enough to go to kindergarten. Sholl did."

"Really?"

"Mhmm, I tell you no lie. How ya momma doin'? And what about dat knucklehead Will Sr.? He still up to no good?"

Will's smile weakens. "My mom, she cool. My dad . . ." His words trail off.

"Unh-unh, quit all that mopin'." She pauses, opens up the floor freezer, and hands each of us a thrill: Will, pineapple; Jacob, red; Princeton, grape; and me, blue raspberry. Jacob and I stare at each other feeling hood-rich and grateful.

Will plays with the frozen cup of sweet and with the

Popsicle stick frozen in place until he sees us twirl until it swirls freely in the red plastic cup. Princeton already has his out the cup, sucking and crunching at the syrup-sweet bottom. Edda Nae hands us a five-dollar bag of Albert's Fruit Chews, four Hot Mama pickles, and four bags of Flamin' Hot Cheetos. I do the quick math in my head.

"Eleven fifty," I whisper to Jacob.

Princeton, always doing the most, hands Edda Nae a twenty-dollar bill, but she slaps his hand away.

"Did I tell you it was eleven fifty?"

"No, ma'am. I'm sorry. I didn't mean to—"

"Sunshine ova there done already paid it." She smiles at Will.

He takes a bite of the sweet frozen bottom, then looks up, eyes sunlit. "Ma'am?" he says.

"Nothing, baby. Today, it's my treat. For old times' sake."

"Thank you," we chime in unison.

Edda Nae winks at Will and then says, "You keep ya head up, heah?"

"Yes, ma'am," he says.

"Alright, nenh. I done said enough and then some. Now, y'all get goin' and you come back 'round and see me again soon, okay?"

"Yes, ma'am," we say, like "amen" at the end of a prayer.

Before we go, she gently waves me and Jacob over. "Have y'all spoken to your father now that he's out?"

The words surprise me so much, I accidentally step back into Jacob. It isn't our first time being asked after our dad, but it is the first time I realize he's already out of prison, which means at any point he could pop up out of nowhere without warning. Edda Nae saying it made it real in a way that I can't shake off, in a way that hurt.

Jacob is the best of us. He comes in for the rescue. "No, ma'am, but our ma keeps in touch."

"Oh, okay." She nods but sees through him with her weathered eyes.

We nod respectfully and walk toward Will and Princeton. I try to console Jacob, put my arm around his shoulders, but he's a little too tall for me to do it comfortably. He chuckles, puts his arm around me instead, and I rub the center of his back. His smile returns. Mission accomplished.

Sugar-drunk at Edda Nae's, Will and Jacob's groupies stay behind when her grandson, Husani, who looks like Jody from *Baby Boy*, rolls up with his crew on lowrider bicycles, their chrome, overspoked wheels, sparkling.

"I'mma catch y'all lata, too," Princeton says, dapping up Jacob and Will. He hugs me, which catches me off guard. "Don't forget . . ." He grins, then leans in closer. "And just so you know, if you eva need advice or anybody to talk to . . . you know . . . 'bout that thing I was right about . . . I gotchu." He hints over at Will.

"Furreal, furreal?" I say, kicking off our signature phrase we came up with on one of his hospital visits.

"Furreal, furreal, furreal," he responds.

I pull him in, just like he did me. "Thanks, Princeton. I mean it . . ."

He looks at me suspiciously.

"And if you ever need me to teach you about the birds and the bees, I'm here." I motion over toward the girls clearly waiting for him to come back and join them.

We both chuckle as he runs in their direction.

Cooled by the cotton-candy underbelly of a cloud, Jacob, Will, and I slurp and crunch in cadence, sucking the slush from the Popsicle sticks until Jacob pops his tongue so loud, it surprises even him. We laugh for at least another block.

I move to shoulder-bump Will and catch his attention, but the Virgin Islands beauty named Saturday—everybody's crush—runs up with her crew, snakes her arm inside his, and offers him a bag of Albert's Fruit Chews. When he smiles, sending his spotlight her way, my legs pull me farther away, and I'm drifting again. I wander, stranded in a never-ending no-wanted-man's-land, beating away the thoughts that threaten to drown me for being and feeling stupid, gullible—again.

Am I so desperate to outrun the ache in my heart that I'm seeing attraction, connection, when it's not there? Leroy made me feel this overwhelming, irresistible desire for him to give me the one thing he won't give anyone else, and even someone like Will, who seems so different, feels a little like how I was with Leroy.

Will's got his own kind of magic, though. He isn't Leroy; I

don't want him to be. At least I don't think so. Do I?

Will shoulder-bumps me, knocks me out of my thoughts. He's smiling, and Saturday and her crew are walking in the opposite direction. His spotlight has returned, and suddenly everything feels warm, nice—different. Yeah, I'll settle for that instead: not Leroy, just different.

As the sun melts into the horizon, we walk until our calves hurt, until our soles ache, until the streetlights come on—and when they do, Will hangs from our shoulders, each of us with an arm across his waist, my left hand holding his skateboard. We talk about everything and nothing at the same time. In the rhythm of dragging feet, gentle jokes, and almost touches, we braid a rope.

"Justin William Alexander," a woman's voice yells, walking toward us from the direction of our house. She's Black-momma-walkin'—wide strides and full hips—in a sunflower dress that blows behind her in the wind.

Will squints. "Mum?"

I chuckle at the way he says "Mum." Makes me want to ask if his family is British or something.

Jacob and I release our arms from around his waist. Miss Rosalind's voice crashes into us before she anywhere near us.

"Didn't I tell you to keep your phone on you?"

We try to step aside, but Will holds us together, his shield of brotherhood. We resist—ain't that much loyalty in all the world.

"I did," he says, leaning behind me.

"Did you? Then check your pockets. Go 'head, show me." She waits, hand on her hip, eyes narrowed, lips pursed. She's beautiful like Momma, just a shade darker but with light brown eyes. Her hair is tied up in a battle ponytail. Small strands fall loose and long as they prepare for war.

"Hey, Jay . . . Jacob," she says.

We wave shyly, trying to make sure he's the only one in trouble.

"Wow, y'all look just like him . . . It's crazy."

Jacob and I look at each other, hoping it ends there. We don't want to be reminded of our father again.

"Did you find it?" She looks at Will, ready to pounce.

Will pats his pockets in vain, looks up slow, and smiles nervously.

She holds it up, a silver Motorola Razr. Jacob and I look at each other, impressed that he has the newest phone out right now and forgot to even bring it.

"Jay and Jacob," she says, smirking.

"Ma'am," we say in unison.

"On the count of three, grab him and I'll get you both anything you want."

We grin and look at Will, proving we have no problem with being bought. He backs away, eyes ready for the challenge.

"Three," she says.

Will darts back, dodging Jacob's hands. I hand his skateboard to his mom, ready to join in. She doesn't hold on to it. She places it down, reaches for my shoulder to steady herself.

"Hold on, baby," she says, slipping the straps off the back of her wedge heels, until her French-manicured toes are glimmering against the asphalt.

Will is barely able to dodge Jacob when he sees her walking his way. "You joinin' in, Mum? You ain't neva gon' catch me." He play-jukes, left and right. She doesn't flinch, just watches.

"Honestly, you can do that all you want but you can't run forever." She hikes up her dress to just above her knees the way only a former athlete would. "Thanks, boys, I got it from here."

We back away in amusement, curious of how it will end.

"You ready?" Will asks.

"Born ready," she says.

Will runs toward her, and in a split second, he's gleefully in a headlock that they both convert into him giving her a piggyback ride. Jacob and I are smiling so hard, our faces hurt. Of course she is Momma's friend; they act just the same—lead with tough but always end in laughter and love.

All smiles, we journey home to the soundtrack of giggling crickets and cackling birds, past Miss Rosalind's SUV packed to the brim with stuff.

8

Leroy

The whole fuckin world shakes and crashes. I wake up to Taj's hand ova my mouth. He points at the motel room door and window. There are two figures: one in front of the door, the other in front of the window.

On the otha motel bed, Night, Taj's best friend, is laser-focused, movin closer wit a Glock tight in his palms. We know whoeva shot up the house is lookin to finish the job. So, while I was in the hospital, Taj snuck into our old house and packed what little bit he could, and we been bouncin round different hotels and motels the past two months usin Rissa community connections to keep err-thang low-profile. Cuz Taj the highest-rankin YG, Rissa the only one allowed to know our location, and that aint her and Benji out there.

There's a tappin on the window and scrapin on the door. Night creeps even closer but stays far enough away to remain out of sight of the two figures peerin through the blinds.

Taj pulls me off the bed, and we hide behind it as he gives me his piece and grabs the extra one from the nightstand.

Somebody knocks on the door again.

"Remember the plan," Taj says. "Stay ova in that room and don't come out."

"No, come wit me. Aint no reason fuh you to be in here."

"We aint got time fuh dis, Lee." He grabs the back of my neck, kisses me on the forehead hard, and pushes me toward the door to the otha connecting room.

I know I agreed every night he made me repeat the plan back to him, but it's different when you gotta do it furreal. Don't nobody know he in here. He can leave, too. Aint nobody gotta shoot or get shot, and don't nobody need no heroes.

"Come on," I mumble, pullin at him. "They open the door and see we aint here, aint gon be no problem."

"Lee." He glares, but that shit won't work on me tonight. He knows it, too. "Okay. Let me get my bag, and I'll go wit you. Damn."

I put on my backpack, and he grabs the duffel.

"We gon hide in the bathroom like I told you." Night looks ova and nods at me, then at him—permission. He gon stay behind just to make sure we get in there safe, then he comin, too.

"Behind the door, lights off, door open, I remember," I say, finishin his sentence. I walk into the next room, but then he closes and locks the door behind me.

My heart drops. He won't neva comin in the room.

Night knew it, too.

He just said all that to get me to do what he wanted. On the otha side of the door, something drops, and then there is yellin. I try to listen, but I can't hear shit besides my heart beatin through my ears.

It's as if I'm back in the house in the kitchen wit Jay all ova again, wit Jacobee tryna pull him out my arms and Taj shootin back. I remember all the blood, how errthang felt wrong, smelled burnt and sweet at the same time. What if somethin happenin to Taj and I just can't hear it? What if he hurt and can't protect himself? While I'm hidin in the bathroom, like he could be in the otha room fuckin dyin.

Somethin slams against the door. Then there is mo yellin and a scream.

I know what Taj told me to do, but I can't, not if it means leavin him behind.

I hold the gun wit two hands like he taught me: one hand high on the grip but not too tight, last three fingers round the base. I square my shoulders, ground my stance. I aim at the door, make sure I aint too close. I get ready to kick, aim, and shoot when somebody knocks on the door from the otha side.

"Lee, get in here. It's Brown Brown and PYT. We good; it's safe."

I don't move. I can't. I just stand, barely breathin.

"Lee, you hear me? Lee, you—"

"I'm comin," I blurt out, shakin but tryna hide it.

Sharp pain races down my shoulder and my side. I can

still hear errthang: Jay's screams, Jacobee's face, and Taj yellin to get help, his voice almost hoarse. I open the door and walk through befo the memories swallow me whole.

The rest of Taj crew here: Brown Brown and PYT, his otha eyes and ears on the streets. It used to be that I would see them only every now and then, but now I'm wit em all the time, which is cool cuz we've gotten close.

"Welcome back, baby!" Night bear-hugs me. He saw how scared I was, and I wonder if he feels bad for trickin me, even if it was to keep me safe. He finally lets me go, then sits next to Taj on the bed closest to the window.

Night damn near covers half the bed, cuz he the biggest, even tho he only twenty years old, the same as Taj. He got his nickname, not just cuz he tall as fuck, muscular, and dark-skinned but cuz in a world of shit starters, he the finisher—the one-hitta-quitta that'll make em see night no matta what time of day it is.

I sit next to PYT, who layin on his stomach readin his favorite manga, *Fruits Basket*. He's Dominican and Puerto Rican wit long black hair that's always in cornrows or pulled back in a ponytail and wrapped into a bun. He the youngest—the same age as me—and the prittiest nigga I eva seen in my life, befo I met Jay. When he talk, errbody round him melt cuz his voice is so deep. But don't let his pritty face fool you.

"You good, Lee-Lee?" He the only one I let call me that,

and even he can't do it too many times.

"Yeah, I'm good."

"No, you aint. Here." He reaches in his bag and pulls out a bag of salt-n-vinegar chips and two packs of Pecan Spinwheels.

"Aye, whey mine at?" Night says.

PYT shrugs. "Iono. Starve, nigga." He throws him a bag of Flamin' Hot Cheetos befo he gets to poutin. Then tosses Taj two Honey Buns—the kind wit the icing on top—so he can put em in the microwave.

Brown Brown walks ova from the desk he was sittin at and reaches into PYT's bag, pulls out a pack of barbecue sunflower seeds. Errbody look at PYT to see if he gon flip, but he don't. Night shakes his head but don't say nothin. Errbody know: PYT gotta soft spot for me and Brown Brown.

Cuz of PYT errbody smilin, feelin betta. Don't matta how big or how small, he know just what to do to make you feel good. That's how he got his nickname.

On my sixteenth birthday, he came to celebrate wit us. Errbody was drunk, damn near passed out, when the Michael Jackson song "P.Y.T. (Pretty Young Thing)" came on the radio. PYT hopped up and started dancin; he dragged me outta my chair, put my hands round his waist, and told me not to let go. Next thing I knew errbody was dancin, all smiles, like I aint neva seen them do befo. After that, errbody called him PYT instead of Enzo, his real name. Later that night, when he was comin outta the bathroom, I told him I thought I loved him cuz he was pritty and I couldn't stop thinkin bout him, and it was fuckin wit me. He kissed me on the cheek and said, "Dass wassup, but I gotta girl."

Brown Brown brings a magazine ova to where me and PYT are at, then lays across the foot of the bed. He pulls out a coupla wine-flavored Black & Milds and starts to "freak" em, removin the filter paper. Eva since he turned nineteen last year, he been buyin and lightin em even tho he don't really smoke. He say it aint neva been bout smokin, it's the vibe. He aint one to talk a whole lot, but errbody we meet always tryna holla cuz he brown-skinned wit green eyes. He stay mean-muggin, but when he wit us, all he do is grin, like he knows a secret don't none of us know, and he don't eva plan on tellin.

There's anotha knock at the door. But it's softer.

"I got it," Brown Brown says, takin his slow-ass time. He pimps ova, looks through the peephole, then perks up.

Taj and I look at each otha, nervous. It's a false alarm, but the fear is real.

"Wass good?" Brown Brown says, laughin.

Rissa rolls through in hair rollers and a bonnet, lookin happy but nervous and outta breath.

"You aight? Whatchu do, run up the stairs?" He hugs her tight.

"You plannin on lettin go anytime soon?" Benji says,

walkin in behind her. No matter what he is wearin, he always rolls through like a bodyguard in all black, except in the restaurant, where he always wears an apron. He is Rissa's foreva boyfriend and aint gon let nobody eva forget.

"Where's Lee and Bittersweet?" Rissa says.

"We good, Auntie," Taj says, givin her a hug. She squeezes his cheeks and smiles.

"Boy, you see me ova here worryin bout you. Get ova here." She laughs.

I walk ova, let her grab my face, too. She holds on to both of us. Since the shootin, she aint really been the same, eitha. Even when her laugh rocks the room, somethin bout it feel forced, like she hidin a sadness she don't want us to see.

Brown Brown and PYT ova whisperin to each otha, lookin at the front side of the door.

"Yall good?" Benji asks.

They shake their head, wave him ova. He goes to them, then comes back in, grabs a pad and pen from the stand near the bed befo goin back out front. Sound like he drawin on the door or somethin. When they come back in, he holds it up so me, Night, and Taj can see it. "Yall remember seein this on the door?"

On the sheet of paper is the letters "D" and "K" written close together. On top of the "D" is a jagged crown, real sharp, at an angle, like how you would rock a fitted.

"Naw, what is it?" Taj says.

Me and Night don't answer, we just stare tryna connect the dots.

"Could it have already been there and we just aint see it?" Night asks.

Benji shakes his head. "I thought that, too, but when I rubbed my finger ova it, looked like somebody had just done it."

Night and Taj look at each otha.

"What's that supposed to mean?" I ask, hopin it's not what I think. But the look on Night and Taj faces shows they already know.

"That means somebody was here, somebody *just* did this. And if they did, it's possible they were the shootas or they know who is."

"That's why we rushed ova here so fast," Rissa says. "One of my folks stayin near yo room said there were two people in masks knockin on yo door."

"I knew it," PYT says. "Brown Brown, didn't I say somethin felt off? That's why we came back so quick."

"Whatchu mean?" Taj asks.

"We was on the way to the store, but somethin aint feel right. Can't explain what it was. Brown Brown aint want us to come back wit nothin, so he was sayin we should go, just make it quick. But I couldn't, so we just ran back here."

Taj wipes his face wit both hands, tryna keep his cool. The mo we hear, the mo worried he gets. We was this close, again—and all it took was a second. If PYT aint get that feelin, who know what coulda happened.

"Don't worry, Bittersweet," Rissa says. "Benji got a few guys from his unit together and they walkin round to see if they still here. I was scared outta my mind."

Taj cocks his piece. Night and Brown Brown do the same. PYT reaches for his bag, grips something that might be bigger than a pistol.

"Whoa, whoa," Rissa says, movin in front of the door. "Pump yo brakes. Where you think you goin?"

"To handle this, whatchu think?" Taj says louder than he should.

PYT stands near me. Benji tenses for a second, but Rissa puts up her hand.

She knows what he thinkin, but she aint havin it. "So you go out there and then what? You don't know who you lookin for."

"But the longer we stand here, the mo time we wastin. They came up to our room, Auntie. They woulda killed us if they aint get spooked. We could be dead."

"Don't you think I know that? I'm not sayin you don't handle this, but lemme chat wit some folks in the hotel, see what they saw. One of them might have seen their faces."

"How long's that gon take?"

"A little while, but it would be better than—"

"I aint bout to be waitin all night for some snitches," Taj interrupts.

PYT and I look at each otha. Taj aint neva interrupted Rissa like that.

"Well, if we don't, yall trigger-happy asses gon walk into a bloodbath. You worked too hard to get where you are in the BDs to throw it all away. Befo you, nobody even thought the gangs could be united—but you did. You were the one who made it happen . . . to keep errbody you love safe. We'll find out who breakin the truce and why, and we'll fix it—togetha."

"Auntie . . ." Taj shakes his head, not convinced.

"Bittersweet. No. I can't let you throw your and errbody's life away just cuz you tryna get even. You not usin yo head, and it's gon get you and errbody you love killed."

"Auntie, it aint yo decision to make."

"Excuse me?" Rissa says, hand on her hip.

"Taj, chill. You aint thinkin straight," I say.

"Auntie, I love you—God knows I do—but Imma need you to get outta my way and let me handle this. It's outta yo hands."

"First of all, in the BDs and in every day of *yo* life, I'm the OG, not you. So, aint nothin outta my hands concernin you. Second of all, let's say you go out there and get killed, what bout Lee? What happens to him?"

"You got him, dontchu? You can do what you been doin."

"Do I look like I was put on this earth to serve you? I took care of both of you since you were young outta the kindness of my heart, but don't for a second get it in yo head that my whole world revolve round you, cuz it don't."

"It aint my fault she aint want us. We aint asked to be born to a crack—"

Slap! Nobody sees it comin, but we feel it just the same.

"Watch yo fuckin mouth," Rissa says through gritted teeth. "I'll tell you what. You do what you want, but if you walk out that door, you takin Lee witchu."

"The fuck I am," Taj shouts, water in his eyes.

"The fuck you *will,*" Rissa says. "If you wanna go out there on some dick-measurin contest to see who bigger and badder, by all means. But don't come cryin to me when you look at Lee and see him followin down the same path. It's the same shit that got Faa killed, and now Rouk runnin round here wit the wrong crowd."

"I aint the one who killed him!" Taj says.

"I didn't say you did, Bittersweet." Rissa shakes her head, frustrated—Taj aint listenin.

"You know what? Maybe I did, even tho I aint the one who pulled the trigger. I shoulda stopped him—I knew what he was doin was too dangerous."

Taj and Faa were workin together? But why he aint neva tell me? If whateva they was on to got Faa murdered, whoeva killed him could be waitin for Taj right now. They could be behind the shootin, settin a trap to get Taj pissed, and make him run out here without thinkin.

"I gotta do this, Auntie. I promised Faa I would keep Rouk safe, keep him and Lee out of all this. I can't protect nobody if I don't know who I'm fightin."

"But if you go out there without thinkin and get killed, what's the first thing *yo* brotha gon do, huh?" Rissa says.

"Taj, let's just wait a minute. She got a point, man," Night says.

Taj shakes his head. He aint havin it.

"Yo, Taj." Brown Brown touches his shoulder.

"What the fuck *I* say? I was the one in that house watchin Lee in a pool of blood. Nobody else. Me! And I say we handlin this shit right now. Aint gon be no fuckin tomorrow. And anybody stand in my way—"

"Taj," PYT says, standin up.

"No!" Taj jumps in his face, but PYT aint tryna fight. He puts his hands up and backs off, defeated.

Now errbody can see it: the anger boilin to the top, almost outta control cuz it's been two months, and Taj aint cry, get angry, or lose his temper. He smiled through it all, but he barely sleep, and he can't do that without callin and leavin voice mails in the middle of the night, beggin for Jacobee to pick up. And when he do sleep, he wakes up screamin my name. They don't see that if somebody don't stop em, he aint gon make it back alive.

He walks like he goin to the bathroom, but I know betta. I tackle him to the floor, at first, just to stop him, say somethin different, but then I start wailin on him. The first few punches catch him off guard, but he blocks the last few, stares back like he don't know who I am.

"What the fuck, Lee?"

But I can't stop. Tryna save him, I broke somethin in me.

It takes Brown Brown and PYT to pull me off him while Taj just stares at me in shock.

"Why the fuck you keep tryna leave me," I cry. "You said you'd neva do what Ma did!"

"You lied." *I need you here wit me.*

"You lied." *Please, don't leave.*

"You a fuckin liar." *If you don't want me, just say it.*

I kick, claw from beneath PYT. My body feel like it's burnin from the inside out. PYT and Brown Brown drag me into the otha room. There, on the floor, PYT folds me into his chest, wraps me in his arms, and I hold on to him cuz I'm afraid of drownin and he the only one keepin me afloat.

When I wake up, I don't know how much time has passed, but errthang is quiet. PYT is still here, and Taj is sleep on the floor in front of me. Night and Brown Brown feet hangin ova the bed closest to us.

If none of this went down, I woulda already found a way for Jay to help me wit my essay and would be lookin forward to startin the GED program at C-Pote Tech. But till we catch whoeva after us, all that gotta stay on hold. And if what Taj slipped and said is true, maybe this aint related to the gang war, maybe it's bout somebody tryna get away wit murderin Faa, the pride and joy of K-Town.

The problem: all we got is this DK symbol; aint no name to focus on and no otha leads to follow. There aint no way to figure out who's behind it. But whateva is goin on is big—somethin so big, Taj and maybe even Rissa know mo than they lettin on. I gotta figure out what it is; I gotta find some way to help so all of us can get back to livin our lives.

I watch Taj open his eyes. He takes a minute to say somethin, but even when he do speak, it aint wit words. He grab my hand, does a one-sided secret handshake he makes up, pulls at my fingers but neva lets me go. Then he mouths, *I'm sorry.*

I don't say nothin, I just look back at him, thinkin. I can't remember the last time Taj eva had a reason to be sorry to me—it's usually the otha way round. I'm always the one fuckin up, gettin in trouble at school, not doin what he need me to. Errtime, he forgives me, hugs me, and asks me to do betta.

I whisper, "Me, too." I pull pack at his fingers, do my own one-sided, made-up handshake.

Slowly, errbody wakes up sayin the same thing: we hungry as hell. So when Rissa calls the room and says to swing by the restaurant for some food and updates, the only person who drags his feet is Taj. I don't think he know how to face

Rissa after errthang he did last night. I don't blame him, but we aint got no choice; when Rissa say come, we go—no questions asked.

When we all pull up at her diner, aint no customers, and won't be for anotha coupla hours. Since the shootin, Rissa only opens the diner for lunch and dinner, in case we wanna eat breakfast. When she sees Taj, she points to the back room wit all the supplies, a small cot, and a desk where all the business happens. He goes into the room and waits for her without even lookin at her or us. Then, Rissa joins him.

Iono what they talm bout but when Taj finally comes out, they both all smiles and forgiveness, wit one arm round each otha waist. It don't mean she gon forget what happened, just that she gon give him the one thing he wants most in the world in this moment: the chance to make it right.

"I got some good news and some bad news. Which tea yall want first?"

It don't matter, cuz Rissa always starts wit the bad news so the good sounds better. We smile, not even choosin.

"Fine. Turns out, somebody at the front desk saw one of the guys befo they put on their mask in the parking lot."

"That sound like good news to me," Night says, stuffin his face wit a waffle and a drumstick.

"It would be, but they don't know where the guy stays or who he reppin—may not even be from round here."

"So what's the good news?" PYT asks.

"The front desk clerk says she saw him hangin out wit one of her cousin's friends who works as a bodyguard ova at the O Lounge."

"Talm bout that club on River Street?" PYT says.

"Yes, but you can't just up and go to the O Lounge, cuz it's run by Lady Tee. Plus—"

"Lady Tee? Who dat?" Night says, gulpin down sweet tea.

"You don't know Lady Tee?" Brown Brown asks.

"If I did, would I be askin?"

"Aint she Prince Ten's old lady," PYT says.

"Who?" Night still aint gettin it.

"He run for Daniel Lee. He like the new Jacobee—at least, he tryna be," Brown Brown explains.

Night nods his head, puttin the pieces together.

"All I know, she hella connected," Taj says, as we watch Night fold two pancakes in his mouth, damn near swallows them whole.

"She knows a lot of people you don't want to cross, and they protect her cuz she protects them," Rissa says. "Plus, the O Lounge is a neutral zone, so you can go there and know you're safe. That's why I called her and told her what's goin on."

"You think she might warn ol boy?" Taj says.

"That aint how she works, boo. I've known her a long time, and she mean what she says. But that also mean we gotta roll up in there on her terms. She said meet her at the club round nine p.m. since the lounge opens at ten. Befo we do, let's check yall outta the motel. Imma set yall up at my house, and me and Benji gon find anotha place until this blows ova."

Taj shakes his head. "Ion want none of this to blow back on you. I'll find somewhere else."

"I'm not askin, Bittersweet. The motels and hotels aint workin. Plus, if yall stay at our house, you don't have to keep movin cuz it's also in the neutral zone, right on the border of K-Heights, and not far from D and D's Grocery. That way, Lee can be close enough to Trish and you will have everything you need without havin to look ova yo shoulder every minute."

It would be good to be able to see Trish again. I been missin her like crazy the past coupla months and aint really been able to see her since she visited me at the hospital.

Taj nods. "That's why we gotta figure out who was at the motel to begin wit."

"And who might know what that symbol mean," I say.

The whole table looks at me, then Taj.

"Nah . . . you gon stay out of it," he says, lookin at me.

"But, Taj—"

"You heard what I said, right?"

I look ova at Rissa, hopin she'll change his mind.

"Don't worry, Lee," she says. "Between the bodyguard and Lady Tee, somebody gon give us some answers."

Taj looks at me, then looks at Rissa. For a second, I can see it in his eyes: he worried. Then Rissa gives him a look, both of us, to let us know we in this togetha.

It's one thing to hear somebody important; it's anotha thing to see it for yaself. The only businesses that can afford to be downtown on River Street are the ones that got mo money than just bout errbody else—which is usually the Bainbridges, one of the richest families in Savannah. They call themselves one of the foundin families, so they got benches in all the downtown squares and a floatin hotel across the river.

Wit they hand in just bout any and errthang business related, from the ports to the warehouses to the big arts college, it seem like they don't know how to do nothin but make money. Only that money don't neva seem to make it back to the people who need it the most, which is why the BDs keep an eye on errbody they can, especially the mom-and-pop shops people tryna buy out to build mo hotels and condos on the river. In my opinion, the only good things bout bein on River Street is the Savannah Riverboat Cruises, saltwater taffy, and them twenty-five-cent oysters in the summer that be hittin.

Tryna drive round them damn squares is confusin, and parkin on Broughton Street wit all them parkin meters that take yo quarters is a ticket waitin to happen. Taj used to say, them cobblestone roads was how Black people got back at the white folks who enslaved em; we mighta been forced to design em and lay em brick by brick, but only after we put a lil juju on em. White people can drive fast, actin like this world is theirs all they want, but them cobblestones fuck up they axles and shake they cars down to bits till all they can do is walk or take the City Kitty bus that only come when it wants to.

We pull up near the place. The smell of saltwater taffy and candied apples points us in the direction of her building. We don't see no sign that says "O Lounge." The storefront sign we do see—"Lady Tee's African Imports"—don't look like much. But when we get past the bodyguards and walk through anotha door that leads to a second building, we shocked the moment we get on the floor.

The O Lounge aint just some place wit drinks, it some high-class exclusive-type shit I aint neva seen befo. Then we hear Lady Tee befo we see her, the sound of money, dozens of silver and gold bracelets and cockleshells that chime err-time she takes a step even tho it seems like her feet neva even touch the ground.

Lady Tee looks like somebody's queen—like that bride on *Coming to America*—she even got the African accent. The only difference, she aint jumpin on one foot barkin at no nigga command; when she walk in the room, she give mad don't-fuck-wit-it vibes. She kisses Rissa on the cheek, holds her hands, and smiles like they childhood best friends. Then, only Rissa, Lady Tee, and Taj get to go upstairs.

At first, I feel some type of way bein left out, but Rissa says they don't want the bodyguard to feel like some shit is bout to go down. Lady Tee opens us a tab and tells us to have fun eatin all the free hot wings, fries, and oysters we can handle, and that the O Lounge got an eighteen-and-up night once a week we can always come back to. PYT and Night try to sweet-talk the bartender and waiter into lettin them take a shot, but they aint even tryna hear it.

When the DJ plays "P.Y.T. (Pretty Young Thing)" by Michael Jackson, it goes down. PYT gets it all started, standin up from his barstool, eatin wings ova errbody shoulders as he dances and mouths the words. Next thing I know, what happened a few years ago happens again; each of us is up shakin they ass and jumpin round havin fun. I'm the last one PYT pulls from my seat. At first I say no—hell naw, actually—but I aint neva been able to turn him down.

PYT is the first nigga I eva had a crush on; Jay is the second. But I don't know if I'll eva be able to see Jay again, or if he even wants to see me. If Jacobee is ignorin Taj, I know Jay aint tryna fuck wit me no mo. I want to tell him how aint no way in hell I wanted to break up wit him, how I still think bout him every day so much it hurts. But if I can't even protect me, I can't protect him. Until I can, this is the only way.

But then a ghost walks through the crowd—from a past I

thought I was gonna have to leave behind: Jacobee.

"I'll be right back," I say to PYT.

He looks at me, then looks at who I'm goin after, and nods like he knows somethin I don't. I run down some stairs and see Jacobee slip into a hallway. At first, I'm scared of somethin I don't even got a name for, but I don't really need no words. I shake it off, do it scared.

"Yo, Bee!" I say, so he knows it's me and nobody else.

He turns round, stares back like he seein a ghost. Not one that scares him—one he mighta been hopin for, too.

"Lee," he says, standin there. He could ignore me, ask me to go home, to get lost, but he don't. He walks up to me, and when I try to dap him up, he hugs me instead. "You look like shit," he says, laughin, still holdin on to me. "You been goin through it, huh?"

"Nah," I say, tryna hide it. I tell him the same lies I tell myself. "I'm okay. It's nothin."

"You a bad liar, you know that?" He tilts his head, grins, like he already knows what I don't want him to know. "Lemme get one of em hugs up outcha." He pulls me in again.

That's when it happens: My eyes water. My chest aches. My throat tightens. My hands are shakin. I let go, but he won't. He holds me tighter.

Tears fall. I wipe them away real fast, try to ignore em, wait for em to pass, but they don't. It only gets worse. The truth comes out lil by lil: *I ain't okay. I'm scared. It hurts too much. Iono if I can keep doin this. And somethin wrong wit Taj—and iono how to fix it.*

Standin in front of Jacobee I realize I ran after him for Taj, but for me, too, cuz he be givin me the one thing I neva really had—hope. Jacobee makes me think it aint enough anymore to just survive. It aint enough to just be safe. I wanna live, and to do that, I need my brotha. I need Rissa. I need Night, Brown Brown, and PYT. I need Jacobee.

But most of all, I need Jay.

9

JAY

I wake up, but I keep my eyes closed, listening. I don't hear anyone, no steps against the floorboards, no cooking utensils clanging or skillets hissing with joy. I wait, listen, for someone, anyone. But the stillness, the quiet is deafening. I get up, scratch my throat with my tongue, and hum to shoo the silence away.

Jacob's room is my room, too, now that Will has been staying with us. The three of us helped move most of my stuff to Jacob's room before we helped move a few boxes into Will's room, equipment and things he said he needed, but I haven't seen what it looks like with everything unpacked quite yet. I follow the trail of nothing to my old room, but the door is closed. I put my hand on the knob, dare myself to turn it, but something crashes into the front door downstairs.

I run down, look through the peephole. It's Will. He's fumbling with a bike. I open the door.

"Whaddup, Jay?"

He's crouched over his upside-down bike, fixing the chain or the tire or both, half-naked in some white swimming trunks because it's morning but it's still hot and humid and because he can.

"Where you headed?" I ask, curious.

"I dunno. . . . Wanna come?" His grin promises an adventure, maybe even a little danger, if we're lucky. He flips the bike right side up, wipes the sweat from his forehead, ignores the rest worshipping him from all sides.

"Maybe . . . how? On that?" I point at the bike, like it's a piece of futuristic machinery.

He nods, strokes the seat, hops on, then rolls down the driveway, all smiles, bobbing up and down before doing a circle and riding back up to me.

"Hop on . . ." He angles the bike so I can see the seat, but all I see are the muscles in his back and how the trunks seem to get shorter by the minute.

"As in . . . get on the bike with you?"

He nods.

"How?" I measure the nearly nonexistent space that would be between us and worry about what would happen as he pedals up and down so close to my lap. I'm not afraid of touching—I just don't know what to do when it happens.

I want to trust Will, but I don't want to risk being wrong and having to deal with the hell that will come with it. Plus, that would be a really bad start to a long summer of him living with us.

Yes, he kissed me when we were little, but it was on

the cheek and, since then, he's never even mentioned it happened. Maybe it was something he did to everybody—a kissing phase.

"No, I'm good," I say.

"You sure?" he asks.

Yes. No. Yes. Maybe. "I don't know."

Will grins, straddles the bike, and glides. Every time his feet touch the street, it flexes his calves, setting off a chain reaction that reveals more golden skin.

"What I gotta do to change yo' mind?"

I don't answer. It's getting harder to pretend. He chuckles, shakes his head, and holds back something I want to hear.

"What? You laughing at me?"

"Naw, sorry, I'm not really good with words when it comes to stuff like this. What I'm tryna say is . . ." He ruffles his curls, then keeps his hands there. "Wanna kick it with me today?"

"Huh?" I want to take the sound back, cram it into my mouth, swallow, and then try again.

"Want to?" he asks again. His voice does that thing mine does when I can't get words out. He never finishes his sentence, just slow-pedals to a yes that doesn't require words.

"Alright, let me get dressed." I run upstairs, dizzy with joy. When I look back, he's smiling bigger than I've ever seen. I smile, too, because I'm—no, *we*—are going on an adventure.

By the time we stop to take a break, we're almost on the other side of K-Heights, farther than I've ever been. I've walked all over Savannah, except K-Town, but only where Jacob went. I soak it all up, the new and the familiar, try to remember every little thing.

Will stops on the corner of Cedar Street, near a phalanx of white pampas grass. We walk, his bike steadily ticking beside us, pointing at things neither one of us has seen before: a mailbox in the center of a rosebush, a secret bamboo garden, a row of mini mansions each more different than the rest. When we follow them, we come out on the other side of Daffin Park, near an army of southern oaks, stretching almost three blocks, equally spaced out, their branches overhead nearly touching. Will parks his bike gently under a majestic, humpback oak in the center and sits on one of the roots. He touches the trunk, feels its bark, marvels in silence.

He turns around, shoulder-bumps me but keeps his shoulder connected to mine. "You sure you don't mind me usin' your room? I told your mom I don't mind sleeping on the couch."

"She ain't letting you sleep on no couch." I chuckle. "She'll build another room by hand and attach it to the house herself before she does that."

He laughs, envisioning it. "I believe you. My mum is the same way."

On the wind, a fragrance finds us, a special kind of sweet.

Will sniffs as it arrives. "That you?" He leans in toward my neck.

I lean back, laughing. "It's not me . . . it's those."

I point to bushes lining a fence and softly whisper the name, like the flowers are old friends: sweet olive. They flirt back, another wave of their aroma caressing our senses.

Will grins, leans closer. "You know a lot about flowers, huh?"

I nod, but a tinge of pain in my chest hijacks my smile. I don't want to think about it, but at the same time I do. "My dad . . . he knew a lot about flowers, was kind of famous for it."

"Furreal? Nice! My mum would mention him but never any details."

Miss Rosalind talks about my father? I knew she was close to Momma, so I guess it makes sense, but I didn't realize she knew him enough to talk about him. While I wrestle with my own questions, I wait for him to do what everyone else does, to ask my dad's name, his whereabouts.

"How you know that flower? Is it special or somethin'?"

"It's the first flower he taught me the name of." I look away, don't want him to see the regret on my face, to mistake it for having anything to do with him.

The leaves and Spanish moss above our heads flutter, gossiping in the wind. They know the story, remember one of the many newspaper headlines about my dad's fall from grace. The one Momma tried to hide but couldn't after the

Avalon Park Neighborhood Association delivered one hundred of them on our doorstep, so we'd never ever forget:

FAMED LANDSCAPE DESIGNER SENTENCED TO SIX YEARS IN PRISON AFTER ATTACKING COUPLE IN AVALON PARK

I brace myself for the questions on his tongue about to jump the space between us.

Will stands up, holds out his hand. "Come on, let's go home. I wanna show you somethin'—the room, now that I set up everything this mornin'. It's a little bit of me, since you shared a little bit of you."

Will pulls back up to the house. There is nowhere to lock his bike out front, so he walks it in and props it in the hallway.

"Okay . . . where is everybody?"

"Shopping . . . my mum's been begging all morning for a girls' day out before she leaves tomorrow. I guess she finally convinced yours."

I shrug, wondering where Jacob might be as well.

As we walk upstairs, I check my and Jacob's room, but he isn't there. When I turn around, Will is standing in the doorway of my former room, with the smile of a showman. I walk in and can't help but smile, too.

Will's room looks like it's a part of a different house. On one wall he has posters of Prince, Aretha Franklin, and

Marvin Gaye. On the other side: Aaliyah, Pretty Ricky, Trina, and Lil Wayne. He has a collection of fitted hats spanning all colors and stacked neatly. Almost as high as my waist along the walls are shoeboxes of Air Forces, Jordans, Timbs, and other shoes I have never seen before. But what blows my mind is the sound system with two turntables next to crates of records stacked higher than the shoes. I'm so caught up in looking at the different covers that I forget Will is even here. One record calls out to me, reminds me of Momma, Nina Simone's *Broadway—Blues—Ballads*.

"Whatchu know 'bout dat?" he says with the second-biggest smile I've ever seen on his face.

I blush, hand it to him to play.

He flips switches, works his own kind of magic. "My mum says Nina is every woman's medicine; she knows what it's like to be broken—"

"And to be forced to live with the pieces." I finish his sentence without thinking, like a memorized prayer.

Will stares at me in a way I've never seen. "How you know that? Don't tell me you can read my mind."

If I could, what would I find?

I shake my head. "My momma used to say the same thing. She would play this album, well, the CD or cassette, whenever she was sad and missed my dad, which was a lot."

His eyes light up, knowing. He moves the tone arm toward the center. "See-Line Woman" hums through the speakers. I am speechless. It's the song my mom always listens to. Then

Will flicks and rolls his shoulders to the beat. I wish Jacob were here so he could coax me into dancing, but a different wish is granted. Will reaches out his hand to me.

Without thinking, memory begets movement and movement begets words; I start to say by swaying and, as Nina chants "yeah," our bodies become sweating semicolons, a decision to keep going when the sentence, the moment, could end. Our eyes lock, and a nothing gives something until I pull back. Will plays it off by sliding by me to grab another record before he flips another switch. Nina Simone's "Baltimore" two-steps between us.

"Who taught you to dance like that?" I ask, trying to think of anything but him standing in front of me.

"My mum." He smiles with his eyes.

"C'mere . . ." He turns to face one of the two turntables. "You ever mixed a track before?"

"Of course . . . not."

"I'mma show you how. Pick a song from what you see here." To the right, another stack of records, dozens. Even has current artists in record form, like Three 6 Mafia, Ciara, Lil Wayne, and Beyoncé, which I didn't know was possible. Another older record calls out to me.

"This one, Donny Hathaway. Play 'Giving Up.'" Momma likes him, but so did Dad and Jacob. We used to listen to him Saturday mornings as Momma and Dad cooked and Jacob and I cleaned, before everything changed.

Will stares at me, speechless.

“Not that one?”

“Oh . . . nah . . . I mean, it’s cool . . . I just . . . I mean . . . Gimme a sec.”

He turns more knobs, adjusts the tone arms. He starts his record on the left first, “Beauty” by Dru Hill. We both nod to the smooth, let it vibrate in the air around us.

“Close your eyes,” he says, pausing the song.

“Why?”

“’Cuz you’ll hear it better, feel exactly when to play your song.”

I’m not sure.

“Come on, trust me. It ain’t something you do with your head, you gotta feel it.”

I nod. He starts the song over. I listen, let the music move through me, and press the button right before the hook. Donny Hathaway’s voice booms through the speakers slow and deep, weaving between Dru Hill’s lyrics—want on the brink of need. The bass dips from “Beauty” and slow twerks against “Giving Up”; hope turns desperate.

I freeze when his hands leave the turntables and land on my waist. When I feel his lips, I pull away, dizzy.

“Oh . . . I’m sorry . . .” He stops the song, but the horns still echo. “I ain’t mean to . . . ,” he says, hands up, surrendering.

An awkward silence dances offbeat between us.

I stare at everything but him, clutching the back of my neck where I can still feel the wet heat of his lips. Why did he do that?

Will takes a deep breath and swallows, then goes into the bathroom.

I didn't know Will could get flustered. I assumed he was like Jacob or Leroy, smooth without even trying, but when he comes out of the bathroom, he's changed into a white tank and basketball shorts, his cheeks are a blushing red. Suddenly Will isn't the unreachable; he is just as nervous and confused as I am. It's a relief, well, as much of a relief as I can have in this moment.

I giggle at the sight of our truth. I don't mean to; I can't stop myself.

"Chill, man," he says, covering his face. "Ain't shit I can do about it. I waited in there for it to go away, but it's gon' take a minute." He laughs at himself. "Shit's mad embarrassin'. I'm over here lookin' like a strawberry."

"More like a maraschino cherry. . . ."

"Damn, you gon' laugh at a nigga when he down?"

"I'm sorry." I can't stop laughing. He chuckles, too, then sits next to me on the bed, slowly, keeping his distance.

"It's still red, ain't it?" He cups his face.

I nod. "What's it like?"

"You ain't neva blush before?"

"I mean, yeah, but my face doesn't turn red."

"Feel it," he says, grabbing my hands and putting them to his face. I almost pull back because it's so sudden.

"It's really warm."

"Yeah, feels like my head is 'bout to explode and my heart." He moves one of my hands from his face to his chest. It's racing just like mine.

I can't concentrate. The more Will tries, the more he shows the softer parts of him, the closer he gets, and the closer he gets the more I want to trust him, for him to win, even if it means my own defeat. But I don't want to be hurt by Will like I was by Leroy. I just want to feel, fly with someone without being afraid to fall.

"Jay . . . Jay, you hear me?"

I snap out of it, but the questions cling to me. "No, I'm sorry. What did you say?" I rub the back of my neck again.

"I said I'm sorry and I ain't mean to . . . I just . . . Well." His voice is softer than I've ever heard it. "I thought I could keep it under control, but when you chose the song my mum and dad fell in love to, it just . . ."

"It's cool, I know you didn't mean it. . . ."

"Whatchu mean?" Will says.

"Nothing. I'm just saying, I get it. You don't have to apologize. I know you just got caught up in the moment and—"

"Nah, that ain't what I mean."

"Oh, I'm not saying you're . . . I'm just saying I know sometimes—"

"Jay, what the fuck?"

"What?"

"I don't just do that with people."

"I didn't mean it like that. . . . I'm just saying I know it isn't a big deal. . . . We can be—"

"I still like you," he says, with a record in his hand. A fact, not a question. No *but* anywhere in the sentence. "I always have. Don't you remember?"

My mind goes blank. I just look at Will, wondering if it is the heat that has me hearing things. He couldn't mean it. Boys like him, if they even like boys, choose boys like Jacob, Leroy, or boys who look like him. Not me.

"Remember . . . what exactly?" I move to one of his other stacks of records so I don't have to look him in his eyes as he responds. I'm embarrassed enough.

"Fuck it, I'mma just say what I gotta say." He takes a deep breath. "I been feelin' you since we were little. That's why I wanted to come, to see if you were still the same, if you remembered. When I saw you at the pool, I knew it was you instantly." He stares at me, tries to read my face for any kind of reaction. "I just don't want you thinkin' I'm this smooth operator or shit like that. . . . I don't go around kissin' on people."

I chuckle, nervously. "Wow . . . you quoting Sade now? Really?"

"You know what I mean. I just feel like . . . Can we start over? Not over over, but over. We can be cool, but I won't—I'll try not to make no more moves . . . unless you want me to."

I don't know how to look or what to say. I can't help but

think of Leroy. Is it okay to like two people at one time?

"Ahh," Will yells, rolling on the bed. He covers his face with his pillow. Somewhere an answer settles and a part of me melts like a thrill off the Popsicle stick, but I can't tell him.

"I wanna do-over, man. Just forget this ever happened," he says through the pillow.

I pull the pillow from his grip. "It's cool. You're forgiven."

"Furreal?" He looks up from underneath his damp curls, eyes ablaze in the light brown.

I nod.

"Wait, don't forgive me just yet." He kisses me on the cheek.

Now, I'd like to think we are matching maraschinos, so I do the only thing I can do while trapped between his lips and a hard place: I hit him with the pillow until he apologizes but refuses to say he'll never do it again.

I won't tell him just yet, but if he means it, if he really likes me, I want him to kiss me as many times as he wants, if it means he can distract me from everything that hurts—the memories of peppermint and Cool Water, of fights in the dirt, of silent car rides, of Leroy's lips, arms, and voice ringing in my ear whenever it is silent. But I don't say anything.

I want to wait and see, keep my heart just out of reach from anyone until I know for sure I won't get hurt—just in case.

After the pillow fight, Will finishes getting changed, and

then he opens both doors to his closet and asks, "You like anything in here?"

Every kind of clothing I can imagine, from graphic tees to jerseys to letterman jackets to polos and jeans and khakis and even Dickies. He has more clothes I can't see stored in tons of plastic containers.

"Come look. When you find somethin' you like, go ahead and change, and we can head out."

"You want me to wear your clothes?"

"Only if you want to. I was thinking about going to the mall real quick and getting some stuff. Wanna come?"

"But you got the whole mall right here."

We both laugh.

I don't want to at first, but some Girbauds with white straps are calling my name. I don't have to say a word before Will has me in the jeans and an XXL white polo with a matching fitted. He lets me borrow some Timbs since my feet are too big for the other shoes. After we finish, I look in the mirror, search hard for the boy I used to know. The boy who didn't think he was worthy of being seen. I realize he knew better all along, which is why he stares back at me and winks.

"Let's go . . . my treat," Will says, staring at me longer than I would expect.

Will gets me some ice cream from a Dairy Queen store look-alike and an almond pretzel from Auntie Anne's. He stays close. Well, closer than close, sometimes even accidentally bumping into me from behind or shoulder-bumping me.

"You think our folks did the same thing we doin' now? Walking in this food court, talking with an almond pretzel?" Will asks.

"Our moms?" I smile at the thought.

"Yeah, but our dads, too."

"What do you mean?"

"What? You didn't know our dads were close, too?"

I look away from his eyes, not just because he mentioned my dad but because I didn't know something so important. It makes me wonder if I ever really knew my dad at all.

"I don't know a whole lot myself—my relationship with my dad is real complicated—but my mum used to talk about the four of them all the time. How she and your mom were best friends since middle school, then how they met your dad in high school, and eventually my dad came later, when he visited one summer. They spent time together, kind of like me and you are right now. They danced and sang and went to parties." He giggles.

The memory sounds cool, and I smile at the thought. I didn't grow up hearing those stories, from my mom or dad. But this past week, I've learned so much from Will based on the stories Miss Rosalind told him.

"What happened?" I ask, no longer embarrassed by what I don't know.

"I dunno. Not even my mum will talk about it. I just know

one minute it was all good, the next minute it wasn't." We stand near the carousel, grinning at a little kid whose face looks like he's on the Ring of Fire roller coaster at the Coastal Empire Fair, holding on for dear life.

"I guess that's why Mum wanted to visit, to fix things."

There's so much more I want to know about who they used to be, all four of them—my parents with Will's parents—and what changed. I want to know what they haven't told us, in hopes of figuring out something I've always wanted to know: the whole story of why my dad did what he did, to me and Jacob, to the couple in Avalon Park. No matter how many times I've read the articles, it never makes sense. How can a person change into a monster overnight and no one notice it? It makes me wonder if there are more secrets behind why things are so different from what they were.

Will nudges me, asks if I want to sit down—staring at the carousel is fun for only so long. When I do, he pulls his chair to the other side of the table so it faces me, and places the bags of shoes and clothes between our legs.

It doesn't take long for me to notice all the eyes staring at us: a group of girls giggling; a few different guys who lick their lips and rub their hands to get Will's attention from the other side of the food court. I'm reminded: Will is the sun, and I, a lesser planet.

When he goes to the bathroom and one of the giggling girls is talked into finally walking over to me, I think about whether I should take her number if she wants to give it to me to give to Will or if I should politely turn her down on his behalf.

She comes close, in a pink halter top, white jeans, and pink-and-white high-top 1s.

"Hi," she says, half giggle, half greeting.

"Hey . . . ," I say, smiling.

She seems nice. Will might like her, which makes it harder for me to think about what I should do.

"What's yo' name?" she asks.

"Joseph . . . but you can call me Jay."

"I'm Sierra."

"Nice to meet you, Sierra." I brace myself, wait for the question I've been dreading and just plan to tell the truth. *Will isn't looking for—*

"Can I have your number?"

Wait, what? I stare at her, unsure I heard her right. "Huh?"

"Let me get your number," she repeats, more confident this time, with a little more spice.

"I . . . umm . . . I . . ."

"Take mine instead." She slips me a sheet of paper, then disappears as quickly as she came. I stare at the paper in disbelief.

Before Will comes back, another girl and a guy give me their numbers as well.

Will sits down, glowing, but I'm terrified. Do I tell him? But how do I describe the impossible? This whole time I assumed they wanted Will, but they want me, even though all I want is to be wanted by him. Will leans in close enough to kiss, chuckles. But I stop, because for a second, I see him—Leroy—across the food court near the gumball machines looking at me—at us.

"You alright?" Will asks.

I nod. But when I look back over to where I saw Leroy, he's gone.

Home smells like a gingerbread house, and the kitchen table is covered in the small white boxes we had folded for Momma the night before to place her cookies in.

I know how tired she is when she doesn't say anything as we close the door behind us. She sits in the middle of the long couch in her black hair bonnet and her favorite baking clothes: a turquoise T-shirt that reads "Proud Mama, #1 Cook" and pink leopard-print pants. Will runs upstairs to the bathroom as I crawl beside her, lay my head gently on her lap.

"Hey," she says, eyes still closed.

I melt in the palms of her hands as she strokes my cheeks with one hand and massages my scalp with the other.

"You're happy," she says, smiling softly, eyes still closed.

I nod, soaking up whatever brown sugar magic is left in her hands.

I take a deep breath and sigh. "Where's Jacob?"

"He's upstairs sleep. Got in late from his new job."

Momma's fingers pick up where words drop off.

"Another one?" I say.

Momma scoffs. "I keep telling him he's not Superman. But he won't listen."

I look up, put my hands on top of her hands, send some love to chase away her worry.

"You know just what to do sometimes, you know that?" She smiles. "I knew it from the moment you were born that you were special. The doctor pulled you out and put you on my chest, and you just pushed yourself up on your hands and looked me right in the eyes—your daddy my witness. That's when we knew. Mhmm . . ."

My smile wanes; he's my kryptonite.

Momma sighs, this time for a different reason. "You ever think about calling your dad? He's been out for over a month now. I'm sure he'd like to hear from you . . . and Jacob."

I groan, turn the other way.

"Alright, alright. I'll leave it alone. Just remember: he's your father, which means he can teach you things I can't. Just promise me you'll keep the door open when it's time—or at least think about it."

"I'll think about it," I say.

I have questions I want to ask her, but looking in her eyes, I know better. Some truths are better off never being told. I wonder if that's the reason she kept secrets of her own.

"You done eavesdropping, Jacob?" she says.

Suddenly he pops his head out so we can see him at the top of the stairs, where the banister begins and the wall ends.

"Since you're here"—she turns my head to face hers—"tell Jacob to quit sneaking all that money into my purse. It's enough he pay the bills behind my back."

I look over at Jacob's face, and it only says one thing: guilty.

"He's not gonna listen to me," I say, pretending to chide him. Momma clearly doesn't know Jacob gives me the money to sneak into her purse or that I'm the one who steals the bills from her dresser and passes them to him.

Jacob comes down the stairs, pretending to be a spy while humming the *Mission: Impossible* theme song. I join along, making hand signals along with the notes. Momma joins, too, adding what she thinks is the high part, but is off-key.

She bursts into laughter, knowing. "It was worth a try."

Jacob crawls on the other side of Momma, tries to put his head on her lap, too, but I block him with my hand. When Jacob holds Momma's hand, pulling it to his face, I grab it, too.

"Unh-unh, whatchu doin'? She not done with me yet. You have to wait."

"Says who?" Jacob says.

"Momma, tell him," I say, trying to coax her. "Ouch . . . My head hurts, so you have to keep massaging it. Tell him . . . he gotta wait."

"Ma, tell him he being selfish. One hand each. Lap rules."

"Those ain't no lap rules. You makin' stuff up," I argue.

"Last I checked, these are my hands, and this is my lap," she says, "so can I say what I will and won't do, please? Thank you."

She tries to push us both off, and me and Jacob bump heads trying to make her stay.

In between our flailing, I see Will peek his head from above the banister as well. "Hey, Miss Julia."

"Hey, baby."

"Can I join y'all?" he says.

"You know you don't have to ask. This is your home, too. You still want them cornrows?"

Will's face lights up. Mine does, too. I didn't even know he wanted them.

"Go get that bottle and bowl I showed you—and don't forget the gel and the rattail comb. It's the one that's half comb and half metal pick."

"Got it," he says, running down the stairs.

Momma pats the front of the sofa, so he sits on the floor between her legs. She rubs her fingers through his curls, which stretch longer than I thought they could. "Is this your first time getting cornrows?"

He nods. "Mum don't know how to braid. She tried one time and . . . well . . ." His smile says it all: it didn't turn out too well.

"You don't have to tell me, baby. Lin can do many things—but hair, well, let's just say that and cooking is my territory."

They both chuckle, knowing. I watch closely, curious

about how it'll turn out. I've never seen Momma braid hair before, besides her own.

"I gotta warn you, though. When I'm done, we gon' have to beat those girls and boys off you with a stick."

Girls *and* boys? I look at Jacob, shocked that Momma said that.

She looks over at me and Jacob. "What? Don't look at me like that. Will is the one who told me he doesn't discriminate." She looks down at him. "Did I explain that right, honey?"

Will puts out his hand—she low-fives it, laughs.

My chest feels warm, the good kind. Jacob grins at me and the possibilities before hovering closer so he can watch Momma.

"What time you gotta work tonight?" she asks.

"Seven to midnight. Should be back by one."

"Oh, okay . . . make sure they don't keep you late like last night—unless they are paying you overtime. You hear me? Time *and* a half."

He nods, looks over at me. His eyes say there's more to the story but that he doesn't want to talk about it.

"Where you work?" I ask.

"The O Lounge, Princeton's ma's place, Lady Tee."

"The really fancy club?"

I knew Princeton said she was hiring, and I remember telling him Jacob was looking for a new gig, but I didn't know he'd gotten in touch with Jacob or that his mom had hired him already.

"What do you do?" Will asks.

"Bartender."

"Nonalcoholic bartender," Momma corrects him.

"I learn how to make real drinks, too," he says, proud.

"Do you?" Momma says, giving him the eye.

He slides out of her grasp, just in case, grinning.

"Just kidding . . . I wouldn't know an alcoholic drink if it was in my hands and I was drinkin' it."

Momma pretends like she's going to pop him, breaks out into laughter instead. "You keep on. You forget me and Lady Tee went to high school together. I knew her when her name was just Theresa, okay? Don't make me pick up that phone and get you fired."

Momma picks Will's curls loose, which stretch to a much bigger 'fro. When she presses down with her hand to begin sectioning it into parts, his hair covers everything on his face except for his lips.

"Let me know if it's too tight, okay?"

Will gives her the thumbs-up.

Momma continues, and it's clear cooking isn't her only gift; with her rattail comb, she parts and commands Will's sandy-brown sea, rolling and weaving with her fingers, revealing parts of him and us through stories: how Miss Rosalind was there when Jacob was born; and that Jacob used to call both me and Will his little brothers, and wherever someone took us, he followed as a dutiful five-year-old protector. But behind every heartwarming story, a question lurks in the back of my mind: If she and Miss Rosalind were so close, why haven't we seen them together in ten years?

"Jay, got get the mirror," Momma says. "Oh, shuckie, duckie nenh. I think I've outdone myself with this one." She stands Will up and slowly turns him around as she smooths in sweet-smelling oil and sprays spritz so the braids really shine.

I hand Will the mirror, watch him scan as he checks all the angles, his smile growing wider with every move of the mirror. His beauty is beyond words, described only by Momma's whoops, Jacob's hollers, and my silence.

As he carries the supplies up the stairs, he grabs me with his eyes and won't let me go. And for no reason I can explain, I feel fully moved and forever blushing.

10

Leroy

K-Heights is different from K-Town—still loud, but instead of racing cars, shoot-outs, and winos sing-cussin in the streets—there are mo kids playin, block parties, and nosey-ass neighbors who drop off food and tryna get all in yo business. It aint bad; it just aint the side of town we grew up on.

Rissa still cooks and checks in on us every day, keepin the fridge full and Taj tryna slowly get back to his normal self, laughin and talkin shit, even play-fightin wit me without it always endin up too serious, but he a long way from bein happy—all of us is. I thought runnin into Jacobee again would make things at least feel betta, but for me, it only made things worse, like findin somethin you aint know you needed and somebody takin it back.

Jacobee is somebody I can talk to—like furreal, furreal—somebody who gets where I'm comin from cuz Taj don't always got time to just sit and listen to me, not while he tryna figure out who after us, who tryna break up the alliance wit the gangs, and whether the two are connected. I can talk to Trish, and I can always lean on Rissa for advice, too, but some things I wanna be able to say, to feel, in a way I only been able to wit Jacobee.

I aint neva tried to talk to Jacobee bout Jay, not since askin him to give Jay that letter tellin him we can't be togetha. But after today, I gotta try. If Brown Brown won't there wit me in the food court earlier today when I saw Jay all hugged up wit some ol light-bright, iono what I woulda did. And what really gets me is, even if I wanted to run up on them and regulate, I couldn't do shit but watch cuz Jay aint mine.

When I come back from the bathroom, I know somethin aint right when I see Rissa and Taj in the kitchen by themselves and Night, Brown Brown, and PYT doin their thing in the livin room.

"Bittersweet, how long you gon be able to keep this up? It aint safe," Rissa yell-whispers. "This aint gotta be yo whole world."

"What aint safe?" I'm tired of tiptoein round. If decisions are bein made, I wanna be part of em, even if I aint a YG.

Taj gives me the look, but I aint bout to back down.

"What? Why can't I know?"

"Not now, Lee. Go in there for a minute."

I shake my head and lean on the wall wit my arms crossed.

"Lee," he growls.

"Bittersweet, let him stay. He need to hear this, too."

"Auntie, he don't need to be in this."

Even if Rissa says it's okay, Taj expect me to do what he

says, no questions asked.

"Be in what?" I say.

Taj turns toward the sink and starts washin dishes already clean.

"Lee, Taj and I have been talkin, and—"

"No," Taj says. "Please . . . Ion want him in this till I make a decision."

Somethin bout the way he say "please" scares me.

Rissa gets up, puts her hands on Taj's shoulders, and talks soft like Ma used to. Rissa faces me. "Lee, wit all this goin on—"

"It's okay, I aint gotta know. Imma —" I say, tryna leave.

"No, Lee, stay. It's important. You should hear this, too."

I wait for Taj to tell me what he want me to do. He turns round, nods for me to stay.

"Wit all that's goin on, I think it's time for us to move," Rissa says.

"Where? You bought anotha house?"

"No, sweetie. I'm talm bout move to anotha city."

Her words hit me so hard I can't see straight, and I hear errthang sideways.

"I don't know when it will happen. I just know it could be soon."

What bout Jacobee?

"You know I've been meetin wit some people—investors—who wanna turn the diner into a restaurant chain."

What bout Jay?

"They made an offer and we negotiatin and they talm bout a lot of money."

What bout Night? Brown Brown? PYT?

"Since there's so much heat on Taj right now, I could put it to a vote wit the otha OGs and have him take on a different role where he aint workin so close wit the gangs or, better yet, he aint gotta do nothin wit the BDs at all."

What if we don't wanna go?

"Bittersweet wouldn't have to do what he doin now. He could put them leadership and money skills to use workin wit me, managin the restaurants."

She turns, faces Taj. "You could get back to trainin as a boxer, as long as yo hands stay fast enough to protect that handsome face." Rissa smiles, hopin he will, too. "You and Lee could do college together, if yall wanted."

All I know is here. Errbody we need is here.

"It's not safe here. Not no mo. That's why me and Benji want yall to come wit us. We lookin at houses big enough for all of us, or we could get yall yo own place near us."

I shake my head and wait on Taj to do somethin, anythin. But he don't.

I leave the kitchen, walk into the livin room, and stand in front of Brown Brown sittin next to PYT, who ignorin Night. I grab Brown Brown by the arm, try to pull him to his feet. I ask him to get me outta here. He goes into the kitchen, says somethin to Rissa and Taj that sound like a promise to keep me safe.

PYT sits up on the couch, mouths, *Are you okay?*

I nod cuz it's too much to explain.

I don't have a word for what I'm feelin, but "hurt" aint big and bad enough. I'm losin errthang and errone all at once, and there aint nothin I can do bout it.

Brown Brown comes back from the kitchen, grabs his keys. I don't have to tell him where we need to go. He tells me: we goin to see Jacobee.

"Chill out, nigga. Be cool." Brown Brown elbows me at the bar, knocks back Sprite like it's a shot of gin or somethin. He needs to be sayin that to himself, lookin ova his shoulder every coupla seconds.

Reyna, at the front desk, said Jacobee would be workin tonight but he aint here yet.

To kill time, Brown Brown orders XXX hot wings, somethin errbody braggin bout when they come here. We both take one, bite into it, slurp the sauce. It goes down like gasoline lit wit a flame, got us both chokin like we some lightweights.

After we chug down three glasses of water each, the lights shut off. I'm bout to bug the fuck out when I hear "Kissin' You" by Total play through the speakers.

The lights come on slow, and that's when I see Jacobee walkin through the crowd and over to the bar in an Egyptian god costume. The way he get to shakin and stirrin and pourin drinks while dishin out winks, you'd think he was makin drinks wit alcohol, but since it's eighteen-and-up night, he servin mocktails, while makin errbody drunk on somethin only he has.

Brown Brown gets up. "Watch the rest of my wings, I'm bout to take a leak, and don't eat none of em, eitha—I know how many I got left."

I shrug, already thinkin bout how I can steal one anyway.

It's so much screamin and crowdin, I don't even notice Rouk comin up behind me. He pushes my shoulder a lil too hard, but I keep my cool. By the sweet smell on his breath, he drunk on somethin that aint Jacobee's mocktails.

"Why you aint tell me?" His words slur, hit my ears upside down.

"Oh, now you talkin to me? Man, go on somewhere wit that."

"Fuck you."

"Whatchu say?"

"You heard me. . . ." He stumbles. "You was supposed to be my boy . . . to look out fuh me, but you knew Faa was diggin up dirt on the BDs and that Taj found out. That's why he did it."

I knew what Rouk's been sayin bout Taj since Faa died, but to say that shit to *my* face is different. How could he even think Taj would eva do somethin like that to Faa? But it aint just that. It's one thing to doubt Taj, but it's anotha thing to doubt me, my loyalty, and errthang we been for each otha.

"Taj aint do no shit like that and you know it, cuz if he did, I woulda known. And fuck you for doubtin me. If that's all you gotta say to me, take yo ass on."

I aint excusin the fact that Taj won't talk bout the shootin or what's really goin on wit the BDs—he got secrets on top of secrets. But that? He wouldn't, he *couldn't*.

Rouk pushes up on me real close. "Well, that's why I did what I did."

I push him off me. "Did what? Man, I aint followin you up. Getcho drunk—" But then I look at him, like really look at him, and I think bout what he sayin. He talm bout the shootin?

"Wait . . . run that back. Whatchu mean?"

He don't say nothin. He don't have to, cuz his eyes say it all. Two guys I don't recognize wit locs walk up behind him, try to pull Rouk back and calm him down, but when Rouk snatches his arm away, the guy wit the longest locs grab him hard and says somethin else in his ear.

Whateva it is, Rouk stops buckin, he just looks down, quiet.

I try to talk myself outta doin somethin stupid. Rouk could just be lyin to make me lose my shit. But what if he tellin the truth? What if he been close to us all this time and was willin to believe the worst of Taj—enough to turn on us? What if he aint the only one?

I try to unhear it, but I can't. All I can see is Jay on the ground bleedin, Jacobee cryin and his hands shakin while he talkin to 911, Taj shootin back, screamin for the ambulance, and the blood, so much blood, and all I can feel is the pain burnin through my arm and leg.

I bum-rush errbody, shove one of the guys pullin Rouk and, befo I realize it, I'm on top of Rouk, screamin and swingin.

I'm tired. I'm gon end this shit right here, right now.

Somebody grabs hold of me, they so strong my feet barely touchin the ground. At first, I think it's Brown Brown, but when he drags me in anotha room and throws me down on a sofa, I see who it is—Jacobee.

"What the fuck, Lee?" he yells.

Brown Brown runs through the door, shoves Jacobee back. "Imma need you to calm the fuck down and keep yo hands to yaself, Jacob."

"Brown Brown, it's cool," I say.

"Nah, Lee, it aint."

Jacobee glares at him, lookin ready to stomp Brown Brown into the ground for touchin him the way he did. Wait, how Brown Brown know Jacobee's real name?

"Bee, I'm sorry, I aint—"

"You bein stupid and reckless and it's gon get you killed," Jacobee cuts me off.

"You aint hear what he said, Bee. He fuckin said he was behind the shootin."

Brown Brown looks at me, shocked. "He did what?"

"And you believed him?" Jacobee spits back. "Errbody in

here know that today, mo than any otha day, Rouk is gon do anything he can to not deal wit the pain he feelin cuz it's Faa's birthday and he aint alive here to celebrate it."

Shit, I forgot. How could I forget Faa's birthday?

"If yo way of figurin all this out is to hit first and ask questions later, you do you, but stay the fuck away from me *and* Jay." Jacobee walks toward the door, turns round. "Just go home . . . both of you."

"Not till yall talk. That's why we here," Brown Brown says.

"I said what I said, aint got nothin else to say," Jacobee says, pissed.

"Then fuckin listen."

Jacobee walks up on Brown Brown, breathin like he gon knock him on his ass, but Brown Brown is ready for whateva.

"Bee, Rouk *is* behind the shootin. He the reason me and Jay got hurt. I can't just let that ride. You wouldn't if you'd heard him. You woulda knocked his ass out, too."

Jacobee walks off, slams the door so hard behind him it rattles.

The moment he leaves, Brown Brown face changes. "I'm gone for one second and you throwin bows wit Rouk? In the neutral zone?"

"You won't there, you aint hear what he said."

"Nah, I didn't. But you know Rouk mo than anybody. And as much as yall done scrapped ova any and errthang, you know he willin to say anything to make you feel what he feel. He's not the shooter, Lee."

He aint see Rouk's eyes. He won't sayin it to get under my skin. He meant it. I know he did.

"Come on." Brown Brown opens up the door. "We gotta go out there and figure out a way to squash this."

At first, I think he gon walk to the otha side, where Rouk and his crew at, but Brown Brown walk up to the bar instead. He sits right in front of Jacobee station and asks for two orders of barbecue wings and two Shirley Temples wit extra cherries, like aint shit happen. I sit next to him, confused. Jacobee walks to the otha end of the bar, like he plan to ignore him.

"How you know Jacobee real name?" I stare at him, waitin.

"Whatchu lookin at me for? You need to be thinkin bout how you gon walk ova there and make that shit right."

He wastin his breath, and he know it.

"You really wanna know that bad?" He shakes his head, grins. "Aight . . . long story short: Back when I ran track, I knew bout him, Jacob. We competed against each otha a lot, was actually the two fastest sprinters in the city. Taj came to one of my meets, and that's when I realize he was feelin him. At first, I thought it was cuz he saw Jacob in that tight-ass uniform. But then I realized we had already met Jacob years befo."

"Yall already knew Jacobee?"

"Somethin like that. We was all bout twelve or thirteen hangin outside the corner store on Peach Street when Jacob came out and Taj catcalled him. Well, let's just say it aint go well for Taj. Jacob always had a bad temper, but they left an impression on each otha."

"Damn. What bout now, tho? You—"

He had been smiling wide the whole time, but it disappears when he see someone walkin up toward us.

"Sup, Leroy. Sup, Darius."

Hearin Brown Brown real name throws me off for a lil bit, but when I realize who sayin it, I aint surprised—it's Lyric.

Brown Brown speaks, but I just look at him. Ion like him, and it aint just cuz he Rouk *new* best friend.

"Just wanted to say, I'm sorry for what Rouk said earlier. He's just been having a real hard time dealin wit Faa's death and he drank way too much. I heard he said some stuff that made it sound like he blamed Taj, but I just wanted to clarify—"

"You won't even there, so whatchu clarifyin?" I spit. I can't believe he here actin like some peacekeepin ambassador again.

"You right. I wasn't, but it's my fault because he's my friend and I threw tonight's party hoping it would make things better, but it only made things worse. So, I'm sorry."

Brown Brown's eyes say it all: *Shut the fuck up and take the apology.*

"Okay . . . whatchu want me to do wit that? Apologize, too? Well, fuck his apology—no offense—and tell *yo friend* to watch his mouth. Cool?"

Lyric nods and then looks at Brown Brown like he my babysitter.

"Again, I'm sorry—I let the bartender know your food and drinks are on me. Sorry for the trouble. Yall have a good night." He backs away, then heads over near Rouk.

The way Lyric puts his arms round Rouk's shoulder, it's like he tryna be somethin he not—me. But it don't matta. If Rouk did what I think he did, he gon pay, best believe dat.

When I look over at Lyric, I notice the guy wit the long locs lookin at me. He winks and blows me a kiss, but it aint on no cute shit, it's a threat. That's when I know: he a shoota, somebody who walks wit death.

"You know them guys ova there sittin wit Rouk and Lyric? The two wit locs?"

Brown Brown looks . . . pauses, like he gon say one thing but don't. "Naw, but I know you need to let whateva you heard go."

"Whatchu mean let it go? He said—"

"Nigga, really? All *you* had to do was squash it, and you can't even do that." He sucks his teeth. But whateva speech he bout to give is cut short.

Jacobee is standin in front of us, pissed off, wit two plates of wings and our drinks. By the way he lookin at us, he might throw em in our face. He motions for us to follow him to a different room, where it's quiet.

We in the same room he pulled me into, wit the couch.

This time, I realize it aint really a lounge, mo like a lil dressin room that smell like flowers and sweat.

"Aight," Jacobee says, ploppin the plates on the wooden table in front of the couch. He sits down, tells us to sit, too, but his eyes say don't get comfortable. "I gotta ten-minute break, which mean you got five."

I jump in, tryna make every second count. "We movin."

"Okay."

"Not up the street, Bee. Like, a whole different fuckin state."

He tenses up, tries to play it off. "When did you hear that? Why?"

"Today . . . and it's complicated. But I need you to tell me what to do. Like, iono, I aint tryna . . ." The words get caught in my throat. I just shake my head and hope he understand where I'm comin from.

"Imma be right back." Brown Brown gives Jacobee a look I can't see and leaves.

Jacobee comes ova, sits next to me. "Lee, I don't have any answers that would make this feel any better. How bout you tell me what you want? If I can help or find somebody who can, I'll try."

"Can you talk to Taj? Like, he don't wanna go, neitha."

"What if yall movin is the right thing to do? You want me to tell him to stay, even if it could mean yall could get hurt?"

"Nah, but if yall gon be here, why we leavin? Maybe yall could come, too."

He shakes his head.

"Why not? Yall need to be safe, too, dontchu?"

"I aint disagreein. I'm just sayin iono. Yall much closer to the danger than we are. Plus, that decision aint up to me."

I can't say nothin else. Shit just aint fair. I wipe a tear wit the back of my fist befo it can dare to fall.

"Look, you said it aint confirmed yet, right? Maybe yall won't have to go."

I nod. "What bout Jay? You really don't want me to see him no mo?"

"Iono what you want me to say, Lee. That's different."

In my head, I jump up, kick the table ova, and scream in his face, askin how it's different. Then it hits me, and I say it out loud cuz I want him to know that I see how he really feel bout me. "You don't think I'm good enough. That's why you don't give a fuck bout us leavin."

"It's not like that, and you know it," Jacobee says.

"Whateva, man. I'm out." I try to walk out, but he stops me.

"Lee, you know that ain't true. I don't want you to leave. I just don't want to give us false hope, cuz even if I do errthang I can, you might still have to go."

He turns me round, makes me look him in the face. When I look away, he holds my face in his hands. "I can't tell you I want you to be wit Jay cuz that aint my decision. It's his. Regardless of whether you wit him or somebody else, I just want you to know I'm here. Aight?"

He grabs the back of my neck and pulls me in.

"I think I love you, Bee." I say it so soft it's mo like a thought than real words.

He hugs me tighter. "I love you, too—but you come round here startin shit again and Brown Brown aint gon be enough to protect you."

I nod, knowin it's true and that I aint gon give him no reason to prove it.

When we leave the room, I see Brown Brown wit Rouk, Lyric, and the two guys he just said he aint know nothin bout. When he see me, he finishes whateva he sayin and walks back ova to me.

"What's that all bout?" I say, suspicious.

He glares back at me. "Whatchu think? I'm doin what you couldn't, makin sure all that shit you just started is squashed, so it's not anotha thing Taj gotta deal wit while tryna keep you safe. Any otha questions?"

I shake my head, don't say nothin.

"Aight, then, let's go."

I follow behind him, but this aint the end. He aint gotta believe me. I know what I know: The shootin won't bout any bigger players. It was bout revenge—Rouk's revenge—and, even if Brown Brown and Jacobee don't believe me, Imma prove it to Taj. And when I do, we gon do somethin bout it so we can stay in Savannah wit Jacobee and Jay, where we belong.

11

JAY

Will and I are masters of mischief as we sneak out for another early-morning adventure. This time on foot. The way Will jumps in the air in his emerald short-shorts and winks makes me giddy. He guzzles more water, until his lips shine full and pink against the white of his teeth.

We don't say anything for the next block, just walk the old path me and Jacob took when we went to school together, slow while the world moves fast. Every now and then, Will catches me looking at him—then he grins and shoulder-bumps me.

We cross the street. Next to us is a hill of houses with their yards on a higher foundation. A stone wall lifts the trees and bushes above our heads like mistletoe, flowers at the base and in hanging baskets explode pink, purple, and white, tickling our shoulders and the top of our heads. I pluck a few of the lavender-blue blossoms, then a white azalea, and hand them to Will.

"You givin' me flowers?"

I grin but don't answer.

"I like 'em. Never seen them before." He smells them,

braids the stems together, then hands them back to me.

"Petunias . . . they come in all kinds of colors. I heard they attract butterflies and hummingbirds," I say.

"Furreal? I've only seen hummingbirds on TV."

"They're much smaller in person. I've only seen them on accident. They bring good luck. It's hard to see them up close, though."

He nods, looks around for one—a hummingbird miracle.

"You alright?" I scan his face for a hint of whatever might be hurting him. Sometimes, like now, Will stares off into space, on the verge of crying. He never talks about it—what happened in New York for him to have to escape here for the summer.

"Whatchu mean?"

"Just looked like you were a little sad, or like you got a lot on your mind." I hold the flowers out to him like a microphone. "Wanna talk about it?"

For a second, he finally looks like he'll tell me what's on his mind.

"I got a better idea," he says, pointing at a little store on the corner, across the street. When there are no cars, he grabs my hand and we run.

The store is no Edda Nae's, but I manage to buy a red and blue Fanta and a bag of candy. I hand Will a box of Jujubes and laugh when he dumps the little box in his mouth in one go. I shake the bag, show him there is more where that came from.

Will says there is a place he wants to take me—somewhere

he found while wandering the streets, something he says he used to do in New York to learn his way around. I tell him not to do that here, to be careful. He nods, half listening.

He leads me back to a playground not far from the church. It has tall swings that squeak when you sit in them and a merry-go-round that's dark brown, speckled with old red and yellow paint. It's the slide that catches my attention. It's high and has enough room for both of us to lie down and stretch out. Will climbs up, breathes in deep, and smiles. Because of the shade of the trees, it's cooler.

I sit beside him, then he leans back onto my lap, closes his eyes. At first I'm surprised, but every second that passes is like a new normal in the making. I adjust his head, scoot closer so he'll be more comfortable. I try to ignore how the fabric of his shorts fall away, revealing the golden hairs on his legs that disappear at the inside of his thighs. When I look down, he is staring up into my eyes. I'm deep-sea diving in the browns, greens, and specs of blue.

I graze his chin with my fingertips, turn his face up toward me, stroke his temples. As if by muscle memory from a future we might have already lived, I sit him up, shift his legs, and pull him back onto my chest. Our bodies—his back, my chest—push and pull until they simmer with the heat of late summer, until he pulls himself higher, puts his head just under my chin and falls asleep.

I don't know how much time passes—I nod off a little, too—but I stare into the pale blue sky and the cotton spooled into bumpy thread behind small planes flying in cursive. I get nervous when Will stirs, wonder if he means to nestle my hand between his thighs. His eyes flutter open.

"How you sleep? Good?" I ask.

He nods, sees where he's holding my hand. "My bad. I dunno why I—"

"It's okay. I like it . . . hearing you snore a little."

"I don't snore." He smiles like he knows better and leans away.

"Where you going?"

He closes his legs, hides where he is growing. "I've been on you too long, might be too heavy."

"It's okay. I don't mind."

"You callin' me heavy?"

We chuckle apart. I pull him closer so we can chuckle together. Somewhere above our heads birds sing to each other, loud then soft. He looks back at me, leans into my neck again.

"Dayum . . . That's you?" he says, sniffing.

"Me what?"

Was I musty, sweaty? Please. God . . . no.

"That smell."

I imagine myself as Fred Sanford, clutching my chest. You hear that, Elizabeth?

"Is that cologne?"

"Maybe . . ." My heart slows down—maybe next time, Elizabeth.

"Smell good as hell."

I grin, and he leans in closer than he ever has, stares at my lips. With my hands around his waist, him folded into me, I want to kiss him, but when he doesn't, I don't.

"You real cute, you know that?"

I shake my head. "I'm not, but thanks for saying that."

"Whatchu mean?"

"What?"

"You don't think you cute?"

The vase in my chest cracks. I shrink a little to keep myself safe, whole. "We should probably get going."

If only he knew what I have heard, he'd change the subject. Better yet, he'd know not to bring this up at all. But looking like he does, he wouldn't understand.

"Wait . . . What goin' on? Did I do somethin' wrong?"

"No . . . I just figured you—" I stand facing him on the stairs, ready to climb down. Rays of sun cut through a passing cloud and the trees, worship the gold that's him, like a god among mortals. It only makes it hurt even more.

"Jay, wait. Is this cuz I complimented you?"

I can't look at him. "Can we change the subject?"

"What? I don't get it. Don't you know how people look at you?"

"Not like how they look at you." Something in me flares up, bares its teeth. I rein it in, try to stop it.

"What's that got to do with anything?"

I climb down, while he slides down the other side.

"Wait . . ." He stands in front of the chain-link fence at the entrance. "Just talk to me. Help me understand."

I kick twigs at the blue wooden fence behind us, rub my chest, try to soothe what's being stirred up. "People only want boys who look like you or Jacob or Princeton." I look away, don't speak for a while. "I'm not saying I'm ugly, just that I'm not . . . pretty . . . like you."

He hangs his head, looks like he's holding something back, too.

"Come on . . . we should go."

Will won't move; he just looks at me. Then he steps to the side and follows in silence, close enough so I know he's there but far enough so I can breathe.

With every step, there's another memory I've spent so long trying to forget, but their words are hounds of hurt, chasing me until my feet reach an imaginary cliff.

In eighth grade, when one of the football players called every cheerleader over to the cafeteria table where I wouldn't let him copy my homework and asked them if they'd ever date me. Their responses: "Boy, puh-lease." "I think not." "Not in a million years." "I'll pass." The head cheerleader never stopped laughing.

I don't know why but something about me always seems to bring the worst out of others, makes them want to hurt me, tear me apart until there's nothing left. Maybe it's me. Maybe I deserve it. Maybe that's why Leroy eventually let me go, too. Maybe he never really—

"Fuck 'em," Will says, pulling me still from behind, stopping me in my tracks.

"Huh?" I say, trying to turn around, but he won't let me.

He leans closer, the breath of his words tickling my neck. "If they call you anything but beautiful, it's 'cuz they need you to shine less to feel better 'bout themselves." He turns me around, pierces me with his gaze. "But don't let 'em dim you. Shine brighter, even if it hurts."

A tear falls without my permission, he wipes it away. Then, like he did ten years ago, he kisses me on my cheek, resurrecting the hummingbird of hope in my chest. He doesn't say anything else. He just stands there, arms draped around my shoulders, becoming my place of rest.

As we walk back in the direction we came, I know Will won't ever understand what it's like to be me. But for the first time, I don't want him to. I want to see what he sees when he looks at me.

Will brushes me back into the present. "I think my mum is why I like you so much."

"Okay . . ." I don't know what to say, so I don't. Just feel the floodwater of questions rise.

"She always says it wasn't supposed to happen, her meetin' my dad."

"Why not?"

"She was a mahogany beauty wit a boyfriend, and he was the secret redbone son of a rich white family who only visited Savannah in the summers."

Did his dad's family not accept his mother? Is that why he never talks about him?

"If it wasn't meant to be, how did they finally meet?"

Will smirks. "I think he went to a club she was singin' at. Mum says he sat in the front row, cried when she sang 'I Put a Spell on You.'"

"Nina." I grin, putting the pieces together.

"Yup. She thought he sat in the front 'cuz he was a fan, till he got up and performed after she did, singing, 'A Song for You' by Donny Hathaway. Mum said that night she kissed him because his pain was the same as hers—seen and unseen—which was why it was love at first song for them, not sight."

I nod, trying to take it all in.

"I know it's a lot . . . I ain't even mean to say all that, just wanted you to know. Clearly, I wasn't there when all that happened, but sometimes when I look at you, I can see what it musta felt like, seein' somebody like my mum."

"I can't sing, though. . . . If that's a requirement, I might not be what you're looking for."

"That's cool. You're more than enough, definitely what I'm lookin' for."

All I can offer is a nod and a grin growing wider by the second. I like hearing Will say I am what he wants. Even if he can't piece together the broken pieces of what Leroy left behind, Will shows me he's willing to try, if only I'll let him.

"Can I hug you?" I'm surprised by the words, and that

they come from my mouth.

He chuckles, stretches out his arms, all wide and dramatic. I reach for his waist, pull him in to me in a way I haven't before. I lean in, kiss him on the neck, right where his tattoo reads, "Kiss me." I try to let go, but he won't let me.

"Hold up . . . ," he says.

"What? Something wrong?"

He shakes his head. "Nope. Just gimme a second . . . a minute."

It takes a second, but soon I realize why: he's hard. I look down and then back up at him, suddenly feeling victorious.

"Your face is red again." Right before I'm about to pull away, he kisses me. Not like he did all those years ago—no peck on the cheek—on the lips.

He pulls back, reads my face. His lips are a question. I lean back in with my answer.

When we pull apart, it's the opposite of what I've seen in movies—there's no staring in each other's eyes; no one whispers, "Let's get it on," and Maxwell's "This Woman's Work" isn't chiming in the background (although it's on my list to do). It's simple. We giggle because it's funny. Because in each other's arms, nothing matters more than this, even if we haven't figured out what *this* is or is becoming.

12

Leroy

Taj is bangin on the bathroom door, pissed. I woke up late again. Well, not late accordin to my standards but late as hell based on his. It's only 9:30 a.m., and Jacobee said he won't gon be ova here till 11:30 a.m. I'm tryna make up for lost time, aimin wit no hands while takin a piss and brushin my teeth.

After I spoke to Jacobee that night at the O Lounge, he called Taj the next day. Iono what he said, but I'm assumin he aint bring up what happened between me and Rouk. Ion think Brown Brown did, eitha. It seem like both of em wanna keep me from gettin in trouble wit Taj, so he has one less thing—one less person—to worry bout. I hope they keep it that way.

I need stronger evidence befo I can talk to Taj bout Rouk, otherwise he just gon ignore me like Brown Brown and Jacobee did. But on the flip side, Jacobee did agree to come ova for breakfast, so that must mean somethin. Maybe things are gettin betta between them? I hope so, cuz like Ma, Taj holds grudges, and his petty game strong.

"Lee, what I say?" Taj is on tha side of the door tryna hide how mad he is, like it's gon make me pee any faster.

"Gimme five minutes and I'll be down."

"You sure you got errthang when yall went to the store last night? I'm bout ta check."

I finish. Not a drop on the toilet seat—yeah boy.

"Yeah, I think so," I say.

"Which one is it? Yeah or I think so?"

I stare at the door, mouth, *Really, nigga?* I spit out the foam, rinse my mouth, then gargle.

"Lee," he snaps, like he could see the look I gave him through the door.

"Yeah, you can check. Night bought errthang on the list."

"What bout the oil . . . you get that canola or olive oil? Jacobee don't like that vegetable shit, it aint healthy."

"You told us that already—we got both."

I rinse my face one last time, then straighten up the floor mat and shower curtain. I aint tryna give Taj no mo reasons to be on my back bout nothin else.

I open up the door, and Taj already fully dressed, fitted n all. Only thing left for him to put on is his front grills and throw on his Chicago White Sox Jordan baseball jersey.

I read errthang and start doin all the steps scribbled down on Rissa's sheets of paper while he goes on and on bout not havin enough time to get errthang ready. Iono what we was thinkin. Can't neitha one of us cook nothin but Oodles of

Noodles and PB&Js. Taj just had to flauge, sayin he'll cook Jacobee eggs and grits, bacon, and even French toast.

When the smoke alarm beepin, Taj gets in my face screamin. There's all this smoke and ioeno if I'm gon accidentally burn the house down, so I do what anybody in my situation would do. I run out the front door befo Taj get to scrappin ova burnt bacon and charcoal eggs.

"Chill, man," I shout, tryna keep enough distance between me and Taj as he start chasin behind me.

"Man? Who the fuck you callin—" Taj sprints, almost catches me. He glarin at me, chest heavin, like I'm the one who did somethin wrong. He the one who put all the cookin on me and expected me to get it right.

I'm standin in front of the curb, damn near hopscotchin across the asphalt burnin the bottom of my feet. "I'm just sayin. I did do like you said, I put the stove on medium."

"Then why was it on medium-high? All you had to do is watch it."

"I was watchin it."

"Stop fuckin lyin," Taj says. He fakes a lunge. I jump backward.

All of a sudden, I spot Jacobee gettin outta his car while I'm runnin for my life.

"That's a lot of smoke," he says.

Taj looks ova at Jacobee. He nods, walks toward him but stops short. Neitha of em seem to know what to say or how to say it. Errthang must feel different for them, too.

"Imma go check," Taj says, turnin and runnin into the house.

"Yo, Bee," I say from the street, eyein the doorway of the house to see if it's safe for me to come closer. I jog ova, grinnin. I pull him in for a hug.

"That's for us?" I point to the grocery bags in the back seat. He opens the door, and I snake my arm through as many of the plastic bag handles as I can, beamin wit pride.

"You know, I can help," he says, grabbin the last two.

"I got it, I got it. Gimme those, too."

Taj comes back out, and I hide behind Jacobee. When it looks like Taj bout to make a move, Jacobee slides the two bags I can't carry onto Taj's arm, but one of the bands gets stuck and his hand is trapped in Taj's while he try to untangle it. Taj's eyes say it all: he couldn't be happier.

Taj play-punches me as I try to squeeze by wit them distracted. "I aint forgot."

"Fuhgive me already," I sing, waddlin into the kitchen weighed down by the bags.

While Jacobee walks in and looks round, I wonder if he can smell all the history and memories. Rissa always says real homes smell like tough love: hugs and ass-whoopins melted in sugar and vanilla.

While me and Taj go through the house slappin the remainin smoke outside wit towels, Jacobee makes dishwater and lathers up a rag, then wipes down the counters, tables, and stove.

He just visitin, but I bet Jacobee settlin in to the kitchen real nice wit all the handwritten recipes; alphabet magnets on the fridge; the mason jars linin the wall on the right side of the sink wit labels readin "grits," "sugah," and "rice."

I jog in from the livin room, all laughs and jokes and sweat after a towel fight wit Taj. That's when Jacobee sees them: my bullet wounds. One on my right shoulder, and when I turn sideways, you can see the exit wound on my back.

"I'm sorry," Jacobee says, tryin not to look.

"Nah, it's good. Lemme go put on a—"

"Lee, no. It's cool. Relax."

We look round in the silence until we find our way back to each otha.

"Does it still hurt?" he asks.

"Sometimes. Might have some tinglin or a sharp pain every now and then, but nothin I can't handle."

He holds somethin back, swallows the words. I think he was gonna tell me bout Jay, but I aint for sure. I just nod, hopin at some point he tells me whateva it is so I can stop wonderin.

"We was hopin to make some breakfast, but it aint work out too good," I say, chucklin.

"I see. Shit led to yall throwin hands—or should I say, spatulas?"

We laugh. It's the corniest shit eva, but somehow it make things feel normal, or like we could get there one day if we all tried.

"Want me to help you cook?" I ask.

"You sure you want to?"

"Hell yeah, if it means I get to eat as we go instead of starvin out there."

Our smiles reflect a need filled between us—for me, a softer touch than Taj's tough love, for him, ioeno, maybe somebody else to protect, to feel connected to.

While I fry sausages, chop onions and green bell peppers, he rinses and sifts the chaff from the grits. As the grits cook, he makes the batter for the catfish, spicy to match the sweet. Last, we make the biscuits from scratch. We whisk the baking soda, sugar, baking powder, and flour. I grate the frozen butter, and as I stir, he pours in the cold buttermilk. Together, we fold the dough and add flour when it gets too sticky.

As we sit at the mini table while the biscuits bake, there's a long silence, but I use it to say what I been wantin to say to him for the longest. "I'm sorry. None of this woulda happened if me and Jay won't there that day. He woulda neva got hurt if—"

"You didn't do anything wrong, Lee. What happened, happened."

I aint convinced.

"Did you shoot yourself? Did you shoot Jay?"

"Nah, but I shoulda been able to . . . ," I say but my words trail off and into the beep of the oven timer. I put on the sunflower oven mitts and bring the biscuits to the table, admirin the golden-brown color and the cinnamon.

"Good job," he says. "You'll be able to burn befo you know it."

I brush the biscuits wit anotha layer of melted butter, like he showed me.

"The flashbacks are the worst part. The spasms seem to be hard, too," Jacobee says suddenly.

I agree, then realize what he means—he talkin bout Jay. I lean forward, going back and forth between worry and wonder.

"Most of the time he can sleep well, if I'm in the bed wit him, but he still screams from time to time, fights in his sleep. Sometimes I think he hits me on purpose cuz he knows he'll get away wit it."

"That's what I would do," I say, grinnin.

"Me, too," he adds. "He doin okay, tho. Hangin in there. So, you might wanna step yo cookin game up, cuz he's become a decent burner, too."

"Fuck that, my biscuits go hard. And you can tell him I said that."

"Where's Taj?" he asks.

I'm blowed when I realize he been upstairs the whole time. What's the point in tryna make sure errthang is perfect if the only thing he planned to do was run upstairs? I hope he'll come down soon, cuz he aint the only one who need this—I do, too.

"He in his room, must not be feelin good. I think he might want you to go check on him."

"Naw, I think he might want you to check on him," he jokes.

"He tired of seein my face. G'on head. I'll watch my biscuits and fix our plates. Just don't take too long or Imma smash this withoutchu."

As Jacobee heads up, I stand at the foot of the stairs, wonderin if Jacobee know that, when it come to Taj, you gotta listen for what he not sayin, watch what he don't do as much as what he do.

Jacobee stands at the top of the stairs in front of Taj room. "Hey," he says. "You should come down and—"

"I'm good," Taj say, cuttin him off.

"Okay, well, we'll be downstairs," Jacobee says, givin up too quick.

"That's all you gotta say to me?"

"What else you want me to say, Taj?"

"Why dontchu act like you miss me? I been callin and callin, losin my mind tryna keep it all togetha wit all this shit goin on and you—"

"Taj, I told you why . . . we needed space."

"No, *you* did. You aint neva ask me what I needed."

"You right . . . I'm sorry. I'm here now, tho. . . ."

Taj musta got up, cuz Jacobee looked like he was bout to turn round and decided to wait.

Taj is stubborn as fuck, but I'm happy he won't let that get in the way of what they got, what they tryna keep that they almost lost. Maybe this is when they both realize how they really feel—

Taj slams the door so hard I can hear the windows shake.

Maybe not.

At the foot of the stairs, I wait for Jacobee, half surprised and half sad. Iono what to say.

I guide him by the shoulders to the livin room, where I fixed three plates and filled three cups wit sweet tea. I move the third plate to the side, and after a few bites, Jacobee fork-blockin, protectin his sausages and grits from my hungry ass. It's so good I keep wantin mo and mo, but it aint just that. I want him to know, even if Taj don't act like he need him, I do. It aint just bout him, it's bout me, too.

"You don't really want them grits, bruh," I say.

He blocks my third attempt. "I do, tho. I think it's cuz they taste better on my plate than they do on yours." He mocks me, eats em real slow, licks his lips.

"Come on, quit bein stingy. You aint make enough, so you gotta gimme some of yours."

He bites into anotha sausage and hunches ova his plate. "Nah, I'm good."

"Not if you aint sharin." I smile. I can still see that look in his eye, the sadness, cuz I got the same thing, I think we all do. I'm just happy he aint leave.

I gotta prove to Taj that Rouk did this; that it aint no gang war or whoeva killed Faa comin after us like he prolly thinkin. It's the only way all of us can get the chance to figure all of this out—no matta how long it might take.

Together, we wrap Taj's plate, along wit my leftovers, and wash the dishes. When we finish, we sneak an extra biscuit from the stove befo we walk to the door, slowly, feelin our way for the end that's a not-goodbye and not-see-you-later but feels good, possible. I just hope he don't leave and neva come back.

"What's the name of that stuff you made again last time wit the noodles and chicken?" I ask, knowin already but needin somethin to say or do befo he put his hand on the doorknob.

"Yock."

"That shit was fiyah."

"You liked it?" he asks, grinnin.

"Yeah. It aint look like it would be good, but it was."

"If I teach you how to make it, you gotta guard it wit yo life, cuz it's a family secret."

"Aight. I gotchu. Just lemme know . . . when you wanna teach me."

"I will." He smiles, and it's like the light in his eyes chase away the dark I'm so afraid of.

Our laugh becomes a tight hug. He opens the door, and there is Night and PYT, wit Brown Brown laggin behind as they walk up from the driveway, starin at Jacobee's car.

When Jacobee speaks, PYT nods, Night does, too, no problem. But Brown Brown don't do shit, just smirks, stands there. I wanna snap on Brown Brown, but if I just go off, he might tell Taj what happened, then I'll neva get Taj to believe the truth bout Rouk.

I wanna say somethin to stop whateva he tryna start, as he stares at Jacobee.

Taj stands in the door. "Yo, you leavin without givin me some love? It's like that, Jacobee?"

Jacobee looks at him, confused.

"I told him you was comin, but he said he had to get somethin outta his car," I lie.

"Lemme walk witchu, then," Taj says, givin Brown Brown a nod as he puts his arm round Jacobee waist and walks beside him.

Brown Brown shakes his head and grins befo walkin inside. Ion like it, the way he can switch faces, go from actin all dirty to clean, and nobody know the difference.

I walk back into the house, tryna shake off whateva it is I'm feelin and peek out the window at Taj and Jacobee in the car, wonderin if they makin up and if Taj finally gave Jacobee the necklace he bought for him a coupla weeks ago.

When Taj hop out the whip and jogs to the door, he smilin. He burst through the front door loud and happy. "I know nenh nigga in heah betta not have touched my plate or it's gon be me n you."

As he runs to the kitchen, I watch Jacobee sittin in the car as he holds up the necklace in his hand. When he smiles, I know there's hope, a chance they gon work it out. I want the same for me and Jay, too, but Rouk is out there. He dangerous, and I gotta be the one to stop him. And to do that, I need to talk to somebody bout Rouk—maybe the only person who will believe me: Trish.

If I was a bagger at D&D's Grocery, I'd be the best one they eva had. I'm packin em faster than Trish can slide em and she makin sure it aint easy since she done won competitions at the National Grocers Association as a top bagger—just something she do in her spare time when she bored. We gettin so into it that a lil kid starts throwin errthang he can get his hands on on the belt just to see how fast we can do it. His ma bout to have a heart attack, clutchin her food stamp card.

"It's alright, ma'am, whateva he throws on the belt is free of charge." Trish got pull like that, since Darryl and Derek—the names behind the D&D—are her uncs. When I trip up for a split second, the game is ova and I lose, makin me the second-best bagger D&D's Grocery has eva seen. It's all good, tho, I gotta a new fan name Tywon who tipped me twenty-five cents of the two dollars he got from the tooth fairy; he was that impressed. Can't nobody tell me nothin.

"I keep tellin you, that weight distribution will get you errtime. Gotta have a plan *befo* you pick up the product." Trish plays wit her ear piercin, a small chain connectin the earrings from the top of her ear to the bottom.

"Yeah, yeah, yeah," I say, smilin and stallin.

Trish faces me, eyes waitin for somethin I owe her.

"I'm sorry, Trish," I say, meanin it.

"And . . . ," she says, smirkin.

I take a big breath, knowin she wanna hear me go through a list of all the wrong I did, so she can tell me how I need to make it right. "I'm sorry for goin so long and not lettin you know I was okay—"

"Damn right . . ." She purses her lips. "And what else?"

"And for usin you like that . . . to make somebody jealous. Will you forgive me?"

She looks up to the right like she deliberatin wit the angels or devils on her shoulder. "If, and only if, you model in my senior fashion shoot."

"Come on, Trish—"

"And you wear somethin I design at the next skatedown."

I look at her, try to make the saddest but cutest face I can to convince her to not be so hard on me. It aint that I don't want to, it's just that errthang Trish want me to wear usually showin way mo skin than I want people to see, unless . . .

well, you know, they gotta reason they seein it.

"Unh-unh, you can't get outta this Mr. I-do-Trish-so-wrong-twice-and-too-scared-to-make-it-right. It's eitha this or I guess I can't answer what you obviously came to ask me . . ."

"Aight, aight, aight. I'll do it. But I aint walkin round in no thong."

"Boy, puhleese, aint nobody tryna see that. I got mo taste than that . . . I'm thinkin less thong mo corset and briefs but right now, I'm designin evening gowns—"

"Trishhhhhh . . ."

She gives me that look. "I know it's hard to skate in a gown . . . I wouldn't do you like that. But lemme hear ya words, you gotta officially sign the verbal contract."

"Aight . . . anything for you . . . I'll rock it all, just long as you fuhgive me."

She giggles the way she always do, eva since we was little—in a way that makes her whole face shine and her dimples come out. It's contagious. Like every otha time, I giggle, too.

"Trish . . . go on break," Darryl says, wavin down at us. Taj and Night still in the office wit him upstairs prolly still talkin business. I look through the store window, still see PYT and Brown Brown chillin out front in the car keepin watch.

D&D's Grocery is one of the only spots we can grocery shop at on our side of town wit errthang goin on. We also goin here cuz Darryl and Derek were good friends of our pops and they look out for us.

Trish takes me ova to the mini diner where Derek is makin some of his specialties and pushes a chair back to take a seat. "So, what's on ya mind?"

Iono what to tell or not tell her, so I just tell her bout what happened at the O Lounge: what he said he did.

"Lee, Rouk is a lot, I agree, but this? Are you sure?"

"Trish, you know me. I wouldn't just say this if I aint believe it was true. But I saw the look in his eyes, and if I believed somebody killed Taj . . . I woulda did the same—ion put that kinda hurt past nobody."

Trish get to shakin her leg, chewin the inside of her cheek. She know somethin.

"What?"

"Nothin, just thinkin."

I reach across the table, put my hand on her shoulders so I can look her right in the eyes. "Tell me. Whateva it is."

"If he did this, Lee, it's really fucked up. Like, on so many levels."

"That's why I need yo help . . . ," I plead.

"Okay, so . . . Rouk called recently."

Tha fuck? This whole time he been ignorin me.

"I know whatchu thinkin, it won't like that. I was surprised, too. He aint exactly been returnin my calls, eitha."

I wanna flip the table, but I gotta listen now; I can feel later. "What he say?"

"Well, he invited me to his birthday party, but somethin

in his voice sounded off, I figured it was cuz of Faa's birthday just passed the week befo. I thought he was gonna ask how to make things right between yall, so I went. . . . But when I get there, Rouk drunk, and all up on me from the moment I walk in the door, talkin bout how much he miss me. I let him take me to get something to drink and, while I'm tryna get him to sit down, I see a tattoo peekin from under his sleeve—and you know he always been afraid of needles. I push up his sleeve so I can see it. But he gets mad and walks away.

"Then, later, me and this girl name Dana dancin on the little stage they had up there, and these two guys come behind us and, since they were cute, you know . . . we showed out a little and that's when I saw the guy she was dancin wit had the same tattoo on his chest."

"Did they have locs?"

"Yeah, they both did. The one that liked me had the longest locs but when Rouk saw me dancin wit him, he came and pulled me away, said I had to go. I asked him what was wrong, why he was actin weird. But he wouldn't say. When we got closer to the door, he told me not to tell nobody bout the tat and to go straight home."

Now both of us are quiet, chewin on the inside of our cheeks. "You remember what the tat looked like?"

"Yeah, gimme a sec. I can sketch it real quick. . . . I been thinkin bout it the last couple of days cuz it reminded me of

Donna Karan, the designer, well, her initials."

Trish draws a "DK" wit the jagged crown, just like the one we saw carved into the door at the motel. But hers mo detailed. "If you look at it real close, it looks like one of them old seals or sigils. The kind that eitha protect you from magic or give you powers."

"Yeah, you right."

I look at it closer, as she fills in even mo details. It don't just look like a regular tat, looks like somethin older. Suddenly, the thought of the masks comes to me. I aint neva seen none like em and can't really remember what they look like. Just the colors: two were red and the one at the back door was black-and-white.

"You aint show nobody else this, right?" I ask.

"No . . . why? You think this is proof of what you told me bout Rouk?"

"Iono . . . maybe."

If Rouk and the guys wit locs had the same tat, then it's prolly the same guys I saw at the O Lounge. And if that's true, it definitely means somethin.

"Just to be safe, keep this close to yo chest. Iono what it means, but listen to Rouk—don't let nobody know you seen it."

I stare at the sketch puttin togetha the pieces. Iono nothin bout no magic but I do know when two or mo are tatted, a gang—or some pain—gon follow. The problem is—as far as I can tell—don't nobody use that tat in Savannah, which mean they must be from the outside.

The count don't exactly add up all the way, eitha: Yeah, the number of people wit tats is the same number of masks durin the shootin. But there were four at the O Lounge: Rouk, the two guys wit locs, *and* Lyric. . . . Only Lyric can't be involved—he aint the type. And no matta how hard he pretend to be, if I'm being real, Rouk aint neva been a shoota, tho, which means the two guys wit the locs probably the ones who were in front and at the back door, the one wearin the black-and-white mask who had a chance to shoot but didn't would have to be—

"Aye, Lee," Taj yells from the front of the store. "Come on. It's time to roll."

"Aight, remember what I said, okay?" I say to Trish, as I hug her ova the table.

"I will—lips sealed. Call me if you find out anything else. And I'll let you know if I hear from Rouk again."

I nod, hopin like hell she don't. And even if she do hear from Rouk, I hope by then I will already have figured errthang, befo it's too late. But as I walk toward Taj and think bout how it's all connected, I can't shake the feelin that I'm missin somethin. I'd assumed the shootin was just Rouk actin out, but if he's tied up wit an outside gang, they aint bout to help him outta the goodness of their hearts—they gotta have their own agenda.

It's gotta be bigger—the thing I was too quick to dismiss. What if the gang war *is* behind it like Taj been thinkin only not the way he been suspectin? What if Rouk recruited an outside gang wit a lot of muscle, a crew big and bad enough to not just move in but take ova? And in order to do that, they gotta get rid of the only person who could stop them, the one powerful enough to unite the gangs—Taj. Cuz if they can take down him, they can take down the BDs. I hope like hell I'm wrong, but the fear in my gut says I'm right.

On the way home, the AC in Night's car takin too damn long to start workin, again, which means no matta how high he kicks up the fan, the hot keeps gettin hotter, punkin out the lil bit of cold his car can manage. I stare out the window, silent, glad we at least dropped PYT and Brown Brown off at they crib, so I got some elbow room in the back of this hot-ass car.

Like I told Trish to, Imma keep what I learned bout the symbol and the tats to myself. I'll tell Taj when I know what it all means, when I know he'll believe me. I may not be a YG, but I can help keep errbody I care bout safe, in my own way.

Almost outta K-Town, Night takes Oak Boulie since it's the fastest way to K-Heights. He slows down, then honks his horn when two cars are shootin the shit like they on somebody patio instead of in the middle of the road. Up the corner, across the street and beneath one of the biggest

Southern magnolia trees I eva seen, a redbone guy on a bike goin too fast, then flips ova and not only busts his ass but scratches up somebody car in the process: a black BMW.

Three guys get outta the car: Rouk and the two guys wit locs. I feel nervous, like I can't sit still. Up until now, even if Rouk was the one who lost his mind and shot up our house, hyped on gettin revenge, it would be dealt wit, but at the end of the day, it's still Rouk. But it aint that simple, it aint *just* Rouk. If I'm right, he aint just make a mistake, he rollin wit shootas—people who kill and ask questions later—and iono what to do wit that.

Taj strokes his chin, squintin. "Hmm . . . Night, tell me somethin: Rouk, a nigga who aint neva had no crew and barely any street cred, sittin in a brand-new black BMW?"

"That's what I'm tryna find out. Thinkin what I'm thinkin?" Night says, starin like a hawk.

"Yeah, Rouk done got himself caught up wit the wrong people, might be in trouble." Taj shakes his head. "Fuck, aight, let's check it out. He might need our help—and I promised Faa to always look out for em, no matta how much he claim to hate me."

There's only one thing that black BMW round here means: money, power, and resources. And if what I'm thinkin is true, the proof is not just the matchin tattoos and the BMW, but the two guys wit locs who might be mo than what we think they are. On the surface, they look like they the same age as

Taj or Night, but they eyes hint at the truth of whereva they come from—a crew wit enough bite to take on the BDs and not even flinch.

I look closer and notice the redbone they talkin to is the guy Jay was wit. I aint gon hold it, a part of me wants to tell Night to drive off and let his ass get scooped up. But I know betta.

"Light-Bright ova there is real close to Jay and Jacobee," I tell Taj.

Night parks a house or two down so we close enough to hear and see without drawin too much attention.

Rouk rubs the dent and scratch on the side of the car like it's a tender wound.

"My bad, I didn't meant to—"

One of the guys wit locs kicks Light-Bright's bike down, and he almost falls wit it.

"Aye, man."

"What?"

"You don't have to—"

His wack-ass kicks it again, watches Light-Bright's face to see what he gon do. Light-Bright aint stupid, he glares back at the guy, but he know whateva he say to the two wit locs gon be the difference between him limpin away wit hurt feelings or bein carried away in a body bag.

"Whatchu gon do bout this?" Rouk says, starin at the scratch.

"I dunno. . . ."

"You betta think of somethin."

The guys grin at each otha, say somethin wit their eyes. Light-Bright looks round for somebody, anybody, but errbody on Oak Boulie know to stay hidden cuz there's consequences to bein found.

"Get in the car," the guy who kicked the bike says, movin toward him, but Light-Bright don't move.

"Come on." The same guy opens the door. "Leave that."

Rouk looks nervous, like what might happen next, he wouldn't wish on his worst enemy. As Light-Bright watches them, he see who got the real power to stop them—it aint Rouk.

"Nah, I'm good. Whateva you gotta say or do, just do it right here," Light-Bright says.

"What?" the guy says, walkin toward Light-Bright.

I feel a chill against my neck. "Taj, somethin aint right. We gotta stop em."

Night and Taj nod, already thinkin what I'm thinkin.

The two guys step forward to grab Light-Bright. Night backs up, peels off, kicks up the music so we ride up hella loud.

Errbody stops, waits for the tinted windows to roll down.

"Whaddup tho?" Taj sings. He seems lighthearted, but errbody know Taj aint nobody to fuck wit.

"Whatchu doin here?" Rouk says. I know that look, like he relieved that Taj steppin in. Whateva was bout to go down if

Light-Bright got in that car, Rouk won't down.

"Ya know, lookin out—makin sho you aint round no bad influences." Taj turns the music off, pulls out a stick of gum, slowly unwraps it, and folds it into his mouth. The way he chews hushes even the trees and leaves silent. Taj looks ova at Light-Bright.

"Whaddup, Light-Bright?"

He nods.

"What's yo name?" Taj asks.

"Will."

"Cool. Imma call you Light-Bright. You from round here?" Taj's eyes are an invitation.

Light-Bright shakes his head.

"You know who street this is?"

Light-Bright shakes his head again.

"Use ya words."

"No, I don't. Don't even know the street name, if I'm bein honest."

"Don't use too many."

Taj looks ova at Rouk, stares at him like he tellin him something only he can understand. Rouk breaks eye contact, becomes small.

"Yo, Light-Bright. Get in, we'll get you where you need to be."

"But he fucked up my whip—" Rouk says, forgettin who he talkin to.

"And all yo whinin fuckin up my vibe. But you don't see

me tryna get you to go for no ride or gettin niggas to do shit you can't do yoself."

"They aint mean it like that, Taj." Rouk's lie is obvious and desperate, a shield bein used like a sword. Errbody know he just lyin cuz he mad at Taj.

"No?" The way Taj chews errbody know he aint convinced. "Whatchu think?" Taj points at the guy wit the long locs, the one who aint said nothin the whole time they been out there but who can send threats just wit his eyes.

He stares at Taj but don't say a word.

"Who you?" Night asks, a second reason for the guy to answer.

"Nobody," the guy says.

Taj chuckles. "Mr. Nobody . . . you real funny-lookin, you know that? You remind me of this guy I ran into at a club not long ago who was tryna run up on my boy, Jacobee. He couldn't take no for an answer then, neitha, so I had to help him understand."

Were these the two guys who jumped him the night he was wit Jacobee? Did he know them the whole time?

"That's a real funny story. Can't say I know anything bout that, tho. But I hope yo head is okay. I heard somebody got taught a lesson bout walkin round like they own errthang . . . when they don't. Won't sure if it was you or not."

Taj nods, sayin errthang by sayin nothin at all. Night clenches the steering wheel. If this was any otha moment, he woulda hopped out the car and handled both of em right here and right now. But this aint the time, and he can tell, too: they aint what they seem to be.

"Aint no thang, baby. Aint nothin on this body made of glass." Taj's eyes are a threat as he blows Mr. Nobody a kiss.

"Aint what I heard." Mr. Nobody smiles like he got razors for teeth.

"Rouk," Taj says, blowin a bubble, then makin it pop. "How bout you let him pay for yo car, since he got all that mouth."

"Nah, it's cool. I'll figure it out," Rouk says, pretendin to be harder than he really is.

"Don't wurr bout it. I gotcha, Rouk," Mr. Nobody says, only lookin at Taj.

"We aint got all day, Light-Bright," Taj says.

Light-Bright leaves the bike on the sidewalk. I move to the otha side so he can get in.

Taj turns up the music, pulls away real slow, then speeds off. Behind us, Mr. Nobody still starin. He blows a kiss of his own.

I turn round and see Taj watchin him through the rear-view mirror. Message received.

When Night turns the corner, he lowers the volume. "You went OG, aint it?"

Taj smiles, shakin his head. He turns round in his seat. "Whatchu doin round here, Light-Bright?"

"I was lookin for Edda Nae's. You know, the candy lady?"

"How you get all the way ova here, tho? She on the otha side of Reeds Gate."

He shrugs.

"Nobody told you to go the otha way?"

"No, I was just goin by memory until I wasn't."

"This here Oak Boulie. Can't be round here less you know somebody."

"I didn't know."

"And you damn sho can't be round here dressed like that . . . ," Night says from up front.

"What's wrong wit what I'm wearin?"

"That's the problem—you *aint* wearin nothin."

"What I'm supposed to wear? It's hot."

"Clothes, nigga . . . Clothes, or errbody gon be tryna pull you in they car. You one of them pritty niggas. You gotta be careful, or they'll snatch yo ass up."

The car is swallowed by silence.

"Whatchu need from Edda Nae's?" Taj asks.

"Just wanted to ask her some questions bout something she said the last time I was there."

"Aight. Lee, give Light-Bright yo numba."

I hold my hand out for his phone, add myself to his contacts.

"Call Lee the next time you need to go, and we'll scoop you. They gon be mad and plottin now that they seen you wit us, so don't be runnin nowhere near Oak Boulie less you wit us. Hear me?" Taj asks through the rearview.

Light-Bright nods.

"Use ya words."

"Yeah."

"And if you eva see them anywhere near you . . . give Lee a call. . . . I mean it. ASAP."

He nods, kinda in a daze.

"I'm furreal . . . they dangerous," Taj says wit mo emphasis.

"Okay. You can drop me off right here," Light-Bright says.

When Light-Bright gets out, he locks eyes wit me and nods. I think we both know—whether we want to or not—we gon see each otha again.

13

JAY

Princeton made me promise to make good on my bet of going over to his house today, but I'm in front of the school and he still hasn't arrived yet. I don't know why he wouldn't just tell me the address. So, I balance on the curb, imagining I'm on a tightrope a hundred feet in the air. I hear the audience below gasp in awe and anticipation as I do the unthinkable, the impossible, above their heads without a safety net, teetering on the brink of something, one foot in front of the other. Right. Left. Right. (Whew.) Left. Right. (Almost, almost.) Left. (Stepping over the anthill.) Right. Then a daring 180-degree turn in five, four, three, two, one.

"Whatchu doin'?"

Princeton is so close, I almost lose my balance. "Waitin'."

"For me?"

"Nope . . . somebody else who promised me food if I met them on the hottest day of summer, before you did." I smirk.

He thinks it over, strokes the few bristles defying his baby face. "He look betta than me?"

"What makes you think it's a 'he'?"

He frowns for a reason I don't quite understand.

"I'm playing—where are we going? Do I finally get to go to your place?" I continue the balancing act for my invisible, restless fans.

He smiles. "Get ready for me to blow yo mind. . . . It's Princeton time."

"What?" I laugh.

"Definitely sounded better in my head. . . . Come on, this way."

After ten minutes of walking the exact opposite direction I take home from school, we cross the line into Avalon Park, home of the mini mansions that have more bedrooms than people to live in them. Each looks different from the next, donning columns and colorful doors with flame-lit lanterns, and manicured trumpet, hummingbird, or creeping fig vines over brick faces. Live oak trees and Spanish moss canopies promenade above our heads like nature's chandeliers.

Right before we cross the street and turn right, I see a face I didn't expect to: Lyric. I didn't know he lived around here. But it makes sense. He does go to Providence Prep. Only he doesn't look like he's walking home, more like he's heading somewhere. He almost looks like a different person when he doesn't smile—like someone with too many secrets.

Princeton walks across the lawn of a white three-story house and acts like he's about to knock on the door.

"Whoa, whoa—where you goin'?" I say.

"To my house," Princeton says.

"Come on, Princeton. No more playin', okay? We've been

walking for almost fifteen minutes. Where are you really taking me?"

"To my house . . . for lunch . . . like I told you already." He pulls out a key and opens it. "How 'bout you come in after you pick your jaw up off the sidewalk."

"I wasn't—I didn't think—I wasn't saying you couldn't live here . . . just that . . ." I let my words trail off and just do as he says.

The house smells of patchouli, amid rich layers of browns, greens, and orange earth tones that make the space feel warm and free. You would think we were on MTV's *Cribs*, Princeton is so excited—and to be honest, it makes me excited, too. The more he talks, the more everything about him seems to make sense: his obsession with being the golden child, being the best, and breaking barriers and records in just about every sport he puts his mind to. The only thing he hasn't conquered, it seems, is becoming valedictorian (thanks to yours truly). But beneath his words, I feel the tide of his loneliness, pulling.

In the kitchen, Princeton snaps to get my attention. "Whatchu want? I can make breakfast for lunch, breakfast for dinner, and ramen."

"You're just a Chef Boyardee, huh?"

"Naw, my moms never let me eat those, but if I keep it one hundred witchu, I love 'em." He blows a chef's kiss that blooms into a full grin, then he takes off his jersey and untucks his white tank top. I haven't noticed before, but when he gets lost in thought, he rubs his bare stomach.

"I want those." I point at the box of Toaster Strudel calling my name from the freezer.

"You sure?" he says, skeptical. "That ain't no lunch."

"Maybe not to a super athlete, but to a regular human like me—oh yeah." I jump off my stool and tell him to make the whole box, enough for both of us. And as we eat all six, two at a time, drawing on them with the glaze packets as they cool, I learn more about him.

First, Princeton is actually his middle name. His full name is Brandon Princeton Baxter. To get that information, I tell him my full name: Joseph Theodore Dupresh. His mom is the famous Lady Tee, which I already knew, but his other mom is Eunyoung "Eva" Kim, a trauma surgeon at a nearby hospital. It's still debatable, but he says he actually hates his nickname "Prince Ten" because it makes people only want him for one thing. And although he is the star athlete from Georgia everyone is talking about, he grew up sickly as a kid, so when he was finally introduced to sports, he got obsessed, and that was how he got into his first love, track and field.

Almost an hour has passed before we get down to the last strudel, or, to be specific, the only half of one that's left. I think about swiping it but don't want to deal with him chasing me around the house. I don't have to, though. He offers it to me.

“What?” I ask, as I chew on it skeptically.

“Nothin’,” he says, shaking his head. “Nothin’ at all.”

I watch him, waiting for whatever it is he has to say to come out.

“You made your decision yet?”

“I dunno if I’m ready to go back to writing love letters. . . . I miss it but—”

“That ain’t what I meant.” He shakes his head.

I stare at him, confused.

“I’m talkin’ ’bout my boy Will.”

I roll my eyes.

“What? Don’t act brand-new. I was right, won’t I? He sprung on you already?”

“Whateva,” I say, finishing up the Toaster Strudel.

“You know, it’s okay . . . to like more than one person.”

“But doesn’t that just lead to everybody getting hurt?” I’m surprised I answer him, but a part of me really has been hoping to talk to somebody about this.

“I mean, I think about it like this. You ain’t any more in control of who you like than who you love. And if you both of them make you feel some kinda way, who say you gotta choose one ova the other? Unless . . .”

“Unless what?” I realize I’m hanging on his every word, lost in the silence. I sit up straight, try to pretend it doesn’t really matter. He laughs, knowing better.

“Whatchu like about Leroy? Like, how does he make you feel?”

The words don't come at first, which is why I'm glad Princeton motions for me to follow him into the living room, a huge space with some of the tallest windows I've ever seen. In the back, I can see there's a beautiful garden. He plops down on a sky-blue long sectional, pats the cushion next to him, so I join him, restraining the part of me that wants to jump up and down on it once I feel how soft it is.

"He makes me feel like I can do anything, like I'm safe, protected."

"And what about Will?"

I frown. "He makes me feel like I don't have to be protected, like I can *be* anything—like I already am."

"Damn."

We stare at each other, hanging in the silence, then bust out laughing.

"I hope you don't take this the wrong way," he says.

Immediately the storm gates close and I feel myself preparing to hear something that hurts.

"Yo, chill. You givin' me them puppy eyes. I ain't 'bout to say nothin' mean. Just relax." He tosses a pillow at me. I catch it and smile.

"I just wanted to say, the reason I asked you a while back to write a love letter was 'cuz, iono, eva since I've known you, you looked like someone who has somethin' important to say. You know? Iono if people know how special you are but, I guess what I'm tryna say is—"

The front door opens and closes. Princeton looks and

smiles; it's his mom Lady Tee. He hops up and goes to meet her. She's tall with locs and glides when she walks: I remember her from some of the track meets, especially when Princeton was trying to become a starter with Jacob.

"Princeton!" She's got bags in her hands, looks like vegetables, fruits, and herbs. "I just saw Lyric up the street. He better not have been coming from here. That boy is trouble."

"Ma . . . ," Princeton sings, trying to quiet her, "I don't hang wit him no more. I told you. That's old history."

I walk up, wait until she sees me before I try to introduce myself.

"Hello, I'm—"

"Joseph," she says with a wide smile and an accent hanging at the tip of her tongue.

"Yes? I mean, you can call me Jay," I say, confused. How does she know my name?

"Would you tell me if Princeton was lying?"

"I would, but he's not—I promise," I say. "Can I help with that?"

She reads my face for the truth, then hands me the last small bag in her hand; it smells of fresh basil. "Okay, I'll believe you because Tin Tin can't stop talking about you and I know—"

"Ahh . . . Ma . . . why? Not in front of company." If he could blush . . .

I chuckle. She does, too.

"Now, you got somethin' in your back pocket, if you ever need to get him in line."

"Good to know."

"Anyway, what I was trying to say is that I know your family, you come from good people. I was pretty close with your dad back in the day, before he met your mom. You are just like him."

"But you've seen my brother at the O Lounge; he's the one who really looks like . . ." I don't mean for the words to come out like they do, soft and small—weak. The one thing he never wanted me to be.

"I'll let you in on a little secret, as someone who knew both of your parents when we were all high school versions of ourselves. Jacob may look like your dad on the outside, but he's got your mom's competitive spirit. You have your mom's beauty and refined posture, but you feel like your dad. He always had this ability to make everyone feel comfortable around him, because he was a great listener."

Her words are like a spell, strong enough to keep all the bad feelings away, so I can hear her, meet another version of my dad, the man I once looked up to, before he . . .

"Is this where you tell us we related?" Princeton says, looking at her suspiciously.

"See, him—that's all of me. Nothing but." She giggles. "No, you are not related. I knew Jay's father back when he went to Providence Prep."

"What? My dad went to Providence? I thought he went to Daniel Lee with my mom and Miss Rosalind."

"Yeah, he did. But he didn't leave Providence until he was a sophomore in high school. So, from middle school, which is when I met him, he was an artsy—albeit, still athletic—writer. That's what he was actually known for in school, before he took up sports. He's one of the most beautiful poets I've ever read. That's how he got your mom. After she became his tutor in biology—or so the story goes—he wrote her love letters. I know because he'd let me read them, and I'd give him a pointer or two."

Princeton and I look at each other. "What?" we say in unison.

"Yes, it sounds crazy. He had a gift."

I can't believe it. Not only was my dad a writer, he wrote love letters, just like me—or do I write love letters just like him? And where Lady Tee used to help him, her son, Princeton, helps me. I don't know if there's such a thing as fate or karma or whatever name it goes by, but I wonder what it all means. Is it possible to be just like someone and nothing like them at the same time? I don't know, and, honestly, I don't want to think about it.

"Why did my dad leave Providence Prep? Isn't it the one school everyone wants to be in?"

Lady Tee reaches for the bag of ginger roots, her smile fades. "Well, at Providence the kids have more than they could ever need but more isn't always better." She shakes her head, and I can almost feel it, the weight of everything she's not telling us. I don't know about Princeton, but I've heard the rumors. Most of the students there are white, so, although every kid not white isn't poor, the color of their skin is always held against them because the standard is one shade, not the beauty and strength of many.

"Your dad, he always knew who he was. So, when others would do anything and everything they could to blend in and curry favor, even if it meant compromising everything that made them unique, he wouldn't. And it came at a cost. They tried to break him, tried to threaten him into submission, but he always stood tall, no matter what. When he couldn't take it anymore, he went somewhere that would treat him like he deserved. And Providence Prep and Daniel Lee High have been fierce rivals ever since." She giggles—a joke to mask her pain.

Is that why Dad did what he did? Because everywhere he went, people were trying to break him. And when he couldn't take it anymore, he eventually turned on us—those he loved—when the whole time he wanted to attack those who hurt him, those he hated, like the couple in Avalon Park.

It don't make it right what he did to us, but I wonder if what happened was the result of them winning.

"Jay, would you like me to make you something to drink?"

Princeton stares at her suspiciously, wondering if she means what she says. I half expect a legion of maids to appear in the doorway, even though we're already in the kitchen.

"What do you all have?" I say, wiping my forehead. I'm sweating. I try to breathe in deep, exhale. I don't want it to happen. Not here.

"Everything." Princeton smiles. "Ma can make just about any drink you can think of just using the flowers and herbs from the garden. If somethin' is hurtin', even better, she'll be sure to fix it."

There's a pain in my chest that almost knocks the wind out of me, but I breathe through it. I close my eyes a little bit, try to keep my composure.

"You okay, Jay?" Lady Tee says, walking closer. "You're sweating."

Princeton puts his hand on my forehead to test it. "Yeah, man, you good?"

I nod, move his hand. "I'm okay, it's just . . . nothing . . . it'll pass." I keep my eyes closed to hide that I'm in the full throws of a panic attack. It feels like silver ants are biting me all over and I can't see anything, even when my eyes are open.

It's okay. It'll pass, it always does. Just a little bit longer.

I feel Lady Tee moving closer, but I can't see her. "Jay . . . can you hear me?"

"Yes, ma'am."

"I want you to listen to me, know that you can trust me, okay?"

I nod, a little nervous.

"Are you having a panic attack?"

I freeze, unsure of what to say or do. I've never told anybody before, always been ashamed. The only people who know are Momma and Jacob, and that's because Jacob has them, too. I don't want their pity. I just want—

"I have 'em, too," Princeton says. "This helps me—" Princeton holds my hand, begins rubbing my back. I want to pull away but don't because I can't see and don't want to alarm anybody. Then I remember, in front of the school: this isn't the first time Princeton has seen me have one. I take a deep breath, relax. No need for secrets, not if he already knows.

Slowly, I feel my vision coming back. I open my eyes, take a deep breath. Princeton's eyes are locked on me like they were when he was in front of the school that time. He smiles, ol charming ass.

"Can you walk?" he asks.

"Yeah, I think so, just a little shaky."

"Cool, let me help." He puts my arm around his shoulder, his arm around my waist. "Let's go out back, the garden might help. It's where I go when I'm havin' it rough."

I thought the front of the house was impressive, but the back garden is a work of art. In the center is one of the tallest

Southern magnolias I've seen, its branches stretching up to the sky like it's in the middle of a dance. At different corners, there are date trees, which fill the garden with a sweetness that seems to blend with beautifully colored bushes all around the perimeter. Not far from the patio, right under a white wooden structure covered in sweet-smelling vines, are three lawn chairs with a table in the center and a trickling pond nearby. That's where we sit, shaded just enough. Before sitting in his chair, Princeton cuts on two cooling-mist fans and points them at both of us.

In addition to the fans, he drops a sandwich bag of folded sheets of paper. "More requests for letters. And here's the cash. It's almost three hundred dollars."

I gasp. "What? Why did you take their money? I don't know if I can—"

"How can I explain if you don't let me? Breathe." He grins.

"Okay, I'm breathing," I say sarcastically.

"Breathe some more, you still got a little too much sarcasm, which means your brain needs more oxygen."

I kick at his lawn chair, accidentally scuff the cushion with dirt.

"Oh shit . . . I'm sorry, I didn't mean to—"

"Jay, it's fine, really." He brushes it off with his hand, dirt disappears.

I take a deep breath. I don't want to damage nothing in or near this house—don't know if we could afford it. Might force me to be Princeton's letter writer forever. I chuckle to myself.

"I told people you weren't gonna write any more letters, at least not till we got back in school."

"Really?"

"Yup, but that only made people want to buy more. So, they upped the price, wrote some notes, and asked if I'd just pass it along. I didn't make any promises, but a few hundred dollars ain't nothin' to sneeze at."

I nod, agreeing.

"I'm not tryna pressure you; it's the last thing I wanna do. If you don't want to, you don't have to. I know everybody on the list and where they live. I can personally send them all their money back. But all I'm saying is try. Read a couple of the notes and you might change your mind. Plus, now that I know we have this cosmic connection across generations, I know it's written in the stars, an enterprise with our name on it. One school today, five schools tomorrow."

I look at Princeton, right into his eyes, and I see it: he's genuine. I also realize he isn't our class president for nothing.

I shake my head, moved. There's something about the blank page that scares me, how it soaks up the ink, swallows the words. But I know it's all in my head. The reason I'm afraid to write has nothing to do with them, it's that I suck at "like" and have no track record when it comes to love. I wonder if that's why my dad and Lady Tee were connected.

Like Princeton, she brings the clarity, helps the pen—and ink—work its magic. Maybe I should write because both of us together can help each other.

"Just think about it," Princeton says. "You gotta numba you can call. If you need me to, I'll climb through your window and help you write 'em myself."

"Jacob would kill you if you climbed through my window. Actually, to find me, you would have to climb through Jacob's window now since we're currently sharing a room."

"He wouldn't kill me, I'm too lucrative. And you done already seen it—he like my dance moves. I been teachin' him a li'l somethin' on the side, too. See? I got skills *and* I got you three hundred dollars, just off my good looks and charm. He ain't gon' waste that."

I nod, knowing the truth.

"But I'm furreal, don't overthink it . . . the letters, I know you do that, too, don't want you to be writing anything too potent, then you gon' have to go in hiding 'cuz you got half the school pregnant from your letters."

I stare at him, terrified.

"Could that happen?"

"Nah . . . no? Well, maybe?" He chuckles, throws some pink petals from a fallen flower at me.

Lady Tee arrives with a silver tray with what looks like four cocktails. I watch her approach, my eyebrows rising at the thought.

"Before you get excited, they are nonalcoholic," she says.

"Ahh . . ." I smile. "These kind of like the drinks Jacob makes?"

"Exactly . . . official term 'mocktails,' some of them even taste better than the real thing, but don't tell any of the adults who come to the O Lounge that. I need them to keep spending over twenty dollars per drink." She giggles.

The longer I look at Lady Tee, the more I see where Princeton got his charm and his beauty. She speaks like she can command the elements, and when she smiles, you feel it: blessed and highly favored. Princeton has the same thing, he makes you want to ask him to hug you and never let go. Mere mortals like me don't stand a chance. But maybe I do, now that I know I come from a different cloth, too—Momma and Dad, their own kind of magicians.

"What's this one?" I ask, reaching for one of the four options.

"That's a special turmeric and ginger iced tea with floral ice cubes."

"As in, flowers in ice cubes?"

She nods, proud. I sip it, prouder. It's smooth with a kick but rushes through my whole body, makes me feel calm. I nod, thoroughly impressed.

Princeton takes one, his has the same kind of ice cubes but is made with rosemary, tangerine, and cranberry and another that's rosemary and basil lemonade. The final one, which

Lady Tee sips, is iced rose lemonade, with literal rose petals in the glass. I sip, watching them sip, wondering if this is something I can look forward to.

I look above us and see star jasmine vines. On the left side, behind us are orange sunset lantanas, red bee balms and daylilies, with stocks of yellow chrysanthemums. In the center, a transition from the warm colors to the cool—lavender, coneflowers, and salvia—that transition to the white queen of the meadows, Cape jasmine, and white azaleas.

Suddenly, I remember Dad's voice, hear him talking about the sun and moon garden he wanted to make, half with flowers that bloomed bright like the sun and the other cool like the moon. It was meant to be the garden for us, his sons, so that we remember the light and dark of our world, the rich parts of who we are.

I sit up, feeling hot again all over, the heat and the sweet, as sweat drips down my face and back. Momma already said he was out of prison, but she never said where he was, but then again, me and Jacob never asked. But the more I sit and think, the more I connect the little things, like petals pointing to a path that leads back to him and, slowly, emotions flood my mind and body, as I remember him helping me memorize the names of flowers, Saturday mornings where he'd experiment with me, Momma, and Jacob, as we tried his mysterious herb teas, like turmeric and ginger, even that one time he showed us how to make floral ice cubes, a thing he'd become obsessed with.

Up until now, I didn't want to see him, I didn't want to meet him, I didn't want to know where he was and how he was doing. But somehow, *not* knowing feels worse. It fills me with dread, only reminds me of the monster he left behind, not the father he'd always been. The words come out before I have a chance to smother them. "Do you still keep in touch with my dad, Lady Tee?"

She doesn't answer at first. Princeton looks at her, wondering.

"I do. . . . As I'm sure you figured out, you're sitting in the garden he wanted to make for—and with—you and Jacob."

I look down, feel myself slowly falling.

Lady Tee reaches over, touches my leg. Just like that, I'm back, under her spell, staring down into an abyss of my nightmares made real. But I'm sitting here, just out of reach, safe.

"Jay, I'm going to say something, and I want you to know that I respect whatever decision you make because it's not my place to feel otherwise. But as someone who knew—and still knows—your father, if the sadness in your eyes has anything to do with him, I know he'd want a chance to make it right. Regardless, if there's anything you ever want to know about your dad, your mom, or anything I can help with, you can always come and ask. I'll always be here. We both will," she says, looking over at Princeton. "And when you're ready to talk to him yourself, here's where you can find him." She hands me a business card; it has the name of an apartment complex.

LAVENDER TERRACE,
1220 WILLOW TREE BOULEVARD

"If the name sounds familiar, it's where your father started—how he got his nickname as the 'Lavender Man,' able to grow it almost anywhere."

I nod, remembering. Not much, but enough.

I stare at the white card and the violet writing and the logo of a lavender plant, and I slip it into my back pocket. I don't know why, but everything I felt, the fear, the sadness, the anger, the betrayal all melts away. I hold my glass, rub the condensation, feel the cool between my fingertips. I know the feelings are still there, just further away. But as I listen to Princeton and Lady Tee joke about whether she actually spiked his drink—and that, if she didn't, could she—I'm reminded that in front of me is something I never thought I'd have but I always knew I needed. I chuckle, keep the truth trapped between cheek and gum like a chewy candy so I can savor it.

When it's time for me to head back home, they both walk me to the front door, and I smile because Princeton, or Tin Tin, as I call him in jest, keeps thinking of all the reasons why it makes more sense for me to spend the night and go home tomorrow.

"I hope to see you around here a lot more often, Jay. You're the first person he's ever brought here, did you know that?" Lady Tee grins.

My eyes grow wide in surprise.

"Maaaaa, please don't. You really blowin' me here," Princeton says.

She winks at me, proof that there's nothing more exciting for parents than embarrassing their kids in the best way. "What? Jay . . . I'm just saying . . . I have this one photo of him as a baby where's he's naked on the couch with—"

Princeton practically drags me out the front door onto the porch. She stands in the doorway, all smiles.

I wave at her. "I'll be back. . . . I want to hear all about that picture—and copies, I want copies—preferably that can be used in our senior yearbook!" I laugh so hard I want to cry.

Princeton is staring at me, unamused but clearly blushing. "You would really do something like that to me?"

"Of course I would. That's what friends do, right?"

We smile at each other; listen to the ring of a new word we've never used to refer to each other before.

As I walk back toward the school, my heart is full and my step is light. I feel for the card in my back pocket, and I'm okay, fine with it being on me but not feeling like I have to do anything with it just yet.

When I'm finally in front of Daniel Lee, I stare at it, wonder what it must have been like when my mom and dad and Miss Rosalind went there. Did it have the same green doors?

Did the trees chatter and gossip alongside them as they gathered out front? Or were they other types of plants or trees? Even though I have even more questions than I started with, I feel good knowing where I can get some answers.

For old times' sake, I decide to take the shortcut home near the church. Everything feels the same, untouched by the phantoms of me and Leroy wrestling in the field. But like a daydream made real, Leroy appears in front of his powder-blue Cadillac. When he sees me, something inside me roars to life, and I feel like our bodies are embers daring to flame again.

Instantly I imagine a sign flashing in neon lights saying, "NIGGA, TURN YO BLACK ASS AROUND *AND RUN*," as a ratchet choir ad lib explains to me all the reasons why I should leave all of this alone because it won't work out anyway. A reminder that there is Will and he deserves a chance—the one that Leroy let go of—because he makes me feel like I don't have to be protected, like I can *be* anything, like I already am. And if I know better, I should do better, or at least do things differently.

I will, I tell myself.

I'll do better.

I'll be different.

So, with the squirrels and the trees and the leaves as my witness, I turn around and walk the other way.

14

Leroy

Jay looked at me and just turned round.

If he woulda at least said somethin like he did last time, cussed me out, pushed me, anythin, I woulda been okay wit it. But to just look at me and not say nothin? That aint right.

If I just figure out who really behind all of this, usin Rouk like a puppet, and what "DK" means, I can prove it to Taj and end this. Then I can finally tell Jay the whole truth bout errthang that happened and why I had to let him go, to keep him safe. But how I'm supposed to prove it when don't nobody know nothin?

I gotta find a way—cuz without it, Jay might neva wanna see me again. And if he still don't like me, I just wanna know he safe, cuz that's what real love is, aint it?

When I get to Rissa's house, where she lettin me and Taj stay, she is just pullin into the driveway, which is weird cuz she usually at the diner preppin for dinner. She runs to the door.

Shit, I know whateva's bout to go down can't be good, but I hold on to the promise I made to myself: I'll fight to figure this out so I can finally show Jay how much I like him, how much I wanna be wit him, how much I love him.

"Yo, Rissa!"

She don't even look at me or speak. I hear Taj yellin from inside, then see the otha car in the driveway: a burgundy Toyota Camry—it's Ma.

"You don't get to come back. Leave." Taj is standin in the doorway of the kitchen, pointin at the door we came in from.

Ma across from him in the middle of the livin room. The louder he gets, the mo Ma look like she bout to tear some shit up.

"You don't get to tell me what I can and can't do. I'm the momma, you the child."

"Rissa, she tryna take Lee away from me. Tell her to get the fuck out."

"Who the hell you think you talkin to?" Ma rushes toward Taj, but Rissa makes it there just in time. I slip behind Rissa and get in front of Taj to make sure he don't say nothin else stupid.

"Tanya, just wait. . . . Let's talk it out. I'm not tryna stop you—I'm just sayin we can't go bout it like this," Rissa says.

"I preciate errthang you do for me and the kids, but I can't let you take *my* kids to some city I aint neva been. What kinda motha would that make me?"

"How you know bout that?" Taj asks.

"I told her," Rissa says. She looks beat-up and tired, and a hit aint even been thrown. "She yo momma, and she got a right to know."

"Since fuckin when?"

Rissa looks ova her shoulder at Taj. "Walk."

Taj sucks his teeth. "Man, I aint—" He stops talkin, squeezes by the lil space between Rissa, Ma, and the wall near the sofa. "Aint you said it's too dangerous for me to be out on the street like that?" Taj turns round, walks back into the livin room.

"Go to the kitchen, then."

"But I aint—"

"Shut up and come on. . . ." I pull Taj outta sight. Some of Rissa's apple crisp is coolin off on the stove, and we listen to it call our names.

While Rissa talks Ma down in the livin room, we smash the apple crumble and rolled oats and brown sugar in spoonfuls, tryin not to hear too much of Rissa yell-whisperin and Ma gettin louder and louder. We eat cuz we hungry, we eat cuz we nervous, we eat cuz it's the only thing we can do besides feelin helpless.

It's been two years since I last saw Ma, but she got a way of makin it feel like aint nothin changed, like we still live together and her and Taj still wake up errday arguin bout lil things. Sometimes I think me and Taj trick ourselves into believin time don't exist cuz we have to, so errtime we see her, we pick up where we left off. When she disappear again—cuz she always choose a man ova us—we try not to miss her too much by tellin ourselves she'll be home soon.

"Why you think they always at each otha throats?" Taj chews wit his eyes closed.

"Iono." I think it got to be cuz of somethin aint nobody sayin cuz Ma stay mad even tho Rissa always been there when we needed her, always took us when she didn't have to. "Maybe they both still sad bout Pops, like this the only way they know how to miss him—to be like they was when he was here."

I plot how to swipe one of them corners, but Taj blocks my spoon.

"Them yours, these mine."

"Yours got mo apples than mine."

He moves some of the apples to my side. "Quit whinin."

I don't remember Pops too much, but I know Taj still looks up to him, tries to be as big as the shadow he left behind. And I know Ma wants wuteva she'd had befo Dad went missin. But no matta what guy she wit, it always ends the same: Taj bleedin.

The last time, we aint have to leave, cuz Ma left us. After a week and she still aint came back, Taj said she won't worth his tears.

Rissa and Ma call us back in the livin room. When they get to talkin again, it aint perfect, and it aint quiet, but it's betta than what we walked in on. But it don't take Taj long to explode.

"Taj, just hear ya mom out."

"Nah, I aint goin back wit her."

"Lee?" Somethin in Rissa's eyes is beggin.

"He aint goin back, neitha," Taj says.

"I'm sorry to break it to you—this aint a choice," Ma says.

"Taj . . ."

"No, Rissa. You seen what happens errtime. The moment a nigga come round, she start actin brand-new."

"Right . . . Cuz you don't neva do nothin wrong, Taj."

"Imma kid, I'm supposed to fuck up sometimes."

"*Then do as you're told,*" Ma screams so loud it makes me jump.

But Taj just stares through her. He don't even blink. "I'm done playin this game witchu. I aint gon let you keep hurtin Lee."

"Who the fuck are you? Huh? You aint got no fuckin right. You don't know shit bout what I had to go through to raise yall."

"Tanya . . ." Rissa's face looks like it's breakin, like if she moves her lips to speak, she'll crumble to pieces.

"No, you don't get to tell me to calm down. This shit is yo fault." Ma turns to Rissa. "You aint neva like me, aint neva think I was good enough to be wit Tré. That's why you egged him on, kept his nose down in community work so he aint neva have no time for me or his family."

Me and Taj look at each otha, confused. What she mean?

"Tanya, I aint neva had a problem witchu. Stop sayin that."

"It's the truth. You aint neva want us to be together. But you aint had to force Tré's hand the way you did."

"I had nothin to do wit what happened between you two, Tanya. I wanted him to do mo, but I told you when you first showed up that you was always gon be second to the purpose he believed he had."

"You shoulda talked sense into him. My family needed you, needed you to show him that being a father to his kids was enough—that what he was doin was gon eventually get him killed foolin round wit these people. His blood is on yo hands. Cuz of you and the BDs, he had a target on his back."

Rissa shakes her head, looks at me and Taj like somethin between all of us might break.

"Don't look at them, tryna make me out to be a liar. Did you or did you not try to stop him? There's somethin you coulda said, somethin you coulda did that night. I just know it, and if you would have, he would neva went missin tryna stop yo ass from being beat cuz you—"

"*Ahhhhhh!*" Taj roars, so loud it sucks the air outta the room.

Ma and Rissa just stare in the quiet that's still ringin. I fight back the tears comin from a place I don't understand. Taj gets up and heads toward the door. Befo leavin, he turns round, look like he bout to say something, but he don't. He walks out, and I follow.

On the porch, he lights a Black & Mild. He tries to play it off, but I can tell his hands are shakin. "I'll be back," he says, walkin to the driveway. He stops me when I try to follow.

"What? Why I can't go?"

"Stay here, Lee."

"Where you goin? When you comin back?"

"Why you wanna know?"

I look down, hide the truth.

"You pick her ova me errtime," Taj says.

"It's not like that. It's just . . . I wanna make sho she don't have to be alone."

"I aint tryna hear that. You made yo choice." The cigar hangs on his bottom lip by an invisible string. "Go back in the house."

"It's just for a few days. I'll be back befo—"

"Don't."

"Whatchu mean? Don't say that."

"Bye, Lee." He walks toward the driveway. I pull at him, tryna stop him, but I can't. He know how I feel bout goodbye, why it cuts me up on the inside so bad. It's the only thing I rememba bout our dad, that he used to say, "I'll be back, Lil Lee Man," but neva did.

Rissa leaves for the diner, not too long after Taj, to get her mind off errthang that was happenin, so I grab me a bag of clothes and sit in the car watchin the house get smaller and smaller in the rearview. Suddenly, I wanna do errthang different cuz errbody you love don't always come back after you hurt em, whether you mean to or not. I hope he'll be here when I get back, that he won't give me the silent treatment or shut down on me like he does Ma, so I don't have to do crazy shit just to get him to speak to me.

We aint even off the block and I wanna ask Ma to stop the car so I can tell her how we live different when she gone; how Taj started every mornin back when we lived in the old house; how he got up real early befo the sun came up, cleaned up her room even tho he neva let it get dirty; how he made the bed up just like she used to, tucked both the top and bottom of the sheets befo foldin the big throw blanket into a diamond. I wanna tell her that the secret to makin a house smell like she neva left is sprayin Chanel N°5, her favorite perfume, five times in every room—and on the worst days, seven.

I wanna tell her so when I get outta the car and run after Taj, she know it aint cuz I don't love her, I just need Taj different. I don't know how to live without his fussin and cussin; the slaps upside my head; the hugs; our routines—him knowin that when he leaves he needs to tell me exactly when he comin back, cuz he knows how scared I am of the quiet when he gone.

But I neva say nothin. Instead, I promise to get on my knees and beg Taj to forgive me the next time I see him cuz Ma is the only person strong enough to make me break my promises, to make a liar outta me even though Taj spends his life tryna make sure I live by nothin but our truth.

When I make it to Ma's place, I can understand why she wants us so bad. Although errthang and every place Ma eva been felt warm, like the sun followed her, it aint the same. Except for a love seat and a recliner in the livin room and a table wit a few chairs in front of the kitchen, there aint much: no bookshelves or wall unit, no Dollar Store picture of Black Jesus hands wit words to the Our Father prayer. There's nothin and nobody.

I wake up to Ma's special mornin alarm: bacon. Ma aint neva been a good cook, even though she brags bout it all the time. Errthang she cooks smells like burnt bacon, even vegetables. But it don't matta—tryin is the only thing that counts. I don't peek my head from beneath the comforter tho. Iono why . . . well, I do; I aint ready to face that my heart hurt cuz Taj aint here, and I want Ma to take me back.

I keep tryna sleep it off, hopin somethin gon change, but I know betta. Between somebody dog cussin at us from the otha side of the wall and this one ray of sunshine that keep tryna blind me through the curtain and the comforter, I can't get comfortable or find the best spot on the couch, where my legs hang just right. I get ready to say the words, even tho Ma gon get to cryin and askin why I can't live wit her. I rather be wit Taj and Rissa and in danger than comfortable here without them. I hope she understands.

"Lee . . ." Ma is hoverin next to my head on the couch.

I slowly peel the comforter down and sit up. She look nervous. Does she know what I'm bout to say?

"I think we should go back for Taj," she says. "Somethin just don't feel right."

Am I hearin her right? I sit all the way up, try to listen better.

"It's just a momma thing. . . . I kept thinkin bout him all night. Taj should be here, too. We a family. We gotta stay together."

"You think he gon come?" I try not to get our hopes up. I wanna go back and try to convince Taj, but I know what I'll do if he don't.

"We gotta make him." She stands up, mumbles under her breath. I aint neva seen her like this.

"What's wrong?"

"I don't know. Just something aint right. Come on, get up. We gotta go get him."

In the car, Ma really only talks to herself, talkin through the same question: Will Taj come stay wit us, and if he doesn't want to, can I convince him? I neva say nothin. Cuz if I can't, I'm stayin wit him.

When Ma pulls up, it's like déjà vu. Rissa has just rolled up, too, and barely stops near the curb befo she hops out of the car and runs straight to the door. Rissa aint look that scared since she showed up at the motel that night. I'm already out the car and runnin behind her.

When Rissa screams, the house shakes.

I want to know what she sees, but my legs stop behind her, and fire shoots down my arm and side again. I can't breathe.

Ma runs in behind me, and she neva stops, don't even seem to think bout what she do or don't want to see. She screams, but no sound comes out at first, as she pushes past the couch that is flipped ova, the glass livin room table that's smashed, and the smears of red on the walls near the kitchen and the stairs.

There are streaks of blood errwhere, like there was one helluva fight, but there are no bodies. When Ma comes back down, her face is pale and wet wit tears. She walks to me, says somethin I can't understand, then walks to Rissa.

"Rissa . . . Where's . . . Tell me where my . . . I came to get him. . . . He not here. . . ."

Rissa shakes her head, but she aint cryin no mo.

"Rissa, you gotta fix this. You gotta promise me . . . to bring back my son."

"I will, Tanya," she says.

If this is connected to what happened at the motel, there's gonna be proof. I run to the front door and open it. Then, I see it: the "DK" and the jagged crown, freshly carved.

I look at Rissa and nod—she already knows.

Whateva made her scream is gone. Now, she looks like the woman we know, who helped raise us: Rissa, president of the Black Diamonds, heart of K-Town. This house, her house, was considered neutral ground. Errbody who anybody knows there are some places no kinda beef is allowed to get cooked. This attack means war. Not just against the BDs, against all of us.

After the popos stop by, Rissa drives me and Ma to the diner. Ma takes a nap on the bed in the office, while me and Rissa sit at the counter. Befo we left, Rissa called one of her connects to do a background check on the detective in charge of the case, Detective Dane, to see if he can be trusted. She stands near the cash register, movin the card between her acrylic nails.

I don't know what she thinkin bout, but I need to tell her errthang I know. Aint a doubt in my mind that Rouk and Mr. Nobody did this.

"Rissa," I say. Tryin my best to find the words.

Even if she gets pissed and blames me for not tellin anyone what I knew—I'll deal wit it. I'll do anything, if it means Taj will come back home.

"Yeah, Lee? You hungry? Lemme fix you something—"

"Naw, there's somethin I gotta tell you. Somethin that may gotta do wit Taj goin missin."

She stands up, squints. "Do you know who did it?"

"I do. . . . Rouk and his—"

"Lee, I don't think—" She stops herself, but it hurts just the same—she don't even wanna let me finish. But there's no goin back. I need her to hear me, to really listen.

"Just hear me out, then you decide."

I tell her errthang I think and errthang I know. No mo secrets that might get in the way of her thinkin of a way to save Taj. It seems stupid now to worry so much ova whether he would have believed me, when at least he coulda been warned. I wait for her to explode, to say errthang I already said to myself: call me stupid, ask why I aint say nothin sooner. But she don't say nothin at all.

"Anything else? Anything?" Her words are soft and weary, too tired to be angry.

"That's errthang, I promise."

She grabs her purse and keys. "Imma keep this in mind when I go talk to Detective Dane. Stay here, look out for Tanya. Don't say nothin bout what you told me to nobody. Understand?"

"Yes, ma'am." I nod, too scared to look her in the eyes, to see the disappointment I know she must have.

"Lee, look at me."

I do, tryna hold back the tears in my eyes.

"Thank you. But you gotta let me take it from here—it's the only way I can keep you safe."

Standin there, watchin Rissa as she walks out the front door, I hold back the tears, push down the rage. And just when I start feelin hopeless in the quiet, I say a little prayer, hopin it's not too late.

***

It's been two days, and nothing from Rissa. Errthang is "Wait a lil longer," but I can't wait no mo. I wake up early and plan to start at the beginning, to go back to our old house and look for clues. I come to D&D's to get the sketch from Trish and see if lookin at the version she made will help me figure out what the symbol means so I can tie it all together. Brown Brown and PYT wait in the car out front.

There was a lil bit of relief when PYT and Brown Brown finally picked up their phones after we found out Taj and Night was missin. They told us Taj and Night sent them to D&D's to buy some stuff for lunch befo any of it even happened. But after forty-eight hours and no sign of Taj and Night—and no leads from the popos draggin they feet—they just like me: willin to do anything but sit on they hands. I keep thinkin we shoulda just met Trish at her spot, but she said she left her notebook here.

"Sorry," Trish says when she finally runs ova wit her sketchbook in her hand. "I actually came here first, but when I couldn't find it upstairs, I realized I left it at home."

"Aintchu supposed to be workin today?"

She aint wearin her uniform.

She looks round, like she aint hear me. "Yeaahhh nnnnooo?"

"Trish."

"Look, if Taj and Night are still missin, you need as many hands of help as you can get and—"

"No, Trish. It's too dangerous."

"Well, all the mo reason why I gotta go witchu." She stands up, puts her hand on her hip. "Otherwise, it's gon be real hard wit you lookin for clues without this sketch."

I think bout snatchin it and runnin. But she hides the notebook behind her back.

"Fine, we goin to my house," I say.

"Why?"

"This all started when they shot it up. If I'm right and this is all connected, then there should be a 'DK' symbol at the house, too. We don't have much to go on, but it's a start. If we can figure out what 'DK' means, I know it'll lead me to Taj."

We pile in the car, and PYT peels off like there's no tomorrow. In the passenger seat, I turn the symbol every possible direction to see if anything pops out.

"Don't think too hard," Trish says, behind me. "Otherwise you only gon see what you wanna see, not what you need to. Just wait till you get to the house, maybe something will come back to you."

I nod, hopin she right, secretly cussin out the scared voice in my head tellin me I aint neva gon find a clue and Taj is gon die cuz of it. When PYT pulls up, I take a deep breath and we all run to the front door, lookin for any sign of the symbol.

"Do you see it?"

Me, Brown Brown, and PYT must look all kinds of crazy

in front of me and Taj old place huddled and squintin, tryna see if the symbol is there.

"Nah, ion see it. Do you?" Brown Brown face get any closer to the door and his nose gon eitha become a key or a second doorknob.

"Lemme see." Trish closes the car door and runs up behind us wit her sketch.

"I really wish you woulda stayed at the store. I told you, it's dangerous," I say.

"Well, who you know wit the most detailed sketch of the sigil?"

"Sigil?" PYT face a whole-ass question mark, just like mine was.

"A sigil, somethin folks think got magical powers," I say.

"It's not here," she says.

I shake my head, ready to scream, swing, or both. "It don't make sense. It's at the motel, so why it aint here?"

We back up, give each otha space to breathe. I kick at the pine needles and twigs and stare at the switch bush, Savin Grace.

"Is this the only place it could be? What if they put it somewhere else like—"

"Shit!" I say, remembering the third masked figure. "The back door."

I run round the back, and errbody follow. At first, it don't look like nothin there but when I stoop down, get real close, and wipe away some of the dust and pollen that got caked on it, just under the doorknob, we all see it at the same time.

"What now?" PYT asks.

The truth? Iono. My questions got questions. It just aint bout Rouk and the guys wit the locs, all carryin the same symbol as a tattoo. It's bout who they workin for. I got the symbol, and it's connected to all the places. I know it can't be none of the gangs here cuz don't nobody recognize this. And the popos say it aint a gang outside of Savannah, like I thought, cuz even when Rissa told the detectives, nothin popped up on their database—the only useful update she managed to give me in the past two days.

If it aint one of the gangs here and it aint a gang tryna move in, then who the fuck is it?

"Ion get it." I aint mean to say it out loud, but I did anyway.

"Get what?" Brown Brown asks, waitin on me to finish. PYT goes back to the front door to look again, to see if we mighta missed somethin.

"Why take the time to scratch somethin into a door? Why not just do what you here to do?"

Brown Brown nods like he thinkin. He leans back on the side of his car. Me and Trish pick thorny leaves and fold them into small squares, thorns facin out.

"Well, sigils were sometimes like seals or crests, maybe it's no different from that . . . to show they were here, to make their mark." Trish shrugs, not sayin that's what it is or aint.

"Maybe it's a warning," Brown Brown says. "So errbody know."

"But we was barely able to find it, and we was lookin for it. The popos prolly don't even know it's there. Yo people on the force say anything bout it?" I ask Brown Brown to double-check.

He shakes his head, frustrated. Although he comes from a family of popos datin back to "The Original Nine," he hasn't been able to get no info, which is weird.

"So, why do it?"

"What if it's personal?" PYT joins us at the bush. "Think bout it like a tattoo. You get it for personal reasons, and even tho you might tell people a story behind it, it's yours, somethin you only know the meaning behind." He shows us the one on the front of his hand, a rose growin out the mouth of a skull. "Somebody got down and carved it into the door on purpose, but at the same time, they aint like none of the gangs or crews we know who tag a spot then be all out here wit loose lips. If I took the time out to do somethin like that, it aint bout street cred, it's bout doin a deed and knowin I'm the one who did it."

We look at each otha. That kind of truth don't bring no comfort or no ease.

Trish phone rings. Outkast's "Hey Ya!" plays. It don't change what we know or feel, but it helps. I take a deep breath, let it out, and stretch my fingers. I aint even realize

I had them balled into a fist the whole time PYT was talkin.

"Hey, Uncle Darryl," Trish says, smiling, nervous. "Unh-unh . . . Well, I meant to tell you but— . . . Uh-huh, no I— . . . Okay. Yes, sir . . . Unh-unh . . . On my way. Sorry." She hangs up.

"You aint even tell him you was comin, did you?"

"Yeaahhhh nnnnoooo?"

I shake my head. "Aight, let's go. We'll be back at the grocery store in five, just in case yo unc calls back."

I wrap my arm round Trish's shoulder, doin my best to hide the truth of what I gotta do next. I can't let this all lead to a dead end, I gotta talk to somebody hella connected—somebody who might have a clue what these sigils are and who this symbol might represent. And I know exactly who—and that ain't nobody gon like my plan.

"I need to see Lady Tee."

Reyna at the front desk just stares at me, battin her long eyelashes, the makeup round her eyes painted emerald and gold. "Okay . . ."

"Can you call her? It's important."

"I'm sorry, Leroy, but she's not taking any visitors at the moment."

I look at Brown Brown to my left and PYT to my right to see if they got any ideas. Yeah, I prolly shoulda thought this through a lil more, but it was hard enough waitin until 9:00

p.m. just to get out here befo the lounge opened.

Brown Brown licks his lips and tries to put on the charm. "Come on, Rey, he just needs—"

A few dancers walk through the front door. She scans their IDs, taps on her keyboard, and presses a button that unlocks the black door behind the bouncer next to her. He waves them in, tells them to keep their IDs so they can be scanned at the next door.

PYT leans in real close, whispers in my ear. "There's bout six guards between us and the club entrance. If you really need to get in there, I can make it happen."

I shake my head and walk back up to the counter.

"Please?" I say, desperate.

Reyna chuckles, almost charmed. "Cute, real cute. But the answer is still no. . . . I'm sorry. I can leave her a message, though."

"But it's bout Taj," I blurt out. "He missin."

"I hear you, Leroy. And Lady Tee is on it. That's why she can't speak to you. She's been in meetings all day, even met with the police chief to put pressure on him to find a lead."

"How she—" I smother the words befo they come out.

Of course Lady Tee know what happened. She prolly the first person Rissa called. But if she talkin to the police chief, she prolly don't know no mo than they do.

"She gon wanna speak to me, then," I say.

"Why? If she's already spoken to—"

"Cuz I got this." I hand her Trish's sketch. "And if she don't already know what this mean, she don't have a clue who took my brotha. But I do, and I'm only talkin to her, directly."

Reyna looks at the symbol, then back up at me. She picks up the phone, then presses a button, tells Lady Tee, then just hangs up. "She'll see you—but only you."

Reyna buzzes me inside, but I walk into a different entrance than the last time. Instead of goin straight across into the club part, the bouncers make me go right to some elevators and up to the sixth floor.

When the door opens, I aint sure I'm where I need to be, but I step out anyway and follow a long hallway covered in African masks and art pieces, till I see an office. From the outside, it don't look big as nothin, but when I walk in, it's huge. In the center is a big black marble table. Each of the chairs round it are different, like thrones fit for kings, queens, or knights. I don't know what chair to sit in, so I just stand and wait.

"Take a seat, Leroy." Lady Tee's standin behind me in an all-white dress wit specks of gold that match all her bracelets. She walks to the head of the table, sits at the only all-black chair that looks like it's made of stone. I sit in the chair closest to the door, not directly across from her but off to the right.

"Sorry to drop by unexpected but—"

"Tell me what you think you know." Her bracelets sing as she crosses her wrists.

"You first." I'm the one wit the information.

She studies me, smiles. "I think you're here because you've hit a brick wall trying to find out who kidnapped your brother—and you're willing to do anything to find him, even if it means recklessly flaunting that symbol."

"You know what it means?"

"See, Leroy? You don't know *what* you don't know. So I'm going to tell you what Rissa and Taj haven't in hopes of keeping you safe because you keep doing what you're doing, you're going to get yourself killed."

I sit up in my chair, listening. "Okay, tell me."

"No, you first," she says, grinnin.

I wonder if she would be doin the same thing if somebody she love was missin, and she aint know if they was alive, gettin tortured, or worse. But I keep my cool and just answer.

"I think Rouk and his crew did this. They all share the same tattoo, this symbol. It's the same symbol carved into our old house, the motel where they tried to finish the job, Rissa's home when Taj and Night was kidnapped—errwhere we eva been attacked."

"What else?"

"Ion think they did it alone. Somebody backin em."

"Who?" she asks, watchin me closely.

"Whoeva carries this symbol. I know it aint no outside gang or one from round here. But iono mo than that; it's why I wanted to talk to you."

She nods. "I'm looking into it, too. And you're right—

somebody is behind them. I don't know who yet, either. The key to figuring this out isn't just asking who is responsible, it's figuring out who benefits."

I don't know what she means, and I aint tryna hide it. I just want her to get to it and quit speakin in riddles.

"Your dad created the BDs to protect the community from one of the main ways we've been stripped of our power, money, and wealth—our property. For years, they've been working on a plan that nobody can know about because it'll not only help us protect what's ours—but it will also ensure we can build and access our own generational wealth, and never be taken advantage of by these people again. That's why Taj, in particular, has been having such a hard time. The stakes are high and the stress higher, with no room for failure."

"I thought it was cuz of the gangs, the cease-fire, and—"

"Think bigger. Those are just tactics they are using to attack the BDs, to make people lose faith in them and destroy them from within because there are a lot of people who stand to lose millions if our plan works. I think that's what's really at the heart of all these attacks."

"So Taj and Rissa knew exactly who been after us? They been lyin the whole time?"

"I told you, Leroy. I don't know, *we* don't know who is hiding behind this symbol. And we didn't know about Rouk, but if what you said is true, then now we have a lead."

I shake my head, exhausted. "So what now? Just tell me what to do and I'll do it."

"When it comes to this symbol and what you know, let Rissa and the BDs handle it. You've done more than enough on that front."

"I can't do that; they need my help to stop this."

"I agree, but not by focusing on this symbol. I think you can do the one thing no one else can—find out who is behind everything—and you can do it with this." Lady Tee holds up a blue flash drive.

"What is it?"

"I don't know. It was in my mailbox this morning, which means it was hand-delivered because there's no postage. But the return address was Faa's, and I think this might be the key—the evidence to prove who has been behind all of this. That's what Faa was working with Taj on before he was murdered and what he died for." She holds up the flash drive between us. "It's encrypted, and I need the password to access it. Did he ever mention something like this to you or Taj? Do you have any idea what the password might be? We've tried everything: birthdays, streets, names. Nothing works. We suspect it might only be numbers, but we can't say for sure."

"No, he neva said nothin to me—and Taj aint round for me to ask. I don't know nothin bout no password."

"Well, take this and keep trying. Without your brother here, you're the only one who was both close enough to Faa that I can trust and might be able to figure it out. But, Leroy, a word of advice," Lady Tee says, puttin the drive in my hand

and closin it into a fist. "This is the biggest weapon we could have to fight against whoever this is, so keep it close—and trust no one."

"How I know I can trust you?"

Lady Tee lets my hand go, smirks. "You don't. But right now, I'm the only one you can."

I look at the drive in the palm of my hand, unsure of where to even begin. But I gotta trust myself, cuz back when Taj mentioned he and Faa worked together, I knew that whoeva killed Faa might have been after Taj—after us. I got so focused on Rouk, I let myself forget what my gut knew and neva realized it was the missin piece.

I can't do that again—too many lives at stake. It won't happen again cuz Imma keep tryin, and aint nothin gon stop me.

"Whatchu mean there's no updates? It's been seventy-two hours," Rissa yells into the phone.

Me, Ma, PYT, and Brown Brown sittin in the diner at the counter starin at her in shock. It's goin on day four and don't nobody still got no answers. It's almost like there aint no trace or no place—like eitha Taj and Night disappeared off the face of the planet or they don't wanna be found.

"Come again? Get me Detective Dane. Tell him Rissa callin bout Taj Booker and Kasim Brathwaite who goes by 'Night.'"

"Tell him you called yesterday, and he told you to call

back today," Ma says, hopeful.

"I'm not callin back. Somebody from there told me to call back yesterday and the day befo that. I'm not hangin up till I talk to Detective Dane, who told me personally to call him if I had any questions."

Benji tries to calm her down, rub her shoulders, but she shrugs him off.

"No . . . No . . . Mhmm . . . Yes, Detective Dane . . . That's fine, just get me somebody else to talk to, then . . . What? Do I have to do yo job for you or are you gon finally act like you give a damn bout Black children? Now, let me tell *you* somethin— . . . Hello? Hello!" Rissa slams the phone down on the receiver ova and ova till Benji pull her into his arms.

Ma wipes away silent tears. I put my arm round her, let her lean in. "If it was bout drugs or a shootin they woulda found them befo we even got up there, but since they the victims they draggin they feet."

Errbody looks when they see somebody walkin toward the front door of the diner, but it's only Jacobee.

"Hey, sorry I'm late. Any new updates?" He daps Benji, then side-hugs Rissa.

"No, it's that police chief. I swear I don't know who side he on," Rissa explains.

"Or who pocket he got his hand in." Ma rubs the top of Jacobee's hands on her shoulders.

Errbody shakes they head in silence. Aint the first time

the popos aint care nothin bout us missin. It's a miracle they found Faa at all, and that's only cuz he was loved by errbody.

Jacobee stands behind me, hugs me from the side. "Feelin betta?" he whispers.

I nod. Last night, Jacobee drove wit me for a few hours so I could cry, cuss, and fuss till it was all outta my system. Part of me feel like he let me cuz he wanted to do it, too, but couldn't. He been round mo eva since Taj went missin, even been to me and Ma's spot, helpin her cook so stuff that aint bacon don't taste like it. And on days that Rissa havin it hard cuz she missin Taj, he steps in at the diner wit Benji, gets all the food to the tables wit that irresistible smile.

Brown Brown gets up and walks outta the diner, pissed. PYT runs out to catch him or at least see what's wrong, but he waves him off. He hops in his car, peels off without eva sayin where he goin or what he doin. The stress don't do nothin but get worse the longer Taj and Night are gone.

Brown Brown been takin it harder for a reason he won't explain. Iono if it's cuz he don't like Jacobee bein round so much and gettin so close to errbody or if it's cuz he don't feel like he doin enough. For some reason, errbody he know on the force still keep ghostin him and eitha won't tell him nothin or threaten to tell his folks to get him in trouble for mindin errbody else business.

"That's it. I aint waitin anotha minute. Benji, getcho keys. You find Dane, and Imma call an emergency BD meetin,

OGs only. If the popos gon pretend they don't know what's goin on when I know they know betta, we gon do it *our* way."

Me and PYT stand up, too.

"Where yall goin?" she asks, one hand on her hip, her purple purse hangin from her elbow.

"We goin witchu."

"No, you not. I need yall to stay here wit Tanya, keep her safe till we know who is who and what is what."

She right, and I know it, but don't make me wanna go wit her any less. I wanna be where she at if there's half a chance that it gets her closer to findin Taj.

"We can go together *after* I chat wit the BDs and know where to—"

Rissa's eyes go to the parking lot. Two black Mercedes-Benz cars and a G-Class SUV pull up out front. Their windows are slightly tinted, but there's someone who looks like it could be Taj, but aint nobody gettin out. Then the doors open, and men in dark blue suits get out and stand on all sides.

"Benji, we got company," Rissa yells.

She pulls Ma ova to her, and Jacobee pushes me toward the kitchen. PYT moves behind one of the columns near the diner. He reaches into his bag, pulls out a Glock wit a long clip.

"Wait," Ma screams. "That might be Taj, that might be my baby."

"Tanya, we don't know that yet. I promise, we'll wait and see. But I need you safe."

Ma nods, breathes deep. Benji comes out the back wit a vest on, and a few mo in his hands. Rissa gives one of the vests to Ma, helps her put it on.

"PYT," Benji yells. He tosses one ova to him; PYT catches it. Puts his on, too. Jacobee sees two extras on the shelf in the room wit the cot, gives me one and puts his on.

"Any movement?" Benji shouts.

"None yet. They just standin there, doin nothin," PYT answers.

Benji has two guns in his hands, and anotha two in holsters. He turns to Jacobee, hands him one. "Know how to use this?" he asks.

"Point and squeeze to shoot?" He flips the safety off.

"Pretty much. Yall stay back here. If anything goes wrong, go down this hatch and lock it. Follow the lights, and you'll end up on the otha side. My guys will be here in two minutes to help us out."

"Tanya, I put one in ya purse, too," Rissa says.

"I won't need it," she says. "I just want Taj. Don't let nothin happen to him."

"We won't," Benji says to her. "But be ready to protect him, if you need to."

"I will. You don't have to worry bout that." Beneath the tears, the exhaustion, Ma still there—and she aint neva been weak.

One of the SUV's doors opens, and Taj steps out. Once

the door closes, the guards hop back in, one by one, and then, the cars and SUV speed off.

My feet won't move. I can't tell if this furreal or a dream.

Benji and PYT wait behind the columns, watch as Taj walks up to the diner and opens the door. Errthang is clear and the cars seem to be gone. But Benji and PYT stay posted up, ready for anything that might pop off. Ma runs up to him, pulls Taj into her arms, as Rissa cries holdin them both. When they let him go, Benji moves to bear-hug him, and PYT pulls him in by the shoulders.

"Where's Night?" PYT asks.

"He home, got dropped off first," Taj says, holdin him back.

Jacobee walks up to him, pulls Taj in, holds him close, longer than I eva seen him do befo.

I still can't move. I'm too scared to speak, too scared to blink, worried that if I do, he might disappear, and I'll wake up trapped in a nightmare where Taj is still missin and there aint no hope in findin him.

Could-be-Taj stands in front of me, lookin me in my eyes. He smells like peppermint and Cool Water cologne—the way it smells only on Taj. He stares at me just like Taj does, eyes soft, face hard, except for the almost smile. But I still won't move, won't believe it. I don't wanna risk it not bein real, even as my eyes get blurry and my lips quiver and I tilt my head up so the tears don't fall.

Could-be-Taj puts his hand behind my head, pulls me to

him, even tho I resist cuz all I know to do in this moment is stand still and hold it all in, just in case.

Could-be-Taj kisses me on the forehead, hugs me tight like Taj would, like he sayin he won't let me go, like he sayin he missed me. Could-be-Taj holds on to me till I know: it's really him.

"So, who was the entourage," Rissa says, eyes scannin Taj like a lie detector.

"Iono . . . they aint say much. All I know is they saved us. Chopped down whoeva it was surroundin the house and pulled us out befo they made it thru the front door."

Errbody stares at Taj, waitin on the rest of the story.

"There was a lady wit em. Rose, or somethin like that; she aint say who she worked for, just that they been keepin an eye on errthang, had to jump in when they saw what was comin. Iono if she the one in charge, but errbody listen to her—and only her. She said she'd be in contact."

"Rose, huh? You sure? It doesn't ring a bell. I know some folks with similar names but not that one." Rissa nods, thinkin. "I'll see if Lady Tee knows who she is, will pass the name round some otha contacts. Benji, can you ask round, too? I doubt she runnin round wit that many men and nobody heard of her."

"What's next, Taj? You look like you got a plan," Benji says, arms crossed.

"Wait, befo you get to that. There's something I gotta say. Lee, come here," Rissa says.

I slowly walk ova, not sure what she wants me to do or say.

"You were right," Rissa says. "And I want errbody to know. I'm sorry I didn't pay mo attention to what you said bout Rouk and those guys in his crew. I asked round, and nobody could give me a name, but the two guys always wit him have been seen errwhere. And not just recently, maybe even nine months ago round the time of—"

"Faa's murder?" I say.

Rissa nods. "Yeah. There's no proof they did that, but I want you to know the BDs are on it."

Taj looks at me. "You knew all this?"

"Yeah," I say, tryna keep my words straight. "But I thought that if I told you errthang without any proof, you wouldn't believe me."

"Lee, don't eva think that. Eva . . . cuz what you know might be the one thing we need to save somebody's life," Taj says. "It's alright, tho. Now that we know bout Rouk and these two guys, we'll figure out a way to catch them, together—like always."

15

JAY

I've been looking for Will everywhere, but I can't find him. I consider walking to the other side of K-Heights to Daffin Park, where we went bike riding, but I haven't seen his bike for a few days, so the only place left to look is the playground. I hope wherever he is, whatever he's feeling, he'll talk to me.

Not far from the slide, around the corner of one of the buildings, I hear something. It sounds like it could be Will's voice. I follow it quietly, just to make sure. I don't want to see anything I'm not supposed to if it doesn't have anything to do with him, so I stay out of sight. The voices get louder, and then I hear scuffling. I peek around the corner, *CRASH!*

Will slams so hard into me, we both tumble, but he quickly yanks me to my feet. "Run!"

Behind us: three guys are chasing, gaining on us fast. Will darts right, jumps over a neighbor's bushes, and we sprint through the backyards, leap over toys, flowerpots, even a weight bench.

I lead us down the other side of the apartments, toward the playground we'd visited before, run into the entrance under the slide to a big cone tree in front of a wooden fence. There I see it: a hole big enough for each of us to crouch through.

We slip through just in time and run down the side of a ditch. Right before we have to decide to go left or right, I see the street name: Willow Tree Boulevard. It sounds familiar—it's Lavender Terrace, where my dad is. That's not far, maybe a block or two, less if we cut through the back of the apartment complex in front of us. Turning around isn't an option. Do I lead us across the complex, into Lavender Terrace? Whatever is waiting for me there is sure as hell better than whoever is chasing us.

I look at Will, panting, with cuts and a bruised lip. "Follow me!" I say.

We weave through houses built similar to the other complex. We don't stop, even when Will trips, even as we're slapped and whipped by bamboo trees—the only barrier between this complex and the next. We keep going, until we see a maintenance shed painted purple, off in the distance, on the other side of the complex.

Then I see him: well, I spot a man standing, watering lavender blossoms, his back to us. But I'd recognize his back and shoulders anywhere—from my nightmares and daydreams.

"Dad," I scream. More desperate than I want to. "We need your help!"

When he turns around and I see his face, every bone in

my body shakes, but now isn't a time to be scared, I need to protect us, to survive. Without saying a word, he pulls me and Will toward him, then pushes us into the shed, locks it from the other side.

"Wait. . . . It's dangerous," I yell-whisper.

Will taps my shoulder. "What's the name of these apartments?"

"Lavender Terrace, on Willow Tree Boulevard," I say.

He reaches for a phone in his pocket. "We're in Lavender Terrace apartments, on Willow Tree Boulevard, near a maintenance shed, I think behind the apartments across the street from the pool. Hurry!" He snaps the flip phone closed.

Through small spaces in the shed panels, we can just barely see everyone as they walk up. Rouk? Beside him are two guys with locs. I look over at Will, confused. His face says it all: *It's complicated, I'll tell you later.*

"Can I help you?" my dad says casually.

Rouk is winded, but the other guys stand firm, strong. The one with shorter locs speaks. "You see anybody come round here?"

"None but y'all."

The guy with longer locs sizes Dad up, as if he's waiting for proof that he's lying—an excuse to strike.

For a second, I swear Rouk's eyes find mine between the cracks. He doesn't say anything, but I can tell he knows we're in the shed.

"Shit, did you see that?" I ask Will. "I think Rouk can see me."

He shakes his head. "I don't think so, if he could—"

Will's phone vibrates so loud, I swear it's a ringtone all by itself. My heart drops.

"What's that?" the one with the shorter locs says.

"What's what?"

"You aint hear that? Sound like a phone."

"Probably. I leave my phone in the shed all the time."

"That's yo phone?"

"Why? You wanna answer *my* phone?" Dad's voice isn't pretending anymore.

The one with the longer locs finally speaks, and it sends a chill through my body. "Why dontchu go and get it . . . out of the shed. Might be important." His voice sounds like he's seen and done things—and lived to talk about it.

"Probably not. Anybody need me know where to find me."

The guy with the longer locs laughs. "We don't want no trouble . . . but it might find you . . . if I gotta ask again."

Somewhere else, not far from the shed, something falls and breaks.

"That might be them," Rouk yells. "Yall go. We can't let them get away." Again, his eyes find mine and then look away.

I was right, but I don't know why he's protecting us. "I'll get him to let me in the shed. But right now, yall wastin time." The one with shorter locs nods, but the other one stands still, listening. He starts to walk slowly past Dad in the other direction—

Suddenly something slams into the shed door, shaking everything around us. There's grunting, hits landing, more slamming. Wood breaking. Yells. More voices, way more voices. More fighting. Then the sound that makes my heart stop: a gunshot.

I can't take it. I gotta make sure he's—

"You can come out now," a voice says. But it's not my dad's.

Will is about to open the door, I pull his hand away.

"It's okay. I know that voice," he says.

"Jay, you in there?" Leroy says.

I stare at the door, unsure. Why would he be here?

I open it. Leroy is standing next to Taj and some other faces I don't recognize, but Rouk is standing with his hands up next to the guy with the shorter locs, who is on his knees with a bleeding lip.

Taj names the two guys holding guns on both of them—Brown Brown, a face I recognize from Jacob's track meets, and PYT, a lighter-skinned guy with long pretty hair. They walk Rouk and the one with shorter locs in a different direction, but not before Rouk looks at me one last time and nods in a way that confuses me—with no anger or hate, a softness.

Dad is standing on the other side and has the guy with the dangerous smile in a wristlock, who refuses to scream out in pain even though he can't move—not if he wants his wrist to remain intact.

Taj and someone who looks like a bigger, taller, version of him—a guy he calls Night—nod at Dad to release him. When Dad lets go, the guy looks back at him and smirks, then slowly walks by Taj, Leroy, and Night, chin up and eyes narrowed. Taj slaps him upside the head, hard enough to hurt his pride but little else. He stops, looks over at Taj, but before he can say anything, Night shoves him forward in the direction of the others. As Taj leaves, he winks at Will, chucks the deuces.

Will mouths, *Thank you*.

"You good?" Leroy says, standing close but not too close. He looks at me but keeps glancing over at Will.

"I don't know. What just happened?" I ask, looking at Will, then Leroy, hoping either one of them can give me some answers. Dad does the same, his face a labored frown trying to make sense of what's in front of him.

"How did you find me, Jay? You weren't supposed to be there." Will is red in the face, frustrated. "That could've been really bad. You could've gotten—"

"What were you doing there, Will?" I snap back.

He won't look at me. Won't say anything.

It hits me: Will is scared, too. His hands are shaking, but he hides them behind his back.

"There's somewhere we need to be," Leroy says, looking

at Will, who nods. "You know where Auntie Rissa's Chicken and Waffles is?"

Will shakes his head. "But I think I can find it if—"

"No, wait. What?" I say, irritated. "What are you talking about? How did you even meet?" I turn to Leroy. "Did y'all plan this together?"

"Not really, but kinda," Will says, only bothering to answer my last question.

"So you plan to just go to Auntie Rissa's? For what?"

"There's a meeting to talk about—"

"You can't go," Leroy says.

"Why not? You're going. He's going."

"Cuz it aint safe."

"You don't get to tell me what is and isn't safe. You lost that right when you sent me that note saying we couldn't be together."

"I told you why: it wasn't safe then, eitha."

"No, you wrote it. You never said anything to me and I—"

"Errthang I do is cuz I wanna keep you safe. Ion wantchu gettin hurt again—"

"Aye!" Dad yells. Even the bees stop buzzing. "We're all going. And Will and Jay, your moms will decide how involved you will or won't be because I doubt Julia or Lin know exactly what's going on, either."

Will and Leroy nod silently. But I don't. I refuse. My dad's voice still reverberates in my bones, and I can feel the rage coming back, and the fear along with it.

"I'm not going anywhere with you," I growl.

"Jay." His words are calm, but I don't trust them. "That's for Julia—"

"You don't get to tell me what to do anymore, either. Not after what you did."

He breathes in deep. "Well, what do you want, Jay? 'Cuz I don't know how to be anything in this moment but your father, after doing exactly what you wanted me to do: keep you safe."

All I can feel is dread—a heavy, invisible hand pressing down on my chest, squeezing—while I look over at him. The danger is gone, but everything I once felt rushes over me.

Before I know it, I'm running as fast as I can down the street because if I don't, if I don't get away, it feels like the earth will open up and hands of fire will drag me into a fiery abyss.

I hear my dad calling out behind me, "Jay . . . Wait . . . Jay," but I need to go as far away from him as possible, until I can figure out how the monster that was once my dad, after all those years, does the one thing I don't expect him to, without a second thought: protect me.

I end up at the steepleless church next to the oak tree. My hands are trembling, my heart racing, and I just want to scream. But screaming isn't enough. I need to hit, to fight back, in the way I didn't years ago. I need to get this feeling out of my body, this fear, this rage, this yearning for love from him. It hurts, and I want to hurt it right back. Scattered among some branches is a broken leg from a wooden chair. I pick it up, clench it in the sweat of my palm. In my body, I want to cry, but tears aren't enough for this kind of breaking, so I fight the phantoms in my memories.

That night six years ago was like many other nights, but something felt wrong. The man who kicked off his shoes near the front door didn't seem like our dad anymore; his voice was rough, too rough. He smelled off, and he didn't look at me and Jacob like he used to—he just sneered at us and mumbled under his breath as he walked past the living room toward the kitchen.

Jacob motioned for me to turn off the TV so we could go upstairs and let Dad crash on the couch like he always did, but Dad stopped us. He called me over near the part of the kitchen that looked like a bar, mumbled a question I couldn't understand—and this version of Dad never liked repeating himself. When he asked again and I didn't answer, he slapped me so hard I fell to the floor, silent.

"I ain't raise no faggot," he said.

"Leave him alone, you mark-ass bitch!" Jacob yelled, crying. The words weren't his own; they belonged to the hard boys who called themselves real niggas; boys who were thirteen, fighting in the streets to survive.

I sat there, stunned. No tears. No sound. Nothing, until

I looked up at Dad, wondering what he meant by that word, what I did wrong.

By the time I realized what was happening, the barstool crashed into the wooden floor and all I could hear was Jacob shriek.

It could have been a punch or a slap or a grab. It happened so fast I couldn't say. All I know: Dad hit Jacob so hard he couldn't cry, he couldn't breathe, struggled to get loose—Dad's hands were too big, too strong, too tight around his neck. I don't remember what Dad said to him, only the heat and sweet of his breath, after I ran over to him, clawed at his arms to make him let go, but it didn't work. Nothing did. Dad was too much, and we were too little of everything we needed to be in that moment, too weak.

For the first time, our dad's strength was used against us. "Dad" is the only thing I screamed over and over, hoping he would save us from himself. But Dad didn't let go until Jacob passed out and fell to the floor.

Jacob woke up in my arms just as Momma pulled into the driveway. My screams now a tired whimper. Jacob begged me to stop, wiped my face, and told me not to tell Momma what happened. He dragged me upstairs with him while her headlights still shined through the curtains so we could change clothes. His shirt was ripped at the collar; mine was overstretched in the struggle. After we changed into our pj's, I got in Jacob's bed, and as Momma opened the front door, he whispered he believed Dad was sorry and that he didn't mean it. He said the bruises on his neck didn't really hurt.

Like a prayer that wouldn't come true if you didn't believe hard enough in the right god, he said that when Dad comes back, everything will be normal. We'll be a family again, but only if we forget. If we don't remember, it won't be bad enough to tell her. He knew what I knew: if Momma found out, it would hurt her. She needed us, and she needed Dad.

We needed to stay together as a family. He said it over and over until he believed it, until he forgot, until I got better at pretending in the time it took Momma to get from the front door, up the stairs, and into his room. When Momma asked where Jacob got the bruises from, he said it was a fight with some boys in the neighborhood. Ma believed him because she didn't have enough time not to.

The police called Ma when she kissed us on the forehead, and they told her Dad had attacked someone, a white man and his wife, in Avalon Park, the wealthiest neighborhood in Savannah. Watching her fight back tears and sound calm, we wondered even then why she never asked why; why she didn't look surprised; why when they called, the way she stared at the phone before she answered was almost as if she already knew a side of Dad we'd only met in secret.

As she held us and cried, we stretched our arms around her. Jacob promised he would do anything to keep us safe, to make sure Momma never cried like that again, and I promised to do everything I could to never have to feel that helpless.

I swing at the tree, ignoring the shock of what feels like the tree slapping back on the other end of the wooden leg. I flail and fail to do more than chip the bark. I'm a warrior outnumbered and outgunned with nothing but rage to press on, until that eventually breaks after I whack at the metal grates of the sign that reads "Church Parking Only."

I have nothing left. I can barely stand. I don't know if I won or lost the battle, but I damn sure plan on winning the war, even if it means I go down fighting. And there's only one way to do that. I close my eyes, gather my strength. If telling the truth doesn't set us free, and the only thing it does is turn up the heat, then let it at least be worth the burn.

When I walk through the front door, Will seems relieved, but his face is heavy and weary. Mom's eyes are a choke chain that keeps Jacob at bay as he glares at Dad sitting on the couch. I swear every muscle and vein in Jacob bulges, waiting for the chance to tear Dad limb from limb. But Momma's hold on us is stronger than any monster—the ones we know and the ones we don't.

"Jay, where have you been?" she says. "Better yet, what's this meeting about and why in the hell are boys from the neighborhood jumping on you and Will?"

I look at Mom, then at Dad. But all I can think about is that he shouldn't be here.

I move before I lose my nerve, I speak before Jacob loses

his cool. I walk right up to Dad, stand in front of him and look him in the eyes and ask, "Why are you here?"

"Jay," Jacob says, as anger melts into full-on panic, fear. But I won't stop, not now. It's my turn to protect him, to protect us.

"How could you do that to me, to Jacob, and sit here like it never happened?"

Dad shakes his head. "You're right."

"Jay, what's going on?" Momma asks. "If this is about why your dad was sent to prison, we can talk about—"

"You know how bad you hurt me?" I promised I wouldn't cry, I promised I wouldn't be weak in front of him. But all I have is what I got right now in this moment: knees that won't stop shaking, lips that won't stop quivering, eyes that won't stop filling, and a voice that dares to speak regardless.

He nods, doesn't say anything.

"Do you know how it feels to"—my voice breaks—"hate yourself—" My throat aches, and the words won't come out, but I refuse to be silent. I growl through the pain and try to speak.

Jacob walks over, pulls at me to stop.

"No, I need to say this. I need him to—" My voice breaks again. "I need him . . . to know . . . what he did . . . to us."

"Jacob, what's he talking about?" Momma asks, realizing this isn't about what Dad did to go to prison. It's about something she doesn't know about, something she should.

Jacob can't speak. Whatever has ahold of me is gripping him because I can feel it: he's trembling and can barely stand. He came over to stop me, to protect me, but in his arms, I will become his sword and shield—I will do the protecting.

"No, Jacob doesn't have to say anything." I look Dad straight in the eye. "Tell her, tell her what you did to us."

Momma looks at Dad, whose eyes are just like ours, as he wipes away the rogue tears falling from his eyes. He clears his throat, breathes in and out, and tells Momma everything that happened before he left that night, before he attacked the couple—when he hit me, called me a faggot, and choked Jacob for daring to protect me and, in more ways than one, gave up and walked out of our lives.

The whole time Momma listens and nods. She doesn't speak, she doesn't cry, she doesn't do anything, just holds everything, all of us, in the wide arms of her attention until every word is spoken and all that's left is for us to look at her, to see what happens next.

"Boys, go upstairs." She looks at Dad, eyes burning hot like coals. "We need to talk."

In the hallway, I want to go in Jacob's room, but I don't know if he is upset with me for doing something I'd promised I'd never do.

Will and I watch Jacob, waiting. Jacob looks over, lets out a weak grin—permission to enter.

We can't all fit in the bed comfortably, so I grab a heavy blanket from the hallway closet and prop up the fan, so it points in our direction. Will and I sit on the floor, and then all of us, including Jacob, sprawl out and stare at the ceiling.

I can't hear anything Mom and Dad are saying. Part of me wants to listen, part of me doesn't. I just want to stay on the blanket with Jacob and Will and pretend it's a deserted island. If I close my eyes, I can almost hear it: our limbs grazing the blanket, the sound of waves in the ocean; our breath, air currents floating above us comingling with the artificial wind fresh off the steel wings of birds sending signals that something is coming.

Jacob's voice growls in his chest, deeper and hoarse from the strain. "I'm sorry I tried to stop you, Jay. I just . . . I don't know. This whole time, I thought I was the strongest, which is why I had to try to do it all, but I wonder if that's what made me the weakest. . . ." His voice trails off.

"You're here. I'm here. It means we both are strong, even if we don't feel it."

We lie there in silence, under the waves of the wind, listening to nothing, to everything.

Will looks over at me, pushes his arm against mine, reaches for one hand. "I'm sorry, about earlier . . . that I didn't tell you."

For a second I forgot about the whole thing, Will and Leroy knowing each other.

“’Bout what?” Jacob says, looking at both of us.

“Rouk and some of the guys from his crew tried to jump me—and Jay happened to run into us and things got a li’l crazy . . . ,” Will says. “Long story short: they chased us, and Jay somehow led us to the complex where your dad was, and he protected us, gave me a chance to call Leroy and Taj. It was supposed to be a trap for Rouk and his guys, but then Jay got all mixed up in it.”

Jacob’s eyes couldn’t get any wider. He just stares at Will, speechless. “How did you—”

“That’s kind of a long story, too, that you and both our parents are probably gon’ hear tonight when we go to Rissa’s—along with I don’t know what else.”

Jacob looks at me, lies back down, and just reaches for my other hand.

In the silence, it feels like each of us are asking the same questions: How did we get here? What do we do now? The answer: nothing. The only thing we can do is wait for when we get to the diner and everything is revealed—whatever that is.

A part of me is scared, thinking back on the words Leroy said, that everything he did was to protect me. I’m still hurt about the note, but if what he said was true, it might make things more complicated than they already are, and I just can’t take it. All of it is so nerve-racking. I don’t realize how exhausted I am—we all are—until, at some point, we fall asleep. But when we wake up, Jacob is holding me and I am holding Will.

There's a gentle knock on the door. I can tell it's Momma.

Before Jacob and I can sit up, she comes in and kneels down, tells us not to. She doesn't speak at first, just takes it all in, the picture of us holding each other like we did when we were younger. Then she hugs our faces and whispers, "I have so much I want to say. But all I can say right now is thank you and I'm sorry. I know you were trying to protect me, but it's my job to protect you." She pauses, breathes in, holds back tears. "I love you with every fiber of my being. And as long as I have breath in my body, I will protect you from anyone and anything, even if it's from your father."

She kisses both of us on our foreheads, even rubs Will's curls, who is still fast asleep.

"Now go ahead and get some sleep, before it's time to go to the meeting. I just wanted to tell you both that J.D. is gone, and he'll stay gone, until you say otherwise."

"You okay?" Jacob asks, reaching for her hand.

"No, baby, I'm not, but I will be. Just gon' take some time. You don't have to worry about me." She's about to get up and leave but stares at Jacob's hand holding hers. "But you know what would make me feel better?"

Jacob and I sit up, ready to do anything for her.

"Got room for one more?"

We nod and move over as she slides between me and Jacob

until she is holding us and we are holding her. As if on cue, Will turns over and holds me, so he's connected to us as well. On the floor, listening to the rickety fan and the silence that won't stop talking, I know this is just the beginning and that there's a long road ahead of us, but we'll be okay, as long as we have each other.

Auntie Rissa's Chicken and Waffles is a grim, gloomier version of its former self. But Rissa, herself, is still a beacon of light. Where she was once in vibrant colors and every word a song followed by the melodic tap of her multicolored nails, she shimmers black sequins, hair slicked down in finger waves instead of her high bun.

Some of the faces from earlier are there, gathered around the counter: Leroy, the guys he called PYT and Brown Brown, and Benji. There's also a woman I believe is Leroy's mother based on how similar they look and how he hovers close to her.

When Rissa sees us, she comes to life just a little: she hugs me tight to prove how happy she is to see me, even winks at Jacob and Will and does courteous cheek kisses to Momma. The lady near Leroy, who introduces herself as Miss Tanya, is his mother after all. She grasps hands with Momma, flashing a warm smile of knowing. She remembers her, too, apparently.

Still waiting on the guests of the hour, Rissa turns up the

heat just a little and has Benji whip up some appetizers, so there's a little more life in the room, she says. Some cars pull up, two black Mercedes-Benzes and a G-Class SUV. Taj walks in along with Night, five to seven men who look like bodyguards and . . . Miss Rosalind?

I look at Will. He's just as shocked.

Will looks at my mom for answers, but she don't seem to have any, either. He walks up to his mom, but there are no smiles, just yell-whispers back and forth that end with her putting her hands on his shoulders, calming him gently into submission. He smiles weakly, losing whatever battle he went over to fight.

Miss Rosalind doesn't look anything like the woman I saw a month ago who let Will give her a piggyback ride; her free-flowing sunflower dress is replaced with an all-white pantsuit with a light-blue blouse, her hair slicked back into a bun. She looks like a beautiful queen who fixes things—even if it means getting rid of them, regardless of how much it hurts. She glides by me, presses my shoulders, does the same to Jacob.

When she gets to Momma, she says something so softly, it's barely a whisper. Momma's eyes are smoldering embers and hers are kindling, between them a wildfire is burning. Momma nods, letting Miss Rosalind know they need to talk—but not now.

The bodyguards draw the shades and stand at all the

entrances and exits. Two hover within reach behind Miss Rosalind. When Taj and Leroy stand up, everybody waits for them to begin.

"Rouk confessed," Taj says, getting straight to the point. "He had somethin to do wit the shootin at our house a few months ago, his men runnin up on us at the motel. They were also the ones who tried to attack me at home a coupla days ago, but they couldn't, thanks to Miss Rosalind."

Me, Will, Jacob, and Momma look at Miss Rosalind. What does she have to do with this?

"They're behind the DKs, the symbol we kept findin err-where they attacked," Leroy adds. "We don't know what it really means yet, just that it's a 'D' and 'K' close together and a jagged crown, tilted to the side."

Taj continues. "When we realized they were prolly gonna make a move on Will, we set a trap for Rouk and his crew instead."

"What do you mean?" Miss Rosalind's eyes flash at Taj, then at Will. "Why would they do that? What's Will got to do with any of this?"

Will looks down but eventually speaks. "I was riding around a couple of days ago on my bike when I accidentally crashed into Rouk's car. His crew got pissed, and two guys tried to make me get in their car, but Taj stopped them. I think Rouk's crew figured I was somehow connected to them. Taj told me to call if I ever saw them again."

Miss Rosalind and Momma lock eyes, asking each other questions without words. I look at Jacob to see if he knew—nothing.

"I didn't tell anybody because I was embarrassed. But when I saw them again, parked nearby, I called Leroy, and he told me their plan. Things got complicated when Jay stumbled into me, but we were able to get out thanks to his dad and Taj's crew."

"Thank you for protecting Will and Jay, but don't ever involve either of them—are we clear?" Miss Rosalind says to Taj. She looks over at Momma, who nods with approval.

"You know betta," Tanya growl-whispers. "You aint raise no kids."

Rissa glares at Taj, too. She looks at Miss Rosalind and Momma. "I just want yall to know it will *never* happen again, aint that right, Bittersweet?"

"Yes, ma'am. I'm sorry. It won't."

"Does that mean it's over?" Momma asks.

"No, this goes deeper than that," Taj says. "Maybe a year ago, Faa came to me cuz he was workin on a story and noticed some unusual property purchases by a shell company. At first, he was gonna ignore it, but he realized all the properties bein bought up were only in K-Town, and at prices way cheaper than anybody would wanna sell. He aint know who it was, or what they goal was cuz nothing really changed in the neighborhood outside of the property rights exchange.

Won't no rent increases, no evictions, or auctions. So, eventually he brought to me, thinkin it might be somethin' the BDs might wanna look into.

"I knew who it could be, but I needed somethin more solid before I could bring it to Rissa and the OGs. Faa agreed to keep diggin and lemme know what he found. Eventually he told me he aint know who it was—they covered their tracks too well. But I at least had enough to show Rissa and explain why we should figure out how to get ahead of it. So Rissa got the OGs to move some money to buy up open property and protect anybody not tryna sell. I got all the YGs to hit the ground and spread the word so errbody could keep a lookout. Even told the heads of the gangs so they knew wat to look for."

Leroy shakes his head, clenching his jaw. I don't know if he knew any of this, but he doesn't like what he's hearing now. "Yall coulda told me what was goin on. I coulda did somethin, coulda helped."

"We did it to protect you, Lee," Rissa says. "Even we didn't know things were going to turn out the way they did. If we did, we probably woulda made a lot of different choices."

"Faa, he's that young man who was killed last fall, isn't he?" Momma asks.

Taj nods. "Yeah. Don't nobody know how it happened or who did it. But all of a sudden the popos tried to pin it on me—sayin that Faa was diggin up dirt on the BDs and that when I found out, I killed him."

Everyone looks at each other, waiting on him to finish.

"It aint true, tho. They used what little they knew to flip it cuz he called me the night he died, said he finally found something," Taj says, somber. "He said it was somethin the BDs needed to see and he was drivin ova to show me in person, but he neva made it."

"But he was just a kid. Why would they take it that far?" Miss Tanya asks.

"Not why, who," Taj says. "We think it was the Bainbridges."

"Wait. How do you know?" Leroy asks.

"Rouk finally told me. He said that the Bainbridges were the ones who fed him the lies about Faa diggin up dirt on the BDs. He wouldn't talk to nobody, cuz they had him thinkin errbody was out to get him, especially me and Lee. So he stayed away, and that whole time, he aint know they the ones who stand the most to gain from all that's been going on or lose if the BDs stopped their plans."

Momma and Rissa look at each other and don't turn away.

"Y'all know about them, too?" Miss Rosalind says, noticing their stare.

She looks over at Miss Tanya, who shifts uncomfortably in her seat, folds her arms. Miss Tanya looks like she wants to say something but doesn't.

"I know we do—a little too well," Momma says. "I

remember Tré talkin' to J.D. about somethin' like this, maybe ten years ago, when his landscape design business was just takin' off. Tré showed him a list of different people, mentioned how all of them were connected to the Bainbridges.

"Since J.D. knew a lot of them from his days at Providence Prep—some were still good friends—the two agreed to feed each other intel from time to time. Little stuff, just to help the BDs grow and prove they could get a stronghold and protect some of the communities that would have been gone. Back then, J.D. had two best friends who were Bainbridges. They saw things different, knew what their family had been doing and wanted to put a stop to it. So they gave J.D. whatever he needed, and that's what helped the BDs expand and really get in front of some of the stuff that was about to destroy them.

"Then, one day, out of nowhere, they flipped the table on J.D. Something must have happened because they suddenly wanted to use him to take down the BDs. When he refused, they destroyed his business almost overnight. The pressure eventually caused him to hurt our family, and when that happened, I realize now that he was lost. Next thing we know, J.D.'s in a courtroom facing six years in prison, after only pushing a bodyguard and punching his best friend at the time, Louis Bainbridge the Fourth. We watched as people we thought were our friends tried to put my husband away for decades. Fortunately, every judge can't be bought."

The room is silent, heavy, as if everyone else is playing memories of their own about running into one of the richest families in Savannah and living to tell the tale—with their own fair share of scars. I look at my momma, wonder how things might have been different for us, for everyone, if they never did.

"Lawda mercy," Miss Tanya says, shaking her head. "Aint they the whole reason most of us live near downtown anyway? It never ends. You move two steps forward, five steps backward. And for what? Only to have errthang you have taken from you. How is it fair that we make up more than half of this city but we can barely feed our kids?" Her voice breaks. "This shit aint fair—we aint do nothin to them; we just wanna live, and no matta what, they just wanna see us poor and in chains."

Rissa puts her arm around her. PYT hands her some tissues.

"We did errthang we knew to fight them the first time," Rissa says. "But even then, they had the judges, the popos, errbody. We put up a good fight, but they were always a step ahead, mo ruthless and willin to stoop so low—usin all they Red Summer tactics."

"What are Red Summer tactics?" PYT asks. Everybody waits on the answer.

"PYT, I aint surprised you don't know. But Brown Brown, yo folks can tell us betta than anybody can. Errbody I know, from my mom when she was alive to some of the OGs, can tell you: burnin down homes, burnin crosses, leavin dead animals on ya property, even lynchin. It's what happen all ova the country years ago. It still happens now, just not as out in the open with it. When they can't openly use their guns, mobs, and torches, they use the law to be even more dangerous, twisting errthang for their own benefit. But we know it when we see it."

The looks on everyone's faces are heavy with dread. Folks either shake their heads in dismay or purse their lips in defiance. Even though I don't know much about any of this—it's news to me—the adults around the room seem to know personally who these people are and what they can do.

"I'm not at liberty to discuss who, but one of the clients I represent has it on good authority that there's a bigger plan in motion, involving the Bainbridges and their desire to flex their power not just in Savannah but Georgia. It's what caused the Bainbridges to pop up on our radar and is why we moved to intervene. We're still putting together pieces as well, but a common enemy allies us with the BDs," Miss Rosalind says. "Were y'all able to find anything that Faa found? Any evidence of what they're planning that we could use against them?"

"Yes and no," Taj says.

Everybody looks at him, confused.

"What do you mean?" Rissa says. "You know somethin?"

"Rouk was involved but he eventually confirmed a suspicion I had the last time I saw him. He won't really the one in charge. The two guys who was always around him were secretly pullin the strings. They were the ones who told him he should roll up at the house and ask me to my face if I killed Faa. Rouk was down because he wanted to know, even if they had to beat it outta me, but when they got to shootin he realized they were mo dangerous than he thought.

"Eva since then, he been feelin guilty for his role in the shootin, especially when he found out Lee and Jay got hurt. But he was afraid if he said something, they might kill him. So he dropped off an encrypted flash drive he found in Faa's things to Lady Tee, hopin it might have somethin to stop them. She'll let me know when it's been unlocked."

"Did yall already turn Rouk ova to the cops? To Detective Dane?" Brown Brown asks.

Another circle of looks around the room by the adults.

"The two guys, yes. Rouk, not just yet. We gon hold on to him for a lil while . . . make sure he good, especially now. Realizin they used him and lied about errthang got him in pretty bad shape, don't want him to hurt nobody, including himself."

So Rouk *was* trying to protect us from the two guys with locs—I knew it. That's why he tried to get them away from the shed. He knew we were in there. Now it all makes sense.

As everyone finishes up the little bit of food that remains, Rissa and Miss Tanya stuff everybody with some good food, even get Momma and Jacob to whip up quick desserts, the room and everyone's faces are different, like they're heavy but with hope. Everyone uses this as a chance to get to know each other, put stories to faces in the room.

"Did you go to Daniel Lee, too?" Miss Tanya asks Miss Rosalind.

"Yes, I did. Same time as this one." She points at Momma.

"Yeah, I thought I recognized you. Yall two was thick as thieves, weren't you? Tré used to talk about yall a lot, especially your husband." Miss Tanya looks over at Momma.

"When you brought Taj back to us, he said your name was Rose. I shoulda realized it was you." Rissa shakes her head. "Wheneva there was trouble brewin, you were always close behind on the way to clean it up if the price was right."

"Sorry for any trouble it might have caused you," Miss Rosalind says, winking.

"Did you know Tré? Is that why you saved Bittersweet—well, Taj?" Rissa asks.

Miss Tanya's eyes are hanging on Miss Rosalind's every word. The longer she takes to answer the more eyes fall on her, waiting for a reply.

"No, I just represent other interests that are invested in making sure that he stays safe and flourishes—and the BDs along with him."

"Chile, she hate the Bainbridges, too," Miss Tanya says, laughing. It cuts through the tension like a hot fork through butter. "Well, thank you for savin my baby. He a smart knucklehead just like his daddy, this one ova here is, too, and I want them round for a long time."

"Don't thank me, I'm not the only one who believes in him, in the BDs. Looking forward to working with you, keeping you and everyone here safe." Miss Rosalind smiles, gracious.

After more conversations and planning, it becomes clear that for now, we at least know who we're up against and that things can get closer to normal. That's when I feel Leroy's eyes on me, but I look away. He's been watching me and Will the entire time. I don't know what to say or do. But as I walk out of Rissa's, I know: he'll always be there when I need him the most, like he was today—whether we're together or not.

In the parking lot, the night air is brisk and there isn't a cloud in the night sky. I look up at the stars, the past burning bright in our present. On the air, Southern magnolias, a soft perfume lingering. I look back for Will and Jacob.

"So that's why you visited? Brought Will?" Momma says, walking past Miss Rosalind. She's pissed in a way that only Momma gets pissed.

"It's one of the reasons, yes. But—"

"You lied, again, Lin. You didn't have to, but you did." Momma's voice quivers.

I look at Will—at somebody, anybody who could say what's going on.

"Jules, now you know—"

"Don't do that. Don't you dare." Momma walks over to her, words sharp like arrows dipped in poison. "You knew before you came, before you even said you were coming why you would be here. So all that talk about wanting to be closer, wanting your son to experience what we had . . . was all a lie." Momma shakes her head.

"Jules, it wasn't. I meant what I said."

"No, you meant what you did. And again, you lied, so you could leave, and do whatever you wanted because everything is about you, Lin. It always is."

Momma pulls away and heads to the car. Miss Rosalind doesn't follow her, doesn't try to change her mind. She just stands there, watching her.

"Will, it's time to go," Miss Rosalind says, waving him over.

"Okay, I'mma go back wit them."

"No, it's time for us to go back. There's some stuff we need to take care of in New York."

Did she say what I think she said?

Momma turns back, keys in her hand. "Lin, he's fine. He's been great to have around. I don't mind him staying for the rest of the summer, at least to finish up things the way he wanted to."

"Will, come on." Miss Rosalind ignores Momma.

"Lin, he hasn't even had the chance to say goodbye. Let him stay, if he wants to. I don't mind him being here—"

"So everything has to be your way," Miss Rosalind snaps. "No. I get to say that to you, too. We're not kids anymore, Jules. You can't always be right because you want to be."

Momma looks at her, about to say something, but she just shakes her head. "Did you hear what he said in there? They saved each other's lives today. Don't you see? They're close, thick as thieves just like you and I were, and right now, you're doing exactly what you did to me, when you chose him."

Miss Rosalind looks hurt, looks away from Momma. "How dare you? You know this has nothing to do with that."

Me and Will look at each other. Jacob walks up, wondering what's going on. I tell him the truth: I don't know. Momma and Miss Rosalind are arguing about something that doesn't seem like it has anything to do with us but has everything to do with us.

"Ma, I don't wanna go yet," Will says. "I wanna stay, with them. I can just—"

"I'm sorry, baby," Miss Rosalind says. "I don't mean for what's going on between us to affect you. But I think it's best that we go. Take a second, say your goodbyes, and I'll be waiting in the car. We can have your things packed and shipped tomorrow."

Will looks at me, and before I can stop myself, I shake my

head, I ask him to speak to me last, and I step back. He nods, goes to Jacob, and gives him a hug. Momma smears away tears, holds his face in her hands, says something soft, and gives him a tight hug.

"Jay and Jacob, I'll be in the car when you're ready," Momma says, closing the door.

It isn't until I look at Will that I see his eyes are red, tears filling to the brim. It's because he knows something that only my mom knows, something I guess I need to learn, too, when it comes to him: heartbreak. Suddenly I feel like I'm back in front of that tree with the broken leg of that chair, wanting to scream but can't. Wanting to summon enough power for a victory over all the things that hurt me, to slay the whispers that taunt me, reminding me of all the ways my "more" isn't enough. The proof: everyone I love leaves me.

Will grabs my hands. "Jay, do you want me to go?"

I look up, confused. "What do you mean, your mom said—"

"I know what she said. Do *you* want me to go?" His eyes are searching, hugging me long before his hands do. That's when I feel it, the question beneath his question. The decision he wants me to make—the one Princeton said I didn't have to make if I didn't want to. If I tell him I want him to stay, will it be enough? Will it just make things harder?

Over his shoulder, I see Rissa's diner and, through the window, can make out Rissa, Taj, and Leroy talking. And as if my thoughts were a tether, Leroy looks over at me, sees me looking at him. And I wonder what I shouldn't: If I can't say I don't want to be with Leroy, is it fair to tell Will I want to be him?

I look into Will's eyes, his cheeks blushing red, his quivering lips, ready to steel themselves in the face of Miss Rosalind and her wrath. For a moment, I can see it: Will choosing me, choosing us—even if only for a moment—so that I know how much he cares. The problem is my heart isn't as clear, nor as brave; and if I'm being honest, there's so much I want to do, feel, and experience with Will, but I don't know if my heart was ever mine to give.

Will reads my eyes, and I don't stop him. He turns around, sees Leroy watching us out the window. I don't know if it hurts more that he didn't say anything at all or that I didn't try to stop him. He kisses me on the cheek, our history, again, on repeat and he walks toward Miss Rosalind's truck and never looks back. But as I watch him get in the front seat, lean his head toward the window, and cover his face, a part of me whispers for him to pull down his hands, to let me see his face one last time. He doesn't, and I know why: he's crying.

Fall

16

Leroy

"Get out, since you aren't here to learn." The wack-ass instructor points at the door.

"You da one aint tryna teach." I stand up and grab my book bag, pissed.

I aint even do nothin this time, and he still throwin me out. I keep askin for a different GED instructor, but don't nobody listen or care. I did all that work, toughed out writin the essays, got extra letters of recommendation, and got my transcripts only to realize the instructor I got aint like me the moment I walk in.

I thought cuz this program is at C-Pote Tech they would treat me different, betta—I'm wrong; this is a mistake. Taj and Rissa said it was safer now that we know who the enemy is, but now I'm stuck still dealin wit the same shit. It aint fair, and if I don't get outta this classroom, I might forget how hard I fought to be here.

"Don't you understand English? Get. Out," he screams, makin the white kids jump.

I stop, look at his ass to make it clear. Aint gon be none of that. Not today or any otha day. "You betta quit talkin to me like you crazy."

"Do what I said the first time, and I won't have to." He paces, mumblin under his breath again.

I can't find my blue folder wit the math work in it. It's also where I been keepin all the different passwords I've been tryin for Faa's flash drive. I keep it on me at all times, so I can keep checkin and tryna unlock it.

Even tho Rouk been cooperatin wit Taj while keepin safe and out of sight, it aint got us anywhere; he don't seem to know, eitha. None of us do. And since don't nobody know what exactly the Bainbridges plannin, it feels like we all waitin for a big-ass shoe to drop.

I need to get my folder befo I leave so I don't have to write errthang out all ova again. I ask round as quiet as I can to see if anybody sees it. I slam the papers I have down in frustration. I just wanna get outta here.

"Throw so much as a sheet of paper, and I'll make sure they expel you, Leonard. I don't know how you made it in here. You're trouble, just trouble. All of you."

"All of who? And my name aint Leonard, it's Leroy."

"Don't play victim, you know what I meant."

"Naw, I don't. How bout you elaborate." I wait, listenin. I aint the only one waitin on him to explain himself eitha.

"I'm calling security." It looks like he puts a blue folder—my blue folder—in his desk drawer. "Out. Now."

I walk right up to his ass, try to open the drawer. He slaps it closed, almost catches my hand. "Do that shit again," I growl.

"That is my private drawer. You have no right."

"Imma ask you once. Is that my blue folder?"

He goes to the classroom phone, calls somewhere for someone.

I open the drawer, pull out the blue math folder wit my name on the front. I shake my head. "I'm out."

He slams the door so hard behind me, I think the little window at the top almost cracks. It takes errthang in me not to go back in there and get his ass for stealin my shit. But aint nobody gon believe me no way, they neva do. If my name is anywhere near it, they assume it's my fault. But I'm just the only one willin to speak up, not let nobody talk down to me.

I need to go find somebody in the office, beg them to send me to anotha GED instructor. I can't have Taj findin out bout none of this. I aint bout to let him down, not this time.

A man wit salt-and-pepper hair, a polo, and jeans is walkin down the hallway. He looks like he might work in the office or at least know where it is. "Aye . . . excuse me. You know where the office is where they set up classes?"

"Advisement?"

I shrug.

"That's probably a good place to start. I'll walk you. I'm already headed there."

"You a teacher here?"

"I do teach every now and then. What about you? Are you a sophomore, junior?"

"Nah, I'm just gettin my GED. . . . Well, tryna, but the instructor keep kickin me out the classroom, even tried to steal my homework folder."

"That doesn't sound very fair."

"I know, that's what I been sayin. He don't like me, and ion like him, but errtime I try to get anotha instructor, they put me right back in there wit him."

"Is he the only one?"

"Ion think so, but errbody else class be full. Iono how I'm supposed to learn from somebody who be talkin down to me all the time and get pissed anytime I ask a question, like I'm the burden."

I don't know if it's just cuz I'm mad or he just seem cool, but I aint neva talk so much to no adult, at least not a teacher. It makes me wish there were mo teachers like him, or mo whateva he is, cuz havin somebody to talk to who wants to hear my side of the story instead of doin errthang to get me locked up feels different for a change, better.

"Whatchu teach?"

"English."

"Furreal? That's wassup. It's actually one of my favorite subjects. Always wanted to learn how to understand all those hard books, write poetry, even essays and all that. You seem like you a good teacher. You don't be yellin at nobody or callin people names when they don't understand, do you?"

"No, I don't. I'm sorry to hear that's happened to you. I tell you what, let me get back to you on the new instructor placement, see what I can do."

"Furreal?"

He nods. "But let me ask you something: Why are you here? Why now?"

Iono if I should tell him the real reason: Jay. I mean, he aint the only reason but he the main reason. Now that he know errthang I know, and bein round him aint puttin him in too much danger, I wanna find a way to try again. It aint gotta be errthang at once, just something, baby steps, till we find each otha again on the otha side of heartbreak.

Iono if it's gonna work, but I figure, if I finally learned how Jay felt bout me through his words, the best way to get him back, to let him know I'm here, is if I do the same. But I need help. "I aint the best wit words, but I wanna learn how to write a love letter."

He stops. "Really? A love letter?"

"I know it sound crazy. . . . I'm just tryna get good enough so the guy I'm tryna write it to can pick up what I'm puttin down, ya feel me?"

"More than you know."

We turn the corner, and he leads me into the office.

"Lee? Whatchu doin here?" Jacobee looks like he just

leavin. He daps me up, hugs me. I knew he went here but aint expect to see him.

"Wassup? Tryna see how I can change my GED teacher. He buggin, kicked me out. I ask this dope-ass teacher, tho, and he showed me how to get here."

"Teacher? You mean President Henry?"

"President? Of what?"

"The college."

I step back, nervous. "Oh . . . my bad . . . I aint mean to . . ."

"It's cool. Now you know him, too. President Henry, this is Leroy Booker, a good friend and one of the smartest people I know."

He steps forward, offers his hand. I shake it, nervous. "Nice to meet you, Leroy. I hope you don't hold it against me or treat me any differently." His words are warm, like he means em. "Jacob's right . . . in addition to teaching, I do serve as the head of the college. But every now and then, I like to just roam the halls and be of service."

I nod, don't really know what to say or do, just really hopin I aint in no kind of trouble. Standin there next to him, it's like President Henry grows taller, the salt and peppa of his hair looks majestic, like a crown. When he release my hand, I still feel the weight, the warmth—his importance.

"Jacob . . . how have you been? Given any more thought to my proposition? I know you're taking a break from track this year, but whether it be as an assistant coach or an athlete, we'd love to have you, even if it is just temporary until you change schools. I still believe you belong at my alma mater—you already a Wildcat."

"I haven't forgotten—still thinking about it."

"Good to know."

"Lee, how'd you end up with President Henry?"

My words won't work. I just look at President Henry, speechless.

"Leroy was just enlightening me on the challenges of his program and his passion for writing. He's brilliant. Happy to see you both know each other, because you were the first person I wanted to introduce him to."

A lady wit a clipboard waves at President Henry, taps on her watch, like there is somewhere else he needs to be.

"Well, I'm afraid I have to get to my next engagement, but Leroy, take this." He hands me his business card, writes anotha number on the back of it. "I want you to give my office a call. I want to sit down, learn more about how we can improve the program you're in, and see if we can get you in either my poetry seminar or something closer to your liking. How does that sound?"

"I aint a poet, tho."

He puts his hand on my shoulder. "Anybody who has heard you talk knows you're a gifted speaker and lover of words—a poet, maybe even a performer. But don't take my word for it—drop by my class Wednesday morning, see if you like it, and if not, no harm, no foul. My office can set up a free-credit allowance for you to take the class, since you're not a college student here . . . yet."

He says "yet" like he expects me to be there soon, like I can, even though so many say I can't and I won't. "Okay, I'll give it a shot. Thank you, Mistah Prez."

He follows the lady wit the clipboard, waves goodbye.

The moment he disappears into the hallway, Jacobee grabs me. "So you kickin it wit presidents now?" He's yell-whisperin; he's so excited.

"I aint know. He said he was a teacher."

"That's cuz he is a professor here, too. A lot of those real good folks in high positions do it like that—just roam the halls, talkin to people, not really sharin their job titles."

"He mad cool, tho. Almost called him Unc a few times."

Jacobee puts his arm round me, follows me outside. "You hungry?"

"I could eat. You cookin?"

"Naw, don't start cookin till later. Got any mo classes?"

I shake my head.

"How bout you join me at the student union. I can swipe you in."

"Okay, okay. That's wassup."

Jacobee says goin to the cafeteria, but what we roll up in looks mo like the food court at the mall, but it don't take long befo my nose leads me to Jacobee fave spot, a good ol aunt-and-unc restaurant.

All the cashiers and cooks know Jacobee by name, and since I'm wit em, they let me in the back, too, where we get to eat the good-good they aint allowed to serve to errbody cuz of health and nutrition guidelines that don't let you put enough salt or sugar in shit. Kinda feels like I'm at Rissa's the way they hug and pile food on our plates, watch us eat it, but only after we say our grace. Befo we leave, they even give us strips of sugarcane to chew on.

As we stretch our legs and walk outside round the mini lake at the back of the student union, we don't say much at first, just walk, listen to the water, feel the hand of the sun—warm and heavy. Then, we spot a bench near some boulders.

Jacobee sits, but I stand watchin the water do its thing. "What's on ya mind, Lee?"

"Whatchu mean?"

"You been thinkin real hard since we came here. I can see it on yo face."

I shrug. "Iono."

He pulls some leaves from the willow tree above us. I kick up some courage from the grass. Some girls walk by wit eyes and smiles for me and Jacobee—a few guys, too. We must look like we carryin the weight of the world on our shoulders, cuz they neva roll up. I'm glad they don't, cuz they would neva hear the swoosh of these nets—we taken, well, almost.

"Rememba way back, when you made that yock?"

"Yeah . . . and yall almost fucked it up." He laughs.

"Why you left when Taj tried to tell you he liked you?" I shield my face from the light slappin heat through the leaves.

"It's actually yo fault . . . ," he says.

"Why? What I do?"

"Bein loved by Taj was one thing. I think I knew what that would look like."

We chuckle. Somethin floats above our heads—words we aint really gotta say.

"But then you came"—he play-slaps me upside the head—"and you needed me, too. I guess I got scared. I've seen love be one thing, and then you look up and it's changed into something else— someone you can't recognize, can't forgive."

"Like yo pops?"

He don't answer, just shakes his head.

"My bad . . . I just assumed that how it was based on what yo mom said at Rissa's after all that shit wit Rouk went down."

"Nah, it's cool. It is what it is, no sense in hidin it. I just feel like, back then, what me and Taj had was movin too fast, felt too much like somethin that would only hurt in the end, and I aint want that. But that night you came to the O lookin for me, I don't know . . . somethin changed."

I grin. "Yeah, I saw how you was lookin at that necklace. I see you wearin it today."

He sucks his teeth. "Shut up. . . . That's when I realized it mighta already happened, and I was in too deep."

"Love," I say, workin the word in my mouth, tryna understand it—I still can't, don't know if I eva will, but I want the chance to try.

"Or somethin like it."

"I'm scared Imma hurt him . . . Jay." I don't mean to say it, but I do.

Jacobee chews on his sugarcane, sucks the last bit of sweet. "Me, too. Well, I know you will. I will, too. That's the fucked-up part."

"But ion want to."

"Don't matter . . . Cuz you don't want to, you will." He throws the sugarcane under a nearby bush.

I don't like that answer, don't like what it means. If you can't not hurt somebody, then how can you call it love?

Jacobee stands up, stretches. I watch his hands reach into the sky. I do what he do, feelin for a way out.

"When me and Jay were little, like round the time our dad got locked up, I used to run up to him, ask him to forgive me in advance in case I did anything wrong, like hurt him. Each time, he cried. He'd ask why ova and ova. I aint know how to tell him I just didn't wanna be like Dad, didn't want to be the reason he cried. I thought if he forgave me in advance, it wouldn't hurt. Or if it did, maybe not as bad. But I ended up makin him cry twice because I couldn't stand to see him cry once."

We look at each otha, let out a big-ass breath.

"That shit is deep. Got my head hurtin." I aint lyin, seriously.

"Naw, yo head hurtin cuz you was holdin yo breath tryna look good stretchin. . . . You can't do it like me, Lee. Imma pro.

"When's yo first class wit President Henry?"

"Think he said I can swing by on Wednesday. Why, wassup?" I chew and suck on my stick of sugarcane, let it dangle from my lip like a Black & Mild.

"How bout you come ova my house for dinner that day instead of Rissa's. I'm sure I can talk her and Miss Tanya into it so they don't miss you too much."

My words don't work, so I do the only thang I know to do: I smile.

"How do you write a love letter without words?"

Mistah Prez aint playin—errbody face is a question mark. Iono what I was expectin on my first day takin one of his classes, but it's mad interestin. Aint like no class I eva been in befo.

"Let's back up a little. What about a poem?"

"Through sounds?" somebody asks, way up in the front of the auditorium.

"Headed in the right direction. Anyone else? Mr. Leroy . . . What do you think?"

"Iono."

"Think about it. . . . What's the first answer that comes to mind?"

"Iono . . . Just live it." Errbody nods their heads. I'm surprised myself.

"Exactly . . . and how do we know we're living? What does it mean to live? Any takers?"

No one answers.

"Let me ask you this, then. . . . What is love?"

Errbody shoots up they hand, has something to say: carin bout somebody, bein willin to die for them, wantin to protect somebody, feelin attachment. I'm tryna write all of it down cuz some of it I just aint neva really thought bout.

"Here's your homework for Friday: write me a love letter without words. For the smart alecks, you can come to class with a blank sheet of paper, if you'd like, but I'll reward you with a blank space in my grade book. . . . And if you want to get to meet the brilliant mind that inspired that lesson, don't forget to say hello to Leroy on your way out. . . . Dismissed."

Outta nowhere, a bunch of people come to my desk, say they really like my answer earlier, want to collaborate or partner on a piece wit me soon. I nod, but I don't really understand what they mean. I'm still new to the class and to all of this, still don't even know if it's for me, but I'm startin to get the hang of it—I wish all classes I been in was like this, I prolly woulda did much better if I had someone who cared.

"That was real nice, Mistah Prez," I say after class.

"Glad you liked it, Leroy. Great answer, by the way. It really got the class thinking."

"Thanks . . . but iono what the homework really is."

"Sure you do."

"I mean, I get what you said, but what do I *do*?"

"Okay. Another question for you, then: How do you know something is real?"

"Yo, you ask a lotta questions, Mistah Prez."

"The best teachers usually do. . . ."

"Okay . . . Lemme think. . . . Like, period?"

"Yeah . . . in everyday life. Something like this marker. How do you know it exists?" He holds it up, moves it up and down in his hand until it looks like it floppy and rubbery.

"You can see it."

"Yup . . . You confirm with your five senses: touch, taste, sight, smell, and hearing. That's what you'll use to guide you. Yes, you will have to physically write the letter in order for me to read it, but it has to be through the five senses."

"What if it don't come?"

"It will."

"What if it aint good?"

"It will be."

"What if you don't like it, tho?"

"Mr. Leroy . . . you sure ask a lot of questions."

I grin, seein what he gettin at. "The best students do."

"Well said, well said."

I walk toward the door, thinkin bout what I have to do first.

"Leroy, trust yourself. Seeing what's around you requires opening up, seeing beauty in the mundane, the boring, everyday things you never really notice. It's all there, you just have to look."

I aint neva seen a teacher turn somethin I really want to do into a homework assignment. If it means I'll be better at somethin than when I came in, Imma fuck wit it, give it my all. I just don't know exactly where to start. I go to the lake behind the student union, hopin it might help.

At first, I just write down what I know—I scribble down "bird," "tree," "fine-ass girl," "fly-ass nigga," "lake wit lily pads." But when I sit on the same bench me and Jacobee was on a coupla days ago and I get still, like real still and close my eyes, it's a lil different. A bird aint just a bird, it's a song; a tree aint leaves shakin, but leaf wings flutterin; a girl or a guy aint just what I see—they the ring of bracelets, click of heels, scrape of shoes, glow of tats brought to life by the sun.

By the time I get to really thinkin bout love, my hand is achin from writin so much so fast. From what I know, love aint no one thing—it's how people make you feel, what they leave wit you when they witchu, and what you remember when they gone: Ma's Chanel N°5 and peppermints; Taj's fussin and boxin; Rissa's jokes and banana puddin; Jacobee's hugs and catfish; Trish's sewin machine and bomb advice; Jay's errthang: his eyes, his lips, his voice, his smell, his waist, his giggle, his smile, his . . . listenin . . . his touch. I almost finish my first couple of lines, but then I look at my watch and realize I'm late for dinner at Jay and Jacobee's.

I knock, then stare at the blue door, listenin for any clue of who might be openin it first. If it's Jay, Imma say somethin sexy, but if it's his moms, I wanna say somethin respectable like, "How you doin, Miss . . . Miss . . ." Shit. I don't know her name.

The door opens.

"Hey, Leroy . . . come on in," Jay's mom says, wearin a white apron wit purple letters that say "Love." She a different kinda pritty, like Ma, but wit eyes that make you tell her things—you can't lie or run, even if you want to. "You can call me Miss Julia. Jacob said you were comin. Him and Jay will be here any minute. Want anything to drink, baby? We got water, juice, tea, soda, whateva you like."

"No, ma'am. I'm good."

The house smells like cinnamon rolls.

Miss Julia looks natural in the kitchen, kinda like Rissa. Then I realize that's who Jacobee get it from, makin magic in the kitchen; he looks like her.

"Leroy, I know you're waiting, but—" She reaches for my hands. "But do you think I can borrow these? A man with strong hands should neva go to waste."

Her hands are warm, soft—like they used to makin people feel better, fixin what might be hurt, broken. I don't wanna let go or say no, so I stay wit her in the kitchen.

"You know, I had no idea you and your brother were Tanya and Tré's sons. We all went to school together. I met your mom a few times back then. . . . She's still gorgeous. I remember she always talked about going to nursing school."

I aint know that. "She a nurse now."

"Is she? Oh good. And Tré, he was so smart. He could do things with numbers that would make your head spin. He had his own language . . . when he finally got to talkin', that is."

She gets quiet, must remember what happened, that he went missin and was neva found. She looks at me like it hurts. "I'm sorry, baby. I didn't mean to—"

"It's cool. . . . I aint really know him, don't even rememba what he look like. I was real young. My brotha knew him, tho."

"Taj, like the Taj Mahal, right? One time when he was talking to J.D.—I heard him say you and your brother were the eighth and ninth wonders of the world."

I aint know that, eitha.

"How's Mr. Eighth Wonder holding up? Seems to be doing pretty well after finally figuring out everything that was going on."

"Yeah, he good. Just tryna get life back to normal."

"Are y'all both math geniuses like your father?"

"He is, got a photographic memory and errthang."

"What about you?"

I shrug. "Iono. Aint really good at nothin."

"You are. . . . You just don't know it yet."

I can feel her lookin at me, her eyes sayin somethin I need to hear.

"You're going to need this." She hands me a light-blue apron.

She shows me how to sprinkle flour on the counter in front of us, and then she moves the dough from the mixer.

"Hands tell you a lot about a person: what they're used to, what they think they're good at. I didn't spend a lot of time with your father, Leroy, but one thing I do remember is his hands, and how similar they were to the men's hands I grew up with, men who used to knock things down because they had to. But when you open them up, see the soft of the palms—shows you can do other things with them, too: build, smooth, even heal. See?"

She shows me her palms, reaches for mine, and rubs her hands across mine so I remember, as she talk me through kneadin the dough. She says you have to fold it ova and into itself, pay attention to how much pressure is needed to know when it's done, cuz all things need both: hard and soft—us, too.

"Feel it?" She smiles, pressin the dough and waitin for it to push back.

I grin. The dough is ready to rest, so it can rise. We take a break, lean back on the counter.

"I told you, Leroy, you're a builder, an artist—that's your gift, and it's all in your hands. You're a natural, must know your way around a kitchen."

"Ion really know how to do that. . . . I can make some grits, as long as you don't mind them bein a lil chewy and burnt at the bottom."

She makes me wanna show off, even though I don't really know how.

"Yeah, grits are tricky. . . . I learned how to cook them real well from J.D. The key: cream instead of water." She winks.

"That's how I learned. . . . Jacobee—I mean, Jacob taught me that."

"I bet he's cooked a lot for you, hasn't he?"

"Huh?"

"G'on 'head . . . you can tell me. . . . Tell the truth and shame the devil."

I giggle. "Maybe."

"Look at you—loyal to a fault. Long as he didn't give away none of my secrets, it's fine by me. . . . You should know something, though."

I look up, wait for her words.

"When we cook, people fall in love."

I grin cuz I know.

"Jacob told me he started cooking at Rissa's diner," she says.

"Yeah, got his own dish. . . . I named it."

"He told me. He was so proud, Ain't No Mo' Catfish."

"He tried to play it off like it won't no big deal."

"I'mma tell you somethin' about my boys—and I can talk about them because they not here—they look tough, and Jacob look the toughest, but there's one way to get 'em: grilled cheese with sweet milk." She nods so hard, my head does the same as she talks.

"That's it?" Iono bout that.

"Oh, you haven't had my grilled cheese. That's why you don't get it."

"Furreal?" I say.

"Mmhmmm . . . You should come over again, and I'll make some for you."

"Okay, I will."

She pulls out some dough she musta been workin on earlier, cuz it's already done. We pinch off pieces, and she shows me how to roll them into balls, then dip them into melted butter and a brown-sugar mixture she made befo we put them in the bun pan, one by one.

"How did you meet Jay?" she asks.

I think bout how we first met and don't know if it's best to tell her the whole story, so I keep it vague. "Met each otha round the way."

"Hmm . . . and Jacob let you get anywhere near him?"

"Only after I got to know him, too." I chuckle, knowin what she gettin at.

"I thought so." Her laugh is a lot like Jay's, how it floats above your head, makes you feel light on the inside.

"Yeah, he don't play when it come to Jay . . . believe that."

"I bet your brother, Taj, is very protective of you, too."

I neva thought bout it, how similar Taj is to Jacobee, but it's true: nobody gets to me without goin through him. "I guess you right."

"I can tell. . . . You look like somebody who got a lot of love growing up, even if it wasn't from the places some folks might expect. It's a good thing to be loved like that. Probably means you do the same for others—love real hard."

The door opens and Jay stands there, in shock, while Jacobee grins, laughs all the way to us.

"Lee, you look good in that blue, baby boy," Jacobee sings.

I can't help but smile.

"What about me?" Miss Julia says, posin for a camera that aint there.

"Heavenly . . ."

We all chuckle. He right, and we all know it.

Jay shoulder-bumps me. I wonder if he knows how much I been waitin to see him. Miss Julia watches us, smilin at somethin only she knows.

Two hours flies by. Aint till Rissa and Taj call and check to see where I am that I see how long it's been. Furreal, furreal, I don't wanna leave, cuz a few mo loaves of the monkey bread is comin outta the oven, and Miss Julia got to makin those grilled cheese sandwiches and the sweet milk. I aint neva tasted somethin so good.

When it's time to go, she gives me my own loaf of monkey bread, tells me to share wit Ma and Taj. She sends anotha one to Rissa through Jacobee, who leaves a little befo to go back to the diner since he on break.

At the door, Miss Julia stops me, hugs me like my own ma do. "Leroy . . . ?"

"Ma'am?"

I wait for her to ask what she already know—prolly from the moment I showed up, lookin for Jay.

"You get what you need?" she says, smilin.

I nod. "I think I got mo."

When Jay comes out, and she goes in, he don't say much, just stands in front of me.

"Can I ask you a question?" Jay's eyes hold me hostage. "Why'd you do it?"

His words hit me like a switch—quick slap followed by a sting. I knew he would ask, I been thinkin bout it a lot myself. But errthang I practiced, errthang I planned to say won't come.

"I mean, I know what you said in your note, the one you gave to Jacob, but why a letter? Why not tell me in person?"

I don't know why but I remember Jacobee at the top of the stairs in front of Taj, him sayin how Jacobee made a choice, a decision, without eva askin what he wanted or needed. I aint realize I did the same thing until just now. I wanna say the right thing, but I just say what I know and hope he hears me.

"I aint think I could . . . if I saw you, like I'm in front of you right now, aint no way I woulda been able to leave you. But I know I had to . . . even if you would hate me for it. I aint mean to hurt you, but it was the only thing I could do . . . if it meant you'd be okay, safe. It's the hardest thing I eva had to do, not bein able to be next to you."

Jay looks at me, quiet. I don't know what I thought tellin the truth would do, what it might change, but I aint ready for the silence. For him to look at me and not say something—cuss, swing, cry, yell, anything. He just nods and says what I least expect, "Thanks for telling me. . . . I gotta go."

Frozen in time without no sound, I watch as he disappears behind the door. What hurts the most is it don't take away from the truth I been thinkin since I saw him on the street and he walked away, left me there: when I see him, errthang in me shakes, cuz aint nobody like him, nobody. And I aint gon let time pass me by. Imma do something real big, so I can show him how much he means to me. That way he don't eva have to worry bout me leavin him again.

In the car headed to Rissa's, for the first time, I feel like writin—like I can do it, and maybe even be good at it, if I really try. I hear the first sentence, *I think I love you, cuz it hurts to say goodbye*. I feel like if ion write it down right now, I might lose it. So I pull ova near the church that started it all. I get out and go to my favorite lil spot, in the cut, where the trees hang ova a bench. But now the words won't flow.

I pull out the letter he gave me—well, the one I found in the back seat. I kept it wit me this whole time. It's why I wanted to write in the first place, the reason why my letter needs to be perfect. But mine is nothin like his, just seems like a bunch of ramblin, strugglin. Then I realize, I aint neva gon get nowhere if I'm worryin bout how my letter don't sound nothin like his. I gotta speak to him in my language.

When the words finally get to flowin, it's errthang that hurts and errthang that makes me feel good all in one place: short but honest.

Mistah Prez's got the love letter I wrote for Jay in his hands.

The way he readin it, you'd think it was a test that was gon determine my final grade he lookin at it so close. But that's a good thing—it aint just for no grade, it's for Jay's heart—and mine, too.

"Looks great. . . . You're going to really give it to him, right?"

I sit down, realizin my legs was shakin waitin to hear if it was good or not. Now, all of a sudden I'm tired, exhausted—worried. "What if he don't? What if it aint good enough to him?"

"I don't think that's possible." Mistah Prez laughs. "But on the off-chance he doesn't, all you can do is deliver the message. The rest is up to him.

"Why do you spell 'pretty' the way that you do? I'm assuming that's intentional?" Mistah Prez asks, handin me back my letter.

"Iono. I always did that. Just look betta to me, like it's prettier than pretty, on a different level errbody can't understand. Somethin you just know when you see it. . . . Ya feel me?"

Mistah Prez smiles. "Tell him that. I think hearing that from you, knowing how little you speak because of how much you care about your words, would help. You've written it perfectly—now you just have to give it to him and say what scares you the most."

"Iono, Mistah Prez. That's a lot." I exhale, feelin the heat in love's kitchen.

"I can always change the weight of the assignment to a quiz grade."

"Mistah Prez? Come on, man."

He laughs, but that shit aint funny. I can't get a zero ova somethin like this. The stakes already high enough.

"You said you planned to give it to him at a skating rink?"

"Yeah. My auntie Rissa, his brotha, Jacobee, and even his homeboy Princeton gon help convince him to come to the skatedown tomorrow at Da Rink. If he go, then Imma give it to him after, when it's just me and him."

"Wow. Good luck. I'm rooting for you."

"Thanks, Mistah Prez. Furreal. Like, iono if I coulda been

able to do it this fast if I aint have yo help."

As I walk out his office, I read the letter ova and ova so many times I can almost repeat by memory. Iono if it's perfect, but if I learned anything bout love, it's that honesty is required. So, this letter is me offerin myself up, lettin him know that if he choose me, if he say yes, I'll do like I said befo all this went sideways: I'll run to him, not from him, if he let me.

17

JAY

The morning sun is a heavy-handed prankster, shining too bright and a little too long against the backdrop of birds heckling in the trees near my window. I roll until I'm a cocoon of sheets and comforter and pillows, but I can't outrun or outsnooze the morning sun and its cackling band of feathered misfits.

It's been a month since I last saw Will—and he never even called after Rissa's. All the while, Leroy and I are just beginning to reconnect, but things are still a bit awkward. There's always this aching in my chest every minute of every day, either feeling guilty about not choosing Will or feeling too nervous to do anything that cements choosing Leroy instead. I peel myself out of my cocoon feeling like everything but a butterfly.

It's supposed to be the first day of my senior year, which means I can finally wear regular clothes instead of a school uniform. On a hanger is a new outfit that Jacob put together for me to wear because he says I've been looking down: a white polo with the silver stripe across the chest, gray

Girbauds with the white tabs, and the metallic silver and white Air Jordan 20s. I pinch myself to see if I'm dreaming.

Jacob skip-limps into my room, smelling of bacon, that's when I know it's real.

Mom yells up the stairs from the kitchen, "Jacob, he up yet? I'm almost done with the grits."

"He up," Jacob yells back, smiling. "You gon' look at it or you gon' put it on?"

His catfish grin matches the smell along with the cheese grits Momma is making. He doesn't wait for me, though. He is all hands, pulling my shirt over my head and trying to smooth a new white tank down my torso with my arms still up.

"Jacob, I can dress myself."

He ignores me, reaches for the drawstring of my shorts. "What? It ain't nothin' I ain't seen before."

I block his hands again. "True but let me get this."

"Why? It ain't the first time you had mornin' wood."

I look down, cover myself, then snatch the pants from the hanger on the doorknob and run into the bathroom, away from the sound of his laughter. I want to run out of the house, but I need clothes on to do that.

Jacob knocks a rhythm into the bathroom door. "Don't take too long handlin' your business. I'll wait for you downstairs."

I cuss him out under my breath.

"You hear me, Jay?" Jacob is still snickering. Asshole.

"No, I don't hear a word you're saying!"

I change into my pants right when Mom announces the food is ready. After I scarf down the catfish and grits, kiss Mom on the forehead, and then get coaxed into kissing Jacob on the cheek to end his season of pouting, I'm speed-walking, trying to not scuff my new shoes or wrinkle the new outfit. I imagine a trail of frankincense, sweet myrrh, and cloves tantalizing everyone and everything behind me, compliments of Jacob lending me some of his oils.

I don't know why, but at the light in front of the gas station I look for Leroy, hope he is waiting for me in front of the hood of his car, arms crossed and gleaming. He isn't, but Princeton is there, decked in a white and red Dwyane Wade Miami Heat jersey with dark blue acid-washed jeans, a red belt, and the Nike Air Max Goadome Scarface-edition sneaker boots, which aren't supposed to be released for another month.

He grins. He already knows the chorus of oohs and aahs he will get in addition to the usual hugs and dick grabs he already dodges.

To say Princeton is staring is an understatement. "Dayum, you look weird as fuck!" he says.

I frown and wait on the ground to open up and swallow his hatin' ass. His words sting more than I expect them to, and my eyes water. I walk past him but make sure my eyes send him a clear message: *fuck you*.

"Aye . . . aye . . . aye . . . I ain't mean it like that."

I ignore him and the feeling like my cheeks and whole face are on fire. If I stop, if I turn around, I'm pretty sure—no, I know—I'll swing.

"Jay . . . Jay . . . Come on, man, quit trippin'. I'm sayin' you look good, damn. What's the problem?"

I stop, chest growing warm after the correction. Out of nowhere, my shoulder aches, not far from where I was shot. It's been doing that a lot lately, whenever I'm stressed, nervous, frustrated—anything really, like my body is punishing me for not being stronger. I shake it off, make sure he gets a good look at the new flawless temp fade and the fit.

"I don't look good. I look dayum good, now keep up."

There is a glimmer in his eye, a challenge he accepts without me knowing what it is. I remember the last time we were at his house, the tenderness he and Lady Tee showed me when they realized I was having a panic attack. Princeton is a good guy, I tell myself. He didn't mean it. In my head, I pardon him, since it's his first offense.

"Aight—I see you, Mr. Dayum Good." He takes three big strides and is already at my side.

"Wanna kick it again at my crib?"

"Why would I do that?" I grin.

He jogs in front of me and blocks me. "Whatchu mean?" His grin is gone; he is serious.

It catches me off guard, his hurt feelings.

"I'm just playing—sure. Lady Tee gonna make us some more of those mocktails?" I say, trying to make it right or at least make him feel better.

He pulls out a wave brush, strokes the waves in his hair, and never answers.

"Oh, you giving me the silent treatment now?"

He snatches the binder I'm carrying.

"Princeton . . ."

"I'mma carry this. Better yet, gimme that book bag." He pulls at the loop behind my neck.

"I'm good. . . . Let go."

"Naw, not till you give me the bag, too."

I glare at him. Yes, it hurts; no, I don't want him to know. I'm not helpless. To prove a point, I think about making a break for the school, leaving him in my dust.

"You could try," Princeton says, reading my mind, "but I beat Jacob's record in the hurdles last season, so best believe I'mma catch yo' ass."

"You're an asshole," I huff, slipping my arms out of the handles against all good sense.

"Thanks for the compliment—one asshole to another."

We stop, look at each other, then burst into laughter. We both know what he means, but it definitely doesn't sound right.

The closer we get to school, the more I realize everyone

around us changes, even Princeton. He goes from walking beside me to in front, moving people out of my way. When someone accidentally bumps my left shoulder, he blows up on them, screaming, "Watch where the fuck you goin'."

If anyone stares (boy, do they stare), he always has something to say. He's worse than Jacob when he used to go to school with me. Every few minutes: "Gotta eye problem, lil bruh?" "Whatchu lookin so damn hard fuh, lil bruh?" "Back up, lil bruh, give a nigga some room."

By the time we get to the front of the building, and we're swallowed by the just-before-the-bell-rings, first-day traffic, he puts my book bag on the front of his torso, pulls my hands around his shoulders, and cuts a path through the crowd to my locker. When a tall guy I don't recognize with tats pushes up on me real hard from behind, I almost fall. The tall guy steadies my waist, then asks my name.

"Don't worry 'bout it, nigga," Princeton growls. "Gon' 'head and take yo' no-free-throwin' ass on."

"What? Say that shit again," the guy says. "Ol goofy-lookin-cock-blockin ass—"

I turn around to face him. "He didn't mean it."

His eyes soften. "What's up witchu?" His smile is a vortex pulling me in.

Princeton reaches back, grabs my hand, and pulls me the rest of the way before he can finish his sentence. I blush when the guy winks, and all I can wonder: Is this a prank?

At my locker, Princeton is still mean-muggin'. His face melts when I open my locker, but then he almost picks me up and moves me to the side so he can put my books in. It takes a second for me to realize all the fuss is directed around me not putting too much weight on the side that was shot. His thoughtfulness—although still obnoxious—is his way of trying to keep me safe, comfortable. I don't know whether to be annoyed or touched, so I settle for a mixture of both.

"Wanna tell me why you're doing this?"

"Doin' what?"

"Doing everything I usually do for myself, like—"

"That all you got to say to me?" he says.

I squint my eyes, try to make my face into a question mark. "Thank you?"

"Really? That's it?"

"There's something else going on with you. What am I missing? Oh, I know: Is today the day?"

"What day?" Princeton says, curious.

"Oh, you forgot one of our many conversations this summer where you told me about your crush on Christina, how you were going to shoot your shot senior year."

"Man, whateva."

"It's okay, Princeton. Don't fret! Today *will* be the day that Christina will leave her boyfriend, Lyric Bryson the great, and choose the new golden boy of Daniel Lee High, Princeton 'Tin Tin'—"

"Forget it. I'll see you lata, *after* I'm done seeing Christina at lunch." He makes to walk away.

"What? I thought the joke was funny." A part of me wants to chase after him, needs to know if I really needed to say something he wanted to hear or if he was just being dramatic. The more I've gotten to spend time with Princeton, the more I realized there are two parts of him—like all of us—the strong, confident, impenetrable front we show to others and the tender, vulnerable, actual version that yearns to be seen, loved on, and heard.

I want to get it right because Princeton is my friend (still feels a little weird to say, but I'm glad I can). But happy or not, it's getting harder to concentrate. I need to take some painkillers. My shoulder is throbbing, and my left arm is starting to hurt more. No amount of smiling is going to play this kind of pain off.

Princeton reappears at my side, shaking a mini bottle of pills. If he wouldn't get weird about it, I would hug him out of thanks and delirium. "Yougonlemmewalkawaylikedat?" he says, blurring all of his words together.

"Huh?" The smile I've been holding hostage breaks free. Then the bell rings.

"Not going to even bother to ask a single question about my plans."

I hold out my hands. He places the painkillers and a pineapple Fanta in them. The Fanta is cold, and so is the bottle of pills, which means he's had both the whole time we've been walking. It could be the pain, could be the rush of adrenaline, maybe even the way he knows how to flood my senses with his dopamine charm, but how I see Princeton begins to change. I think it's quite possible Princeton might become more than a friend: my best friend.

"Meet me out front at twelve, and don't be late," Princeton says.

"I will, but I'll have to head out . . . somewhere . . . right after."

"I know, I know. I understand I can't be the only apple of your eye."

I suck my teeth. "Really? The apple of my eye?"

"Don't try to change the subject. Where you goin'? Whatchu doin'? *Who* you doin'?"

"I should be asking you that." I roll my eyes. "What's with you being all up in Christina's face, huh? Telling me you're meeting her at lunch, then demanding I find you at the same time, too?"

"It ain't even like that. It's about a business proposition. Don't you know? I'm always workin' with the business in mind. It ain't gonna grow itself and, although you got all the writing skills, we gotta keep you as undercover as possible. That means, I'm the face—I shake the hands, kiss the babies—well, the ladies . . . and . . ."

I turn toward him, wait for him to say what else he does

or doesn't kiss, curious. "Go ahead, I'm listening."

"Well, I don't know where I was goin' with that but . . . just make sure you meet me at twelve p.m., right when the bell rings."

Before I can answer, he's already down the hall. Then he turns around, makes a megaphone with his hands, and yells in front of everyone rushing to get to class, "And don't be late, issa best friend date!"

I ignore the warm butterflies fluttering in my chest and, instead, knock back two pills with a swig of Fanta, making sure under no circumstances he sees that I'm doing my best to hide the biggest fucking smile.

Christina smells like fall—pumpkin pies, cinnamon sugar, and nutmeg—against the high school cacophony of slamming lockers, scuffing sneakers, and murmurs of who might be nominated for homecoming king and queen, even though it's only the first week of school. I hear her voice aimed at my ears, soft and deliberate, like a silk pillow fight.

"You're Jay, right? The boy who writes love letters?"

I nod slowly, confused. When I close my locker, she snakes her hand around mine and walks with me to the front entrance of the school. The only boys she talks to are like Jacob. She doesn't even look twice at Princeton (but don't tell him that), and he's the golden boy. What does she want with me?

She looks forward, chews the inside of her cheek. Her lips shine and sparkle. "I have a proposition for you—inspired by Princeton—but I want to make it directly to the man with the pen. If I help you expand your love letter business, even outside of this school, would you promise to do something for me?" Her hair gets caught in a necklace, she fixes it, hides it under her blouse.

"That's a cool necklace. . . . I thought your initials were 'CC'? What's 'DK'?"

"Oh, it's just a gift from the boyfriend, supposedly some kind of family thing, you know."

But Lyric's initials are "LB." Why would he give her a necklace that says "DK" and say it's a family thing? Could it— *Nah*. That's behind us now. No need to look for coincidences where there ain't any.

"Jay?"

"Huh? Oh, sorry. Was thinkin' 'bout somethin'?"

"What? My proposition? So what do you say?"

"Maybe. . . . What do you have in mind?"

Her eyes are calculating, sizing me up. "I need a breakup letter, not a love letter. You think you can write it?"

"I could. . . . Never really did one, might need a little time. When you need it?" I ask.

"Homecoming."

I stop in my tracks again. Christina is by far the most popular girl in our school, but her boyfriend, Lyric Bryson, is the most popular guy at Providence Prep. Together, they are like a celebrity couple, well, in our case, a Romeo and Juliet, since our schools want to destroy each other in just about every school sport, academic club, you name it.

With a plan to break up with Lyric just before or after the homecoming game, against the rival team we'll be playing, the social fallout from that kind of drama will corrode the hallways until Thanksgiving break. And if Lyric thinks I have anything to do with it—

A boy bursts out the doors behind us. I pull Christina close by the waist on instinct, as we walk out of the double doors and onto the tree-lined promenade. There is sweet in the heat but still a cool breeze; everything and everyone is buzzing since it's our first day as seniors, which means we get dismissed early.

"I'm sorry, I didn't mean to—"

She clears her throat, smirks, like she's confirmed something. "How much?"

"I don't know. . . . Whatever Princeton said he'd charge. That's how you know me, right?"

"He'd probably offer to do it for free."

"Yup, I would, but it ain't up to me." Princeton smiles, appearing out of nowhere. He whips on his blinding charm, but Christina seems to be wearing invisible shades that make her immune. Perhaps this why Princeton can't get enough.

"I see she told you about my proposition. See? I told you."

"What do you think, Jay?" She stops, stands in front of me, arms crossed. She taps her nails to a beat I can't hear. There is something playful and mischievous in her eyes, like she's testing me. So I answer like Jacob would, with a confidence I don't already have.

"I'm too good to do it for free."

Princeton makes an audible noise, somewhere between an "oooo" and "damn."

"Are you?" Another grin.

I wonder if she can see my leg shaking. "But if you bring us new business, at least three big spenders from nearby schools, I'll consider it."

"Okay, okay, I see you. Negotiatin'," Princeton says, impressed.

I feel I'm on the verge of passing out after overdrafting on swagger. Luckily, I see Leroy coming to save the day . . . I think?

"Whaddup, Tina?" Leroy strolls up slow; his smooth scent follows.

"Hey, Lee . . . Whatchu know good?" She hugs him.

"Chillin' . . . Chillin'."

She turns to me. "If you that good, I wanna see it for myself. Gimme a peek on Monday."

I look at her, mentally swatting away the growing list of reasons I probably shouldn't even get involved. "Okay," I say, more fearless than I feel. But not before that number one reason comes strolling through the crowd out of nowhere, hugging her from behind.

"Lyric?" she says, a lot less happy to see him than I thought. "Whatchu doin' here? I thought you had practice?"

"What? I can't surprise my baby?" He looks over, sees Princeton standing next to me. They both look at each other but don't speak. Whatever bad history is between them, it shimmies proud and rude in the silence.

Christina picks up on it, suddenly wears a different kind of smile, one he probably believes but is far from true.

"Hey, I'm Lyric. You're Jay, right?"

I nod, surprised. "How do you know my name?"

Leroy puts his arm around me, but I'm not sure why.

Lyric looks at him, his eyes a switchblade, but then he smiles at me. "Let's just say you've made an impression . . . on me."

"Okay. Wow. I didn't know my name got all the way to Providence Prep."

"You'd be surprised. . . . Word travels fast. You write the love letters, right?"

"Maybe . . . maybe not." I say, half swagger, half curious but thoroughly confused. Suddenly I realize Princeton may know about Christina's proposition but not what she wants in return.

"With our fourth anniversary coming up"—Lyric squeezes Christina, pecks her on the lips—"I might have to come see you about one."

I nod, my eyes dancing between the truth of her eyes and the daggers in his smile. I don't know what's going on between him and Leroy or between him and Christina, but a part of me feels like it would be best to steer clear of all of it.

"Well, we won't keep you, Jay. Bye, Lee," she sings, her French-manicured tips twirling in the air above her head.

"Am I the only one who saw that? Looks like trouble in paradise." Princeton daps Leroy and does a special handshake I don't recognize. "Nice seeing ya, Leroy, but I'mma leave y'all to it. And Jay, don't forget by Monday, she wanna peek and you betta give it to her." He winks.

"She want a peek of what? Was I interruptin somethin?" Leroy smiles, like he is thinking things he couldn't tell me.

"I don't know . . . maybe." I'm really starting to get the hang of this half swagger maybe. How did I live without it?

"It's like that? Tina real cool . . . but she aint me."

I don't know how to really respond to that, so I don't.

"Plus, it would be kinda awkward, if yall, you know."

"Why?" But I connect the dots: he's already slept with her.

He nudges me wit his shoulder. "Getcha mind outta the gutta. It aint nothin like that."

"Why would it be awkward, then?"

"Cuz I like you—that's why."

It feels too hot, and the sun isn't to blame.

I've never heard him say it before: that he likes me—he still likes me. Then it hits me. In order to see me and

Christina, he had to have already been waiting, had to have seen us talking. Maybe that's why, even as he jokes, he stays closer than close, his words trying to leave a stamp that he's here, he's waiting.

The leaves beneath our feet chatter in dissent, proof of the time that's passed. It almost feels unreal, the silence of the last few weeks. No attacks, no interruptions, nothing.

This is really our first time meeting in person like this. Usually, he might swing by and visit me and Jacob, or we'll see each other at Rissa's, especially since Jacob works there. But it usually feels too weird to be just us. Sometimes, it feels like it's my fault, like I'm the one holding us up, confused. But I just don't want to get hurt again—better yet, I don't want to hurt him, either.

In the time we've spent together, even if it's been with others, I've learned so much, parts of him that I knew existed but never saw: like the fact that when something is really funny, he lets out a high-pitched giggle; that he is ticklish; that he talks so little because he thinks so deeply about everything. What I've learned more than anything: sometimes, to communicate what he doesn't know how to say in words, he touches—brushes, leans on, even nudges—so that I know he still cares. Every time we meet, we get a little closer, talk a little more than we did the time before; we create our own tongue, a language fit for us that doesn't always require speaking.

We arrive at his powder-blue Cadillac. And the first time

in a long time, he opens the door for me, I get in, and it's like we're back where we started months ago. As he drives, we steal glances of each other, say a few words to make it feel less awkward, until it feels good, normal.

To me, Leroy is a map full of adventures, but sometimes I'm afraid of what I'll find, of triggering a booby trap or a curse. The last time we touched, like really touched, even kissed, our lives almost ended. Then when we crossed paths again, not too soon afterward Rouk attacked me and Will.

Every time we touch, something bad happens, and I don't know if it's a sign that we shouldn't or if the storm that's been surrounding us has finally passed. It's not that I don't want to try . . . to get closer—I just don't want to be responsible for what happens next. It's hard to think of beginning when all I can think about is the end.

We enter Rissa's diner together, but I can feel us drifting apart. Leroy smiles when he sees everyone, but something isn't right. We sit at the counter, close to where Jacob is cooking. He comes to the other side behind me, as always, and bear-hugs me. I can tell he feels the difference in me, too. He always does—it's just that when *he* keeps smiling, most people believe him.

"How was school?" Jacob almost pulls me out of my chair.

"Caught Christina tryna spit game," Leroy says, half irritated, half proud.

"Who? Christina, Christina? Homecoming queen?"

Leroy nods.

"What she want?" He looks at me, grins. "Wait, she ask for your number?" He's too excited.

Leroy play-punches him at the thought.

"What?" Jacob smiles. "Aight, I'm playin', I'm playin'."

"That's how you feel?" Leroy pouts again.

"What? I took it back." Jacob throws his hands up in surrender.

"Whey my hug at?"

"Taj got one for you. Don't he?" Jacob says it loud enough to reach Taj and Rissa, who must be doing business in the back.

"Somebody call me?" Taj comes from the office. Rissa is next to him, smiling.

Before Leroy can get away, Taj bear-hugs him, lifts him up out of his chair. Leroy hates and loves it at the same time. He tries to get Taj to let him down quick. "Aight, aight. I'm good. That's too much love."

"Nah, nigga. Can't neva have too much," Taj says, scheming. In a matter of minutes, Leroy giggles and hits all kinds of high notes till he is all laughed out and blushing.

"What?"

"You just let him do me like that?" Leroy sits next to me, his own shade of red, and stares at me, feeling betrayed.

"What could I do? If you can't take him, you know I can't."

"You neva know till you try."

"Haay, Jay. He treatin you good ova here? If not, you lemme know, cuz I'll get him." Rissa leans in, seeing everything on our faces but not saying it.

"Yeah."

"What if he aint treatin me right?" Leroy don't look up, just draws symbols in his notebook.

"Same goes fuh you. You lemme know, cuz I'll get him." She puts a hand on each of ours. "But I know I won't have to, cuz yall will figure it out."

Jacob brings two finished plates to the counter for us, pancakes for me, catfish for Leroy.

"Rissa, you doin anything special this weekend?" Leroy asks.

"Why you askin like you don't— Oh." She looks over at me. "Of course . . . What about you, Jay? Whatchu doin tomorrow at about six p.m.? Might be good for you to get rid of all that stress and shake a lil somethin—you know, letcha hair down."

I look at both of them, even Jacob, as he leans in, looking guilty. I know already that whatever they are about to say is his fault.

"Rissa, lemme get anotha plate of that Ain't No Mo'," one of the elder regulars gruffs. Two more tables ask for the same.

"In a minute, I'm tryna talk this fine man right heah into a double date—well, a triple date—at Da Rink."

"Tell 'em to hurry up and say yes—we still hungry." A

little boy dances in his seat as he finishes the rest of his fish.

"So, whadduyasay, good-lookin?"

"I guess I'm goin' skatin'," I say.

She smiles as the restaurant thunders in full-bodied laughter.

I guilt Jacob into either buying me something new or letting me borrow something out of his closet. Judging by the outfit on the hanger, I don't know if it was a good idea.

It's unlike anything I've ever seen him in: a white silk short-sleeved collared shirt, dotted with sky-blue flowers, and fitted gray slacks and white dress sneakers with blue treads that match the color of the flowers. A month ago, this would have been okay, although still a bit different. But Jacob has been having me work out and lift weights with him, which means I'm a little bigger—got mo' curves, as Rissa says.

Jacob doesn't say anything as he sees my eyes stare at it over and over. But I know he's got a plan because he even cuts my hair, lines up my wannabe mustache and the shadow of my nonexistent sideburns. I beg for the slit in my right eyebrow—he says I don't need it—but when he does it, he grins so hard I don't have to say anything to get him to do it to the other one.

After I get out of the shower, he dabs my lining with alcohol, chuckles when I suck my teeth as it licks fire up the back of my neck and face. Then he sprays me down with the olive oil Pink hair spray. He stands there, arms crossed, staring at me like I'm his greatest masterpiece. While he lines himself up and showers, I change.

With the look fully assembled, I can see my body in ways I hadn't before: the muscles in my arms, broad shoulders that start wide and then narrow at my waist, and thighs and hips and other things I'd prefer stay hidden. Because of Jacob parts of me blossom into being, and I find it hard to look, because I don't know the boy in the mirror. But at the same time, I can't *not* look, because no matter how much I struggle to believe it, the boy in the mirror *is* me.

Jacob comes out in a similar outfit, but in a green dress shirt, khakis, and brown dress sneakers like mine. When Momma sees us, she tears up and takes a million photos with her disposable camera. She has us posing all over the house, outside in front of the car, the trees, the bushes, even in front of the mailbox. Just when we think she's done, we hear the winding of the camera, then *click*. But when we pull up to the Da Rink parking lot, I panic.

Most, if not all, of the guys wear Timbs or the latest kicks and T-shirts and jeans or Dickie suits of all colors, designs, and sizes. More important: their clothes are baggy or loose-fitting. While Jacob parks, I try to think of how to break it to him that we need to change, that I need to change to feel comfortable, safe.

Everyone knows that, at Da Rink, attention is currency; how you look matters because the goal is to make everybody look at you. But there's a catch: they have to look at you for the right reasons, because all attention isn't created equal. Some know how to make anything different seem dangerous, to make enough people believe the very things they love about you they should hate. And when that happens, your ability to restore the balance is based on how much you are willing to bleed—and in their eyes, the more the better.

"Aight, a few ground rules." Jacob brushes his waves to perfection. "One, don't drink nothin' I ain't buy you, and even then, finish it—don't put it down or somebody may slip something in your drink and try to have their way with you. Two, stay close where I can see you at all times. Remember: we neva know what can happen next. We're safer together."

I reach out and hug him out of fear of everything that could happen, and when I see people staring as they walk by the car, I bury my face into his neck.

"Aye." He holds my face, makes sure I look in his eyes and hear every word. "Ain't nobody gon' ever look or be like you, so rock yo' shit like they wish they could. Aight? Don't worry 'bout it. I ain't gon' let nothin' bad happen to you."

I nod, still unsure.

We get out, smooth the wrinkles from our clothes, and walk to the front, shoulders back, eyes straight ahead. When I walk to get in the line that zigzags over itself and into the parking lot, Jacob stops me, tells me to follow him. He gives the security guard our names, and the burly guy waves us in.

Where school feels like a watering hole you survive every day you go for a drink, Da Rink is more of a block party with two newly built rinks—a bigger one for the adults and a smaller one for itty-bitties or beginners. In the far back, the DJ booth and a small VIP section sit elevated, and to the left, a mini arcade with tables and chairs near the concessions stand. Farther back are lockers and an area to rent skates.

With his arm over my shoulder, Jacob and me are treated like royalty—not a coming-out but a showing-out, where everyone wants to be invited in. Yet again, Jacob's gravitational pull keeps me safe, extends me grace and privilege that isn't my own.

But it changes when Jacob goes to get our skates, leaving me behind. Without him, I feel like an astronaut whose suit cord is cut, and all I can do is drift alone into the abyss. Suddenly, it feels too crowded, too loud, too much—like an astronaut whose suit cord is cut—and all I can do is drift alone into the abyss.

Someone bumps me so hard I almost fall. I only catch the back of his jacket, a light-blue letterman but with the white letters "LB" on the back that light up in the black light.

I close my eyes, breathe in and out, try to block out the voice within that only wants to hurt me, see me suffer. My collarbone and arm begin to burn from the inside out, from where the guy bumped me. I focus:

In . . . out . . . *You have to leave. Nobody wants you here.*

In . . . out . . . *Everyone's laughing at you, again.*

In . . . out . . . *Without Jacob, you're nothing—and you never will be.*

It isn't working, I can't fix what is breaking, and I only feel worse after trying until I back into the wall of *him*, the scent of peppermint gum and Cool Water. His arms wrap around my shoulders, like clouds blocking out a harsh and unrelenting sun.

I feel Leroy's smile, even though I can't see it.

"You a li'l close, ain't it?" Jacob's voice pierces the haze, brings back a different kind of light.

Leroy releases me, then daps and hugs Jacob. He stands beside me, every now and then brushing his body against mine.

"Taj ova there lookin fuh you."

"Where?" Jacob says.

"There." He points. "Rissa got us the VIP. I saw yall when you came in, came to get you."

"Y'all rented skates already?" Jacob hands me mine: black with red wheels, size eleven, while he holds on to his, a size twelve.

"I brought mine."

"Look at you talkin' like you know what you doin'."

Leroy smiles, accepts Jacob's silent challenge. "You sure you don't need me to show yall the ropes over there in the kiddie rink?"

"Nah, but you can go ova there and brush up on yo' skills. Would hate for us to make you look bad," I say.

Leroy looks at me. "You can skate?"

I nodded. "A li'l bit."

He doesn't know me and Jacob used to win roller-skating competitions each summer from when I was eight to twelve years old, which was when Jacob had to quit to take track more seriously. We had choreographed moves and everything, and because I was so young and could do it all, I was his secret weapon. Skating was one of the few things Jacob and I were equally good at, together.

"You skatin in them clothes?" Leroy scans my body, gets stuck at my waist. I try to turn away, hide, cover myself.

"Yup," Jacob answers for me.

"Okay . . . okay . . . I see yall tryna distract people."

"Making up excuses so you won't have to look bad?" I say, excited at the thought of being underestimated by him, by everyone.

"Oh, it's like that?" He nods, smiles. "Gotchu."

After we lace and get the numbered signs to pin to the back of our shirts, we head toward the rink. The next time I see Leroy, he is ready to put on a little performance of his own. Before, I only remember him having on an unbuttoned red baseball jersey, some jeans, and red Air Force 1s. Now he's in a mesh red-and-black ribbed tank with just a strap on one shoulder and a section missing on the other side, revealing his tats underneath. It hugs and exalts him, matching his sagging pants with a red fitted. His tattoos glitter like enchanted armor in the lights. His skates are all red with black wheels, and when he smiles, the light sparkles on his vampire-fang grills. When he glides by and winks, a part of me swoons and can't stop staring—and he knows it.

"He came here to stunt, ain't it?" Princeton smiles, standing next to me. He's glowing in a light-blue ribbed tank and white pants, fitted like bell-bottoms. Everywhere he goes, a trail of eyes follow, and I don't blame them.

"I didn't know you were going to be here," I say, surprised to find him next to me. "I see you. . . . I see you."

He grins, blushes. "Well, when I heard you would be here with Jacob and Leroy, I had to come with all the bells and whistles. I'm glad I did. Otherwise, I woulda been jealous. Kinda am actually."

"Aww . . . whateva," I joke.

"You sure you good wit all these people? I figured it would be a little rough . . . you know." Princeton leans on the barrier with his elbows, so I can't run from his eyes.

"I'm not gon' lie. I definitely had a moment when we first came in with Jacob. There was this guy who bumped me. I don't think he meant to, but it was pretty hard."

"Who? You remember what he look like?" Something in Princeton changes, like it did yesterday, ready to go to war over my discomfort.

"Chill. I'll tell you if you don't make a big deal of it."

He looks at me, agrees begrudgingly. I look around, then realize who it was wearing the letterman jacket: Lyric Bryson.

Princeton follows my eyes. "Lyric? He the one who did it?"

I nod, confused by the truth, too. "I don't think he meant to."

"Nah, he prolly did. He can be a li'l moody like that. I tell you what, that nigga do it again, you let me know. He already on my shit list anyway."

"Why? What do you mean?"

"Well, iono if you know this—don't tell nobody cuz I ain't supposed to know, either—but the main reason Lyric struttin' 'round here like he always got something to prove is because he a Bainbridge, but they don't claim him."

"What? Really?"

"Yuuuup . . . hear Ma talkin' on the phone in her study but the door was cracked: Louis Bainbridge the Fourth was a rolling stone. But Lyric gets the short end of the stick 'cuz his mom used to be Louis B's secretary. When they found out she was pregnant, they cut her a check, made sure she ain't neva speak of their connection. As long as she does that, they keep the money flowin'—the cost of her silence—but if it ever gets out . . ." He shakes his head.

"Hmmm . . . that sucks. That's not a way to live, not being

able to be who you are," I say, thinking about him differently, wondering about the layers of his past he might be hiding. A Bainbridge who isn't white, that I didn't expect.

"Look atchu, all sensitive seein' stuff from his perspective. Does this mean I can go punch him in the face now?"

I shake my head, chuckle. "No, I say. You need to stay standing right here and never leave my side until it's time for me to skate. And when I do, I want to hear you cheerin' so it feels like you are out there with me. Best friend duty." I wink.

"Werd?" He smiles with both rows of teeth. "Heard. I gotchu."

Rissa grabs the mic. Turns out she's the much-anticipated MC for the night. "Wayment, wayment . . . Hold up, hold up. All these fine people in heah skatin round and round, I know you can do betta than that. Stay quiet if you ugly!"

Everybody roars and claps.

"That's what I'm talkin bout." She scans the crowd, finds me, smiles. "Hayyyy, errbody. Yall ready for a skatedown?"

Everybody stamps their feet.

"Gooood. Here's the tea: errbody with pro-level skills will come to the rink and put on a number. Pro-level means anybody confident enough to show off and not fall. For now, only fourteen and up. We have a special skatedown coming up next fuh the little ones. In case this is your first time, here's how it goes: the DJ is going to play two songs, and while they're on, the rules are simple: look good, have fun, and whateva you do, don't fall.

"At the end of the second song, we'll close out wit a skatedown train led by my very own nephew Leroy Booker, the fine one wit the vampire fangs—and no, he can't bite you; he's already spoken for, so don't ask. At the end, our judges will write down the numbers of their top picks, and then we crown the winners, bow down for a lil minute, and enjoy free food and a free beverage compliments of yours truly."

The hungry and happy room hoots and hollers.

"Alright . . . Go, DJ."

The crowd responds, "Cuz that's my DJ."

As we skate slow and wait, the beat to Juvenile's "Back That Azz Up" flirts through the speakers, and the air in the room changes from chill to hot and hormones-threatening-to-take-over.

Rissa jumps back on the mic. "Wayment, wayment . . . Mistah DJ Man, Mistah DJ Suh. You can't do that."

The crowd bursts into laughter.

"You almost had people twerkin down these walls. Look ova there, already got some people ready to hang upside down and pop in a headstand." She pauses, looks at him. The crowd knows why and laughs. "Mistah DJ Man, Mistah DJ Suh . . . Can I ask you a question? . . . Watcho name is?"

A really tall dark-skinned man with a shaved head and

white headphones stands up in the DJ booth so everybody can see him. When he speaks, his voice rolls like thunder, to which Rissa immediately keeps responding.

He says his name, DJ Harold. Then licks his lips.

"I'm sorry," Rissa coos, clutching invisible pearls around her neck and fanning herself with the oohs and aahs of the crowd. "DJ Harrrorrr." She purrs like Eartha Kitt. "Can I give you a nickname?"

"Depends on what it is."

"The spirit within me told me I should call you . . ." She pauses, looks over at everyone in the rink as they hang on her every word. "DJ ThundaMakeYaWonda." She sings it to the crowd and they go wild. "Whatchu think, Harrrrold?"

He looks out at the crowd. "I like it. . . . I like you." Then he kisses her on the cheek.

The crowd screams, claps their hands, and stomps their feet. Rissa pretends to almost faint, then whispers into the mic, "Benji . . . if you're out there . . . I love you."

Everyone laughs; some even wipe happy tears from their eyes.

"Alrighty, errbody, it's skatedown time. Mistah DJ Thunda-MakeYaWonda, drop that track on em nice and slow."

He bops his head and lets it ride.

Jacob glides beside me, says to just do the moves he tells me to when he gives me the signal, just like old times. I nod, petrified, knees clacking like hair knockers. But when a chopped and screwed remix of Shaggy's "Mr. Boombastic" dribbles with bass from the speakers, and everybody sways, skates braiding to the beat, something crawls up the base of my spine and vibrates all over my body: first cold, then warm.

If attention is currency, I want the swagger trapped in my bones to seep out like magic conjured by ancestral tongues made foreign, a different kind of rich.

When Jacob skates on Leroy's left, I go to his right, and, together, we grind low, shoulders, then hips, a roll, then legs, left and right, as our knuckles almost drag to the floor, our backs undulating back up. If Jacob and I are the chants, then Leroy's body becomes the beat that, in another time, might have summoned the rain, as we become a triad wielding wiles beyond our years. Leroy does light jumps, skating on one leg at a time, down then up, picking up speed. We follow, swerving in and out of people, guided by the sway of his legs, the heat of his suggestion.

Jacob gives the signal, and I race ahead of Leroy, switch strides and skate backward near the center, where there are fewer people.

Leroy catches up. "Show me whatchu got on the next song. It's my favorite."

Purple Ribbon All-Stars' "Kryptonite" sweeps through the speakers as Leroy flashes a smile.

I wait, then ride the beat, knees bent, dipping and rising,

drawing a figure eight with my hips, in and out, until I'm spinning, my hands following the curves of my waist, my chest, my legs, the circle getting smaller and faster before I break loose and skate forward. Somewhere there are cheers, yelling the number on my back in place of my name. Leroy watches me, ensnared by the glimpse of who I can be, what I want to offer him and only him.

He nods, says something I can't hear.

Rissa grabs the mic, says it's skatedown train time.

Before I can turn around, Leroy's hands find my hips, pushes me forward, matches my stride as everyone gets behind him, dozens upon dozens laughing, skating, emanating a joy I've never felt but can't help but be enveloped by. Then something catches my eyes. Amid the crowd, the dancing, there's Brown Brown and Lyric talking. But it's no everyday chat because Brown Brown's face is tense like a pit bull. He gets up, walks out slowly, with Lyric following closely—too close—behind. Just as they leave, I see PYT keeping his distance, watching everything they do.

Leroy pulls me closer, and instantly I'm back where I belong, with his hands around my hips, holding me tight, for everyone who is anyone to see. In my ear, he whispers, "I'll never let you go," and I believe him.

18

Leroy

Me, Jay, and Jacobee are crowned "Kings of the Skatedown," and Da Rink get even mo hype when they find out issa three-way tie. But none of that even mattas to me, cuz I got to do somethin I been dreamin of doin, skatin, flirtin, and holdin Jay in front of errbody so they know who he wit and how special he is. I aint know how it was gon turn out. I thought he won't really into me anymore and, I aint gon lie, seein him at the skatedown had me so nervous.

I always knew Jay was pritty, but only recently I feel like he started to see it a lil bit mo. But I won't prepared for when he rolled up at Da Rink in his fit. Thought I was gon have to start knockin niggas out left and right, cuz I aint like how they was lookin at him like a piece of meat. Well, ion mind them lookin, it's how they was lookin, like if he won't careful, they won't gon just look. But when I had em droolin wit Trish new fit, it was on. And I aint felt so good in a long time.

When Rissa makes the announcement, I make sure Jay gets some time to hug and errbody do what they gotta do befo I pull Jay to the side. I ask em if he wanna go somewhere wit me, where it's just us, and the look in his eyes makes me wanna just grab his hand and run. I give Rissa, Jacobee, and Taj a heads-up that we'll be slippin out for a second but that we will come back in like an hour. I aint let nobody know bout my plan—not even Jay, until he see me pull up at Rissa's diner.

Ion think he really believes we are goin in without anybody bein in there cuz I aint park right in front of the diner like I normally do—aint tryna attract no attention. So I park on the otha side of the street, near the gas station, and we run ova and enter through the back. I keep all the blinds down and the lights off, except way in the back, where we're near the kitchen and the room in the back. There, I walk him into the room, turn him round, and do somethin I been wantin to do for the longest: I kiss him, really kiss him. Get so lost in his lips I forget the whole point of bringin him here won't the kissin—although I hoped he would want to—but the love letter. It takes errthang to pull away from his lips, to keep it togetha.

"You okay?" he asks, his arms round my shoulders. "Did I do something . . . wrong?" He pulls back, nervous.

"Nah, not at all. I just wanted to do this right. I been waitin so long to give you something. . . ." I hand the letter to him, watch as his face frowns, then turns into a smile when he realizes what it is.

"This whole time . . . eva since I met you, it's like I aint have no words for you, for how you make me feel." I'm tryna say it real smooth, like I practiced, but my hands are shakin. I try to hide them but Jay sees, reaches for em, holds them while I speak.

"Even right now, you doin this, and I'm nervous, cuz iono if I can really say it in a way you really get, so you feel what I feel. It's like, when I wake up, I'm reachin for you when you not there. And when you here, even right now, I'm tryna get closer, cuz when I'm round you, the shit that I don't talk bout, that hurts, don't hurt as much. That ache right here, in my chest, turns warm when you smile, and I feel light, like if I stretch my arms out, I could fly away.

"I aint gon lie, iono what's in front of us, and if it's anything like what we been through already, whew."

We both chuckle.

"But I wrote it in a letter—I'll say it to you now: I think I love you, cuz it hurts to say goodbye. So I don't. I spray the last of you—" Lookin at him, watchin him take in my words throws me off and—*fuck*—for a second, I forget the words.

Jay smiles, unfolds the letter in his hands, puts it in mine. "Here, read it to me?"

I nod, but lookin in his eyes, the words come rushin back. "I spray the last of you on my sheets, breathe you in till I see you in my sleep. Yo eyes, yo hips, till all that's left is yo name and my name on our lips. Rissa called you mine befo I knew what to do wit it, but when time stood still, I knew. Since I found yo letter in the back seat, I feel like I only belong to one person: you." I take a breath. "PS, this might sound lame or silly, but you da first person I eva wrote a love letter to, cuz, yeah, you that pritty."

Between us, it's like the words echo round us, and I can read them in his eyes, I can feel them on his skin, and can hear them in my ears. And even though he just heard me say the words, he takes the letter from my hands, leans back on the desk, and reads. Half standin, half sittin on the desk, he don't look comfortable, so I pick him up, sit him on top of the desk proper, so I can watch him read it, face to page, lips movin, recitin the same words in a soft whisper. And as his eyes leave the page, they read me instead, and he kisses me, pulls me closer.

Then, we hear somethin. We freeze.

I lean back, see headlights in the front, in the diner parking lot. But aint nobody supposed to be here, not at least for a coupla hours.

We look at each otha, listenin. Somebody rattles the front door, plays wit the lock, but the only people who got a key is me, Jacobee, Rissa, and Benji. So, if they gotta work it, try to pick it, they aint supposed to be here.

I grab Jay's hand and pull him toward me as I cut off the light just befo the back door opens. I gently close the door a lil bit mo in the room we in. I look round, tryna figure out where we might be able to hide, just in case they be comin in here. There's a closet, not far from the door, big enough for both of us to get in.

I move Jay in front of it, whisper for him to get in and I'll get in wit him. He gets in first, I back in so, if the door open, they'll find me first, not him.

Outside the room, we listen, tryna figure out if we bein paranoid or if somebody really broke into Rissa's. The footsteps are quick, and it don't take long befo whoeva it is finds the room where we at. I hold the doorknob of the closet where we at, feel Jay's arms pullin me back into him, his hands round my waist, so I stay close.

"I keep lookin, but I don't see it." It's Brown Brown. But why—

"I just told you. I aint one of yo lil goons you can order round and tell what to do. If I told you I'm in the diner lookin for the drive, I mean it. I aint got no reason to lie."

"Wait, what? I can't hear you. . . . The voice modulator sound off, I can't hear you. . . . You sound muffled. Why don't you just— Wait . . .

"Aight, I gotchu on speakerphone. Whatchu say?"

"You said it was there. That means if it's not there, either you're lying or you don't know as much about them or the BDs as you claim to." The voice sounds like a robot, but at the same time, you can almost hear—it's a voice like his, not too deep, not too soft. Who is it?

Jay holds me tight. I can feel it in his grip, he shocked just like I am.

"What I say just now? If you wanna come here and look,

by all means, you can skip yo ass on in here and look yaself. I keep tellin you, I aint yo 'do' boy," Brown Brown says.

"Okay, then. You be sure to remember those words when your dad doesn't get that chief of police position he's been working his whole life for. And, better yet"—the voice pauses between threats—"when they find evidence of his corruption—well, not just his, your aunts' and your uncles'—we'll see what decision they would have preferred you make."

"Yo, fuck you."

"Does that mean you'll try harder and keep looking? Or is this the best you can do for me? 'Cuz Darius, at this rate, you're going to have to make an uncomfortable choice: end up like Rouk or end up like Faa."

I hold on to Jay this time, squeeze him as much as I can without hurtin him, wishin I could at least use my words. Iono how much mo I can take, hearin this nigga voice like he own the world and Brown Brown bein stupid enough to betray us ova his family. Brown Brown aint go to the school he chose cuz they had the best track team, he went cuz his folks won't gon pay for him to go to Providence Prep if he kept hangin out wit Taj and us—if he aint cut us off and plan to go into law enforcement. They aint neva cared bout him, or went to none of his meets, they neva showed him love, not since he told them he aint neva wanna be a cop.

How can he betray us, when we the ones who protect him, look out for him, pick up the phone errtime he calls Taj from somewhere drunk cuz he can't take bein in the house wit his folks or even on that side of town? We aint gotta be blood to be a real family, we just gotta be willin to go to the ends of the earth for each otha and back again.

"Wait . . . I think I found somethin. Looks like it's in a binder. . . . I dunno, looks like some kinda plan. This might be it. I'll bring it wit me. I don't see the drive, tho. Maybe this is better—their plan to protect the neighborhood."

"Remember: No traces. If it gets back to you, there's no way the Diamond Kuttaz can protect you. In the meantime, see if you can find out where they're keeping Rouk. He's a loose end, now that he's turned on me. Now that their lil truce is falling apart, Frank and Myrrh were able to confess right on time, so they can handle Rouk as soon as they get out on bail. Then, you might be able to get your own DK tat, once you prove your loyalty."

"Whateva, I'm out." Brown Brown leaves, closes the door behind him, and locks it.

I can hear him move to the back door, too. I hear the lock.

I slowly step out of the closet, help Jay behind me. His eyes look like mine—confused and in a daze. "Are we sure that was him?"

"Yeah," I say. "I know Brown Brown voice anywhere. It was him. It was *fuckin* him. This whole time. This *whole* time? Shit!" I punch a wall and accidentally scare Jay.

"I'm sorry. . . . I aint mean to, I just—"

He comes up behind me, puts his arms round my waist. I'm happy he here wit me, that I can feel him next to me.

"Do you know who he was on the phone with?" Jay asks.

"Nah, I couldn't really make out the voice. Iono, it could be anybody. Hell, it could be somebody else in the BDs for all I know. And that shit bout Rouk and Faa—"

Words won't come out; all I can do is stand still and clench my fists so hard it feel like my nails are cuttin into my palms. It's fucked up what Rouk did, and honestly, iono if we gon eva be the same, but hearin whoeva that was say them two guys gon kill em when they get out, shit just aint right. Not after they killed Faa and used Rouk's pain so he couldn't see straight. Ion agree wit what Rouk did, shit was all the way wrong, but I can't say I wouldn'ta done the same. If somebody killed Taj or Jay or Rissa or Jacobee, and I believed it was somebody I thought I trusted since I was little, I wouldn'ta stopped until they blood was on my hands—and then some. It just aint fair.

So much fucked-up stuff has happened to Rouk and Faa, from their ma dyin while givin birth to Rouk to their pops dyin from an overdose cuz he couldn't live wit the pain. Errthang kept gettin harder and harder, till we finally met each otha the last day of the Coastal Empire Fair. And even tho we barely knew each otha, the moment Faa beat Taj on that shootin game and won Rouk the blue teddy bear I begged him for, we became inseparable. We spent all night together, tryna see who was better, who was stronger, who could go on the scariest ride, the Ring of Fire, the most amount of times until all we could do was enjoy each otha and crowd on the Ferris wheel, goin round and round till—

"That's it," I say.

"What?" Jay asks.

"The password! I think I know what it is. It's the one date me, Faa, Rouk, and Taj all had in common, the first day we met each otha and became friends."

"You sure?" he says.

"Yeah. I think so. It's the only thing it can be." Glad I still kept the flash drive in my pocket, in case I needed it. I pull it out and cut on Rissa's computer. Once it loads up and I plug it in, it asks for a password. I type in the numbers: 11500. It still don't work. I shake my head, frustrated.

"You sure it's just the date? That might be too easy. What if it's the date and your initials or something? Jacob and I used to do that, make passwords based on our initials all the time, our own secret code."

"Iono, I don't think so." Think, Lee. Think! Back then, Taj and Faa were obsessed wit who was the oldest. And Taj and Faa did have a thing for numbers, I just won't round them enough to know since I aint really understand computers like that. It's worth a try, tho. But what order? Do I add it at the end, in the middle, start at the front?

The longer I stare at it, the mo I realize it's mo simple than it seems. Between the dates, there are four spaces I could put each of our initials: befo the month, befo the day, befo the year, and after the year. I plug in the letters and numbers and hold my breath as I do it: F11T5L00R.

It still don't work.

"Try writing it using two numbers for the month and day and four for the year."

I do what he says, retype it: F11T05L2000R. Suddenly, I'm scared to press Enter, cuz if it don't work, iono what I'm gon—

Jay presses Enter for me. I look at him, surprised.

"Trust yourself." He grins.

The screen unlocks.

"It worked," I yell-whisper.

"Yes!" Jay says.

There's a shit ton of folders errwhere. Some are labeled specific years and dates, articles, property purchases, but one folder stands out: "BPD." When we click it, we learn what the letters mean: Bainbridge Promise Development. We click on the first thing inside, which turns out to be a map of Savannah.

At first, it look normal, so I'm bout to click out, but Jay says, "Something's missing. Maybe if you zoom in, we can read the—"

"K-Town is gone." I say it befo I realize what it means. Don't take long for the truth to slap us upside the head ova and ova: it aint the same map cuz it's what they plan to turn Savannah into. "They tryna get rid of K-Town and call it

'Promise Heights'?" I say, thinkin out loud.

"Hold on. Look there, not just Promise Heights, the full name: Savannah-Bainbridge Promise Heights, a city within a city, one completely made ova, erased. High-rises, entertainment centers, a luxury resort."

I shake my head, overwhelmed and furious. "This is what Faa found, proof that they won't just tryna move us out of K-Town but get rid of it—and the people who live there. Just so they can get mo rich? Guess it don't matta if they scatter us to the ends of Savannah. They don't give a fuck, long as they get what they want."

Jay watches me, but this time even he aint got no words. So he points instead. "Back out a little. This tells us the Bainbridges are involved but it don't really tell us why they would hurt Faa. I mean, think about it, if you released this to the media, what would they do?"

"Not a damn thang."

"Right, some people might be pissed, but that can't be it—can't be enough to kill somebody over. But that might," he says, showing me where to click. Next to the map is a folder called "BPD Roster."

When I click, what we find shocks us both into silence. It's a list of names, hundreds, just like the BD network, except all the people on the list are in high positions, from the heads of neighborhood associations and church groups to city council and errthang else you can think of. Next to each name is money they've given and the promises they expect.

If you only count half of em, just the big ones, it's already in the millions. The closer you look, you see this aint no regular investment, it's the proof that all paths, all companies, all names—no matta how regular or fancy, some even connected to the BDs—lead to the Bainbridges, which means so does all the money. And at the top of the list is a name we both recognize.

"It's him," I say, lookin at Jay. "The same guy yo ma mentioned, the guy who was best friends wit yo pops from Providence Prep: Louis Bainbridge the Fourth."

"And he's the person who benefits the most from this, the one who stands to gain tens of millions alone. *That's* more than enough of a reason to kill Faa and do everything else."

I nod, and it hurts. But it don't explain errthang. "But a guy like that aint gon be talkin to Brown Brown on nobody phone, robot voice or nah."

"No, he won't. Because he doesn't have to."

I look at Jay, confused. "Then who was he—"

"Lyric," Jay says, so soft I barely hear it.

I shake my head. It couldn't be Lyric. Sure he hung round Rouk, but there's no way some kid from Providence Prep is behind this. How would he even be involved wit the Bainbridges?

"Why Lyric? He just Rouk's groupie."

"You don't understand. I saw him leavin Da Rink with

Brown Brown not long befo we did. I also saw PYT; he was watching them, too. I think he followed Brown Brown to see what he was up to. And earlier tonight, Princeton told me—"

"PYT followed them? Was he wit them, or was he followin them?"

"I don't know," Jay says. "Didn't look like he was with them, didn't look like he wanted to be seen, either."

"But why Lyric? It don't make sense. Rouk confessed; Rouk was there. Yeah, the loc guys tricked him into doin some of it, but they all got the same DK tat, the Diamond Kuttaz. Lyric aint got no tat, at least ion think he do—"

"He wouldn't need one. Lyric *is* a Bainbridge. *And* Rouk hung around him."

My heart drops. "Where you hear that at?"

"I was trying to tell you. Princeton told me. He said no one was supposed to know. He only knows because Lady Tee. But he said Lyric's mom use to be Louis Bainbridge's assistant. He's not allowed to talk about it either, because if he does, he'll lose everything. They're keeping him a secret."

All the pieces begin to crash together in my head so fast I get light-headed.

"And you know how you've mentioned the DK tattoo?" Jay grabs some paper from the desk, draws out the symbol. "Did it look like this?" His crown don't look as jagged, but it's pretty much it.

"You seen this befo?"

"Yeah. On a necklace that Christina has."

"Daniel Lee Tina? Lyric's Tina?"

"Yeah, *that* Christina. This whole time, there was somebody who was close to everybody. It's him. Lyric is the one because you said it yourself, he's Rouk's groupie. But what if that's just what he pretends to be because no one knows the truth?"

Shit! If I woulda paid attention, I woulda saw how easy it was for Lyric to be trusted by any and errbody, so he could be errwhere and nowhere at the same time—makin him the Bainbridges' secret weapon, usin his desire, his pain, to finally be accepted, as an excuse to get him to do the dirty work: to put a hit out on Faa, when they realized what he found, and—

"Lee, you smell something?" Jay shakes my shoulder, interruptin my thoughts. His face is turned up, sniffin at the air.

Now that he mentions it, there's something off, almost like Rissa forgot and left the burner on, but Jay realizes what's goin on first.

"Lee," Jay screams, pointin to the door. "Look!"

There's a light near the bottom of it and smoke. Fire.

Tha fuck? I run up to the door, beat on it, but it's locked from the outside.

"Why is it locked? We neva locked the door cuz . . ." It's Brown Brown, he had to do this. But why? Why would he burn down Rissa's— "No traces," the voice said. They wanna cover they tracks so nobody know what Brown Brown took from the diner.

We gotta get outta here so we can tell somebody what we know.

I kick the door. Try to run my shoulder into it, but ion do it right cuz a sharp pain shoots down my side and I can barely move it.

"Leroy, hold up. Let's think for a minute. Is there another way out?"

"Nah, ion think so. The only otha way is the underground tunnel in the otha room. But we gotta get through this door first to get to it."

"Okay . . . okay . . . Ummm . . . okay," Jay says, thinkin on the verge of panickin.

I hold him by his shoulders, look into his eyes, and say what I need to hear, too. "One thing at a time. We gon figure this out. But we gotta keep the smoke on that side of the door. I'mma look for stuff to put under the door, you call nine-one-one, and any- and errbody you can to see who can get here first."

I grab what I can and start stuffin it in the crack beneath the door.

"Wait," Jay says. "We gotta get the drive."

I hear him but I don't hear him as I try to keep the smoke out.

"They won't pick up; it's just ringing," Jay yells.

"Who?"

"Nine-one-one! Can they—why won't they pick up?"

"Don't worry. You call errbody else you can, and Imma call, too."

I look for my phone but can't find it. I look at the door and the small puff of smoke sneakin its way into the room. I hear Jay callin and dialin, callin and dialin, and I can't help but think of errthang I didn't do, again—errthang I didn't see that I shoulda.

Lyric was the one always close: befriendin Rouk when Faa died and usin Frank and Myrrh to stir up the gangs to destroy the BDs' truce. He could trick Rouk into goin to Taj house, knowin Frank and Myrrh was really goin to kill Taj, maybe even Rouk, too, and make him the perfect scapegoat. And when that aint work, Lyric looked for someone else he could turn and blackmail, like Brown Brown, to find Faa's flash drive and make sure it neva leaked to the media or anybody else. And if he couldn't do that, he could get the Bainbridges the one they aint had but needed: the BDs' plans for how to stop them.

But I can't give up now. Not knowin what I know. This is my chance—our chance—to put an end to this shit and bring the Bainbridges and Lyric to their knees.

I find my phone on the bed and call, too. Together, we tag-team it.

"You call Jacobee; I'll call Taj."

No answer.

"I'll call Rissa; you try Jacobee."

No answer.

They must all still be at Da Rink, not close enough to they phones. We need somebody who aint there right now. Somebody we know could hear they phone when it ring.

"You call nine-one-one, and I'll call my momma," Jay yells.

The line keeps ringin. No answer.

"You call PYT, and I'll call Princeton."

Princeton don't pick up, but PYT does.

"PYT!"

There aint no answer, just heavy breathin. I put the phone on speaker so I can hear him better. We hear PYT scream.

"PYT . . . you there? PYT, call somebody. The diner is on fire and we locked in here. PYT!"

"Nigga, you aint nothin but a snake." It's his voice. "Aint shit you can do. I aint sayin shit. Fuck you!" We hear hits, him grunt. Then the dial tone.

I look at Jay. "Fuck!" I'm bout to lose it. I'm so mad I can't even see straight.

"Just keep callin," I say, so mad, I'm shakin all ova. Iono who hurtin him, iono who tryna hurt us, but I'm gettin sick of bein in situations where somebody hurtin the people I love. When I get outta here—when we do—I aint gon stop till I feel betta or this shit is made right—whicheva take the longest.

"I'll call my ma, you call yours, yo dad, any-fuckin-body. As fast as you can."

Ma don't answer. Night don't answer. Trish don't answer. I call Taj again, he don't answer. Jay calls Jacobee again. No answer. He calls his mom. She picks up. He screams into the phone. Tells her where he is. Lets her know he'll keep tryna call otha numbers. Asks her to do the same. I call 911 again, and they finally pick up. Now both of us is yellin into the phones, screamin for help, hopin it'll come sooner than soon.

But I can't just sit here and wait. What if they don't make it? What if they get here and they can't find us? This can't be it. This can't be how it ends. Not for me, not for Jay.

This was the Bainbridge plan the whole time, to use Lyric to send a message: anybody who dares to right the balance, to question why they get to keep they boots on our necks, gotta pay the consequences. So they toyed wit us, let us think we was safe when we won't. They trapped us in our memories, reminded us we are as helpless as we feel just like me and Jay fightin to keep the smoke out our lungs. But Imma keep fightin cuz they can't win.

I kick the door. If I can't stop the smoke from comin in, then we need to get the fuck out.

Jay helps.

We kick.

We keep slammin, tryna get the door loose, but the smoke is comin in fast, too fast. We can barely see, we can barely breathe. We can hear the cracklin, the fire as glass and stuff explode. I keep kickin, and Jay looks for somethin, anything in the almost dark that we can use to get the door loose.

We cover our mouths wit our shirts, huddle close. Try to kick from a distance, but it's gettin harder to breathe. Instead I hold on to Jay. I don't care what happens, I aint gon let him go—neva.

We stand near the door, hopin somebody will hear us, but nothing. We hear nothing.

The room is dark wit smoke, and my eyes burn. I look round for anything. I pull the sheets from the bed, grab a water bottle sittin on the desk and wet them as much as I can and wrap them round Jay. I pull us back as far away from the door as we can, kick away the chair. Move the desk as much as it will budge.

Jay keeps fallin back into me, fallin asleep.

I shake him, try to keep him awake. I hold him up.

There's bangin on the otha side. I jump up, run to the door, bang back. I hear voices but don't know who.

"Lee!" It's Taj.

"Jay!" It's Jacobee.

They kick hard, and harder, and harder.

It keeps gettin harder to breathe. I grab Jay, try to hold him up, but he can't stand, can't breathe, keeps fallin. I yell for them to hurry up.

"Get back from the door," Jacobee yells. "Benji and his

crew comin wit an ax and a sledgehammer. Get as far back as you can."

I pull us back, as far as I can. I wait for them, for somethin to rip a hole into this smoky darkness and get us out. But nothin happens. The voices are gone. The room gets darker, too dark. And I don't feel Jay tryna hold on anymore.

I shake him as hard as I can, try to hold his face, but he limp. I try errthang I can, hover ova him, cover his face, try to get him to talk. But there's nothin. No sound. Don't even feel him breathin. It's hard to breathe. All of it. It's too hard.

I don't know why, but the mo I try, the mo tired I get, until all I can do is sit pushed back as far as I can near the bed and the desk. I can't see, can't hear, can't feel.

Wit Jay in my arms, the only thing I can think of is when Mistah Prez first read Jay's letter and he asked if I believed in fate, that two people could be connected across time and space, always revolvin, fallin in and out of love across lifetimes. He asked if I believed that maybe I loved Jay in anotha life—and, if given the opportunity, what I would do, be willin to give up, to be wit him. That's when I said *my life,* cuz ion really think I knew how to live befo I met him, cuz I was just survivin. He woke up somethin in me that had been sleep. Somethin that would become bold enough to speak, to feel, to be somethin I neva thought I could be—if it meant I could be wit him.

I said I'd give up my life, not cuz I wanted it to sound

nice, but cuz I've loved Jay since the first time I saw him at Da Rink when he was eight, showin the world that he won't scared to be soft, showin the world he won't scared to be different, showin the world he won't scared to be pritty, showin the world he won't scared.

I'm prepared to die, if it mean Jay can live. But if I get outta this alive, I aint gon let nothin and nobody take him away from me. And no matta how hard it get, I aint leavin. I aint gotta leave to keep him safe cuz Imma do that shit right next to him, so he neva forget I'm here to stay—even if he push me away, even if it gets harder, and there's mo scary shit waitin for us on the otha side.

I hear the first hit on the door, see it come away in chunks, pieces. I cover Jay and our heads, hold us together, tight, until the door flies open, off the hinges. And I see Taj and Jacobee kick the little bit of it that's still hangin as Benji and his friends from the Marines rush in wit the fire extinguisher, pullin on us until they finally get us outside.

Out front, they crowd round Jay as the ambulance shrieks closer. I try to get loose, try to get ova to Jay while Jacobee is givin him CPR, tryna get him up. If I can just touch him, if I can get close enough, then maybe—

I hear it. I see it in the eyes of Jacobee and errbody near him. Jay's coughin. They pull him up, pat him on the back. And I see him look ova at me. Covered in smoke and ash. Even wit all that, he dares to smile. I can't say nothin cuz my throat burns from the smoke and I can barely breathe. So I do the only thing I can, I get ova to him, don't care it feels like I'm on my last breath, cuz even if I am, I want it to be wit him. I hold him tight and cry cuz sometimes, words just aint enough. He holds me, while I hold him, and errbody arms wrap round us, too.

Soon, all any of us can do is watch and listen as Rissa's diner, a Savannah staple—errbody's hope away from home—burns till it can't burn no mo. Then it hits me: the drive, the computer, errthang was inside.

I aint remember to grab it, which means errthang we learned went up in smoke and the only otha stuff we had is in Brown Brown's hands on its way to the Bainbridges. Then, Jay puts somethin in the palm of my hand and smiles: it's the flash drive. And even though I can't speak, even tho errthang hurts, I look in his eyes and think it as loud as I can . . .

They thought they taught us a lesson.

They thought they sent us a message.

They thought they destroyed us.

But they were wrong—and now it's our turn:

Me and you are gonna send the Bainbridges a message they'll neva forget.

Acknowledgments

I give all the glory, power, and honor to the higher power, spirit, and ancestors who continue to guide me.

To my momma, who continues to teach me the power of love, witnessing, and healing. To my two fathers and my siblings, you keep me strong and inspire me to keep going. To my sister-cousin, Tranika Brown, my ride-and-live and real-life hero, and my brother-cousin, Rashawn—yeah, you, too, I ain't fuhget. And cousin Jeanette McKinnon, you all up in and around these pages, too. Thank you for your love and help raising all of us, even when you were still just a child. Six things only we will understand: West Lake, shared water jug, Mrs. Edna, the big park, the little park, and the country sto'. To the rest of my family, friends, and loved ones—thank you for your prayers, they were felt and known.

A very special thanks to Terrance Daye, who spoke and breathed new life into *Pritty*. To KarynRose Bruyning, who first called me a novelist before I knew what it meant—and her many *feelings* that keep me laughing. To Ellen Goff, the best agent ever—*periodt!* To Carolina Ortiz, whose vision, tireless joy, passion, and patience turned this from a manuscript into a real book. To Maria Zoccola, the prolific poet and proofreader, you copyediting guru you. To Jahid A.

Wilson, Jr., the best research assistant in the whole world—not to mention, one of my former youth leaders—thank you!

To my MFA cohort at St. Francis College and the amazing faculty who continue to teach me craft: Theo Gangi, Lincoln Michel, Felice Belle, and Hannah Assadi. To Yahdon Israel, who challenged me to write the book the world needs—and the reason it no longer starts with a bank robbery (inside joke).

To Tasha Wei, the master herbalist who knows all the things! To the youth leaders I've taught at the Deep Center and the many educators, artists, and activists across the country—who continue to teach me—this book is because you are. And to Savannah, Georgia (and my second hometown, Clarksdale, Mississippi), that created a childhood worthy enough to inspire not just a novel, but a movement rooted in an unforgettable truth: When Black and Brown youth/people play, we heal.

And, finally, to six-year-old Keith from the past, who always felt broken, invisible. They were wrong; you were right. We did it, baby boi—and we're just getting started.